"A poignant and uplifting novel, a gentle story about facing death without fear, and a call to arms for living life to the fullest. I defy anyone not to be moved by this warmhearted, deeply compassionate book and its lovable characters."

—Freya Sampson, bestselling author of *The Last Chance Library*

"This book definitely had me thinking and reflecting on my life and made me cry, and I walked away loving the characters and rooting for Clover, feeling very happy with the way the book ended."

—*The Southern Bookseller Review*

"Such a wonderful premise, beautifully executed. I fell in love with Clover, longed for her world to open up, and cheered when she finally realized that comfort zones are designed to be stepped out of. Poignant and ultimately uplifting, I loved it."

—Jill Mansell, #1 *Sunday Times* bestselling author of *Promise Me*

"A beautiful, uplifting novel about unexpected friendship, a decades-old love story, and finding the courage to live your best life."

—Lucy Diamond, *Sunday Times* bestselling author of *The Best Days of Our Lives*

THE
COLLECTED REGRETS
OF CLOVER

MIKKI BRAMMER

ST. MARTIN'S GRIFFIN
NEW YORK

For Carl Lindgren, who taught me to look for the beauty where there is seemingly none. And for the women of Cloverlea, who taught me to look for the magic.

Published in the United States by St. Martin's Griffin, an imprint of St. Martin's Publishing Group

THE COLLECTED REGRETS OF CLOVER. Copyright © 2023 by Mikki Brammer. All rights reserved. Printed in the United States of America. For information, address St. Martin's Publishing Group, 120 Broadway, New York, NY 10271.

www.stmartins.com

Designed by Gabriel Guma

The Library of Congress has cataloged the hardcover edition as follows:

Names: Brammer, Mikki, author.
Title: The collected regrets of clover / Mikki Brammer.
Description: First edition. | New York : St. Martin's Press, 2023.
Identifiers: LCCN 2022056025 | ISBN 9781250284396 (hardcover) |
    ISBN 9781250284402 (ebook)
Subjects: LCGFT: Novels.
Classification: LCC PS3602.R34483 C65 2023 | DDC 813/.6—
    dc23/eng/20221213
LC record available at https://lccn.loc.gov/2022056025

ISBN 978-1-250-87024-7 (trade paperback)

Our books may be purchased in bulk for promotional, educational, or business use. Please contact your local bookseller or the Macmillan Corporate and Premium Sales Department at 1-800-221-7945, extension 5442, or by email at MacmillanSpecialMarkets@macmillan.com.

First St. Martin's Griffin Edition: 2024

10 9 8 7 6 5 4 3 2 1

1

The first time I watched someone die, I was five.

Mr. Hyland, my kindergarten teacher, was a cheerful, tubby man whose shiny scalp and perfectly round face reminded me of the moon. One afternoon, my classmates and I sat cross-legged on the scratchy carpet in front of him, enthralled by his theatrical telling of *Peter Rabbit*. I remember how his meaty thighs spilled over the edges of the child-sized wooden chair he sat on. His cheeks were rosier than usual, but who could blame him for getting excited over a good Beatrix Potter plot?

As the story reached its climax—when Peter Rabbit lost his jacket fleeing the evil Mr. McGregor—Mr. Hyland stopped, as if pausing for emphasis. We stared up at him, hearts thumping with anticipation. But instead of resuming his narration, he made a sound similar to a hiccup, eyes bulging.

Then, like a felled redwood tree, he toppled to the ground.

We all sat motionless, wide-eyed, unsure if our beloved teacher was just upping the ante on his usual dramatic storytelling. When he hadn't moved after several minutes—not even to blink his open eyes—the room erupted with squeals of panic from everyone.

Everyone except for me, that is.

I moved close enough to Mr. Hyland to hear the final push of air from his lungs. As the pandemonium echoed down the hall and other teachers rushed into the classroom, I sat beside him, holding his hand calmly as the last blush of red disappeared from his face.

The school recommended I get counseling following the "incident." But my parents, who were more than a little self-absorbed, noted no significant change in my behavior. They bought me an ice cream, patted me on the head, and—reasoning that I'd always been slightly odd—judged me to be fine.

Mostly, I was fine. But I've wondered ever since what Mr. Hyland would have liked his last words to be if they hadn't been about the antics of a particularly naughty rabbit.

2

I didn't mean to keep count of how many people I'd watched die since Mr. Hyland thirty-one years ago, but my subconscious was a diligent accountant. Especially since I was nearing a pretty impressive milestone—today the tally nudged up to ninety-seven.

I stood on Canal Street watching the taillights of the mortuary van merge into traffic. Like a runner who'd just passed the baton, my job was done.

Amid the exhaust fumes and pungent blend of dried fish and tamarind, the scent of death still lingered in my nostrils. I don't mean the odor of a body decomposing—I never really had to deal with that, since I only ever sat with the dying as they hovered on the threshold between this world and the next. I'm talking about that other scent, the distinct smell when death is imminent. It's hard to describe, but it's like that imperceptible shift between summer and fall when somehow the air is different but you don't know why. I'd become attuned to that smell in my years as a death doula. That's how I knew someone was ready to go. And if there were loved ones there, I'd let them know that now was the moment to say their goodbyes. But today there were no loved ones. You'd be surprised how often it happens. In fact, if it weren't for me, at least half of those ninety-seven people would've died alone. There may be almost nine million people living here, but New York is a city of lonely people full of regrets. It's my job to make their final moments a little less lonesome.

A social worker had referred me to Guillermo a month ago.

"I've got to warn you," she'd said on the phone. "He's an angry and bitter old one."

I didn't mind—usually that just means the person is feeling scared, unloved, and alone. So when Guillermo hardly even acknowledged me on the first few visits, I didn't take it personally. Then, when I was late to the fourth visit because I'd accidentally locked myself out of my apartment, he looked at me with tears in his eyes as I sat down beside his bed.

"I thought you weren't coming," he said with the quiet despair of a forgotten child.

"I promise you that won't happen," I said, pressing his leathery hand between mine.

And I always keep my word. Shepherding a dying person through the last days of their life is a privilege—especially when you're the only thing they have to hold on to.

Snowflakes whirled erratically as I began my walk home from Guillermo's cramped studio apartment in Chinatown. I could've taken the bus, but it always felt disrespectful to slot right back into routine life when someone had just lost theirs. I liked to feel the icy breeze nibbling at my cheeks as I walked, to watch the cloud materialize then vanish with each of my breaths—confirmations that I was still here, still living.

For someone so accustomed to witnessing death, I always felt a little adrift afterward. A person was here on earth and now they were gone. Where, I didn't know—I was mostly agnostic when it came to spiritual matters, which helped me make room for my clients' chosen faiths. Wherever he was, I hoped Guillermo had been able to leave his bitterness behind. From what I could tell, he hadn't been on very good terms with God. A small wooden crucifix hung adjacent to his single bed, the torn, yellowed wallpaper curling around its corners. But Guillermo never looked at it directly to seek comfort; he snuck darting glances, as if avoiding the scrutinizing gaze of an authority figure. Mostly, he positioned himself with his back to it.

In the three weeks I spent visiting Guillermo, I'd learned the details of his living space by heart. The thick layer of grime on the outside of his only window that muted the daylight, rendering the space fittingly somber. The piercing shriek of metal against metal from his decrepit bed frame every time he adjusted his weight. The bone-chilling draft that came from everywhere and nowhere. The sparse occupants of his kitchen cabinets—one cup, one bowl, one plate—that were testaments to a life of loneliness.

Guillermo and I probably only exchanged a total of ten sentences during those weeks. We didn't need to say more than that. I always let the dying person take the lead, to decide if they want to fill their final days with conversation or to revel in silence. They don't need to verbalize their decision; I can just tell. It's my job to stay calm and present, letting them take up space as they navigate those last precious moments of life.

The most important thing is never to look away from someone's pain. Not just the physical pain of their body shutting down, but the emotional pain of watching their life end while knowing they could have lived it better. Giving someone the chance to be seen at their most vulnerable is much more healing than any words. And it was my honor to do that—to look them in the eye and acknowledge their hurt, to let it exist undiluted—even when the sadness was overwhelming.

Even when my heart was breaking for them.

The warmth of my apartment was almost stifling compared to Guillermo's place. I shrugged off my coat and balanced it on top of the mass of winter attire on the rack by my front door. The rack protested, sending my wool peacoat into a crumpled heap on the floor. I left it be, telling myself—as I did with most of the accumulating clutter in my apartment—that I'd deal with it later.

To be fair, not all of the clutter belonged to me. I'd inherited the enviably located two-bedroom from my grandfather after he died. Well, technically, I'd been on the lease since I was a kid. It was a shrewd move on his part to ensure that no amount of New York City real estate bureaucracy could cheat me out of my rightful claim to his rent-controlled legacy. For seventeen years, we'd shared the third-floor apartment in a brownstone that looked comparatively unloved next to its manicured West Village neighbors. Grandpa had been gone for more than thirteen years now, but I still couldn't bring myself to sort through his belongings. Instead, I'd gradually slotted my own possessions in the limited spaces between his. Even though I spent my days looking death in the face, I still couldn't seem to accept that his absence from my life was permanent.

Grief plays tricks on you that way—a familiar whiff of cologne or a potential sighting of your person in a crowd, and all the knots you've tied inside yourself to manage the pain of losing them suddenly unravel.

Warming my hands around a steaming cup of Earl Grey, I stood in front of my bookshelves, which were packed tightly with Grandpa's biology textbooks, musty atlases, and sea-faring novels. Wedged in between them, three dilapidated notebooks stood out, not so much for their appearance, but for the single word inscribed on the spine of each. On the first, REGRETS; the second, ADVICE; the third, CONFESSIONS. Aside from my pets, these were the things I'd save in a fire.

Ever since I started working as a death doula, I'd had the same ritual, documenting each client's final words before the breath had left their body. Over the years, I'd found that people often felt the need to say something as they were dying, something of significance—as if they realized it was their last chance to leave a mark on the world. Usually those last messages fit into one of three categories: things they'd wish they'd done differently, things they'd learned along the way, or secrets they'd kept that they were finally ready to reveal. Collecting these words felt like my sacred duty, especially when I was the only other person in the room. And even when I wasn't, family members were usually too consumed with grief to think about writing down such things. My emotions, on the other hand, were always neatly tucked away.

Setting my tea aside, I stretched on tiptoes to retrieve the book titled CONFESSIONS. It'd been a while since I'd been able to make an entry in this one. Lately, it seemed like everyone had reached the end of their lives with regrets.

I nestled into the sofa and flipped through the leather-bound notebook to a clean page. In my compact scrawl, I inscribed Guillermo's name, address, the day's date, and his confession. I hadn't expected it, to be honest—I'd sensed him slipping away and thought he was already unconscious. But then his eyes opened and he put his hand on my arm. Not dramatically, but lightly, as if he'd been on his way out the door and had forgotten to tell me something.

"I accidentally killed my little sister's hamster when I was eleven," he whispered. "I left the door of its cage open to annoy her and then it went missing. We found it three days later wedged between the sofa cushions."

As soon as the words departed his lips, his body relaxed with serene weightlessness, like he was floating on his back in a swimming pool.

Then he was gone.

I couldn't help thinking about that hamster as my own pets gathered around me on the sofa that evening. George, the chubby bulldog I'd found six years ago burrowing through the trash cans downstairs, rested his wet chin on my knee. Lola and Lionel, the tabby siblings I'd rescued as kittens from a box left outside the church on Carmine Street, took turns slinking figure eights around my ankles. The silkiness of their fur soothed me.

I tried not to imagine whether the hamster had suffered. They were pretty feeble creatures, so it probably hadn't taken much. Poor Guillermo, carrying that guilt with him for fifty years.

I glanced at my phone, balanced on the faded sofa arm. The only time it ever rang—aside from robocalls about car insurance and fake IRS audits—was when someone wanted to hire me. Socializing was a skill I'd never really mastered. When you're an only child raised by your introverted grandfather, you learn to appreciate your own company. It wasn't that I was opposed to the idea of friendship; it's just that if you don't get close to anyone, you can't lose them. And I'd already lost enough people.

Still, sometimes I wondered how I got to this point: thirty-six years old and my whole life revolved around waiting for strangers to die.

Savoring the bergamot vapor from my tea, I closed my eyes and let my body relax for the first time in weeks. Holding in your emotions all the time is kind of exhausting, but it's what makes me good at what I do. It's my responsibility to always remain placid and even-keeled for my clients, even when they're frightened and panicking and don't know how to let go.

As my feelings began to thaw, I leaned back into the sofa cushions, allowing the weight of sadness to settle across my chest and a yearning to squeeze my heart.

There's a reason I know this city's full of lonely people.

I'm one of them.

3

Usually after a job ended, I spent the next day catching up on the mundane domestic duties I'd neglected while working. Household chores and bill paying felt inconsequential when someone was dying. Three weeks' worth of dirty laundry bulged in the basket I was lugging to the basement. Grandpa hadn't just bequeathed me the rare treasure of a rent-controlled apartment, but also one with a laundry room in the building. Saving me from the New York City burden of trekking to the laundromat was one of the small but infinite ways he'd made my life easier, even in his absence.

On my way back upstairs, I stopped by the mailbox to unleash the flow of envelopes and catalogs that always awaited my sporadic visits. I rarely got anything worth reading.

A gravelly voice called from midway up the staircase. "On vacation again, kid?"

The shuffling gait that accompanied it was as familiar as the voice itself. Leo Drake was a sprightly fifty-seven when I moved in with Grandpa at age six, and the intervening decades had barely made their mark, except that his hair was now a little more salt than pepper, and his swagger a little slower.

He was also still my only friend.

"I guess you could call it that," I said, waiting as he made his way down the last few steps. "Though I'd prefer the beach to the laundry room."

As a tall, slender man with high cheekbones, Leo's age only advanced his elegance. It fascinated me how elderly people's fashion preferences tended to stay frozen in a certain era, usually the years they'd been in their thirties or forties. Often it was due to thrift— why buy new clothes when you already had plenty—but for most it seemed to be a nostalgia for what they considered to be their glory days. The time when more of their life was ahead than behind them.

Leo's style was still firmly planted in the sharp tailoring of the 1960s: crisp spread collars, notched lapels, linen pocket squares, and, when the occasion called for it, a well-loved trilby. I'd never once seen him look disheveled, even if he was just on his way to the corner bodega for milk. It'd probably been that way ever since his days working on Madison Avenue. Though he was relegated to the mailroom at first, that didn't stop his astute eye from documenting every sartorial flourish of the advertising executives to whom, as a Black man, he was mostly invisible. And when he eventually did have the financial means, he emulated—and elevated—that style to make it his signature.

All Leo was doing today was checking the mail and he still wore a pressed button-up shirt and pleated slacks. It was a conspicuous contrast to my sweatpants and baggy fisherman sweater. If my theory was correct, my style legacy didn't seem promising.

Leo smiled slyly as he slid his key into the mailbox. "And when is our rematch?"

Grandpa had taught me to play mahjong as soon as I'd come to live with him. It took me four years to finally beat him—he refused to let me win intentionally, insisting that it wouldn't do me any favors. Over time, I memorized all the different mahjong hands and observed each of Grandpa's moves closely, tracking the tiles he discarded. He had only one tell: lightly scratching his neck with his right pointer finger whenever he suspected he might be losing. Leo became his regular opponent after I went away to college, and then continued the tradition with me when I moved back after Grandpa died. We'd enjoyed a heated rivalry for the past decade or so.

"How about next Sunday?"

Sifting through my armful of mail, I found only a single letter worth opening—a check from the family of a man with leukemia I'd worked with a few months ago. Like Guillermo, he'd left the world with an unabated bitterness that stuck with me. When I first started working as a death doula, I'd naively tried to get people to focus on all the positive things about their life—all the things they should be grateful for. But when someone has spent their years angry at the world, death just feels like one final cruel blow. Eventually, I realized that it wasn't my job to help them gloss over that reality if they didn't want to; it was to sit with them, listen, and bear witness. Even if they were unhappy right up until their final exhale, at least they weren't alone.

"It's a date," Leo said, tipping the brim of his imaginary hat. "Unless, of course, you end up with a better offer."

Though he was well aware that I had no other social life, Leo couldn't resist subtle nudges hinting otherwise. I knew he meant well, but it only managed to make me feel more inept. I didn't expect to get to my mid-thirties and still have only one friend. That's the thing about loneliness: no one ever chooses it.

"Thank you," I said, giving him a smile. "But I don't think there's much danger of that happening."

"Well, you never know, do you?" Leo nodded toward the second floor. "Speaking of, did you hear we're getting a new neighbor? Moving in next week. Hopefully they're chattier than the last lot."

Damn. I'd been hoping the second-floor apartment—previously home to a reclusive Finnish couple—would stay empty a while longer. Unlike Leo, I'd appreciated that our neighborly relationship with the Finns was limited to polite head nods and cursory hellos.

Leo had a knack for sourcing neighborhood gossip before it hit the mainstream. On our way back upstairs, he filled me in on all the other tidbits he'd heard since we'd last spoken. The Airbnb drama in the building next door, the messy divorce down the street, the overpriced restaurant closed for health violations after a rat jumped out of the toilet while a customer was on it. A connoisseur of small talk, Leo spent much of his time out and about strolling the surrounding blocks, chatting with whomever was willing to engage. I'd always wondered why the two of us got along so well. A classic harmony of opposites, probably.

The door of the empty second-floor apartment was ajar as we walked back up the creaking staircase. Through the crack, I spotted a cluster of paint cans sitting on the floorboards and a roller nesting in its tray nearby, ready for use at any minute. As Leo gossiped, oblivious, a sense of unease settled into my stomach.

New neighbors were inevitable in New York and I'd endured plenty. But each time someone unfamiliar moved into my building, it still felt like a personal intrusion. On my space. On my routine. On my solitude. It meant a new personality to decode, new greeting rituals to establish, new quirks to accommodate. A new neighbor meant unpredictability.

And I hate surprises.

4

The day I learned that my parents were dead was the same day I learned that pigs roll in mud to protect themselves from sunburn.

It was a Tuesday lunchtime in first grade. I was sitting against the lone oak tree in my elementary schoolyard, tucked between two gnarled roots that stretched across the ground like arthritic fingers. It was where I spent most of my lunch breaks when weather permitted, reading while my classmates played boisterously nearby. That day, I was engrossed in a book about animal facts. I'd almost finished the section on pandas when I noticed my principal, Ms. Lucas, beelining across the playground toward me. The movement of her voluminous bouffant matched the rhythm of her purposeful gait and she clutched her polyester blazer with the air of importance. The back of my neck tingled like an insect was scurrying over it, but when I brushed my hand against my skin, there was nothing there.

Trailing close behind Ms. Lucas in a V-formation were my first-grade teacher and the school's guidance counselor. Since the trio looked like they were on a mission, I calmly placed the book on my lap and waited for them to arrive under the oak.

"Clover, my dear." Ms. Lucas's cloying singsong felt suspiciously like a buttering-up—the tone that adults used when they needed you to cooperate. She bent forward primly, her hands tucked neatly between her kneecaps in an inverted prayer position. "Would you come along with us to my office please?"

I looked back and forth between the women on either side of Ms. Lucas and noted their grim smiles. I wondered if anything I'd done that day warranted some kind of punishment. Had I broken a rule by accident? I tried my best to be good. Maybe I'd forgotten to return a book to the library? Feeling slightly outnumbered, I stayed wedged in the tree roots, grateful for their protective embrace.

"I'd like to stay here under the tree," I said, quietly thrilled by my small act of defiance. "It's still lunchtime."

Ms. Lucas frowned. "Well, yes, I understand that you want to enjoy the outdoors before it gets too cold, but there's something I—we—would like to discuss with you, and I think it's better if we went inside."

I considered my options. Ms. Lucas and her big-bloused body-guards didn't seem likely to leave me alone. Reluctantly, I stood, brushed the twigs from my jacket, and obediently began walking toward the school building.

"Good girl, Clover," Ms. Lucas said.

In the principal's office, I had to hoist myself into the wooden swivel chair. As I sat with my legs dangling far from the linoleum below, the aging springs beneath the leather cushion dug uncomfortably into my scrawny thighs.

The somber-faced threesome sat across from me, exchanging pained glances, as if silently drawing straws to see whom the un-pleasant task would fall upon. Apparently, the guidance counselor had drawn the short one. She took a breath, about to speak, then paused as she reconsidered her words.

"Clover," she finally said. "I know your parents have been away on vacation."

"In China," I added helpfully. "That's where pandas are from." I clutched my book to my chest like a precious treasure.

"Yes, I suppose it is—that's very clever of you."

"Pandas eat bamboo. And they weigh more than two hundred pounds and they're really good swimmers," I said, hoping to cement my cleverness with the adults while I had their captive attention. "Mommy and Daddy are coming home in two days—I've been counting." I hoped they wouldn't forget to bring me back a present like they did last time when they went to Paris.

The guidance counselor cleared her throat and fiddled with the fancy brooch on her blouse. "Ah, yes, about that. I know your parents were supposed to arrive home on Thursday, but there's been . . . an accident."

I frowned, tightening my embrace around the book. "Accident?"

My first-grade teacher bent forward and patted my knee, the cluster of cheap bangles jangling on her wrist. I liked their bright colors. "You've been staying with a friend of your mother's, is that right, Clover?"

I nodded cautiously as my ears started to burn. A prickle of sweat began to ease its way between the chair leather and the backs of my thighs. The rowdy shrieks of my classmates floated through the open window, adding to my discomfort.

My teacher's uncomfortable smile was unnerving. "You're going to stay with your grandfather instead tonight. He's coming up from New York City to pick you up this afternoon. Won't that be fun?"

I really had no idea if it would be fun or not. Since I'd only spent a handful of afternoons with my maternal grandfather in my short lifetime, I felt relatively neutral toward the man. He'd seemed nice enough, even though he didn't really ever say much, and he and my mom kind of acted like strangers with each other. But he did always send me a gift on my birthday—this year it'd been the animal book I now held on my lap. Maybe he'd bring me something new.

"Why can't I stay with Miss McLennan?"

The old spinster who lived a block from my parents wasn't a pleasant host, and her house always smelled like roast beef, no matter what was being served. But aside from making sure I was fed and taken to school, Miss McLennan left me to my own devices, usually reading alone in my room while she sat crocheting on her plastic-covered sofa. And since my parents often dropped me off to stay with her for weeks on end, she and I had learned to peacefully coexist—even though I'm pretty sure she did it for the wad of cash my dad always tucked into her palm before he left.

My teachers exchanged bleak glances and communicated in some kind of secret code using only their eyebrows, culminating in a heavy sigh from Ms. Lucas.

"Clover, I'm sorry to say this, but your parents are dead." The other women sucked in sharp breaths, stunned by my principal's callous delivery of such delicate news.

Equally shocked, I sat, eyes wide. The women hovered nervously around me like they were trying to anticipate the movement of a wild animal.

Finally, I managed a whisper. "Dead . . . ? Like Mr. Hyland?"

I thought about the episode of *Sesame Street* the school showed my class after our teacher's dramatic demise, where Big Bird grappled with the passing of his friend Mr. Hooper.

"I'm afraid so, Clover," Ms. Lucas tutted, trying to make up for her abrupt revelation. "I'm very sorry."

Sitting next to my grandfather as the Metro-North chugged from Connecticut toward Manhattan in the remnants of the afternoon, I realized I hadn't said goodbye to any of my classmates. But since they barely ever spoke to me, it likely didn't matter. Before our kindergarten teacher's sudden death, the other kids hadn't given me much thought, but my curious reaction—mostly the fact that I wasn't freaked out by it—had alienated me. After one boy began to spread rumors that I "hung out" with the dead, I was officially cast as a weirdo. They probably wouldn't even notice I was gone.

Grandpa had arrived at my school just as the bell echoed through the halls at the end of lunchtime, holding the small sky-blue suitcase I'd taken to Miss McLennan's. After a brief conversation with my teachers, spoken in mumbled tones I struggled to decipher, Grandpa guided me solemnly to a cab waiting outside the school gate.

En route to the train station, he'd given me only a few details about my parents' accident—it had involved an old boat, a tropical thunderstorm, and something called the Yangtze River. I'd just nodded in response, secretly wondering if my parents had spotted any pandas swimming in that river. But as I watched suburbia slide by on loop outside the dusty train window, reality began to percolate.

To die, I knew, meant you were never, ever coming back. From that moment on, you only existed in people's memories. I remembered my mom impatiently herding me out the front door on the morning they left for China. And the distracted kiss she blew in my direction when she left me with Miss McLennan and told me to "be good" as she fussed with her reflection in the car window. My father might have waved to me from the front seat, but I couldn't be certain. That morning, as usual, they seemed to have other things on their mind.

I also knew that it was important to cry when somebody died. After Mr. Hyland's heart attack, I'd seen the librarian sobbing in the hallway. And when Grandpa and I sat down on the train, I noticed him slide his thumb beneath his eyes several times and wipe it on his sleeve. So I waited expectantly for the first tear to spill from my own lashes and I even pressed on my eyelids a few times just to check. But no tears had fallen yet.

Two hours later, we stepped out of Grand Central Station into the dark clutches of evening, the wind gnawing my cheeks and the chaos of traffic seizing my eardrums. This was my first time in the big city—I wasn't sure if I liked it.

Trying to anchor myself amid the unfamiliarity, I gripped the bottom of Grandpa's coat as he thrust his arm high in the air and whistled. It must have been some kind of magic trick, because a yellow cab materialized in front of us. Although I hardly knew my grandfather, somehow I was certain that I was safe. Besides my blue suitcase, he was the only familiar thing I could hold on to.

The scene speeding past the taxi window was worlds away from the repetitive suburbs of the train ride: soaring buildings, pulsing lights, throngs of people weaving among one another on the sidewalk. I wondered how Grandpa could possibly be ignoring it all. But he just stared blankly at the back of the seat in front of him and mumbled something about needing to pick up milk.

When we arrived in front of a narrow brownstone, Grandpa handed a neatly folded bundle of bills to the driver.

"Say 'thank you,' Clover," he instructed me as he pushed open the cab door.

"Thank you, Mr. Driver."

The garlic-scented grouch in the front seat grunted in response.

Inside the brownstone, I counted each step out loud as we climbed toward the third floor. Just as I announced number fourteen, a man in a brimmed hat came swaggering down the stairs.

"Hello, Patrick," he said to my grandfather before noticing me peeking out from behind his thigh.

Grandpa put down my suitcase to shake the man's hand.

"Leo," he said. "Meet my granddaughter, Clover."

Leo gave Grandpa a brief, sympathetic glance, then bent down and offered his hand to me, his broad smile punctuated by a single gold tooth.

"Pleased to meet you, kid," he said, the overhead light reflecting in his eyes like sunbeams on an unopened Coca-Cola bottle. "Welcome to the building."

I shook his hand as firmly as I could, admiring the amber warmth of his skin. "Nice to meet you, sir."

Leo stepped aside, sweeping his arm up the stairs like a theater usher. "I'll let you be on your way," he said, tipping his hat. "But I look forward to seeing you both soon."

On the third floor, I watched Grandpa sift through keys on a ring attached to his belt, then click open the procession of locks. As he hung our coats on the rack by the door, I looked around his living room with wonder. Floor-to-ceiling shelves lined the walls, overflowing with all sorts of objects—precious rocks, animal skulls, creatures in jars. It was like Grandpa lived in the museum I'd visited last month on a school field trip.

And now I lived there too.

After a dinner of baked beans and toast, and only a few words spoken between us, Grandpa led me to a small room at the end of the apartment. An enormous wooden desk sat in one corner, with stacks of papers and books lined up like chimneys on top of it. In the other corner was a single bed and a nightstand with a green banker's lamp and a small vase holding a lone peony.

"This will be your room," Grandpa said, then gestured to the piles of books. "We'll take care of all that tomorrow."

He pulled out the bentwood chair from the desk and set my suitcase on it. The sky-blue vinyl glowed against the room's muted palette of mahogany, leather, and tweed.

"It's been . . . a big day. If you need me, I'll be in the living room." He patted me stiffly on the head then quickly returned his hands to his pockets. "Goodnight, Clover."

"Goodnight, Grandpa."

I stood in the middle of the room, absorbing my new reality. Did I have to brush my teeth every night now that I lived in the city? Miss McLennan was a stickler for teeth cleaning. A lot of things might be different now. Who would take me to school? Would my new school let me borrow books from the library? Would it have an oak tree in its yard?

I decided, as a test, to "forget" about teeth brushing for the night. Sliding down between the bedsheets, I inhaled the scent of unfamiliar laundry detergent seasoned by mothballs. The bedding was tucked in so firmly around me that it was difficult to roll onto my side. I imagined that was what it felt like to be held in a tight hug, but since I hadn't experienced many of those, I wasn't completely sure.

I reached over to the nightstand, slowly pulling the edge of the discolored doily to grab hold of my animal almanac without toppling the vase. Lying back against the lumpy pillow, I rested the book on my chest and flipped through the pages to the section marked *P*.

Satisfied that I knew everything about pandas, I began to learn all I could about pigs.

5

Except for running into Leo at the mailboxes the day after Guillermo died, I managed to go the next five days without interacting with a soul. But extended solitude was always a fickle thing. At first it soothed, swaddling me from the chaos and expectations of being human. Then, in an instant, it shifted from rejuvenation to numbing isolation.

Sitting on my sofa as the sixth day of seclusion ticked by, unable to remember when I last washed my hair, I felt the beginnings of that shift. It was like the telltale tickle of the throat before tonsillitis. The onset of symptoms began like it always did, with my viewing habits. Of course, there's nothing wrong with losing yourself in a romantic movie or TV narrative—that's the whole point of them. But even I knew there was a perilous line between watching something vicariously and watching it to replace real-life emotions. The sign I was toeing that line was whenever I began to compulsively rewatch the same romantic scenes over and over, trying to squeeze more out of the narrative than existed—as if, on the hundredth replay, a new scene might magically appear. Today I'd watched the most romantic parts of *Practical Magic* at least twenty times each. But instead of the pleasant spread of oxytocin I usually got from watching movies,

I felt a yearning in my chest, as if Sandra Bullock's emotional peaks and troughs were my own.

When you grow up as an only child, you learn to inhabit your imagination almost as frequently as you do reality. No one can let you down—or leave you—when you're in control of the story. So when the constant rewatching of a love story no longer fed my ache, I'd often continue the narrative as a fantasy in my mind, envisioning the characters' lives long after the final kiss and rolled credits.

That's when I'd know I needed to get out of the house and reconnect with the real world.

As I reluctantly pulled on my coat, a light flickered on in the apartment across the street. Dusk still flirted with daylight, so the reflection of the remaining sunset against the window made it harder than usual to see inside. But I still recognized the two figures shrugging off their own coats and snuggling up together on the sofa. In the four years they'd lived opposite me, Julia and Reuben hadn't drawn their shades once—I wasn't sure they even had them. It seemed less a symptom of exhibitionism and more a sign that they were so content in their intimate bubble that they didn't give a thought to who might be watching from afar. As I observed their blissful embrace, I wondered what it must be like to be so caught up in someone else that the world outside didn't matter. Then the angle of the sun shifted, casting an almost-blinding reflection into my eyes and severing my view into their living room. Sighing, I pulled down my own window shades and forced myself out the door.

I never agreed with New York's problematic reputation as a melting pot; my New York was more like a chunky vegetable soup, where people mostly floated in proximity without interaction. I often liked to slip into a weekday screening at the independent cinema on Sixth Avenue, alongside other solitary filmgoers—the closest thing I felt to a gathering of kin. Scattered at uneven intervals in the rows like beads on an abacus, we could be alone together. And as the projector clicked to a stop and the lights reignited, everyone shuffled out and continued on their lonesome way.

But that night, I knew the idea of watching a movie with the slightest trace of romance—even in the company of others—would only fuel my compulsive behavior. So to pry myself from my solitude, I got on the F train toward Midtown, headed to the only kind of social gathering I ever really frequented: a death café.

I first attended a death café while backpacking in Switzerland in my early twenties, where I spotted a ragged flier taped to a lamppost, inviting passersby to a "café mortel." Who wouldn't be tempted by that? The casual gatherings usually took place at restaurants and had been developed by a Swiss sociologist named Bernard Crettaz as a way of normalizing conversations around death. Complete strangers got together to ponder the intricacies of mortality over food and wine, and then went their separate ways. Genius. A British guy called Jon Underwood had since evolved the idea into an informal network of what he called "death cafés" across the world, and they'd begun springing up in New York City in recent years. I usually attended one every few weeks, comforted by the balance of human interaction without emotional investment.

Plus, death was the one topic I knew by heart.

The overstuffed F train was a tangle of arms gripping poles, faces dodging backpacks, and eyes avoiding one another. Most people loathed the forced surrender of personal space, the feeling of another body pressed against theirs. I found it quietly thrilling. Except for when I was tending to my clients—holding their hands, mopping their brows, rubbing their backs—I rarely got to exchange physical touch with another person. It had always been that way—I didn't even know if I was ticklish. Aside from the occasional pat on the head or shoulder, Grandpa had shown his affection for me in more practical ways, like equipping me with essential life skills. As a result, I savored any chance to feel another body in contact with mine, even if it was fleeting.

The train groaned to a halt at Thirty-Fourth Street and the sea of commuters parted briefly. As I slid my hand along the overhead pole, a lean man in a navy suit and gray tweed coat slotted in beside me, a folded copy of *The New York Times* in his hand. The doors closed and the commuters compacted, as if someone had pulled an invisible rope around them like twine on a bundle of sticks. The momentum pushed the man closer toward me, my face now inches from the meticulous knot of his striped silk tie. Feeling the warmth from his broad chest, I closed my eyes and inhaled the beguiling blend of sandalwood, expensive soap, and maybe a hint of whiskey. I imagined him wrapping his arms around me, bringing his hand to my hair as I pressed my cheek to his lapel. My heart swelled at the thought.

"THIS. IS. FORTY-SECOND STREET. BRYANT PARK," the automated voice scolded abruptly over the loudspeaker. Pulled from my fantasy, I reluctantly shuffled toward the opening doors. The man in the navy suit didn't look up from his newspaper. But as I trudged up the chewing-gum-scarred steps, I thought I smelled the faint scent of sandalwood on my coat.

6

That evening's death café was held in the bowels of the New York Public Library. I usually avoided going to the same death café too frequently. Though each session attracted newcomers, there were inevitably regulars who would latch on to any familiar face. Luckily, there were enough death cafés held across the city these days that it was easy to remain relatively anonymous.

The room was empty when I arrived, except for a circle of black plastic chairs awaiting their occupants. I never liked the pressure of being the first one in the room. It meant you had to acknowledge each person as they entered and then withstand the threat of small talk until the meeting started. So I hovered next to the nearby bookshelves, pretending to peruse the neatly arranged volumes on aeronautical engineering.

When I finally took up my position in the circle, all the other chairs were filled except for one. It was easy to spot the first-timers; they had the darting glances and fidgeting hands of someone well beyond their comfort zone. As the wall clock nudged past the hour, restlessness plagued the room. The moderator, a cheerful Italian woman, bounced the stack of papers on her knee to signal it was time to begin. I hadn't seen her before—I would have remembered that Roman nose.

"Welcome, everybody," she said buoyantly. "My name is Allegra." She paused, noticing a thirtysomething white man peering tentatively into the room while holding a cellphone to his ear.

"Hello, sir! Are you here for the death café?" It was normal for at least one person to have to be coaxed into the room at these meetings.

He cupped his palm over the cellphone and laughed nervously. "Yes, I think so. I mean, I am," he said. "Sorry I'm a bit late." He nodded contritely at everyone.

"Well, then it's lucky we're saving you a seat," Allegra chirped. I envied her ease—the air of confidence that came from knowing you were well loved. "Come on in! We're just getting started."

The man hurried over to the vacant chair but paused mid-circle, as if just remembering there was someone still on the other end of the phone. "I've got to go, I'm in the middle of something," he whispered into it. "Just make sure it stays confidential." He shoved the phone into his pocket and abruptly sat down without removing his coat, even though the windowless space was stifling. "Sorry," he said, addressing the room again. "Work stuff." His obvious nerves seemed to amplify everyone else's fidgeting, like a meeting of electrical currents.

"Now that we're all settled, let me say I'm so happy to be here with you all for this death café," Allegra said, and I wondered how her honeyed, shoulder-length hair achieved that elusive equilibrium between neat and disheveled. "I understand that this might be the first time for many of you and so I wanted to explain a little about what we do here." She paused to scan the circle serenely, undeterred by the panicked expressions of people—the latecomer included— who looked like they might flee at any moment. "This is a space for open discussion and we follow no set agenda, so we encourage you to bring up any topics or questions related to death that might be on your mind. There are many death cafés across the city, and some of you may have attended those already. The only difference here, since we are in a library, is that we cannot serve food and drink."

One of several reasons why this death café wasn't my favorite—
I'd have to scrounge up dinner when I got home instead of filling up
on appetizers. Fingers crossed there was something in my freezer I
could heat up.

"Now," Allegra said, clapping her hands together. "Let's go around
and introduce ourselves."

The attendees were varied, as always.

A twentysomething man in an emerald turtleneck who'd always
been fascinated by death but found that no one ever really wanted
to discuss it.

An elderly woman in thick red glasses who'd been diagnosed
with early-stage Alzheimer's and was grappling with the reality of
watching her mind slip away.

A theater major who'd been raised an atheist and felt her lack of
spirituality left her ill-equipped to deal with the finality of death.

A Dutch tourist who'd come across the death café flier in the
library and thought it would be a good way to "experience New
York City" while also practicing his English. (Remembering my first
death café in Switzerland, I felt a spark of camaraderie with him.)

The latecomer was up next, his right leg jackhammering. I wasn't
sure if my left leg mirrored his out of empathy or my own nerves.

"Uh, hi, I'm Sebastian." He offered an awkward wave then adjusted the edges of his gold-rimmed spectacles. "I guess I'm here
because my family never really talked about death and so, well, it's
pretty foreign to me. I kind of have an intense fear of it, actually. I
thought by coming here and learning more about it, I could maybe
overcome that."

A few others in the room nodded sympathetically. Sebastian
looked at the woman next to him, hoping to shift the spotlight away
from himself as soon as possible.

As she introduced herself, explaining that she was there because
she suspected her apartment was haunted, I braced myself and silently rehearsed in my head. Memorizing what I was going to say
always reduced the chance of oratory mishaps. I never revealed my

actual profession at a death café—that would only lead to brimming curiosity and well-meaning but invasive questions. Most people had never even heard of a death doula, let alone met one. Instead, I assumed a much more relatable identity. When all eyes finally trained on me, I took a deep breath and mustered a smile.

"I'm Clover," I said, willing my face not to ignite to crimson. "And my grandmother passed away recently."

The circle rippled with mutterings of condolence and I squirmed at my fib. But as always, it was a sufficient explanation for my presence, and the group's attention shifted to the woman on my left.

Allegra began the conversation with an article she'd found about a mushroom burial suit that would eventually turn your body into compost. A passionate debate about burial versus cremation followed, also weighing the merits of being buried at sea or donating your body to science.

"I love the idea of becoming one with the earth as compost," the atheist theater major said. "It's like the earth nourishes us while we're living and then we nourish it when we die."

The Dutch tourist nodded emphatically. "Yes, and much more eco-friendly than cremation—all those emissions."

"So, if I want a sea burial, can my family just take me out on their fishing boat and dump me in the Atlantic?" The woman next to me had a strong pragmatic streak.

"Nah," turtleneck-sweater guy responded. "I looked into it for my great uncle who wanted to be buried at sea. You need all kinds of permits and stuff. But there's a company up in New England that does it—takes you out on a chartered yacht for a full-day cruise with a picnic lunch before they slide the body into the sea."

This back-and-forth was always entertaining—most New Yorkers weren't shy about sharing their opinions. I preferred to respond in my head so that I didn't have to endure the room's collective scrutiny. Plus, I was mostly intrigued by other people's thoughts on death as an abstract concept.

My clients were already in the process of dying and often had a certain clarity about things. Knowing that death was impending seemed to allow them to deal in absolutes—as if they had one last piece to fit into the puzzle of their life and they knew exactly where it went. There was a freedom in having no future to speculate about. But for most people, death was an unknown—an inevitable but nebulous event that could be minutes or decades away. And from my experience, the ones who preferred not to think about it while living tended to have the most regrets while dying.

I liked to play a game with myself at these death cafés: guess the way each person in the room would process their dying moment. Some, like Allegra, would welcome it with grace. For others, like the latecomer Sebastian, it would likely bring panic and regret.

I just hoped they'd have someone like me to help them through it peacefully.

7

A misty rain floated around me as I descended the grand steps outside the library. After the staleness of the meeting room, the damp evening air slid through my lungs like a palate cleanser, my exhale forming a cloud in front of my face.

"Clover!" An enthusiastic voice called from behind me.

This caught me by surprise for two reasons. First, I'd never met anyone who shared my name, so the chances of them (a) existing and (b) being in my direct vicinity were pretty slim. Second, since most of the people I'd spent the past decade with were no longer alive, the fact that someone was calling to me specifically was also unusual.

But as I turned to identify my pursuer, I realized I'd announced my name to a roomful of people an hour earlier—and Sebastian was veering toward me with a slight jog in his step. I reflexively patted my coat pockets to check if I'd accidentally left something behind in the library. Nope, everything was there.

"Clover, hi!" Sebastian's grin signaled he was oblivious to the shocked expression on my face. I began considering my nearest escape. The thing about New York City was that you had to be clever about extricating yourself from unwanted interactions. Never reveal your hand—aka the direction you were headed or the subway line you were taking—until the other person had shown theirs. Then you could choose the exact opposite to avoid any more than a short, polite conversation without seeming rude.

I could have just run without acknowledging Sebastian, but my good manners prevailed.

I smiled weakly. "Oh, hey, how's it going." I pretended not to remember his name—that would just make him think I wanted to talk to him.

"Sebastian." He extended his hand so I had no choice but to shake it.

"Sebastian, right." I said nothing else, praying it would speed things up and force him to get right to the point of whatever he wanted to say. We both cringed at the silence that followed.

He shifted his feet awkwardly and wrung the charcoal scarf he was holding—it looked like cashmere. "Hey, I'm sorry about your grandmother. My grandma isn't doing so well either."

Not the greatest attempt at condolence. But despite what I'd said in the death café, both my grandmothers actually died before I was born, so I wasn't really in a position to criticize.

"Oh, thanks, yeah, she was a wonderful woman," I lied. Grandpa had never said much about his wife, which I'd always assumed was his way of grieving (though he had once mentioned she was allergic to strawberries). Was it sacrilegious for me to lie about someone I'd never met, even if it painted them in a good light?

Sebastian pressed on. "So, I noticed you didn't say anything in there either. It's weird talking about death, right? Honestly, it really freaks me out."

I felt obligated to counter his statement. Silence hovered while I considered whether to blow my cover.

"Actually," I said, meeting his gaze for the first time and noticing the way the youthfulness of his round face countered the flecks of gray in his hair. Combined with his gold spectacles and scarf, it gave him the charming air of an eccentric professor. "I don't think it's weird at all. Death is a natural part of life. In fact, it's the only thing in life that we can really count on."

Sebastian looked a little stunned. "Yeah, I guess you're right." His laugh was jittery. "That's kind of why I came to this thing. I figure I'm going to come face-to-face with death sooner or later, so I may as well try to conquer my fear now so it's not so bad when the time comes."

I nodded, desperately trying to plot my exit without seeming rude. But he seemed eager to continue the conversation.

"So, Clover, what's your story?"

"My story?" This was getting painful. And it made me uncomfortable how he kept using my name, like we were good friends. "Oh, nothing really interesting—just a girl who grew up here in the city."

I turned toward the street, hoping it would be a clear sign I needed to leave.

"You grew up here? That's cool. You don't really meet many real New Yorkers these days. Everyone seems to be from somewhere else—like me."

I ignored the obvious conversational volley. "Well, it was nice to meet you," I said quickly. "But I better get going."

As I started down the stairs, he fell into step beside me. "Hey, which way are you going? Are you taking the subway? Maybe we could walk together?"

I knew the social convention here was to express a sense of good-natured regret, which I hoped my face was conveying. I was never good at pretending.

"Oh, actually, I was going to take a cab." Another lie. The only time I ever took a cab was when the temperature was at frostbite-inducing levels.

"That's a shame," Sebastian said, a little too forthcoming with his disappointment.

I hurried toward the curb, pleading with whichever god might be listening (I figured I must be on pretty good terms with all of them by now) for a cab to whisk me away from this interaction. I thrust my arm in the air with as much confidence as I could. As my prayer was answered, I resisted diving headfirst into the cab and slamming the door shut. Instead, I turned dutifully and offered Sebastian a rushed goodbye. "Uh, see you later."

The cab began to move, but he was still trying to talk to me through the partially open window. "Wait," he called as the taxi pulled away. "Want to get a coffee sometime?"

"No way," I muttered when Sebastian was out of earshot. The driver frowned at me in the mirror and though he said nothing, his judgment stung.

The cab sailed through the yellow light just before it turned red and I exhaled my relief. Through the rain-streaked windows, I watched the city lights blend together in neon smears. Should I tell the driver to drop me at the Twenty-Third Street subway station? No, I couldn't risk it. That was one of the many ways New York could be cruel—in spite of the millions of residents, not to mention tourists, you still often ran into the person you were trying to avoid. There was no way I was going to take that chance, even if it meant splurging on a cab. I mentally struck that particular death café from my list. Now that the concept was catching on, I'd be able to find another one to add to my rotation.

George, Lola, and Lionel met me expectantly at the door when I arrived home. Since I'd fed them before I left, it was comforting to know that their enthusiastic welcome wasn't driven by hunger. I felt missed.

After microwaving a pot pie—the only thing in my freezer—I reassumed my position on the sofa, armed with the remote. But after minutes of scrolling through my Netflix queue, I realized I wasn't taking any notice of what was on the screen. Unease sat flatly across my lungs. Why did that guy, Sebastian, want to talk to me so badly? There were lots of other people at the death café and I'd hardly looked at him except when he was introducing himself, which was the polite thing to do. And I'd made it pretty clear that I wasn't interested in having a conversation outside the library. So why was he so persistent? If there was one thing I was good at, it was blending into the background and slipping through life unnoticed. It was rare that someone actually singled me out, so there had to be a reason for it.

I looked at the line-up of '90s romantic comedies on my TV screen and felt a brief flutter in my stomach.

Was it possible that our encounter on the library steps was . . . a meet-cute?

No, not a chance. Nothing about me was remarkable enough for a man to prioritize talking to me over someone like Allegra. I felt embarrassed for considering it.

Now that I thought about it, that phone call he'd been on did sound shifty. Maybe he was some kind of con artist who preyed on the vulnerable and went to death cafés to find his next unsuspecting mark. He could be a real estate broker or a life insurance salesman, or maybe he was selling overpriced funeral services. I'd helped enough families with funeral arrangements to know it was a ruthless way of draining people of their savings at a time when grief clouded their judgment. I was always on high alert for that type of swindler to make sure my clients weren't taken advantage of.

It all began to make sense. I'd mentioned my grandmother's death and he thought he'd found his next target for whatever scam he was peddling. Jerk. Now I didn't feel so guilty about lying. I snuggled deeper under the thick alpaca blanket and returned to my scrolling, this time with more focus. I was just about to hit Play on *Pretty Woman* when an onslaught of syncopated, irritated honking stopped me. It was so aggressive that it transcended my high tolerance for New York noise. Enveloping my shoulders in the blanket, I shuffled over to the window to investigate.

Like a blood clot wreaking arterial havoc, a mover's truck blocked the narrow one-way street below. A line of burly men dutifully transported boxes like ants, immune to the blaring of horns. For once I could empathize with the honking drivers—who schedules movers for nine o'clock at night, anyway?

My empathy quickly devolved to self-pity as I spotted an unsettling development unfolding in the street below. The industrious trail of movers was leading right up the front steps of my building.

The new neighbor was here.

8

One of the many things I loved about George was that he was never in a hurry to go outside to relieve himself. I suspected he'd trained himself to hold it in out of sheer laziness, even when his last bathroom break was eight hours ago. That meant I could delay our exit from the building until late at night, after the movers had gone. Hopefully the new neighbor would be busy inside their apartment unpacking by then.

I waited until eleven o'clock before I wedged him into his coat and grabbed his leash. Since he usually liked to take his time sniffing the stairwell on the way down, I lugged him in my arms, creeping along the second floor to avoid rousing the noisy floorboards. Enjoying the luxury of being carried, George watched me quizzically as if to point out the ridiculousness of it all. When we reached the mailboxes, I realized I'd been holding my breath the whole way down.

But my attempt at stealth was pointless. As I pushed through the front door, a woman around my age was walking up the front steps, a brown paper take-out bag in her hand. Tucking a lock of dark hair under her wool hat, she smiled broadly.

I felt like a mouse caught snacking in the kitchen.

"You must be Clover!" The woman skipped up the last few steps to join us at the top of the stoop. "I met Leo when I picked up the key the other day and he told me all about you." She stuck her hand out to shake, even though my arms were obviously occupied by fifty-five pounds of bulldog in a plaid winter coat. "I'm Sylvie."

I held on to George like a shield, shifting his weight to my hip so I could extend my hand out beneath his hefty backside.

"Hello," I said, a little annoyed at Leo. "Welcome to the building?" I didn't mean for it to come out as a question, but the slip in intonation betrayed me.

Sylvie's hazel eyes reflected amusement. "And who is this handsome guy?" She stroked the backs of her fingers across George's head and he grinned goofily at her, tongue flopping lazily out the side.

"Uh, this is my dog, George." I cringed. Of course he was a dog.

"It's a pleasure to meet you, George," she said in the kind of cartoonish voice humans reserved for animals and babies. "And you too, Clover. I'm looking forward to getting to know you!"

A stunned half smile was all I could offer. Sylvie was like a bee buzzing erratically around my head—perhaps if I stood really still and ignored her, she'd leave of her own accord. But the clumsy silence didn't seem to bother her and she maintained her expression of mild amusement.

"Well, I can see you and George are on your way out for a walk, so I'll leave you to it," she said, fishing in her coat pocket for her keys. "My pho is getting cold, anyway."

"Nice to meet you," I said, walking quickly down the remaining steps. "Have a good night."

"You too! Oh, and Clover—" Sylvie began searching her keychain for the newest addition. "Let's get coffee sometime!"

"Oh, okay. Sure."

Without looking back, I power-walked as far away from the building as possible before George had a chance to settle on a place to squat. Anxiety gripped my throat and the walk I'd done thousands of times suddenly felt unfamiliar—the streetlights seemed more intrusive, the sidewalk cracks more treacherous. I hurried toward the library, still denying George's attempts to exercise his right to stop and sniff.

I felt ambushed. And annoyed with myself for not being more prepared with an excuse on the spot. My nerves made me agree too quickly to Sylvie's invitation. Once you've had coffee with someone, you can't go back to polite nods in the stairwell. And the more you talk to them, the more reasons they might have to reject you.

I'd made that mistake with Angela, an Australian woman who'd lived in the second-floor apartment ten years ago. A few weeks after she moved in, she'd invited me to try a new teahouse in our neighborhood. Surprised and flattered, I even let myself get a little excited about the idea of making an adult friend who wasn't Leo. As Angela and I sipped on our matcha lattes, I thought our social outing was going well. I wasn't too nervous and I'd even made her laugh a couple of times. But when I told her what I did for a living— essentially, that I chose to watch people die—the conversation instantly became stilted. Out of nowhere, Angela remembered she had somewhere else to be and hurried out of the teahouse without finishing her drink. And for the remaining year she lived in our building, she hardly spoke two words to me.

Now I knew how to recognize that reaction. I'd seen it countless times since then, whenever I mentioned my job to other people. The way their bodies tensed, how they avoided eye contact. The way they mysteriously never had time for a conversation. It was as if my mere presence might somehow expedite their mortality.

I wasn't going to let myself fall into the same trap with Sylvie. It was safer to reject her before she could reject me.

9

"Why do we die, Grandpa?"

I was six years old, sitting opposite Grandpa in a booth of the diner a few blocks from our apartment. In the month since I'd come to live with him, his habitual weekend breakfast spot had become mine by default. He preferred the corned beef hash; I loved the French toast.

"That's a big question for a little girl," Grandpa said. "But it's a very good one."

He dipped his teaspoon into his black coffee and stirred it as he thought. I'd watched him perform the same action so many times in the past few weeks that I wondered if the answers to all hard questions lay in the bottom of a coffee cup. Grandpa lifted the spoon and tapped it three times—it was always three times—on the left side of the cup.

"You see, Clover, with so many people being born every day, there's not enough room or resources for us all on this planet. That means people need to die to make space for other people to be born."

I considered this as I arranged the blueberries on my plate into a smiley face. "Couldn't we just move to another planet? Like Jupiter? Or Neptune? They have rings, so they probably have a lot of extra space. But we'd have to go there in rocket ships."

Grandpa stroked the stubble on his chin—a newly familiar sound that I found comforting. "Perhaps one day we'll be able to move to other planets, but we haven't quite figured out how to do that yet."

He moved a long leg out from beneath the table, flexing it with relief. The cramped booth somehow emphasized his impressive height while making my six-year-old frame feel even smaller. As a pair, we probably looked like a question mark seated across from a comma.

"Eventually," Grandpa continued, "our bodies grow so old that they don't do what they're supposed to." He pointed to the graying hair on his head. "My hair used to be the same color as yours. And my hands used to be smooth like yours are. But I'm getting older, so my body doesn't work the way it used to."

I frowned, then raised my eyebrows in concern. "Are *you* dying, Grandpa?"

He reached for his spoon and began stirring again.

"In essence, yes." Tap, tap, tap. "In fact, we all are."

He reached for a box of the diner's promotional matches next to the condiments. Singling out a green-headed stick, he struck the box's flank and a small flame sprung to life. I watched the stick devolve from a crisp, pale yellow to a disfigured black as the fire slid toward his fingers.

With a brief flick of Grandpa's wrist, the flame reduced to smoke.

"You should never play with matches, Grandpa." I proudly echoed the advice I'd been recently taught to parrot by the teachers at my new elementary school.

A smile flirted with the edges of Grandpa's mouth. "You're right about that, Clover. But we'll make an exception this once so that we can explore your question. Is that okay?"

I swirled my straw around in my orange juice, deliberating. "Okay. But promise you'll be very, very careful."

"I promise," he said solemnly. "Now, let's think about each of these matches as a human life."

Pushing my plate away, I propped my elbows on the table and rested my chin on my hands.

"In theory," Grandpa continued, "each of these matches should burn for exactly the same amount of time, right?"

"Right."

"But sometimes, you strike a match and it goes out almost immediately. Other times, it stops burning halfway."

"And sometimes it breaks when you try to light it."

"Exactly!" Grandpa's approval felt like gold. "So even though they're technically the same, each match is actually very unique. Sometimes it's not as strong structurally, for reasons we can't see just by looking at it. And there are outside factors that contribute—like how hard we strike it against the box, or the dampness in the air, or how much breeze there is when we try to light it. All those things can affect how long a match burns for."

Vinyl groaned as I shifted impatiently in my seat. "But what's that got to do with dying?"

Grandpa struck another match with a flourish. As if proving his point, it fizzled out almost immediately.

"Well, my dear, just as we don't know how long a match will last until we light it, we never know how long a life will last until we live it. And often there are factors that we have no control over."

"So who decides when we die then? Mommy and Daddy weren't old like you—why did they die?"

I watched Grandpa's chest rise then fall. The inner corners of his eyes glistened as if they held tiny diamonds.

He gave a helpless shrug. "Unfortunately, those are more big questions that we don't know the answer to."

"Well," I said, stabbing my French toast with my fork. "Then we've got a lot of work to do, don't we?"

P late empty and stomach full, I watched Grandpa examine the messy handwriting on our check. He raised a polite hand in the direction of the waiter, a freckled beanpole with slicked-back hair.

"Excuse me, sir," Grandpa said, holding up the check. "When

you have a moment, it appears that you haven't charged us for my granddaughter's orange juice."

Surprised at being addressed so politely, the young waiter glanced at the check, then waved dismissively. "Oh, that's cool, man. Call it on the house."

Grandpa pulled out his money clip and looked the waiter in the eye. "Well, that's very kind—but if it's all the same to you, I'd prefer to pay for it."

The waiter frowned, then shrugged. "Suit yourself, man. That'll be an extra two bucks."

Grandpa peeled off several bills and stacked them neatly on top of the check. As he slipped the money clip back into his breast pocket, he met my eyes.

"It's always important to be honest, Clover—even when people don't hold you accountable."

As Grandpa and I stood side by side at the crosswalk outside the diner, I had to crane my neck backward to look him in the eye, like trying to see the top of a skyscraper. My entire child-sized grip was only sufficient enough to grasp two of his long fingers, which I held on to obediently as we waited to cross the road. French toast was great, but I loved the second part of our newly developed Sunday ritual even more.

A small brass bell above the red French doors always announced our arrival into the bookstore. The jingle reminded me of the sound of Christmas—well, movie Christmases, at least, since my parents never celebrated the holiday itself. When questioned, they told me that it was hypocritical to celebrate someone you didn't believe in (I wasn't sure if they were referring to Santa or Baby Jesus).

"Hello, Patrick! Hello, Clover!"

Miss Bessie, the bookstore's owner, was balanced in heels on a stool, rearranging a procession of mysteries on a high shelf. Beneath her tight, polyester dress, her large breasts looked like they were resting on two inflatable swimming rings. I wondered whether it helped her stay afloat better when she went to the beach.

Grandpa tipped his hat. "Hello, Miss Bessie—lovely to see you." He reached out a hand to help her down from the stool.

"Hello, Miss Bessie," I echoed shyly from behind Grandpa.

Miss Bessie beamed at me. "Lucky for you, darling girl, I've got some great new children's books this week." She reached a hand toward me. "Should we go take a look?"

Grandpa offered Miss Bessie a grateful smile, then looked down at me. "Off you go," he said, patting me on the head. "But remember— only one book, *so choose wisely.*"

I felt the weight of his dramatic intonation—this weekly mission was one I took seriously. At least I knew I'd have plenty of time to make my decision, since Grandpa always spent ages in the nonfiction section making his selection. After all, he was allowed only one book too.

As Miss Bessie and I rounded a corner into the colorful children's nook, she reached behind a potted plant and produced a bowl full of candy. Holding it in front of me, she pushed her pointer finger to her lips.

"*Ssshhh,*" she whispered. "I'll let you take two pieces as long as you don't tell your grandpa."

Staring at the candy, I was torn—I really wanted both a Hershey's Kiss and a lollipop. Technically, Grandpa hadn't said I couldn't take two pieces, but Miss Bessie was acting like it was a secret. I rocked on my heels, thinking it over.

"Thank you, Miss Bessie," I said, holding my head high and making firm eye contact. "But I'll just take one."

An hour later, Grandpa and I walked back to the apartment with our chosen books under our arms—him with a thick biography of the scientist Louis Pasteur, me with a comprehensive guide to a mystical village of gnomes. I knew exactly how we'd be spending the rest of the afternoon. Grandpa would sit in his corduroy armchair, I'd settle into a beanbag at his feet, and together we'd escape to different worlds in the pages of our books. And once in a while, he'd pat me on the head, as if to reassure me he was still there.

I walked quickly so we'd get home as soon as possible. Since it was an unusually warm winter's day, the sidewalks of our West Village neighborhood were packed. As I trailed Grandpa's stride, weaving in among the pairs of legs, I examined the people bustling by, imagining each one as a partially burned matchstick.

Gazing up at Grandpa's towering physique, I felt a small pang of panic in my stomach. How much longer would he burn for?

10

I always had the best intentions of putting away my clean laundry, but those intentions usually dwindled somewhere between the laundry room and my front door. So for the past week, the basket had sat in its usual place in front of my closet, ready to be cherry-picked. Lola and Lionel had reclaimed their positions snuggled in among the clean clothes, ensuring that I would continue to be a woman whose outfit wasn't complete unless it was sprinkled with cat hair.

As I retrieved a sweatshirt from between the two cats, I caught my reflection in the mirror hanging on the closet door. I rarely stopped and studied my face, so it almost felt like running into someone after months of not seeing them. I'd always wondered whether age snuck up on you gradually, or if you just woke up one day and looked old. So far I'd escaped any significant signs of aging—the two lines on my forehead were the same ones I'd had since my early twenties and only a few gray hairs had sprung up. I leaned closer, my breath fogging against the mirror as I scrunched my face to see what I'd look like with permanent crow's feet. Distinguished, maybe. Or haggard. Not that it mattered—except for Leo, there was no one in my life to notice me getting older.

I switched my focus to the photo tucked in the corner of the mirror. It was of my parents standing in the door frame of a house that existed to me only in sensory snippets—the itch of the carpeted stairs against my bare feet, the spicy scent of damp hedges outside my bedroom window, the ceiling fan that beat the air like helicopter blades. Grandpa gave me the photo soon after I came to live with him. The few memories I still had of my parents were an amalgamation of what really took place and what I'd conjured from staring at the same photograph for decades. I imagined that the slight smirk on my dad's face was a sign of his rebellious spirit, while the vibrant red on my mom's lips conveyed her elegance. And the way they held hands—fingers interlocked tightly rather than loosely wrapped—signaled their deep passion for each other.

What I knew for sure was that my dad was some kind of lawyer (I liked to imagine it was for human rights, but I think it was closer to corporate litigation) and he traveled abroad frequently. My mom had been a moderately successful ballet dancer before I was born. Based on the few details Grandpa had revealed over the years, my unexpected arrival into the world had paused her career, halting her aspiring trajectory from ballet corps to soloist. It was probably why she preferred accompanying my dad on his overseas trips instead of spending time with me.

Otherwise, my parents were a mystery to me. The photo mostly made me wonder whether I was supposed to miss them more.

When I walked back out into the living room, I almost gagged at the smell—the stagnant odor of cat litter competing with the mustiness of Grandpa's old possessions. How long had it been that way? I was so used to it that I often didn't notice until it was almost rank.

Decades-old paint flaked from the window as I pushed it open. A slight breeze sidled in, dissipating the stale air as I struck a match and held it against a stick of incense until the flame made its leap from one to the other.

I preferred the spiced-wood smell of palo santo, but it felt wrong to use it as a mere room freshener when it was such an important tool in the rituals of the dying. I'd spent part of a college summer vacation studying with a shaman in the Peruvian Andes, learning about the Incan traditions of death. My favorite was that they had sometimes buried their dead in the fetal position, so as to better their chances of rebirth in the afterlife. I loved the idea of preparing someone for a journey rather than simply saying goodbye.

The scent of palo santo always ignited my memories of that time. It was surreal being on a mountain so high that you were above the clouds, as if you were somehow navigating the barrier between the real world and the spiritual. Ever since, I'd found a quiet peace in the ritual of smudging—the process of clearing negative energy with repetitive strokes of lit palo santo or sage—whenever a dying person requested it. I'd studied enough religions and spiritual credos to acknowledge the existence of an invisible energy that coursed through everyone. Even if the clearing of it was little more than a placebo effect, I'd seen firsthand how it could give someone hope and the feeling of starting over.

Or at least letting go.

Setting down the incense ember in a clay pot, I watched the smoke curl its way to the open window like a snake to its charmer. The usual soundtrack of siren wails, over-sensitive car alarms, and aggressive conversation floated up from the street. I never really minded that ambient noise—it kept me company. But then a far less frequent sound pierced through the urban din: the ringing of my phone.

When I unearthed it from under George's belly on the sofa, the caller ID of a hospital on the Upper East Side lit up the screen.

A new job.

Within an hour, I was on the 6 train (which I loathed only slightly less than the R train) rattling uptown. I usually preferred at least two weeks between jobs, a loose rule I'd developed after experiencing a hellish burnout a few years ago. It wasn't being around death that I found taxing—more the burden of being an anchor when everyone else around me, usually grieving family members, was emotionally unmoored.

But this job likely wouldn't last longer than a day. The nurse on the phone explained that the patient, a twenty-six-year-old unhoused woman named Abigail, was brought in after she was found collapsed in an ATM vestibule in Midtown with end-stage liver failure. It was likely a result of cirrhosis—and the entire bottle of gin she'd consumed. Even though Abigail was lucid and talking, the prognosis wasn't optimistic. Her parents were on their way from Idaho, but they'd probably arrive too late.

I wouldn't be paid for this job, but there was no way I could let her die alone. And in situations like these, my task was just to be there as a presence. Hospitals were so full and understaffed that it wasn't realistic for a nurse to stay with a patient around the clock. So they'd begun offering the services of volunteers, some of whom were death doulas like me, to provide comfort to those who had no one else. Or even those who did. Unfortunately, death isn't always the peaceful slipping away that movies depict it to be—often it's prolonged and very unpleasant. The sensory chaos of bodily functions shutting down or going awry. The gasping. The look of panic as people cling desperately to their final moments. Sometimes family members turn away or run out of the room to spare themselves from having such a confronting scene seared into their brains as the final memory of their loved ones.

That's why it's so important to have someone like me there. Someone who won't look away, no matter how harrowing it gets.

Abigail was sleeping when I arrived at the narrow cubicle in the hospital ward. Except for the telltale yellow of her skin and the circles like smudges of ash beneath her eyes, it wasn't obvious that she was nearing death. But I knew how well the body could hide internal tumult—the machines attached to her told a more depressing story.

I settled into the stiff, pleather chair by the bed and pulled out my book from my bulging tote bag. I liked to come equipped with things that might help a dying person feel more comfortable in their final moments. There was a small Bluetooth speaker for playing music or nature sounds, plus an iPad for googling images of destinations that conjured a person's happiest memories, or for reading passages from their preferred religious text. I also packed a scented lotion for massaging their hands, some stationery and a pen for writing letters and documenting final wishes, some small candles to help create a more intimate environment, and my sticks of sage and palo santo. I probably wasn't allowed to burn things in the hospital, but I wasn't above breaking the rules if it meant granting someone's dying wish (once I'd even snuck in a pint of Guinness).

Three chapters of Martha Gellhorn's *Travels with Myself and Another* passed before I sensed Abigail stirring. Disorientation clouded her face, escalating to concern as she noted the tubes creeping like vines along her emaciated limbs. She smacked her tongue against the roof of her mouth, desperately seeking moisture. I pressed the Call button and reached for the paper cup of water beside the bed, positioning the tip of the straw in front of her lips.

Abigail winced as she sipped. "I'm pretty sick, huh?" Her eyes willed me to contradict her.

My heart twinged but I smiled calmly. It was my job to make her last few hours as comfortable as possible, but that didn't mean lying to her. Fueling her fear would do nothing, so I'd learned to be mercifully vague.

"Yes," I said, keeping my tone even. "But the doctors here are taking really good care of you." Her sallow skin aged her well beyond her twenty-six years—alcohol abuse tends to do that. "I'm Clover— I'm here to keep you company. And you're Abigail, right?"

She nodded.

"I hear you're from Idaho," I said. "I've always wanted to go there."

Straight but neglected teeth and swollen gums peeked through her weary smile.

"Yeah, from Sandpoint." Abigail's eyes traced the perimeter of the cubicle where the fluorescent light emphasized every blemish of the curtain and its pallid salmon hue. "I miss home a lot."

She seemed up to having a conversation, so I pressed on.

"What do you love most about it?" I'd learned that helping people visualize a beloved place was a way to calm them, to anchor them to something comforting and familiar—especially when their reality was a sterile hospital cubicle.

"Well, my town is super beautiful. It's surrounded by mountains and it's right on the lake." Her smile disappeared. "But when I was a teenager I thought it was too boring, so I came out here to New York to become an artist."

"That's a cool career choice," I said, silently noting the increasing beat of her heart-rate monitor.

Abigail stared at the beige ceiling. "It was a lot harder than I thought it would be. I guess my skin wasn't thick enough for this city—it kind of swallowed me up."

That made sense. When the hospital admin had finally tracked down Abigail's parents, they hadn't heard from their daughter in five years. She'd cut off all contact after they'd tried to convince her to go to rehab for alcoholism. They had no idea she'd been living on the street for a year.

"New York can definitely be tough." I rested my hand lightly on hers. Not everyone liked to be touched, so it was better to gauge their response. "Have you always been into art?"

Abigail clasped my fingers tightly. "I've been drawing and painting pretty much every day since I was a kid." Her words slowed as she battled to stay awake. "My parents said I used to draw on all the walls and furniture with my crayons. They said the house was like one big canvas to me." Pain stifled her laugh and her face turned solemn. "Are they coming?"

I made sure my nod was confident but casual. "They're already on their way. They should be here really soon. I know they can't wait to see you and hug you."

Hope had a magical way of healing someone—or at least helping them hold on for that little bit longer. It wasn't just important for Abigail to be able to see her family one last time; closure was just as valuable for the living. Being denied the chance to say goodbye to a loved one left stubborn emotional scars. After thirteen years, mine hadn't healed—and I'd promised myself that I'd do everything I could to spare others that same burden.

"That's good," Abigail said, shoulders relaxing. "You know, I thought about calling them so many times and asking if I could come home—and maybe even try rehab—but I was too ashamed." Her eyelids fluttered and her speech became a murmur. "I never realized how much I loved them until I couldn't tell them . . ."

It would be better if she'd stayed awake, since there was a risk she wouldn't regain consciousness. But sleep seized her before I could respond. She didn't even stir at the sound of plastic rings screeching across metal when a nurse whipped back the flimsy curtain.

"She was awake and briefly coherent," I reported to him as he methodically checked Abigail's vital signs. "And still consuming small amounts of liquid."

The nurse's eyes were grim. "It's good that you're here."

Abigail's parents arrived just after one thirty in the morning. Their faces wore the fatigued battle scars of an unexpected cross-country journey and the disorientation of being plunged into an unfamiliar city.

I moved to the foot of the bed, giving them as much space as the cramped quarters would allow. Abigail's heart monitor beeped rhythmically, a metronome keeping time to the hospital commotion beyond the curtain.

"Abigail told me about how she adored being an artist and how much she loved and missed you both." I smiled with my eyes more than my lips—a way of conveying warmth and comfort without denying the sadness of the situation.

Her parents stood frozen, struggling to believe that fate had dealt them such a callous blow.

"You can speak to her; she'll hear you," I said, keeping my voice low and calm. "Messages of love always make their way through, even when someone is unconscious." Unfortunately, it was often the first time that love was ever expressed. "I'll just be outside in the waiting room if you need me."

Nodding, the couple clutched each other like tree branches in a flood—the only thing keeping them from being swept away.

Abigail's sleep became eternal at 6:04 A.M.

Ninety-eight. Once again, my job was done.

11

The frenetic jumble of peak hour, combined with my severe lack of sleep, made the 6 train even more painful on my way home from the hospital after Abigail's passing. As I tried to stop myself from dozing against the pole, I watched a teenaged girl sketching furiously in a notebook. She sat with an almost trance-like focus on her art, oblivious to the impatient commuters and nausea-inducing sway of the train car.

A pang pierced the space between my ribs. One young creative life blossoms as another one ends; there was something beautiful about the tenuous reality of being human.

The morning sun stunned my weary eyes as I climbed the subway steps. I pulled my urban suit of armor—sunglasses and an imposing pair of noise-canceling headphones—from my bag. Eye contact was the gateway to conversation and only the bravest of souls (usually German tourists) were willing to flag me down for directions while I was wearing them. But the headphones were more than a deterrent; they were also a mental retreat. I didn't usually listen to anything—it was the feeling of being enclosed that comforted me. Sliding them on was like escaping to a private space of my own, observing the world rather than participating in it.

I loved how the city moved at simultaneous yet contrasting

paces. One was the slow, mesmerized shuffle of first-time visitors to New York as they savored every detail of every streetscape. The other was a dexterous routine of sidestepping and outpacing those visitors, which locals had perfected to get from A to B as quickly as possible. It was like watching fish darting in and out of swaying seaweed.

As I began to walk, the sun briefly plunged into a gloomy cluster of clouds, creating an ambience more reflective of my mood. Even though it was my job, it was still jarring to watch two people die in the space of a week. From behind my dark lenses, I observed each passerby—their expression, their body language, the way they engaged in the world. All seemed oblivious to the fact that they were burning matches whose flames could unexpectedly fizzle at any moment.

As if underscoring my thoughts, tires screeched and yelling erupted in the street behind me. A man preoccupied by his phone had walked into oncoming traffic, narrowly avoiding a collision with a UPS truck. His flame had faltered briefly, but it continued to burn.

He was one of the lucky ones.

Tendrils of morning light spilled into my apartment as I sat down in Grandpa's favorite armchair to write my notes about Abigail. His broad shoulders had rubbed away the ridges of sage corduroy and the seat cushion was slightly more indented on one side because he always crossed one leg elegantly over the other. Each morning, he'd sit there reading the newspaper, ankle resting on the opposite calf, revealing his day's choice of sock—always some kind of stripe. The steam of his black coffee would dance with the sunlight that always hit that exact spot in the living room.

His armchair had seemed enormous when I was a kid, and Grandpa was larger than life. But when I returned to live in the apartment after his death, it seemed to have shrunk, just like he had with age. A lithe man of six foot five, he'd towered over the rest of the world, so much so that it seemed like his head was permanently bent forward in deference. By the end, he measured closer to six foot two.

I nestled into the armchair like I was leaning back into his embrace and considered what I would write about Abigail. People don't usually realize that the words they're saying will be the last ones they'll ever speak. Usually, those words are pretty mundane, like "It's cold in here," or "I'm tired," or a series of nonsensical phrases brought on by the delirium of death. I still made sure to document my clients' official last words in one of my notebooks, for accuracy's sake. But then I'd elaborate the record with anything else poignant or interesting the person might have said during my time tending to them. After all, it's a little unfair to be remembered for something just because it was the last thing you physically said.

Abigail's last words, though she said them hours before her actual death, were a recurring theme in my REGRETS notebook. If I ever analyzed my records statistically—and one day, I might—that theme would probably turn out to be the one I heard most often.

I wish I'd told them how much I love them.

Sometimes people were referring to parents or spouses, other times it was friends. In almost every case, it was because they'd been so busy in their lives that they took their loved ones for granted.

Or they just never knew how to find the right words.

There are few rawer expressions of vulnerability than *I love you*. At least, that's what I'd gathered from hearing people talk about it—I'd neither said nor been the recipient of those words. My parents weren't exactly forthcoming with affection, verbal or otherwise. And even though I knew Grandpa loved me more than anyone, he'd never said it out loud. But as far as I could tell, *I love you* was one of the hardest things to say in the English language. Not for its pronunciation (*synecdoche* held that title, in my opinion), but for the weight it carried. The way it teetered on the tip of your tongue, like a child on the side of a pool before attempting their first dive. The heart leaps, the pulse thunders, and you wonder if it's too late to turn back.

It sounded kind of thrilling, actually. But, then again, loving someone inevitably also meant one day losing them—if not by rejection or betrayal, then most certainly by death. At least when you're alone, there's no risk of getting hurt. After all, you can't lose something you don't have.

The church bells down the block chimed to signal eight o'clock—three minutes late, like they had for years. I'd always wondered if I should let someone at the church know about the delay, but I liked the imperfection of it all. Proof that we're all living our lives slightly out of sync with one another.

Robbed of a whole night's sleep, I was tempted to go straight to bed, but I knew better than to mess with my circadian rhythm. I'd try to keep myself awake at least until sundown. Watching TV would only make me sleepier, so I needed something that would keep me active.

And I knew exactly what I could do to busy myself.

When I first began documenting the last words of dying people, it was simply to keep a record. A way of acknowledging the life they'd lived—however flawed and messy that might have been—especially when they had no one else to remember them. But in the past couple of years, whenever I was feeling anxious, depressed, or was longing for human company, I'd begun to revisit the entries in the notebooks. Reading people's final words made me feel close to them, like they were somehow guiding me with their wisdom. And focusing on them rather than my own loneliness gave me a purpose, a way to fill my days and pull me out of my melancholy. Maybe by studying what people deemed to be most important when looking back on an entire life and finally connecting the dots, I could find some direction in my own. So once in a while, I'd select an entry from one of the notebooks and find a way to integrate that person's wisdom into my own life.

From the ADVICE notebook, I'd pick an entry and try to live by that guidance for the next week. Sometimes it was as simple as treating myself to a bunch of fresh flowers, even if it was just from the corner bodega—the advice of Bruce, a plumber with a passion for gardenias. Other times it was more poignant, like the words of Dorothy, a dog groomer with charming dimples who told me that the most important lesson she'd ever learned was to listen more than you speak. (Admittedly, when you're an introvert like me, that's pretty easy advice to follow.)

With the CONFESSIONS notebook, I had to get creative. I wasn't sure if I believed in karma, but I figured it couldn't hurt to do something that might make up for the deed a client had confessed to. In Guillermo's case, for example, I might volunteer at an animal shelter to atone for the accidental demise of his sister's hamster. Then there was Ronald, a gruff accountant with lung cancer who admitted that he used to steal money from street musicians when they weren't looking. In his memory, I always carried ten-dollar bills so I could slip them into the musicians' hats and instrument cases whenever I saw one. I tried to do it discreetly, wrapping the ten in a one-dollar bill, so that it was a nice surprise later that day when they were counting their earnings.

From the REGRETS notebook, I'd choose one and try to find a way to honor it—if I could avoid making the same mistake they did, if I learned from their regret, then it wasn't in vain. Since I already had that notebook in my lap, I closed my eyes and let the pages flip through my fingers to choose an entry at random—it always felt more democratic that way.

Camille Salem.

Yes, that was a good one. A bubbly woman whose biggest regret was that she didn't start eating mangoes until she was fifty.

"I ate one once when I was a kid, and couldn't stand the slimy texture," she'd told me forlornly from her hospital bed. The chemotherapy had vanquished her eyelashes, but her eyes were still a bright, sparkling green. "But then my husband made me try one while we were on vacation in the Philippines and I almost had an orgasm over how good it tasted. Think of how many mangoes I missed out on by not eating them for fifty years!"

I was pretty indifferent to mangoes, to be honest. I preferred tarter fruits like raspberries. But today I was going to search the city and find a really delicious mango. Then I'd sit down and enjoy it like it was the best thing I'd ever tasted, letting the juices drip down my chin and appreciating every fleshy morsel. Thanks to Camille, I'd save myself a potential regret.

If only it was that easy to free myself of the rest of them.

12

The Harlem death café was a hassle to get to on the subway. But after I emerged from the urine-laced humidity of the underground and saw the brownstones basking in twilight, I was glad I'd made the trip.

Leo was Harlem-born and -raised. On the occasions he'd babysat me as a kid, he'd taken me to his favorite ice-cream joint, dazzling me with stories of speakeasies and jazz as we strolled beside the row houses. He rarely visited the neighborhood anymore—he couldn't bear seeing the fingerprints of gentrification on the streets he'd loved as a child. But I liked to let him know that some of the places he remembered still remained intact. I thought I might even pick up a pint of ice cream for him on my way home that evening.

The death café was hosted in a drafty community hall with a pervading scent of peppermint. The moderator's family owned a nearby soul food restaurant, so they often served fried chicken and biscuits at the meeting—another reason I considered it worth the arduous subway trip. I arrived fifteen minutes early to tackle the buffet before everyone else crowded around it. With a paper plate piled high (mac and cheese was an added flourish that night), I settled into a chair in the corner of the room and paid closer-than-necessary attention to spearing my food with the plastic spork. As

I predicted, seven people were soon shuffling shoulder to shoulder along the front of the buffet, competing for the choicest bits of chicken.

A long trestle table sat in the room's center with ten chairs positioned haphazardly around it. Aside from Phil, the moderator—a large man whose cherubic cheeks and kind eyes kept him eternally youthful—I didn't recognize anyone. There was usually quite a turnover at these things since the constant talk of death was too confronting for some attendees. Plus, I think a lot of people came to this one just for the comfort food. I liked that Phil never forced me into conversation, even though he knew me as a semi-regular. An exchange of nods was enough for both of us. I sat down and held my breath as if on an airplane right before takeoff, hoping the seat next to me would stay empty. Thankfully, the old man on my other side seemed just as averse to friendly chatter. We sat silently as I contemplated getting one more piece of chicken before the introductions began.

"Clover!"

The back of my neck prickled. That enthusiastic male voice could belong to any number of people, and not the person I was dreading it might be. I began calculating how rude it would be if I didn't turn around and instead just ignored it. Unfortunately, the answer was well below my lowest threshold for bad manners.

Sebastian, the suspected funeral home/real estate/life insurance shark, was removing his scarf when I turned to connect the voice with a face. His wide grin sparked a flash of anger in my chest—was he touring the city's death cafés in search of unsuspecting targets? I was tempted to expose him immediately to everyone in the room, but I would at least need to gather some proof first. A symptom of spending a lot of time alone with your thoughts like I did was that sometimes they could run a little wild.

"Of all the death cafés in all the world," he said, very poorly channeling Humphrey Bogart. I considered myself a pretty worthy judge—I'd seen *Casablanca* at least thirty times and could pretty much recite it verbatim.

I pretended to look confused. "I'm sorry . . . do we know each other?"

Sebastian flinched but maintained his grin. "Yeah! We met at the death café in the New York Public Library, remember?" His smile receded slightly. "You mentioned your grandmother had just passed away."

The nerve. If I really did have a grandmother who had passed away recently, she'd be long buried by now and not in need of whatever he was peddling. Was he just playing the long game and trying to find out if I had any other ailing older relatives?

"Please take your seats, everyone," Phil said, looking pointedly at Sebastian.

As he shuffled his chair closer to the table, Sebastian seemed more relaxed than the first time we met. Probably because he now knew the run of play at death cafés. Or maybe that nervous-newcomer act had all been part of his ruse? He trotted out the same story as last time—that his family never discussed death—during introductions. Likewise, I stuck to my lie about my grandmother recently dying. (I mean, he'd just announced it to the room, so it would've been odd if I didn't acknowledge it.)

Phil was a little more improvisational in his approach than other café moderators. Instead of suggesting a topic to get the conversation flowing, he opened it up to the room.

"Well, then—let's get things rollin'," he said, his Ss catching gently on his teeth. "Who has something they want to discuss?"

A redhead in bright, clashing patterns raised her hand eagerly, waving it unnecessarily since she was competing with nobody. I'd already suspected she'd be opinionated—you could always tell by someone's dominant posture, elbows on the table, and the way they scanned the circle hoping to lock into eye contact with someone.

Phil nodded sagely in her direction, briefly consulting the torn notebook sheet in front of him. I could see he'd drawn a diagram of the table during introductions and written each person's name in their position.

"Tabitha, is it?" The redhead nodded eagerly, like she had a secret she was bursting to reveal. "Well, Tabitha, what do you have to share with us?"

Tabitha clutched the large, pink crystal hanging around her neck.

"So," she said, scanning the rectangle of faces eyeing her uncertainly. "Have you ever wondered if we all have a specific time we're meant to die? Kind of like a set fate? You know when you hear those stories of people who escape death, like in a plane crash or a building collapse, and then they die in a freak accident a few months later? It's like death has their number and they can't escape it."

Though I'd never admit it to her, I'd often thought about the same question. I'd witnessed enough peculiar things over the years to suspect that everyone had a predestined expiration date. A few years ago, I had a client—a stockbroker in his fifties—diagnosed with a terminal illness and given three months to live. To his doctors' bewilderment, he made a full recovery, but then, three months later, fell off a ladder while changing a lightbulb in his lake house and died of a head injury.

"I definitely believe there is," piped up a stocky young girl with winged eyeliner and draped layers of black clothing. "I think it's already decided the day you're born." She leaned over her mac and cheese, lowering her voice for dramatic effect. "The question is: If you could know the date of your death in advance, would you want to?"

The room fell silent. A siren crescendoed nearby as the proposition sunk in. This was a hypothetical I hadn't considered.

Sebastian broke the silence.

"No way," he said, shaking his head. "If I knew when I was going to die, I'd become obsessed with changing the outcome in any way I could. And then I'd end up living a miserable life anyway."

It annoyed me that I agreed with him.

Tabitha looked serenely across the table at Sebastian. "Personally," she said, toying with her crystal, "I think I'd like to know. It would allow me to prioritize things a little. If you knew exactly how much time you had left, you'd be more likely to use it wisely, right?"

At the head of the table, Phil nodded thoughtfully. "That's true, Tabitha. But the thing is, we all know we're going to die—that's guaranteed. So shouldn't we be making the most of our lives anyway?"

"Yes," I said, surprised at myself for speaking up and instantly regretting it as everyone focused on me. "The reason so many people die with regrets is because they live like they're invincible. They don't really think about their death until right before it happens."

What most people don't consider is that death is often random and cruel. It doesn't care if you've been kind all your life. Or if you've eaten healthily, exercised often, and always worn a seat belt or a helmet. It doesn't care that a loved one left behind might spend the rest of their lives replaying events in their head, tormented by the words "if only." People tell themselves they've got plenty of time, until they're at the mercy of a careless action—a driver on their cellphone, a neighbor who left a candle burning. And by then, it's too late.

"It's kind of like that Brad Pitt movie," Sebastian interjected. "The one where he's death in human form and he comes for Anthony Hopkins but then falls in love with the daughter."

My annoyance at Sebastian deepened knowing that he was well acquainted with another of my favorite movies.

The blond, bearded guy next to Tabitha rolled his eyes. "Bro, I can't believe you watched that—it's like four hours long."

"I grew up with three sisters," Sebastian said, shrugging. "And it's actually not that bad. It has a really great soundtrack—Thomas Newman was the composer, I think."

The blond guy shook his head, even more displeased, and dug his spork into his remaining hunk of fried chicken.

Phil tapped his pen on the table. "And who else has a topic they'd like to discuss?" He was purposely avoiding eye contact with

Tabitha, who obviously had more to say and no qualms about dom-
inating the conversation all evening. The discussion moved to more
practical matters, like if it should be your decision whether you have
a funeral.

The blond guy said he didn't want one. "Just have a beer—or a
joint—in my honor instead," he proclaimed.

Unsurprisingly, Tabitha had a counter-opinion. "Funerals aren't
for the dead," she insisted. "They're for the people left behind to
have closure."

Sebastian nodded emphatically. "Yeah, I think it's important that
people have the chance to say goodbye. And besides, it's not like you
have any control over it—you're dead."

I knew it. He'd probably be the type to convince people to buy
extra things they didn't need for the service, like ostentatious floral
arrangements and sappy PowerPoint slide shows. I concentrated on
holding my tongue until Phil called the meeting to a close and invited everyone to help themselves to the remaining food. As I was
about to claim my leftovers, I noticed Sebastian talking to the old
man who'd been sitting next to me. He handed the man his business
card and patted him on the shoulder—I could barely believe how
blatantly he was marking his next target. Appalled, I threw my plate
in the trash and hurried out of the building without any leftovers.

Determined not to get caught lingering outside the death café
again, I power-walked to the subway. I'd have to get Leo's ice cream
next time. MetroCard in hand, I hurried down the steps, my heart
leaping at the sight of the train pulling in as I reached the turnstile. In one motion, I slid my card through the reader and pushed
against the revolving bar.

Beeeeeeeeeeeeeeeeeeeep. The green text on the turnstile screen
demanded I swipe my card again.

My thigh muscle ached from hitting the bar. Rubbing the mag-
netic strip of my card on my coat sleeve, I swiped again.

Beeeeeeeeeeeeeeeeeeeep. The screen instructed me to repeat the
action.

My hands shook with a mix of frustration and adrenaline as I heard the monotonic announcement echoing from the belly of the 1 train.

"STAND. CLEAR. OF. THE. CLOSING. DOORS. PLEASE."

I desperately swiped my card a final time and the screen mockingly flashed its final verdict:

Card already used at this turnstile.

I only ever used curse words in my head, and only rarely. Tonight was one of those occasions.

Fuck.

I should've slipped under the turnstile and sprinted to the diminishing gap between the doors, but I hesitated too long and watched glumly as the train hissed out of the station. The departures screen compounded my disappointment: nineteen minutes until the next train. An arbitrary New York City transit rule meant I couldn't swipe my card again for another eighteen minutes since it was registering as just used. I turned to the ticket booth to plead my case, but it was unoccupied—I was at the mercy of an MTA employee's ill-timed break.

As I considered my options, a disheveled man unzipped his fly and relieved himself on the side of the ticket machine, reinvigorating the scent of urine. A steaming yellow stream arced from between his hands as he tilted his head and sneered at me.

There was no way I was waiting down there.

I power-walked back up the stairs to street level, wondering if I should invest in a fitness tracker to measure all this vigorous exercise. The fluorescent glow of Duane Reade beckoned me in sanctuary. I needed to pick up some vitamins to make up for the recent lack of vegetables in my life, anyway. I set my phone timer for fifteen minutes—exactly enough time to get to the station, with a buffer for any MetroCard mishaps.

A nasal country-music ballad leached from the store's sound system while I perused the rainbow of multivitamins.

"We meet again!"

I allowed myself to mentally curse again.

Sebastian was standing next to me, hands stuffed in his coat pockets.

"Hi." I didn't even attempt friendliness.

"I figured I'd stop by and pick up some allergy medicine," Sebastian explained. "The pollen count is out of control right now, even though it's still winter."

The slight rosy hue surrounding his nostrils seemed to corroborate his alibi, but I didn't respond.

He tried again. "So, you're stocking up on vitamins?"

At the thought of enduring any kind of conversation with him, I broke. "Why do you keep following me?" My exasperation made my question louder than I meant it to be. "I don't want any of whatever it is you're selling!"

Sebastian clenched his eyebrows, confused. "Selling? What do you mean?"

"Funerals, real estate, life insurance—I don't know. Whatever you do to swindle people out of their money. I saw you give that guy your business card."

I jammed the jar of multivitamins back onto the shelf, sending the ones next to it tumbling. We both lunged to catch the cascading jars in a clumsy juggling act.

Sebastian was still shaking his head in confusion as he put the vitamins back on the shelf. "I don't know what you're talking about . . . I mean, I do work at the Federal Reserve, but I'm an economic modeler. That's not exactly swindling people out of money."

As I bent down to pick up the remaining jars, I realized that I had indeed allowed my imagination to cultivate a slightly outrageous narrative about Sebastian.

"Well, why do you keep showing up at these death cafés?" I demanded, too proud to admit I might be wrong.

He shrugged, like the answer was obvious. "Like I said, I've never really had the chance to talk about death before—emotionally stunted family and all that. I heard about death cafés and thought they might help."

The burn of embarrassment crept into my cheeks.

Sebastian looked down at his shoes and scuffed one along the floor. "But I guess you're right—there is more to it than that."

The burn receded. Maybe my narrative wasn't so outrageous after all.

"It's something we kind of have in common."

"Oh?" Now I was confused.

"It's my grandmother. We found out a few weeks ago that she's dying, but nobody in my family wants to talk about it, which is ridiculous, in my opinion."

For the second time that night, I reluctantly agreed with him— not talking about death only ever made it harder. I felt a sliver of compassion.

"I'm sorry to hear that. It must be tough for you."

It was as if my guilt for assuming the worst in him somehow shifted his appearance. The combined bookishness of his spectacles and scarf were suddenly quite charming.

"It is." Sebastian looked at me hopefully. "But I know you can relate, since you just lost your grandmother."

Guilt continued to clench my abdomen. Between the two of us, I was turning out to be the dishonest one. "Well, um . . ."

"Anyway," he said. "I'm really sorry if it seemed like I was following you. I just thought it might be good to talk to someone who'd been through the same thing and it was a really nice surprise to run into you tonight. I live on the Upper West Side so this death café is pretty close to me."

Dishonesty was one thing, but misleading someone who was grieving a loved one felt cruel.

I took a slow breath. "Actually, Sebastian, my grandmother didn't die. Well, she did die—both of my grandmothers did—but it was before I was born, so I never met either of them."

"Oh." Sebastian rubbed his chin. "Why would you lie about that?"

"Because I don't really want to talk about what I do for a living."

"But what does that have to do with going to a death café? No one really mentions their jobs at these things."

"Yeah, but death kind of is my job."

"What are you, like, some kind of hit woman?" His nervous tone indicated he was only partly joking.

"No. I'm a death doula."

"A *death* doula? Wow, I've never heard of that. Sounds kind of ominous."

I fought off competing emotions. Embarrassment for letting my imagination get carried away and for getting caught in a lie. Empathy for Sebastian and his dying grandmother. Nervousness at the fact that a nice-looking man my age was aware of my presence and looking at me intently. My brain struggled to communicate a coherent sentence to my tongue.

The chiming timer on my phone was my savior.

"I've got to go," I blurted abruptly, slowly placing the last jar of vitamins back on the shelf to avoid another avalanche. "Have a good night."

"Wait, could we maybe—"

By the time he finished his sentence, I'd already made it through the store's sliding doors.

13

After a week of grayish cotton wool blanketing the city sky, an infinite stretch of clear blue finally greeted me as I waited to cross Seventh Avenue. I was grateful for the injection of cheer—Sundays still felt gloomy without Grandpa. In the months after he died, I couldn't bring myself to set foot in the diner. Or the bookstore. Continuing our weekly tradition without him was a taunting reminder that I'd been on the other side of the world enjoying myself when he needed me most. That even if there was nothing I could do to prevent his death, I could have at least spent more time with him before it happened.

I've never understood Western society's warped perception of grief as something quantifiable and finite, a problem to be fixed. Eight months after Grandpa died, my doctor suggested I see a psychiatrist because I was still having trouble accepting he was gone. After only one session, the psychiatrist promptly diagnosed me with "persistent complex bereavement disorder," aka chronic grief, and suggested I take antidepressants. Turns out, in the opinion of most medical experts, your grieving process shouldn't last longer than six months. And if you aren't over it by then, there's something clinically wrong with you.

What the hell?

It felt callous to be expected to resume life as normal six months after losing someone whose existence had been so indelibly intertwined with yours. There would never be a moment I wouldn't miss Grandpa. That was one of the reasons I became a death doula—my grief felt more at home in the company of others who were grieving, whether it was loved ones or the dying person themselves grieving a life they knew they could have lived better.

As much as it hurt, I eventually realized that keeping up our diner and bookstore tradition was one of the few ways I could still feel close to Grandpa. Now, every Sunday when I wasn't working, I ate breakfast alone in our favorite booth at the diner and then walked to the bookstore, his absence as conspicuous as his presence ever was. After more than a decade, the pain had dulled slightly, but my grief hadn't diminished. It had just taken a different shape.

I pulled my coat tighter and walked the few blocks from the diner, the grease from my French toast lulling my stomach into a false sense of satiation. Two decades of commercial invasion had stripped the surrounding neighborhood of many of its original gems, but Bessie's bookstore endured. The woman herself, now in her late seventies, remained equally robust—her middle noticeably rounder, her smile as welcoming as ever. And she still tried to tempt me with candy.

"Clover, honey!" Bessie shuffled sideways in the space between two shelves to accommodate her generous girth. "That Georgia O'Keeffe biography you've been waiting for is here behind the counter. You sure do love those lonely pioneering women!"

"Thanks, Bessie." The idea of a solitary life among the mountains and desert of New Mexico definitely had its appeal. "I might just take a quick look around to see what else is new."

"Be my guest!"

I didn't need more books, but I liked the rush of dopamine that came from finding a new title to add to my potential reading list. I gave the science section a wide berth, trying not to imagine Grandpa's tall silhouette perusing its shelves.

Two young men, each of a coltish build, stood browsing the fiction spines between the letters *E* and *K*. The shorter leaned his head on the shoulder of the taller, their pinkies casually laced together. I stepped backward quietly, not wanting to intrude on their bubble. Each man would use his free hand to pull out an individual book and skim its blurb, before slotting it back in with the same hand to avoid breaking the pinkie connection that kept them linked. Every so often, one would pass a book to the other, along with a smile and a whisper of "I think you'd like this one."

I envied their intimacy. The treasure of having someone who knew your taste in books. A shoulder to rest your head on as you browsed.

An emptiness blazed in my heart. I didn't feel like scouring the shelves for new additions to my reading list anymore.

As I rounded the corner from the bookstore, Georgia O'Keeffe tome under my arm, I thought about the entry I'd selected from my ADVICE notebook that morning from Olive, a cartographer with an endearingly loud laugh and an aggressive melanoma. After making me promise I'd always wear sunscreen (which I have ever since), she added a more surprising piece of advice.

"Whenever I moved to a new city or started a new relationship, I'd always change my perfume," she'd told me. "That way I'd be able to look back and relive my best memories from that time whenever I smelled it. So whenever you feel a shift or start a new chapter in life, find a new scent to go with it."

I'd never worn perfume before. And I definitely wasn't moving to a new city or starting a new relationship. But I understood implicitly the way smell helped imprint memories—the distinct spice of Grandpa's aftershave could transport me in a second. And the idea of choosing a scent felt like a way to inject some variety into my relatively monotonous life. I could at least consider sampling some perfumes to find one that fit.

As I started walking toward the nearest department store, I felt my phone vibrating in my coat pocket. I didn't recognize the number, but that wasn't unusual if someone was calling me about a job. Ducking under a shop awning, I steeled myself. Death I could handle; phone calls I loathed. Why couldn't everyone just email?

"Hello, Clover speaking."

A brief silence on the other end, then a throat clearing.

"Ah, hi, Clover."

I recognized the voice immediately.

"It's Sebastian. From the death cafés." A nervous laugh. "And the vitamin aisle of Duane Reade."

I could've just hung up, but curiosity stopped me. Why would he be calling me after I'd made such an embarrassing exit? And how had he gotten my number?

"Hello, Sebastian."

"So, I'm sorry to bother you on a Sunday . . . I bet you're wondering how I found you."

"You could say that."

"I swear I'm not following you. I mean, I kind of am, but not in the way you think." Uncomfortable silence. "After you ran out the other night, I went home and googled exactly what a death doula was. And you know, the more I read about it, the more I realized how great it was."

"I see." His flattery softened my defenses slightly, even if it wasn't directed specifically at me.

"It made me realize that a death doula is exactly what my grandmother needs. I think it would really help her." Sebastian's sentences were gaining pace, like he was trying to get it all out before being interrupted. "She wants to stay in her house and so she has home health aides there to help her around the clock, but nobody like you—someone who can help her through the more, you know, experiential stuff. That's what you do, right?"

"Yes, kind of." I trod carefully. "But how did you get my number?"

Another nervous laugh. "It actually wasn't that hard. I mean, how many death doulas named Clover are there in New York? And I'm pretty good at going down internet rabbit holes."

A flock of boisterous teenagers bustled past me on the sidewalk.

"There are lots of death doulas in the city who could help your grandmother," I said, trying to keep my voice low. "I can recommend some."

"Yeah, that's probably true, but I think she would like you a lot." Sebastian's persistence was a little exasperating.

"You don't even know anything about me. The only thing you thought you knew about me was a lie, anyway." The side of my neck ached from clenching my shoulders.

"Well, are you taking on new clients?"

It was hard to say no to a potential job. Long stretches between clients weren't healthy for my finances, even if I was a diligent saver. You don't become a death doula for the money—I usually scaled my rate to whatever the person could afford. Sometimes, like with Abigail, I even did it for free. But regardless of the payment, Sebastian's grandma didn't deserve a lonely death.

"Yes . . . but I may already have one. It's not quite confirmed yet." I'd never been a liar, but the instinct seemed to emerge whenever I spoke to him.

"I'd be willing to pay more than your usual rate. Just name the price."

"You don't even know if I'm good at my job."

"Actually, I do," Sebastian said with irritating satisfaction. "I found a death announcement online that mentioned you while I was searching for your contact details. It thanked you for your support."

Who could that have been? It was rare that I got any kind of public acknowledgment.

"It turns out," Sebastian continued, "I have a friend who works as a nurse at the hospital where the person, um, passed away, and he asked around for your name and contact details."

It felt a little like an invasion of my privacy. But then again, if anyone else had done the same thing to track me down and offer me a job, I probably wouldn't have thought twice about it.

Undeterred by my silence, Sebastian kept talking.

"You come very highly recommended, which doesn't surprise me, of course. And it would mean a lot to me if you could help my grandmother. I just want to help make this whole *thing* as easy for her as possible."

Part of me desperately wanted to say no. I felt uncomfortable around Sebastian, especially now that I'd been caught in a lie. But it would be unethical for me not to help someone if I could. Even if he wasn't here to say so, I knew Grandpa would be disappointed in me.

Sighing, I relinquished.

"Okay, let me think about it. Text me your email address and if the other potential client I have doesn't work out, I can send you all the usual paperwork and we can see from there." One more lie for the road.

"Great—looking forward to seeing you again, Clover."

A flutter filled my chest. Even if Sebastian had meant it in a professional context, it was the first time a man had ever said that to me.

14

For my ninth birthday, Grandpa gifted me three things: a navy-blue leather-bound notebook, a silver fountain pen, and a pair of binoculars. As we sat at the diner, empty breakfast plates between us, he produced a package from beneath the table and slid it in front of me. "Many happy returns, my dear."

Already giddy with anticipation (I'd spied the wrapped gift tucked under his arm as we walked from our apartment), I eagerly peeled back the pinstriped paper. The asymmetrical folds and liberal use of tape were endearing evidence that he wrapped it himself.

"Intelligence will only get you so far in life," Grandpa said, watching with satisfaction. "And the same can be said for wit and charm. But two things will serve you better than any others."

His emphatic pause made me look up from unearthing the treasures from the paper. Grandpa was a man of sparing conversation, so I knew to listen closely whenever he took the time to impart any kind of wisdom.

"What are they?"

He took a thoughtful sip of coffee. "Infinite curiosity and a keen sense of observation."

I slid the notebook out from beneath the folds and ran my fingers over the smooth leather cover. A strand of the same leather looped around it twice, with the fountain pen hooked over it. For years, I'd watched Grandpa carry an almost identical journal, regularly pausing to scribble a series of notes, documenting life as he saw it.

And now I had my own.

"Thanks, Grandpa! I love them." I raised the binoculars to my eyes and scanned the periphery of the diner.

"You're welcome, dear," Grandpa said. "But remember, those binoculars come with a caveat."

"What's a caveat?"

"It's a condition or rule."

"What kind of rule?"

"You must never use them to invade someone else's privacy." His tone was firm. "I know in this city we all live in one another's pockets. And that closeness can make it tempting to delve into people's lives—or their windows—in ways that we shouldn't. So no spying on the neighbors, understood?"

"Understood." I matched his somber tone, though I secretly regretted giving my word. Watching the glowing brownstone windows across the street every night, each with its own characters and storyline, was one of my favorite hobbies. And the binoculars would have made it even easier to watch those stories unfold.

"Good girl," Grandpa said. He reached into his jacket pocket and produced his own notebook, waving it enticingly. "I thought we could go on a little field trip today. What do you say?"

I sat up straight to convey my enthusiasm. "I say yes!"

Every year, Grandpa found a memorable way to mark my birthday. The year before, it'd been a trip out to the Coney Island aquarium and a lunch of hotdogs and funnel cakes. The birthday before that, we went on an adventure to the abandoned subway station underneath City Hall.

"One more thing before we go," Grandpa said, sliding his notebook back into his pocket and nodding toward the diner's kitchen.

Hilda—my favorite waitress on account of her elaborate hairdos and equally compelling personality—was approaching the table carrying something in her left hand obscured by the plastic menu in her right. She swept the menu to the side, revealing a red-velvet cupcake with a single candle flickering at its center. A sporadic star of off-off-Broadway shows, Hilda commenced a dramatic rendition of "Happy Birthday."

Grandpa's smooth, deep baritone, which he reserved for special occasions, provided the coda. "And maaanny mooooorree."

Celebratory breakfast complete, Grandpa and I sat side by side on the C train as it chugged lethargically toward the Upper West Side. Our binoculars hung around our necks and our leather notebooks rested on our laps.

In the three years since our cohabitation had begun, I'd developed an intense curiosity over the contents of Grandpa's notebooks. Sometimes I'd find one unattended—usually splayed on the side table next to his armchair, leather cord lying tantalizingly undone—and fought the temptation to read it. What could be so important about life that it required such extensive documentation? A tenured biology professor at Columbia University, Grandpa had a passion for categorizing things. Since his study became my bedroom when I arrived to live with him, every inch of spare space in the apartment was now filled with his pedagogical paraphernalia. Crowded rows of jars containing natural specimens lined the bookshelves of our living room. And from the day I'd mastered the use of the label maker, Grandpa enlisted me to help classify the contents of any new jars he added to the collection. He'd slowly dictate the spellings of complicated scientific names while I diligently manipulated the dial back and forth, embossing each letter into eternity. (*Ornithorhynchus* was my most memorable label—although the tiny platypus fetus suspended in liquid admittedly wasn't very cute.)

Getting off the C train at Eighty-First Street, we followed the path into Central Park down into the woodland below the castle. I'd never really found tales of princesses sitting around waiting for princes appealing, but I liked the idea of living in a castle with end-less rooms and dungeons to be explored. Occasionally, I imagined a prince joining me on those expeditions, but I always led the way.

We wandered under the thick canopy of trees until Grandpa stopped at a lamppost.

"What do you notice about this lamppost?"

I examined it carefully, tracking my eyes up and down to take in every detail before I gave my final answer. The only thing that distinguished it from the average lamppost was a small numeric plaque midway down its trunk.

"The numbers?" I offered tentatively, searching for a tell in Grandpa's expert poker face. His smile affirmed my guess, like a hidden door swinging open after the uttering of a secret password.

"Exactly." He hitched up his pant legs and knelt on one knee so that he met my eye level. "If you ever find yourself lost in Central Park, these plaques will help you find your way."

I frowned at the random number sequence. "How?"

"Look closely at the last two numbers," he said, running his fingers over the embossed metal. "If they're odd, that means you're closer to the west side of the park. And if they're even, you're closer to the east."

"But what about the first two numbers?"

"They represent the cross street we're closest to." He rested his elbow on the top of his knee. "So if it says '7751,' what do you think the closest street is?"

I swung my arms from side to side as I thought. "West Seventy-Seventh?"

Grandpa winked. "Clever girl."

As the fresh knowledge took root in my brain, I felt the satisfaction of having unlocked one more of the world's infinite secrets. I skipped after Grandpa as he led me down the path to a small clearing near the lake with a stretch of benches at its perimeter.

He gestured to the end bench. "Let's have a seat."

My legs dangled beneath me as I ran my hand over the curve of the iron armrest.

"This is one of the very best spots for bird-watching," he said, tapping his binoculars knowingly. "And if you point your binoculars at that cluster of trees over there, you'll likely spot a family of ruby-throated hummingbirds."

I positioned the rubber eyepieces snugly in front of my eyes.

"I don't see anything," I whined after only a few moments of scanning the treetops.

"Well, that's because you're missing the most important element of observation."

I peered at him over the top of my binoculars. "What's that?"

He wiggled his eyebrows. "Patience."

Sighing, I refocused my lenses on the trees and waited, determined to show just how patient I could be. Three minutes ticked by before I spotted a flash of crimson moving among the foliage.

"I see one!" I whispered loudly, trying not to startle the creature. "I see its red throat."

Grandpa leaned over and kept his voice low. "That means it's a male. The females usually have white throats. What else can you notice about it?"

"It has a long, sharp beak. Longer than other birds. And it's always moving, not sitting on a branch."

"That's because hummingbirds rarely stop moving. Their wings beat up to eighty times a second, which creates the humming sound that their name comes from."

"Whoa, that's fast."

As the bird disappeared back into the trees, I rested the binoculars on my knees and looked at Grandpa, eager for our lesson to continue.

"The way we understand nature is to observe its patterns. With birds, we know they appear at a certain time of year, and that they prefer certain types of trees and certain types of foods." He slung one long leg over the other, revealing a blue-and-green striped sock pulled above his ankle. "Or take the seasons, for example. How do you know that it's fall?"

"Because the leaves change color and fall to the ground."

"Exactly. That same thing happens every year. And when the leaves fall, it helps us know what kind of coat we need to wear or which vegetables to plant."

"Or that it's almost Halloween."

"Right. So the best way to understand the world is to look for its patterns." He patted his notebook. "And that's what this is for. By noting down everything interesting you see, you'll eventually find that things occur with regularity. And it will help you learn how they work. Shall we take some notes on what we've observed so far?"

"Yes!" I'd been desperate to write in my notebook all morning. I uncapped my fountain pen and began carefully describing the lamppost in my best handwriting.

"You know, it's not just nature that shows us patterns." Grandpa nodded toward the clearing where several groups of people were lounging. "You can also learn a lot about people just by watching them."

I lifted my binoculars to zoom in on a trio of girls gathered on a picnic blanket. Grandpa placed his hand on the barrels and gently pushed them down. "Remember what I said: no spying."

"The cav-e-at." I said, proud that the word had stuck in my memory.

"Yes, exactly, the caveat. But we can observe from afar in public." With his arm stretched along the back of the seat, he pointed subtly to a family sitting on one of the benches on the opposite side of the clearing. "Tell me what you see over there."

I frowned. "A man and a woman with their two kids." I was slightly insulted that he would ask me such an obvious question.

"But what can you tell me about what they're doing?"

"He's talking . . . but it doesn't look like she's really listening."

"How do you know that?"

"Well, her body is turned away from him and she's looking around at everything."

Grandpa nodded. "And you see how his legs are turned toward her and he's leaning into her space, but the more he leans in, the more she moves away?"

"I see it."

"The interesting thing is that neither of them probably realizes that it's happening. You can learn a lot from watching people's body language—often it tells you much more than what they're actually saying."

"I think her body language is saying that he isn't very interesting," I deduced, then paused to note that fact on paper.

Grandpa chuckled. "You might be right."

I looked at the two little girls at the couple's feet. "But she's not taking any notice of her kids either." The observation stung a little—I was pretty sure I'd seen that same look of indifference on my own mother's face. "Maybe she's unhappy. It looks like she doesn't want to be there."

Grandpa opened his mouth to respond but then stopped, as if he'd cast a fishing line and was reeling it back. "Yes, that could be true." He squinted above the treetops. "Unfortunately, there are a lot of people in this world who are unhappy with the lives they've chosen."

"That's really sad, Grandpa." I kicked my legs out in front of me and tapped my sneakers together. "Can't we do something to help them?"

"Sometimes, but it's not always our place to do so."

I peered up at him, dissatisfied. "But that's not very fair to her kids."

He rubbed his stubble for a few moments, thinking.

"I'll tell you a secret about adults, Clover," he said finally. "Even though it seems like they know what they're doing, often they're just trying their best to work life out as they go. And that's especially true of parents—I think every mom and dad probably wishes they'd done things differently at some point, in some way."

I looked back at the woman and her kids. "You mean maybe my mom and dad wished they'd spent more time with me? And maybe taken me with them on their trips?"

"That's very possible." I noticed him grimace slightly. "You know, when your mom was a young girl like you, I traveled around the world a lot for my job too. And that meant I didn't get to spend as much time with her as I would have liked."

"But you were having adventures." I loved the stories he'd told me about his biology expeditions to far-flung jungles and islands. "Maybe they were too dangerous for a little girl?"

Grandpa seemed surprised by my logic. "Yes, that's true. And the same might have been true of your mom and dad's adventures."

I considered that for a moment. "And if they'd taken me to China, maybe I wouldn't be here with you now."

He rubbed his stubble again. "I suppose that's something we'll never know for sure," he said. "But what I do know is that I'm very glad that you *are* here with me."

I beamed up at him, curling my hand under his arm. "Me too."

We sat for a few moments, watching the kids playing in front of their parents until he tapped my notebook with his pen.

"The lesson here, my dear, is that almost anything can be understood if you study it hard enough. Even human beings. Some people have a natural ability to read others and understand them, but for the rest of us, it helps to look for their patterns."

"What kind of patterns?"

"Well, as you meet more people in your life, you'll see that there are many different personalities in the world, and that means you can't approach everybody the same way. For example, you and I like to spend time sitting quietly reading our books, isn't that right?"

"Of course!"

"But for some people that would be misery. They'd prefer to always be surrounded by lots of other people, chattering."

I was skeptical. "Really?" A life without books sounded like misery to me.

"Yes, really," Grandpa said. "So, as you interact with people in your life, take the time to observe them. Look at the way they inhabit the world. Do they like to be noticed or do they prefer to blend in? Do they approach problems creatively or intellectually? What agitates them or calms them?"

My pen hovered over the page, but Grandpa continued speaking. "Learning these patterns will help you be of most use to people. It won't help you ever understand them completely—we humans are a complex bunch—but it will give you clues about what makes them tick."

"People, patterns, clues—got it," I said, noting the words down like a complicated math formula.

I had a feeling this particular birthday lesson was going to come in handy. I didn't know many people yet, but one day I might. And I couldn't wait to find out exactly how I could be of most use to the world.

15

I thought you'd disappeared into thin air," Leo teased as he examined the scattering of mahjong tiles between us on his dining table. He circulated a tile between his finger and thumb, considering his move. "I haven't seen you in a week. Did you even leave the house?"

"Of course I did." My tone was more impetuous than I'd intended, but he was needling me on purpose. "I walked George every day—twice."

"That doesn't count unless you actually interacted with another human being." Leo returned the tile to his lineup and threw out the neighboring one instead. "I don't know how you can spend so much time at home without seeing anybody."

"We're not all as sociable as you are, Leo. Why do I have to interact with anybody? I like spending time by myself."

Leo leaned back in his chair, crossing his arms like a disapproving bouncer. "You know, I can't understand why you keep your world so small. There are so many interesting people out there."

I braced myself. Leo had become increasingly philosophical in the past month or so, like he'd just realized that he was getting old and still hadn't pondered many of life's big questions. Unfortunately, it meant he'd started philosophizing about my life as well.

Shrugging, I picked up a tile from the mahjong wall. "I just like my own company most of the time."

It was almost true. The upside of having lost my parents so young, if there was one, was a fierce self-sufficiency. Too busy with their own lives, my parents never thought to arrange playdates with other kids. So when I reached school age, I hadn't really learned the art, or point, of making friends. When my classmates shunned me after Mr. Hyland's death, I just retreated further into my imagination and became so reliant on myself that I didn't need anyone. Sure, I'd met some interesting people in my travels during college and even kept in touch with them via email for a while—until Grandpa died. I'd learned the hard way that when people ask you how you're doing after a loved one's death, they don't really want to know. They want to hear that you've moved on because they can't stand to look at your pain. And when I didn't move on, the emails gradually trickled to nothing.

Leo didn't let the subject slide. "But you're so good with people—just look at the work you do." He reached over to pinch my cheek, like I was still the little girl he first met. "You just need to open yourself up a little more."

I dodged his hand. "It's easy to be 'good with people' when they're dying. I know I'm helping them and I know what they need: comfort, company, and someone to listen." I counted the items off on my fingers for emphasis.

Leo grunted in dissent. "I think you're underestimating how rare your skills are, kid. Everyone confronts their death differently. Hell, most of us don't even want to talk about it until it comes knocking. It takes a real special person to help someone navigate the dying process in their own personal way."

"Right. But I'm good at it because that's my job." His relentless prodding was exhausting. "There aren't any pretenses with dying people. And there's no pressure to make a good impression because they won't be around to remember you." It also meant that there was no risk involved for me—I knew the outcome of the relationship before it even began.

"That's playing it too safe, if you ask me," Leo said. "What kind of life are you living if you've never let anyone see the real you?"

I tensed my body to stop myself from squirming. I knew his question had merit.

"You see the real me." Again, almost the truth.

"And I'm also more than twice your age—I won't be around forever." He shook his head. "Don't you ever want to settle down with somebody one day?"

I shrugged one shoulder, hoping it seemed casual. "I guess I've never really thought about it."

Of course I'd thought about it. About what it would be like to have someone whose day was better for having you in it. Someone whose mind you occupied even when you weren't there. Someone who trusted that you would treat their heart gently—and would take on the sacred duty of doing the same for you.

"Well, I don't wanna get all grandfatherly on you, but maybe you should. There's nothing like being in love—even if it doesn't last as long as you want it to." Leo's eyes shone as he looked up at the glamour portrait of his wife, Winnie, who watched over our mahjong games. They'd been quite the socialites on the jazz scene in the fifties and sixties, but their enviable romance (which I never got tired of hearing about) was cut short when Winnie died in a car accident at thirty-five. And more than fifty years later Leo still wore his wedding band. I think that's another reason he and I got along so well—our grief could coexist. I loved that he'd kept his ring, even when people suggested it was time he took it off. It frustrated me that society was so determined to quantify grief, as if time could erase the potency of love. Or, on the other hand, how it dictated that grief for someone you knew fleetingly should be equally as fleeting. But while a mother who miscarries might not have ever had the chance to hold that child, they had plenty of time to love them, to dream and hope for them. And that means their grief is twofold—they're not just grieving the child, but the life they never got to experience.

Who are we to tell anyone their pain isn't worthy?

Leo blew a kiss in Winnie's direction then went back to frowning at his tiles. "You know, everyone talks about how they want to live forever, but they don't think about what it's like when your wife and all your friends are dead, and you're the only one left. It's lonely."

An ache welled in my chest. I didn't need to live forever to know what loneliness felt like.

I stood at my stove later that night, warming milk for hot chocolate and ruminating on my conversation with Leo. As well versed as I was in the intricacies of fictional romantic love, I had yet to master it in real life. Or, more specifically, yet to even experience it. My imagination, on the other hand, needed only a glance or a brushing of shoulders to ignite the fuse of a daydreamed crush. I'd had many of those over the years—baristas, librarians, bus drivers, supermarket cashiers—but most of the time, they didn't even notice I existed. And I was too shy to try to get their attention; I wasn't sure I was even worthy of it. So instead, I preferred to live in my head, observing the people around me, and on screens, living vicariously through their relationships. It was safer that way.

Closing my eyes, I inhaled the steam from the milk and cinnamon as it bubbled in a low simmer in the copper saucepan. The handle bore tarnish marks in two distinct places, the result of three decades of use between me and Grandpa. The creamy brown liquid formed a meditative spiral as I poured it from the puckered side of the saucepan.

As I clasped my hands around the ceramic mug, a familiar longing niggled at me. An incongruous tug-of-war between the need for solitude and the craving for emotional connection—I didn't want company, but I didn't want to feel alone.

I positioned a chair at the corner of the window, then rested my mug on the sill and wrapped myself in the alpaca blanket. Extinguishing all the living room lights, leaving only the spillover of the streetlamp, I slowly pulled up the blinds so that the movement was imperceptible from the outside. George ambled over, ready to assume his role in this routine he knew well. I pulled him onto my lap and lifted the binoculars to my eyes.

The light of the living room opposite burned bright, like a lighthouse to my ship. There they were, as usual around this time of night, seated at right angles to each other at their dining table.

Julia and Reuben.

Not their real names, of course. At least, probably not their real names; I'd never actually met them. But I knew them intimately. I knew that Reuben did most of the cooking, but Julia always chose the wine—usually a red—and drank two glasses to his one. That they always stopped for a brief kiss during dinner, like a palate cleanser between the salad and the main course. That when they watched TV on the sofa—Reuben always to Julia's left—he would absent-mindedly rub circles on her back while she would comb her fingers tenderly through his hair.

Tonight I watched as Reuben embraced Julia from behind as she did the dishes, reaching his arm around to pull a stray curl from her eyes so that she wouldn't need to use her wet, gloved hands. Then later, the way they alternated dipping their spoons into the shared tub of ice cream as the opening credits of a movie flickered against their faces. I thrived on their intimate bond—a love that was implied rather than declared—as if it belonged to me.

Gradually, the longing in my chest began to subside.

16

get it. It's a little strange that I'm thirty-six and don't have any friends except for my eighty-seven-year-old neighbor. For anyone who's always had friends, it's probably hard to imagine how someone could go through life without any. But it's actually easier than you might think. The truth is, the solitary life snuck up on me. Kind of like how innocuous drips of water can suddenly become a problematic puddle.

Humans find comfort in habit—that's why you can understand people from their patterns, as Grandpa taught me. The trouble is, once you think you understand something or someone, you're usually reluctant to question that assumption. I didn't spend all my school lunchtimes under a tree with a book because I didn't like my classmates. I did it because reading felt like the greatest adventure—a way of traveling to new worlds and seeing life through other people's eyes. In my mind, I was an intrepid explorer, but my classmates' assumption was that I was a weird loner. And since they didn't engage with me, I didn't try to engage with them.

To be fair, my fascination with death didn't help matters—especially during high school. It probably wasn't smart to focus all three of my ninth-grade social studies projects on death. Or to write a poem for English class from the perspective of a mortician. But since death had shaped my life from the time I was five, I wanted to observe it, to decode it. I wanted to find sense in the thing that felt so senseless.

I did try to make a friend once in high school.

Priya's family had moved to Manhattan from Singapore at the beginning of my tenth-grade year at Stuyvesant High School.

The afternoon the guidance counselor brought her to our social studies class, I'd been staring out the classroom window watching the thunderstorm clouds roll across the Hudson River. The room always had the same scent—the woody spice of pencil shavings competing with the wet-dog-like aroma of teenaged boys.

My heart leaped when the teacher directed Priya to the desk next to mine. The one that was always empty.

"Hey." She smiled shyly as she slid into the chair.

"Hi," I replied just as shyly, trying to hide my shock that she'd spoken to me. "It looks like it's going to rain."

Priya looked awkwardly out the window. "Oh, yeah . . . looks like it." She busied herself arranging her pens—the fancy gel kind—and notebook on her desk.

As I watched her, a feeling of intense gratitude washed over me. A new addition to our class evened up the numbers, which meant that when we had to work in pairs, I wouldn't have to face the embarrassment of always being the one left over. Or endure the look of pity from our teacher, Ms. Lynd, as she appealed to the nearest pair to let me invade and form a reluctant trio.

But Priya also represented a clean slate. She didn't know the social dynamics of our sophomore class. Or that I'd earned the nickname "Clover of the Crypt," which nobody ever said to my face, but which I'd overheard in sniggers and whispers in the hall. So when we joined our desks together for a partnered task, I thought it was finally happening: I was about to make my first friend. Priya was impressed with all the facts I knew about Singapore (Grandpa had told me about a sabbatical he'd taken there before I was born) and was excited that I knew how to play mahjong. And when she told me she loved reading Virginia Woolf and Joan Didion, I knew we were the perfect fit. As I walked home along the river that afternoon, I couldn't help envisioning what life might be like with a friend my own age—and one who was a girl.

I'd noticed Priya's pierced ears, painted nails, and colored lip gloss, and I'd watched the way she giggled and twirled her pony-tail when the boys in our class made jokes. I could definitely use someone to talk to about those things. Now that I was a teenager, I was beginning to suspect that I might be missing out on some vital knowledge because I didn't have a mother figure in my life. So far I'd navigated the obstacles of puberty via books from the school library (Grandpa offered me a scientific explanation of what was happening to my body, and money to purchase the necessary men-strual accouterments, but was no help beyond that). And when my classmates had begun to wear makeup, I'd tried replicating their efforts using products cobbled together from the drugstore. But with no one to advise me on skin tone—or the merits of being light-handed—the results had made me mostly swear off makeup for life. Having Priya as a friend might change that.

But I didn't want to come on too strong—or seem too desperate. So at first, I tried to play it cool. I smiled at her when I saw her in the hall and made brief small talk before class started by recom-mending a couple of books I thought she'd like. I figured I'd wait two weeks and then maybe invite her to Bessie's bookstore after school. And then I could casually suggest we go for coffee or see a movie and our friendship would blossom from there. She might even invite me over to her place for dinner with her parents. I bet her mother was just as sophisticated as she was. I'd probably even need to get a flip phone like the other kids in my class, now that I'd finally have someone who wanted to contact me besides Grandpa. He was still my best friend, and I loved that he always had time for me, but I was ready to branch out and finally make a real friend.

I couldn't remember a time when I'd felt this exhilarated.

❊   ❊   ❊

Two weeks later, I waited by Priya's locker after the final bell.
I'd stopped by the restrooms on my way to double-check that
the clip-on earrings I'd gotten from a stall on Canal Street were on
straight. I hoped she might also notice my new Stellar Strawberry
Lip Smacker gloss.

When she spotted me waiting, she looked surprised.

"Oh, hey, Clover—what's up?" The sparkly sweater she was
wearing looked expensive.

"Hey, Priya." I tried to lean nonchalantly against the locker next
to hers but almost lost my balance. "I was going to go to my favorite
bookstore in the West Village after school and I was wondering if
you want to come?"

She concentrated hard on putting her books in her locker one at
a time. "Thanks, but I can't today."

"That's okay," I said. "We could go tomorrow—or next week
sometime?"

Priya closed her locker slowly, letting the latch click delicately
into place. Then she turned to look at me.

"I'm really sorry, Clover, but I don't think I can hang out with
you at all." She looked down at her pristine high-top sneakers. "It's
really unfair what all the other kids say about you—but I'm trying to
fit in too. I think it's better if we just see each other in class."

"Oh, okay," I said quietly, as the burn of rejection began to sear
in my chest. "I understand."

She smiled meekly. "Thanks—I'll see you tomorrow in social
studies, I guess."

I watched forlornly as Priya crossed the hall to a group of girls
I'd known since elementary school. As they all gathered around to
admire her sweater, I felt a pang of envy, suddenly self-conscious of
my frumpy Old Navy sweatshirt.

That was the day that I began to realize how hard it is to be
anything but what the world already thinks you are.

17

The turquoise paint rimming my cuticles almost glowed under the harsh amber light of my building's front stoop. I'd just finished the abstract painting class I'd signed up for to honor the regret of an eighty-year-old biochemist named Lily. She'd never pursued her passion for painting because of her ninth-grade teacher's frank assessment that she had no talent and should stick to science. A few days before she died, I'd brought Lily a canvas and paints so that she could have a chance to finally unleash her suppressed creativity. But by then her arthritis had rendered her hands so weak and painful that it only made her sadder that she hadn't tried it sooner.

So far I wasn't showing much talent for it myself, but at least I could say I'd tried it.

The spice of Leo's seafood bisque was wafting down the stairwell as it usually did on Fridays, growing stronger as I walked stealthily up to my apartment. I'd managed to go several weeks without running into Sylvie again.

Just as I thought I'd made it safely past the second floor, my relief shifted to complacency as I forgot to avoid the noisiest floorboard on the staircase. Behind me, a door whined open.

"Clover, hey!" Sylvie called across the landing.

I turned reluctantly to face my new neighbor, who was leaning against her doorway in a gray sweatshirt with some kind of band name on it.

"Oh, hi, Sylvie." I was grateful my keys gave me something to do with my hands. "Nice to see you again."

"You too!" Sylvie beamed and I wondered if her enthusiasm level was ever set to anything but high. "I've been hoping to run into you again but I keep missing you. Lucky I heard your footsteps outside my door—I knew it wasn't Leo because he couldn't walk up the stairs that fast."

"Oh, right," I said, disappointed in myself. "So . . . how's everything going?" I couldn't help reflecting back some of her friendliness, like it was contagious.

"I'm finally all moved in! Well, there are still a few boxes that need unpacking. But I'm looking forward to getting to know the neighborhood—and my neighbors, of course."

"That's great—I know *Leo* always loves meeting new people." I hoped she caught my emphasis.

"Oh, yeah, Leo's an old charmer—and he clearly loves seafood," Sylvie said, raising her eyes to the ceiling and wrinkling her nose. "But I want to know more about you. Maybe we finally can grab that coffee tomorrow?"

It was going to be really hard to keep avoiding her. And Leo was right: he wouldn't be around forever and I'd have no one once he was gone. At the very least, I'd need someone to list as my emergency contact on registration forms—it would make practical sense for me to form a new acquaintance for that reason alone. Plus, the idea of spending the next year tiptoeing up and down the stairs and hiding from Sylvie was exhausting. It might be worth trying. I just couldn't get attached—or reveal too much about myself.

"Sure," I said, though I wasn't at all. "That would be nice." There was no turning back now.

"Great!" Sylvie said. "Meet you downstairs at ten tomorrow morning?"

A giddiness spread through my limbs—that same cocktail of

adrenaline and nerves that came whenever I took a risk. It reminded
me how long it'd been since I'd done that.

"Yes, that's fine." I probably should've pretended to check my
schedule.

"Perfect—see you then!" Sylvie flashed one last grin before closing her door.

It was an unusual feeling to actually walk into the café with someone—I was used to heading straight to the single-seat table in the
corner. I looked around at the people clustered in twos and threes at
the nearby tables and envied their nonchalance. Could everyone tell
that this was one of my first real coffee dates with someone? Could
Sylvie?

As we sat down, I began fidgeting with the sugar packages in the
center of the table to distract myself from the nerves pressuring my
bladder.

"So," Sylvie said, apparently immune to awkwardness, "I know
what a birth doula is, but what exactly does a death doula do?"

Leo must have told Sylvie about my job. I braced myself for the
look of judgment and revulsion I'd learned to recognize whenever
I revealed my profession, but it never appeared. Sylvie's expression
was open and friendly, like she was genuinely interested in my answer. I still proceeded cautiously.

"Well, it's basically the same thing when you think about it, but
kind of in reverse," I said, arranging the sugar sachets in a row. "A
birth doula helps usher someone into life, and a death doula helps
usher them peacefully out of it."

Sylvie arched a curious eyebrow. "But you're not a doctor, right?
Do you need to have any medical training?"

"Some death doulas do, but that's not the kind I am. I guess
what I do is more . . . experiential," I said, searching for the right
words. "I'm just there to keep them company and listen, helping
them reflect on their life if that's what they want to do. I also help

them with finding peace with any wrongdoings or regrets—things like that. And if they have nobody else, I'm there to hold their hands as they're dying."

"Wow, that's heavy," Sylvie said. "Don't you find it depressing? I don't think I could handle watching people die over and over again. It would really mess me up."

"I guess I've just learned to shut my feelings off." I was proud of that strength. "It makes me better at my job if I'm not emotionally involved."

Sylvie's brows now flirted with skepticism. "You don't even shed a single tear once in a while? You know, with the super heart-wrenching cases?"

"No," I said, shrugging. "Actually, I don't ever cry."

"Ever? Like, never in life in general? Not even during sad movies?"

I shook my head. "Nope." Another fact I wore like a badge of honor.

Sylvie eyed me curiously. "Girl, I'm not sure that's healthy. Just because you don't feel your feelings, doesn't mean they don't exist."

"It works for me." The defensiveness in my voice surprised me.

"If you say so." But she clearly wasn't convinced. "Anyway, I bet you've heard some pretty wild confessions from people on their deathbeds."

I thought about the books on my shelf. By now I had years' worth of confessions, some more sordid than others. But I took my ethical duty seriously—I'd never reveal a word of them to another soul. "I guess there have been a few."

Sylvie leaned across the table. "Has anyone ever asked you to go out and do something crazy to help them resolve their unfinished business?"

I found myself mirroring her movement, as if we were sharing a secret. "I've helped people make difficult phone calls or write letters to apologize. But it's usually an anticlimax because most of the time they leave it too late and the person can't be tracked down in time."

"Oh, man, that's sad—I hope that never happens to me." Sylvie's cheerfulness dulled briefly. "But then again, I find it really hard to hold grudges. After a few days, I've usually pretty much forgotten what I was even upset about in the first place."

That made complete sense—if Sylvie had a tail, I bet it would be wagging constantly. I couldn't help feeling a little charmed by her general enthusiasm for life. It made me feel better about the world.

I fumbled for a segue to a topic other than me. "So, Leo mentioned you're an art historian?" Most people love talking about themselves, so they rarely noticed when I deflected the focus to them.

"I am!" Sylvie said, then cocked her head and studied me, as though examining an artwork for its meaning. "But don't think I didn't notice you changing the subject there."

"Right, sorry." I blushed, embarrassed that my motives were so obvious. "Are you from New York?"

"Nope—Chicago." A hint of bravado stiffened her posture. "I always swore I'd never live in New York, but here I am. I was working at an art museum in Tokyo for two years and then the Frick made me an offer that I couldn't turn down. Never say never, I guess."

"I love Tokyo. I spent a semester abroad there during college." I hadn't expected to find something in common with Sylvie so quickly.

"Wait—what do you even study to become a death doula?"

I shrunk from the server's scrutinizing look as he set down our coffees.

"Everyone has their different path, like I said." I waited until the server was gone before continuing. "But I did my thesis in thanatology."

"Which is . . ."

"The study of death."

"No way. That's a real degree? So cool."

Cool. Not a word that I'd ever heard used to describe me. "Well, there are lots of things you can focus on, but I studied the death traditions of different cultures. That's what I was doing in Japan."

A series of curse words coming from the next table shifted our attention. A curly-haired British woman was frantically mopping a cold-brew stain that streaked across her white dress while her companion tried to contain the spill on the table.

"Here, take these." Sylvie passed the woman a handful of napkins with a sympathetic smile, then turned back to me. "So, you travel a bunch?"

"Not really anymore . . . because of my job." The woman was just making the stain worse by rubbing it.

"Hard to schedule it around people dying, huh?" Sylvie sprinkled sugar across the top of her latte. "You do realize that I'm going to ask you a million questions about your job now, right?"

That she found me remotely interesting was flattering. "What do you want to know?"

"For starters, how did you go from traveling the world studying the traditions of dying to being here in New York working as a death doula?"

I stirred my black coffee, uncertain whether I wanted to venture further into that topic. "My grandpa died alone while I was abroad," I said quietly. "It made me realize how many people die alone and that I could be more useful to the world by being a death doula than by being an academic who just studies death in the abstract. And I just didn't feel like traveling much after he died—I guess I kind of lost my love for it. Staying in New York has helped me hold on to him."

"I'm sorry—Leo said you guys were really close."

"Thanks, we were." I wondered if there was anything Leo hadn't told her. "Anyway, where in Tokyo did you live?"

Sylvie graciously let my obvious subject change slide this time. "Ginza, mostly. I had the cutest apartment—I'll show you some photos of it next time."

Next time. The thought of hanging out with her again triggered an unfamiliar sense of possibility. It felt like putting on a stiff, new leather shoe for the first time—the right fit, but still slightly uncomfortable.

Was this how the beginning of a friendship felt?

18

When I spotted Sebastian leaning against the wrought-iron fence of a townhouse on West Eighty-Fourth Street, I considered abandoning our agreement and fleeing back to the subway. But then he waved at me, and my legs propelled me forward. Despite his mild-mannered appearance, his was a confident lean, like he was assured of both his place in the world and his purpose in it—one ankle slung over the other in front of him, hands loosely in his pockets.

When no more than three feet remained between us, I stopped abruptly.

"Hi, Sebastian."

Normally, with a new client, I'd assume my professional persona and jump straight into the details, confident in the knowledge that I was good at my job and knew exactly why I was there. But anxiety plagued me more than usual.

"Hey, Clover, great to see you!"

Sebastian took a half step toward me, as if moving in for a hug. But he must have registered the stunned look on my face because he quickly stuck out his arm for a handshake instead.

"So, I should tell you something," he said as we walked up the steps to the front door. "My grandmother knows you're coming, but she doesn't know that you're a death doula."

The mental alarm bells I'd been ignoring got louder. "Who does she think I am then?"

"I kind of told her that you were a friend of mine who was interested in seeing her photography."

"But I don't even know anything about photography." I hated the idea of being forced into a lie—if I was going to be dishonest, at least let it be my choice.

"You'll be fine," Sebastian said with less certainty than I'd have liked. "Once you get her talking and reminiscing, she won't even notice."

I was annoyed that I'd let myself be duped, but it was too late to back out—his grandmother was expecting a visitor.

Sebastian led me through a much grander hallway than I'd expected. The decor was sparse compared to my cluttered apartment, but deliberately so—each object seemed like it was selected judiciously and positioned with precision.

"Your grandmother has a nice house," I said, reminding myself that Sebastian was technically my employer and I should make some polite conversation, in spite of his deception.

"Yeah, I guess she does." Sebastian looked around without really seeing. "My grandfather bought it back in the 1950s, but I think it's at least a hundred years old. I spent a lot of time here as a kid—my parents sent me here for pretty much every school vacation."

Walking behind him meant I could study his appearance surreptitiously. He was probably around my age—with men it was hard to tell—and only slightly taller. Each time I'd met him, he'd worn the same thing: a black button-down shirt, black chinos, and the same gold-rimmed spectacles and charcoal scarf. He was probably one of those guys who bought five versions of everything to keep things simple.

Along the hallway, framed photographs hung at militant intervals. I'd anticipated stuffy family portraits, but the black-and-white vignettes that stared back at me were evocative portals into faraway worlds. A muscular horse raised on her hind legs in a desert, her shining mane trailing in the wind like flames. The searing eyes of a turbaned man, his face carved with the lines of emotional turbulence.

"You said in your email your grandmother was a photojournalist?"

Sebastian stopped to look at the photo I was examining. "Yeah—she was one of the few female photojournalists of her time, actually. Before she married my grandfather, she traveled the world taking photos for newspapers."

"And she took all these?"

"Sure did." His chest puffed slightly as he stood next to me. "Pretty much any photo you see here is one of hers." He continued walking. "I'll give you the proper tour later on, but you should probably meet Grandma first. The garden is her favorite spot."

Through the French doors separating the kitchen from the garden, I saw an elderly woman tucked into a wicker chair. A cornflower-blue shawl embraced her shoulders and a thick, pine-green blanket sat across her knees. With her face positioned toward the sun, she sat, eyes closed, a tranquil smile on her face. It almost felt rude to interrupt.

Sebastian didn't seem concerned.

"Hi, Grandma!" He strode over and planted a kiss on each of her cheekbones. She reached up and cupped his chin tenderly. I could tell the admiration was mutual.

"Hello, my darling." Her clear, robust voice seemed incongruous with her petite, age-worn frame. "I was just listening to the birds and trying to steal some sunshine before the inevitable winter grayness returns."

Sebastian motioned for me to join them. "Grandma, this is the friend I was telling you about—Clover."

"It's a pleasure to meet you, Mrs. Wells." I extended my hand.

"Oh, please, call me Claudia," she said, covering my hand with both palms. "It's rare that I get to meet any of Sebastian's friends."

Sebastian looked between us happily. "Clover and Claudia—it's got a nice ring to it."

"Like a pair of headstrong sisters in a Jane Austen novel," Claudia remarked.

"It's a pleasure to meet you, Claudia," I said, charmed by her irreverence. "I always wanted a sister."

Claudia leaned forward cheekily. "We won't focus on the age difference between us." She gestured to the adjacent wicker chair. "Take a seat, Clover. Sebastian, make us some coffee, will you?"

Nodding obediently, he disappeared back into the house.

"My grandson tells me you're interested in photography," Claudia said, pulling the shawl tighter around her shoulders. The taut fabric emphasized the bony curve of her back.

I felt a flash of resentment at Sebastian for forcing me to deceive such a lovely old woman. I prayed my cheeks wouldn't turn red and expose me.

"I am," I said as casually as I could, which wasn't casual at all. I did find photography interesting, so maybe it wasn't a complete lie. "But mostly I'd love to hear about your career as a photojournalist. It must've been an especially unconventional choice for a woman in the 1950s."

"You're not kidding." Claudia frowned at the sky. "My father almost disowned me when I told him it was what I was going to do. Luckily, my willfulness came from my mother, and she forbade my father from forbidding me."

"Your mother was ahead of her time." I loved that Claudia was wearing red lipstick for no greater occasion than sitting in her garden.

"Yes and no," she replied, wrists draped elegantly together in her lap. "Mother told me to go to college and pursue my passion as long as I was able to—which, in her mind, was until I found a husband. According to her, women's careers shouldn't interfere with their marriages. In fact, women of our social class weren't expected to have careers—unless you count 'society wife' as a métier. I suppose there's a certain skill in organizing galas and hosting fancy dinners, but it wasn't something I ever aspired to."

"And how did you meet your husband?"

"He was my brother's friend," Claudia said. "After college, I got an internship with a news magazine here in the city—I was their first female intern—and he was already living here. My brother and father asked him to look out for me and . . ."

"You fell in love?" The prospect of a romantic story sent a spike of endorphins through my limbs.

"Not exactly. Back then, being in love wasn't a prerequisite for marriage," Claudia said dryly, adjusting her shawl again. "You could say we appreciated each other, but most important was the fact that my parents deemed him a suitable match. And once that was decided, my brief photojournalism adventure came to an end. You young women these days are lucky—you don't have to choose between a career and a husband and kids."

Well, actually, a husband and kids had never even been presented as an option for me, so I'd never had to choose. I guess that made me lucky—or really unlucky.

But I was here to focus on Claudia's life, not mine.

"You're right," I said. "We do have a lot more freedom these days. Though still not as much as we could, and should, have." As soon as I said the words, I regretted revealing my personal politics. I usually tried to stay neutral.

But Claudia's approving smile indicated I didn't need to worry.

"I think we're going to get along well, my darling."

19

Claudia was napping in the sunshine when I walked back into the townhouse. Sebastian had left us alone to "get to know each other" while he tended to a list of various domestic tasks she'd given him. A lightbulb change in the library. A faucet tightening in the powder room.

As I wandered through the house unaccompanied, I couldn't resist peeking into the rooms that branched off the airy hallway. The same palette of neutrals dominated the living room—benign off-white and pale gray tones—and the only hints of color were the meticulously arranged hydrangeas in stark, angular vases. It reminded me of the preserved homes of famous people I'd seen in my travels—of Monet at Giverny, of Elvis at Graceland—where domestic vignettes, cordoned off by ropes, were paused in time as if the occupants had just stepped out momentarily. Everything about this home felt austere, untouched, and completely inconsistent with the warm, vibrant woman I'd met in the garden.

I heard the slow shuffle of footsteps down the marble staircase and scooted out of the living room back into the hallway, pulse thumping with guilt. Sebastian was navigating the last of the stairs with a large cello case, his hands awkwardly around its middle like he was trying to waltz with a voluptuous partner. He grimaced as it hit the wall, though it was unclear whether he was more concerned about the instrument or scarring the pristine white finish.

"Oh, hey!" He rested the bulbous end of the case on the floor. "Is everything okay with Grandma?"

"Yes, she's just napping in the sun. I figured it was better to let her enjoy it." I looked curiously at the instrument case. "Is that her cello?"

"No, mine, actually," Sebastian said. "Grandma likes to listen to me play, so I bring it over sometimes and, you know, serenade her—so to speak."

The tender image softened my annoyance with him. I suppose he had his reasons for lying, just like I did.

"That's very sweet of you," I said. "Music can be calming for the dying."

Sebastian flinched at my last word. "It's only a small thing, but I think it makes her feel better. Sometimes she asks me to play for hours and she just sits and listens with her eyes closed, looking so peaceful—like she's having a nice dream or something."

I offered him an encouraging smile. "Those small pleasures tend to be the most meaningful for people at this stage."

Silence floated conspicuously and we looked everywhere but at each other.

Sebastian looked at his watch. "I'd better get going." He rested the cello against the front door as he pulled out his phone. "Are you heading back downtown? I'll give you a ride."

"Oh, no, that's okay. I'll just take the subway." Sharing a back seat with Sebastian and having him know my address both felt a little too . . . intimate.

"It's no trouble at all. You live around the West Village, right? I heard you mention it to Grandma. My chamber ensemble rehearsal is right by NYU, so I can drop you on the way."

It would be an obvious lie to say I preferred taking the subway.

Maybe I could conjure up some other "business" I had on the Upper West Side. But we did need to discuss my future visits to Claudia—that particular lie had to stop.

"If you could drop me at Washington Square Park, that would be great. Thank you."

Sebastian lit up. "Cool! Let me just call an Uber."

After a brief drama maneuvering the cello into the Uber's trunk, we were headed down Columbus in the backseat of a lavender Toyota sedan. Rhonda, a Texan middle-aged blonde, was at the wheel. As we passed the back of the Museum of Natural History, a pang of sorrow hit me—I'd spent so many afternoons there with Grandpa. Another instance of grief squeezing my heart when I least expected it. I looked across the back seat at Sebastian. Years from now, he'd be able to find solace in the fact that he'd been attentive to his grandmother in this final stretch of her life. But it probably still wouldn't feel like nearly enough.

"So, your grandma said you're the only one in your family who lives in New York?"

Sebastian looked surprised that I'd broken the silence. "Yeah, just me. My mom and dad and three older sisters all still live in Connecticut, in the town where I grew up."

"And they don't come to the city much?"

"They do for holidays and stuff." He fiddled with the button on his shirtsleeve. "My dad came down when we took Grandma to the gastroenterologist—it was a guy he knew in college and I think he pulled some strings to get her in."

"What was the diagnosis?"

His brown eyes dulled. "Stage four pancreatic cancer."

"I'm sorry." I let the words float for a few seconds. "How much time do they think she has left?"

"About two months, at best."

"That must have been a shock for you all. And for her."

"See, that's the crazy thing." Sebastian's body tensed. "The doctor told my dad the diagnosis first and my dad told him not to tell Grandma that she was dying."

"What?" I fought the urge to express my disapproval—it was my job to remain impartial. "That's really . . ."

"Unethical? Yeah. I was so angry at my dad when he made me swear not to tell her. But he insisted that she's better off not knowing—I think it's because he just can't face telling her." Sebastian took off his glasses and began polishing them with his scarf. "I would've argued with him more, but it's his mother we're talking about. And in our family, it's always been the case that what my dad says, goes." I sensed bitterness in his tone.

"But she knows she's sick, right?"

"She knows she has cancer, but she doesn't know how bad it is."

"And even though your family knows she's dying, they still don't visit her more?" I was kind of grilling Sebastian, but I needed to know these things if I was going to keep visiting Claudia. Navigating complicated family dynamics was a delicate part of my job.

He nodded. "Like I said, that's how my family has always dealt with death—by not talking about it and pretending it won't happen. We're not exactly normal."

"Actually, that is pretty normal, in Western countries at least. It's less normal for people to discuss it openly."

The Uber stopped at the traffic lights outside Lincoln Center and Sebastian watched the fountain propel water elegantly into the air.

"They'll probably come when it's getting close to the end," he said as the lights changed. "They tried to convince her to move into a nursing home last year, before all this happened, and she refused. So they arranged for home health aides—Selma comes early in the morning to help Grandma shower and get dressed and all that, and then Joyce comes at six and spends the night."

"And Claudia doesn't think that round-the-clock care is strange?"

"I don't think so. I mean, she hasn't said anything. My dad told her that if she wanted to stay living at her townhouse, she had to accept it. And it's not like she's short on space."

"So why do you need me then?" Claudia clearly had plenty of help from people who didn't have to pretend they were interested in photography.

"Well, Selma and Joyce are great, but they're all about making sure she's as healthy as possible and that her practical everyday needs are taken care of. They're not really into sitting back and having long chats about life."

I felt the need to defend them—home health aides had really tough jobs. "It's hard to do that when you have so many other things to take care of."

"Yeah, for sure." Sebastian was almost apologetic. "I was just kind of hoping that you could help make this easier on my grandma from a more philosophical perspective, I guess. So that when the time comes, she's more . . . prepared."

My empathy swelled again. "She's lucky to have you."

He shrugged. "She was really good to me when I was growing up—kind of my escape, in a lot of ways. It's the least I can do."

"It was the same way with me and my grandfather." As a rule, I didn't share personal details about myself with clients, but the words had just tumbled out.

"You guys were close?"

"He raised me, actually."

"Wow, what happened to your parents?" As soon as he said it, he put up a hand like he was halting traffic. "No, wait, forget it—that's super rude of me to ask."

"No, it's fine. There's no point pretending that death doesn't happen. Plus, I just asked you all those questions about your grandma." I couldn't remember the last time I'd talked to someone about my parents. "They died in a boating accident while they were on vacation in China. Their bodies were never found."

"I'm sorry—that really sucks." The kindness in his eyes felt genuine.

I took a deep breath. "No one wants to lose their parents, but I don't actually remember a lot about them. I was only six when they died."

"Jesus, that's rough," Sebastian said.

Rhonda watched curiously in the rearview mirror. Since I didn't want to dissect my life story any further with two strangers, I steered the conversation back to Claudia.

"I'll be honest, Sebastian—I'm not sure how things are going to work with me visiting your grandma if she doesn't know the truth. Lying about the photography is bad enough. And like you said, it's kind of unethical."

Sebastian grimaced again. "I get that. But could you just give it a couple of weeks? I know she's probably going to find out eventually, but I just want to give her a little bit more time to live in ignorant bliss. Not that what she's going through is blissful."

"I get what you mean." It was hard to deny his good intentions, even if they were morally flawed. "But it seems like a bit of a stretch to tell her I'll be coming to see her several times a week just to talk about photography. And I won't be able to do my job properly—the entire point of my work is to help people come to grips with their impending death, not to deny the fact that it's happening."

"I know, I know." A heavy sigh. "I'll talk to my dad about it, but please say you'll keep coming to see her for now? I just feel kind of helpless. And having you spend time with her feels like something I can do for her without going against my dad's wishes."

I thought about Grandpa. I would've done anything to make his final days—and moments—better. And I could probably ask Bessie to recommend some photography books.

"Okay," I sighed. "I'll give it two weeks."

20

After Rhonda and Sebastian dropped me off at Washington Square, I stayed for a while to watch the social drama of the dog park. It was another tradition Grandpa and I had developed when I was a kid. Each Sunday on our way home from the bookstore, we'd spectate at the dog park, commentating on the social hierarchies of its canine players. There was always that one exuberant, carefree pup that the others followed around in awe, drawn in by its innate confidence. And then there was usually a timid dog who found all the raucous socializing to be too much, standing silently at the edge of the park, resenting its owner for subjecting it to such torture. I could relate to the latter archetype. Participating in the world was overwhelming sometimes.

Since I hadn't gotten around to buying vitamins after running into Sebastian at Duane Reade, I ducked into the pharmacy on my way back down Sixth Avenue. At the end of the aisle, I recognized a familiar silhouette leaning against the counter, charming the young pharmacist with a story about "the good old days." I waited until he'd tipped the brim of his trilby and turned in my direction.

"Hello, stranger!" Leo greeted me with his unfailingly broad grin. Whenever he did that, I always imagined hearing the *ting* that sounded in movies when someone flashed their gold tooth.

I pushed his arm playfully. "Now you're the one who disappeared into thin air." It was unusual to go a week without a game with Leo, or at least running into him on the stairs.

"Yeah, yeah," he said. "You know how it is when you have visitors in town, always wanting you to show them around and give them the 'local's' tour."

Since I'd never had a visitor in my life, I didn't.

I looked at the white paper bag with a stapled prescription bulging in his hand. "Is everything okay?"

"You bet." Leo shook the bag back and forth so it rattled like a maraca. "Just stocking up on the usual cholesterol pills so that I can keep on eating those cheeseburgers."

"I'm not sure that's how cholesterol pills work, Leo. I think the point is that you take them *and* stop eating greasy foods."

"Nah, I like my interpretation better," he scoffed. "Speaking of— what are you doing now? Feel like getting a bite to eat at the diner?"

My stomach rumbled. "Yes, I do." The vitamins could wait.

Except for losing some of its luster, the diner looked almost exactly the same as it always had. The now-faded hues of the Formica and vinyl were like a postcard left out in the sun. I liked that it hadn't changed—a time capsule that also kept me fed.

Leo was in his element, filling me in on the neighborhood gossip. Though Grandpa had always told me not to encourage Leo's idle chatter about other people's lives, I indulged him once in a while.

"Well, first of all, there's the bodega cat drama," Leo recounted.

"Oooh, sounds intriguing." He didn't need much encouragement, but he liked a captive audience.

"You know the fat ginger tabby in the bodega over on Grove?"

"The one who gave birth to kittens between the bags of potato chips?"

"That's the one." He lifted the top of his cheeseburger to remove the pickles and then shot me a cryptic look. "She went missing last Tuesday."

"Stolen or wandered off?"

"Nobody knows. But here's the kicker: she mysteriously returned three days later."

"That's not so mysterious, Leo," I said, pouring syrup on my French toast. "Cats tend to wander off. It's kind of their thing."

"You're right—they do." He doused his fries in ketchup. "But do they come back a different gender?"

"You mean the cat that came back was male?"

Leo sat back against the booth, satisfied with his reveal of the plot twist. "Yep."

"Wow, so somebody switched them." I was hooked. "Who would do that? Don't they have security cameras?"

"Everywhere but the potato chip aisle."

"So, what's your theory?"

"Cat-breeding ring, I'd say. Let's see if there's an uptick in ginger kittens at the pet stores later this year."

Leo's shuffle was even slower than usual when we walked the few blocks home. I was used to reducing my pace while walking with him, but today it felt like I only needed to take one step for every two of his. As I held on to the crook of his arm while we wove through the oncoming pedestrians, he leaned into me more than once.

True to the capricious early-March weather, the sun retreated without warning. Fat raindrops began to splatter the pavement in front of us, escalating from sporadic to relentless within minutes. But when I tried to guide Leo beneath the narrow awning of a jazz club, he resisted.

"It's just a little bit of water, kid. And besides, there are only so many times in your life you get to play in the rain." He turned his face skywards, grinning. "Might as well enjoy it while I can."

I took a mental snapshot of the moment so that I could always treasure it.

"You're right," I said, squeezing his arm tighter and following his gaze toward the heavens.

And for the next ten minutes we stood side by side, letting the raindrops tumble over our cheekbones.

21

Hey C. I'm too lazy to come upstairs and knock on your door. LOL. Wanna come with me to yoga tomorrow? I need someone to keep me accountable, haha.

The message buzzed on my phone early Saturday evening. On the one hand, yoga was a good way to socialize with Sylvie without committing too much—and I was relieved that I hadn't scared her off on our coffee date. On the other hand, yoga wasn't something I'd ever tried and I didn't want to make a fool of myself.

Looking up at my notebooks, I thought about the advice a soft-spoken gardener named Arthur had given me right before he died.

"If you want something you don't have," he'd said, "you have to do something you've never done."

I'd never really spent time with a woman my age (at least, not one who wasn't on their deathbed). This could be my chance to finally form a real friendship.

After rereading Sylvie's message a couple of times, I poised my thumbs to reply.

Sure. What time?

Three dots, then no dots. Then a message.

8am. . . . yikes. Too early for you?

I toyed with the chance to gracefully decline.

That's OK. But I haven't done much yoga before.

Better to manage expectations.

Sylvie's reply came instantaneously and I wondered how she'd managed to type it so quickly.

No problem! I'll give you some pointers. See you downstairs at 7:40. S xx.

Instead of the French romantic comedy I'd planned to watch that night, I worked my way through a series of yoga videos on You-Tube, memorizing some poses so that I wouldn't look like a complete novice. I wasn't the most limber of women—unfortunately I hadn't inherited any of my mother's balletic grace. I did get some of Grandpa's height (five feet and nine inches of it), but as a result, my limbs felt slightly too long for my body.

Sylvie was already standing on the front stoop when I arrived downstairs the next morning. Yoga mat slung across her back and reusable coffee flask in her hand, she was blowing clouds of breath into the morning air like a lithe dragon with a perky ponytail.

"Clover, hi!"

"Oh, hey, Sylvie."

She handed me the flask. "I figured you might want some coffee."

"Thank you—that's really thoughtful." I felt unexpectedly nurtured.

Sylvie made a "forget about it" gesture as she turned and bounced down the stairs two at a time. "It's the least I could do for dragging you out so early."

As we walked the two blocks to the yoga studio, Sylvie continued chattering. "So, let me give you the lowdown on the regulars. I've only been four or five times, but I think I've got most people figured out." A nod from me was all she needed to keep going. "The teacher is great—she studied in India—but the only thing is that she has a New Zealand accent and for some reason it really annoys me during the guided meditation, the way she says 'cocoon.'"

There hadn't been anything about cocoons in the YouTube videos, so hopefully it was something I could improvise. My confidence began to deflate.

Sylvie continued her rundown. "And then there's this really hot guy who's always front-row center and he's *super* flexible. But, then again, he clearly knows he's hot and super flexible, which is, you know, less attractive."

I laughed nervously. "Yeah."

"Oh, by the way, did you know they do doga at this studio? You should totally take George one day! He would looove yoga."

I was certain that George would, in fact, not love yoga.

When we arrived at the studio, which was tucked into the lower level of a brownstone, panic stiffened my already-sore muscles. I'd walked past these flocks of spandex-clad yogis many times, and I'd even enjoyed observing their movements from afar. But to actually move among them—worse, to be seen by them—was slightly petrifying.

The studio door shut behind us and, by some miraculous feat of soundproofing, managed to block the urban din outside. A subtle fusion of eucalyptus, lavender, and maybe myrrh scented the air, thanks to an artfully concealed diffuser. The soothing hum of Tibetan singing bowls drifted from an equally well-hidden set of speakers.

Sylvie flashed a smile at the man behind the minimalist wooden check-in desk adorned with a single bonsai tree. His auburn-flecked beard was alarmingly well-groomed and I wondered if he used the same comb to tend to both his facial hair and his man bun.

"Sylvie Anderson and Clover Brooks," she announced, then gave me a sly sideways glance. "I got your last name from your mailbox."

"Wait," I said as we put our shoes and bags in cubbies beneath a cushioned bench. "How much do I owe you for the class?"

Sylvie shook her head. "Don't worry about it—I've got you. You can get the next one."

Next one? I wasn't even sure about this one.

We shuffled into a room with serene oak floors and artificially weathered concrete walls. A stacked pyramid of uniformly rolled yoga mats sat in a wall recess like fire logs. Sylvie handed me one and led me to one side of the room. "I like to put my mat by the window so there's something to look at if I get bored when they make you hold the poses for ten minutes."

As she began an elaborate series of stretches (I must've missed the video that told you to stretch before a class composed entirely of stretches), I sat on my mat and studied the other people in the room. Their clothing clung flatteringly to each well-honed muscle while their skin radiated either from inner peace or expensive skincare routines.

Sylvie nodded to the center of the room where a muscular, smooth-skinned man balanced on his hands with his shins resting on the backs of his arms. "Super-hot-flexible guy," she whispered. "As soon as it gets even remotely warm in here, he takes his shirt off—for everyone else's benefit, I'm sure. Not my type—I'm more into scrawny, artistic dudes—but maybe he's yours?" She wiggled her eyebrows as she switched her stretch to the other wrist.

I pulled my arm across my chest, trying to stealthily ascertain whether the guy was my "type." I'd never been asked that before.

"It's kind of hard to tell from here," I said, hoping a vague response would satisfy her.

A silky, New Zealand accent interrupted our conversation.

"Good morning, everyone." A petite, sinewy woman, clad in form-fitting white, stood at the front of the room. I pondered the logistics of selecting appropriate underwear for her outfit.

"My name is Amelie and it is such a deep, deep joy to have you all here," the woman said as if lulling a baby to sleep. "Thank you for choosing to begin your day with all of us in this beautiful practice."

Sylvie coughed conspicuously.

I was pretty pleased with myself for keeping up with most of the movements. It helped that we repeated them multiple times and I could copy everyone around me. The challenge was keeping my daydreaming at bay—about why the woman in front of me chose an iguana back tattoo and whether she regretted it. Or how the Himalayan salt lamps were probably just wellness placebos, but maybe I should get one just in case. Sylvie had to nudge me several times when we'd already moved on to another pose. To anchor my mind, I tried imagining the most unstimulating thing I could.

A rock. A brown, boring rock.

"Can I touch you?"

The startling, whispered request came from Amelie, who'd been wandering around the room adjusting people's poses.

Another question I'd never been asked before. My ears began to burn.

"Um, sure, okay," I whispered back, mirroring the teacher's tone since there was obviously an implicit rule against speaking at a normal volume.

Amelie knelt behind my forward bend and placed her hands on my upper back. The warm, firm pressure was an unfamiliar but pleasant sensation and my body buzzed to life.

I was no longer in danger of daydreaming.

"That's right," Amelie cooed. "Just breeaaaathe into the stretch."

I tried to remember the last time I'd been touched in such a prolonged, meaningful way. I often held clients' hands to comfort them, or helped them in and out of chairs and beds, but that was all in their service.

This was the first time in years that I'd been touched with such an expression of care and energy meant only for me.

❖   ❖   ❖

The class concluded with a guided meditation in which Amelie managed to make her voice even more monotone and breathy.

"Imagine yourself surrounded by beauuuuuutiful healing light, like a golden co-coon."

Sylvie snorted.

"That co-coon is your safe, healing space, where nothing can harm you."

I opened one eye to look over at Sylvie holding her nose to stifle her laughter. Her entire body shook.

Amelie's staccato inflection on the word "cocoon" was a little peculiar. Like it belonged in a chorus sung by the von Trapp children as they bade everyone "So Long, Farewell." I tried to resist succumbing to Sylvie's giggle contagion. But the more I knew it was forbidden, the stronger the urge became. Tears trickled, then streamed down my face.

Amelie cleared her throat pointedly. "Let us aaaalllll remember that peace begins within ourselves, inside our golden co-coon."

It was too much for Sylvie. She sat up and touched my shoulder, which was still shuddering with laughter. "Let's get out of here," she whispered.

Avoiding eye contact with each other—and Amelie—we rolled our mats, then tiptoed through the maze of prone, meditating bodies. As we quickly retrieved our belongings and made a break for freedom, I felt the warmth of complicity spill over my guilt for disrupting the class. We jog-walked down the block, as if there was a threat of Amelie pursuing us in a meditative rage.

Once we'd turned the corner, Sylvie slowed to a stroll.

"So, what are you up to this week?" she asked, pulling her hair out of its ponytail and smoothing it back into a new one. "Are you still on 'vacation'?"

"I have a new client I'm going to see tomorrow."

"Oooooh, tell me more."

"It's an old woman on the Upper West Side. She was a photojournalist back in the fifties."

"What? So cool! I'd love to meet her—I bet she'd have to be a feisty old broad if she did that." Sylvie adjusted the strap of her yoga mat across her chest. "How'd you find her? Come to think of it, how exactly does a death doula find her clients?"

"I met her grandson. Apparently no one really visits her except for him."

"Geez, that's so sad." Sylvie's expression morphed from morose to sly. "Grandson, huh? Is he cute?"

My cheeks flamed. "Maybe a little?"

"Maybe? Girl, in my experience, he's either cute or he's not."

I'd considered it, of course. But I'd quickly nipped the thought in the bud when I realized how unprofessional it was to be objectifying my new employer.

I flailed for a conversation shift. "So . . . how's your new job at the Frick going?"

"Oh, you know, good for the most part. Starting a new job is always weird, getting to know the personalities and all that. And there are all the office politics to navigate—the art history field is pretty cutthroat." Sylvie waved at a dachshund walking past, but ignored its owner.

"Yeah, my grandpa was a college science professor and he used to tell me how conniving some of those academics could be."

"Totally. And the worst thing is they're all so passive-aggressive. I'm always one for airing it all out versus bottling it up, but I'm not sure my colleagues could handle my brutal honesty just yet."

I liked Sylvie's frankness because it took the pressure off having to guess what she was thinking. It made it easy to be in her company. I was even a little disappointed when we reached our stoop.

"Thanks for dragging yourself out of bed to come with me to yoga. It was super fun!" Sylvie slid her key into her front door. "I seriously haven't laughed that hard in so long. Let's do it again soon—if Amelie lets us in."

"That would be great," I said, surprised that I meant it.

As I walked up the stairs, my thighs burned from the newly

awakened muscles and my cheekbones were still sticky from crying with laughter. It occurred to me that this was the longest I'd spent socializing outside of my job with someone who wasn't Leo.

I thought about Olive and her perfume advice. I still hadn't found a scent that I liked, but for the first time in years, my life felt like it was beginning to shift.

22

The sunrise of my twentieth birthday spilled across the volcanoes that towered over Antigua, Guatemala, amplifying the deep ochre tones of the city's baroque architecture. My footsteps echoed on the cool cobblestones until I stopped at the ornate iron gate of an interior courtyard where lush foliage surrounded a dilapidated tile fountain. Seated around the courtyard's perimeter were the building's residents—the elderly folk, or *abuelos*, who, with no money or family to care for them, were passing the twilight of their lives in this community nursing home. Some gazed into the distance, while others snoozed in the sun's warmth. As always, the rhythm was slow, the atmosphere peaceful.

I was halfway through a two-month stay between my sophomore and junior years of college, volunteering at the scarcely funded nursing home while lodging with a local family a few blocks away. It was the first birthday I hadn't spent with Grandpa since I'd moved in with him. For the past two years I'd been studying sociology at McGill University in Montreal—a way to stretch my wings a little and experience a new culture while still being within a short flight of New York City. My plan was to follow in Grandpa's academic footsteps, except that instead of biology, I would travel the world studying the different cultural traditions surrounding death.

"Good morning, Clover!" Felicity, the volunteer who unlocked the gate for me, was a med student from Vancouver. She had been volunteering for an entire semester at the nursing home and loved the residents so much that she decided to spend her entire summer vacation here, assisting the nurses.

"Hello, Felicity! You look lovely today," I said as she locked the gate behind me.

Even her off-white scrubs and rubber clogs did nothing to distract from her natural beauty—shiny black hair, glowing skin, and a bright smile. But because her personality was so disarmingly generous and genuine, it was impossible for me to resent any of it.

"Oh," she said, looking down sheepishly. "You're so kind, Clover. You look really pretty too." Though I knew she meant it, it felt like a wild embellishment in comparison.

Felicity looked at her watch. "I'd better go start giving everyone their meds—I'll see you in there," she said and headed inside.

As I walked through the courtyard, a few of the *abuelos* clustered around me excitedly. Since I was still a relatively new face in their monotonous daily existences, my presence was a welcome novelty. The most buoyant welcome came, as usual, from Rosita—a delicate-framed woman no more than five feet tall—who danced toward me, eyes sparkling and toothless grin radiating joy. Though she was deaf and couldn't speak, Rosita had no trouble communicating her enduring zest for life. She wrapped her frail arms around my waist in greeting and I felt my heart swell. I cherished her daily hugs—if only she knew that the thing she so readily offered had been so scarce in my life.

Not everyone shared Rosita's cheerfulness. Other residents sat sedately in their wheelchairs staring ahead stoically as if readying themselves for the indignity of being ignored, knowing they'd already been forgotten by the rest of society. But as I made sure to stop and say good morning to each of them, the stoicism melted and the sadness in their eyes ignited into hopefulness as they appreciatively returned my greeting in murmured Spanish.

The past month had already taught me one of my most important lessons in life. During my first couple of weeks, I'd felt overwhelmed with sadness seeing the unfortunate circumstances of these people, finding it hard to see past their debilitating illnesses and slowly wilting bodies. But I gradually began to realize that pitying them wouldn't take away their pain. The kindest thing I could do for them was to look them in the eye and simply acknowledge their presence as human beings. That's when I'd promised myself I'd never turn away from someone's pain, no matter how much I wanted to.

"Buenos dias, Clover," a distinctly American voice called from behind me.

My pulse thumped in response as I turned around, willing myself to play it cool. "Oh, hey, Tim," I stammered. "I mean, buenos dias."

Tim was another volunteer, from Seattle, who'd started at the nursing home a week after me. Since I'd been given the task of showing him around on his first day, we'd gotten to know each other quite well. It was always much easier for me to interact with people when I had a purpose. Plus, I'd discovered one of the benefits of traveling to a place where no one knows you— the anonymity of being a stranger, the potential of a clean slate. In Guatemala, I wasn't a weird loner; I was fun, confident, and adventurous. At least, that was the persona I'd been trying on for the past month.

"Man, I have the worst hangover," Tim said, even though his tanned swimmer's physique looked nothing but robust.

"Did you go out last night?" I searched for something more to say so I didn't sound like I was interrogating him. "Working with a hangover can sure be brutal." Or so I'd gathered.

"Yeah." He took off his Seahawks cap and rubbed his head. "Me and some of the other volunteers hit up a tequila bar last night."

"Oh, okay." I hadn't heard anything about a night out.

He squeezed my arm. "We totally would have invited you but it was super last minute."

I pinned on a smile. "That's cool—I was busy last night anyway." Busy writing in my journal, but still, technically true.

Rosita, who was still clinging to my waist, reached up and tugged Tim's backpack strap playfully.

Tim looked down at her, as if not sure how to engage. "Oh, hey, Juanita." He looked around uncomfortably. "I'd better go sign in. Gotta make sure it's on the record since it's the whole reason I'm here." He leaned toward me and lowered his voice. "Those big finance firms love their new hires to have good deeds on their résumés."

The morning humidity carried the scent of yellow jasmine, filling the courtyard with a subtle sweetness as I walked inside with Rosita. My shift that day was what was generously named "occupational therapy"—basically helping the abuelos put together jigsaw puzzles or create artworks from donated materials like plastic cutlery, paper plates, and old buttons. More often than not, I was just there to keep an eye on them as they sat transfixed by the glacial pace of the Mexican soap opera on the boxy television balanced atop the supply cabinet.

When I arrived in the room, the abuelos were already busying themselves with their crafts. Each resident of the nursing home was issued the same standard set of clothes—the men wore gray V-necks and slacks, while the women had simple house dresses, all in the same floral fabric. I always wondered what each of these people must have been like in their youth, long before they'd ever considered that society might forget them—or at least no longer value them. I could glean aspects of their personalities from the way they carried themselves. While some had relinquished their grooming habits, or weren't capable of continuing them anymore, others still took pride in their appearance, like José with his short hair slicked neatly to the side and Pilar with her braids twisted up into a tidy bun. And then there were the small but meaningful flourishes that distinguished their otherwise matching outfits— Valería's frilled apron, Carmen's beaded necklace, Fernanda's hand-crocheted cardigan.

What had they dreamed about when they were my age? What did they wish they'd done differently now that the end was near?

In the corner of the room, a round-faced gentleman sat on a battered chair, hands folded tidily in his lap as he patiently awaited my arrival. Arturo had proudly informed me last week that he was a poet, but now that arthritis had commandeered his knuckles, he was unable to put his creations to paper. So I'd volunteered to be his scribe and had spent the past few mornings carefully noting down his poetic observations about life and love.

Today's poem was about knowing there was a great love out there for you, even if you hadn't met them yet.

"Until we meet, I'll look at the moon because it's the one thing we both share," he proclaimed in Spanish, his dark irises shining.

"How romantic," I marveled, enchanted by his unabashed sentimentality.

"I'm sure you've already found someone special," he said, nudging me with his elbow.

"Maybe I have," I replied, nudging him back cheekily.

I definitely had—and I was pretty sure Tim felt the same way. Over the past two weeks, I'd carefully documented all the signs in my journal. The way he'd put his arm around me casually while he was talking to me. Or how he'd ask me to massage his shoulders when they were feeling stiff. Or that when he needed someone to cover his shift, he always asked me first, not because I was one of the best with the abuelos, but because he knew he could count on me. And then there was that one time I did go out for drinks with all the other volunteers, when he made a point to sit next to me and even squeezed my knee when I paid for his drinks because he forgot his wallet.

In the interest of being a modern, independent woman, I'd decided that I didn't need to wait for him to make the first move. And my birthday seemed like the perfect opportunity. At the end of our shift that day, after we'd served the residents their evening meal, I was going to reveal that it was my birthday and ask him if he wanted to join me for dinner to celebrate at the tiny little restaurant on the corner.

And that's when I'd tell him how I felt.

I'd already considered the logistics of how we might keep up our long-distance relationship once he went back to Seattle and I returned to Montreal. It would be a challenge, but I was willing to put in the work. Maybe we could even plan to do our post-grad studies in the same city. There was a good chance he'd end up moving to New York—it was one of the world's financial capitals, after all.

I was actually pretty excited about it. My first kiss, finally.

The clanging of the mealtime bell signaled dinner in the nursing home. Ever creatures of habit, the abuelos shuffled toward the stark dining hall, taking their designated seats at the long communal tables.

I felt a squeeze on my shoulder. My giddiness intensified as Tim leaned close and whispered in my ear.

"Hey, Señorita Clover, do you think you could cover for me for fifteen minutes? I just have to duck out quickly for an errand."

Butterflies tickled my stomach as I leaned in to whisper back, treasuring the intimacy amongst the chaos of the dining hall.

"Of course."

He squeezed my shoulder once more. "You're the best."

It was hectic covering both his tables and mine, serving the residents their standard portions of rice and beans, and then their cup of lopsided flan. But I didn't begrudge it at all. Relationships took sacrifices—this was my chance to show him that I was willing to go the extra mile.

Forty-five minutes later, when Tim still hadn't returned, I volunteered to fill in for him washing the dishes. He must have gotten held up while on his errand—things did move slower in Antigua.

As I stuffed my hair into a hairnet while the cavernous industrial sink filled with hot water, I noticed that the detergent bottle was almost empty. Everyone else in the kitchen looked run off their feet, so I went in search of a refill myself. Stopping briefly to stomp on a cockroach, I navigated the narrow hall that led to the storage room. The door was closed, which was unusual, but it was probably someone's well-intended yet naive effort to keep out such pests. As I jiggled the door open and felt inside for the light switch, I heard a giggle and then a gasp as the fluorescent bar flickered to life.

Huddled in the corner, limbs and lips intertwined, were Tim and Felicity. Even in the harsh lighting, her hair and skin radiated.

Adjusting my hairnet as confidently as I could, I walked in and grabbed the dishwashing detergent from the shelf. Then I exited the room without saying a word, closing the door softly behind me.

Standing outside that storeroom door, my chest aching, I learned a second important life lesson.

Looking other people's pain in the eye was much easier than facing your own.

23

The bottle of pinot noir felt heavy in my hand as I stood outside Sylvie's front door. As the first official time I'd been invited to someone's house for dinner in the name of friendship, it felt slightly momentous.

Since I had no idea about her taste in wine, I'd given the guy at the liquor store a cursory assessment of Sylvie's personality. He suggested the Tasmanian pinot noir as an irreverent but discerning choice.

"Most people play it safe with a Californian merlot or cabernet sauvignon," he said with the unbridled condescension that seemed to be a prerequisite for working in a wine store. "But since your friend sounds like she's well traveled, and a bit of a wild card, this red will impress her."

My friend. I'd let the term roll around in my head and felt a flutter of nerves.

With my knuckles poised to knock on Sylvie's door, I assessed my outfit one last time. I wasn't actually leaving the building, so I didn't want to look like I'd made too much effort. But I also didn't want to look like I didn't care—and my loungewear sometimes leaned slovenly. Jeans and my nicest wool sweater was the final verdict.

I breathed in and rapped three times. My nerves heightened at the sound of footsteps on the other side. The door swung open to Sylvie bearing her usual, sunny smile. Logically, I knew Sylvie always smiled as her natural set point, regardless of who was in front of her. But her warm, studied gaze still had a way of making me feel far more interesting than I actually was.

"Clover! So glad you're here—I've been looking forward to catching up all day." Sylvie stepped sideways and swept her arm out to welcome me inside. "It was a shitty day at work and I just want to forget about it. I'm so happy to see a friendly face!"

"Thanks for inviting me." I wasn't accustomed to enthusiastic affirmations of my presence. I thrust the wine bottle toward her. "I brought you this."

"Aww, thanks," Sylvie said, sliding the bottle around in her palm to study the label. "An Aussie red—you picked me well."

I wanted to claim the compliment, but this was one lie I could avoid. "The guy at the wine shop helped me choose it."

Sylvie squinted one eye. "You mean the one on West Third? The annoying guy who talks to you like you've never seen a grape before, let alone a bottle of wine?"

"He was a little condescending." I was glad it wasn't just me.

"'A little' is an understatement," Sylvie said. "Sometimes I like to go in there and ask about obscure wines just so I can watch him sweat over not knowing the answer. My stepmom is a winemaker, so I trust her judgment way more than I would his." She held up the bottle. "I bet he would've been so pissed if he knew you were buying this for me."

A nervous laugh was all I could muster.

"Let's crack this open," Sylvie said, padding over to the kitchen counter. "Would you mind taking off your shoes?"

Mid-step, I stopped my foot from touching the ground and slunk back toward the door, embarrassed to have violated Sylvie's house rules.

"Of course, sorry." Were socks permitted? I peeled mine off just in case.

"Totally fine," Sylvie grinned. "After living in Japan for a couple of years, I can't bring myself to wear them in the house." She gestured to the bar stools lining the counter. "Have a seat!"

Structurally, the apartment was a carbon copy of mine, except that it had been updated within the past twenty years. (I'd limited maintenance requests to emergencies like flooding toilets so that my landlord didn't have a reason to raise my urban-mythically low rent.) Aesthetically, Sylvie's apartment was the antithesis of mine. We had exactly the same number of windows, with exactly the same outlook, but her apartment was inexplicably filled with much more light, even at dusk.

"Are you still in the middle of decorating?" I asked, surveying the minimalist decor. Not a single shade within its palette deviated from white, cream, light gray, or wood. A lone abstract artwork hung above the sofa, but the walls, a bright alabaster, were otherwise bare. Sporadic stacks of books—spines all adhering to the serene color palette—sat positioned carefully on the coffee table and credenza. The bookshelves were comparatively empty, save for a smattering of well-spaced objects like smooth ceramics, an expensive-looking candle, and a glass vase of dried eucalyptus leaves. And yet it all somehow still felt cozy.

Sylvie laughed. "Nope, this is it—I guess all that Japanese minimalism wore off on me too. Though my taste has always leaned a little bit Agnes Martin." She looked around at her abode. "God, I'm a total millennial cliché, right?"

"You don't collect mementos when you travel or anything like that?" Even if it was just a fridge magnet, I always used to like bringing back some kind of reminder of places I'd visited. For a while I'd collected rocks and shells until I realized the cultural and spiritual implications of pilfering them.

Sylvie scrunched her face. "Nah, I'm not really a fan of *stuff*. I prefer to just have memories of experiences as my souvenirs. The one thing I try to do everywhere I visit is take a cooking class, so I can learn a local dish. Speaking of which . . ." The smell of spicy coconut and lemongrass filled the air as she lifted the lid off a simmering pan. "I hope you like Thai food."

After dinner, which we'd eaten seated on cushions around the coffee table, we perched on opposite ends of the sofa drinking a bottle of Sylvie's stepmother's syrah. My cheeks felt rosy, which meant I was getting tipsy. If I wasn't so concerned about potentially staining my neighbor's pristine furniture with wine, I might've relaxed completely.

"How's it going with that new client?" Sylvie said, her long legs tucked neatly to one side.

"You were right," I said, noticing her elegantly painted toenails and wondering if I should try painting mine. "Claudia's stories about being a photographer are really interesting."

Sylvie peered slyly over the top of her glass. "And what about that grandson? What's his name again?"

"Sebastian." Saying it out loud made me self-conscious, like I was conjuring him into the room. "He's fine. Why?"

"I just thought maybe you were getting to know him a little and that some sparks might fly between you."

"He's my boss," I said, thinking I should clarify that my blushing face was because of the wine.

"Yeah, but let's be real—there's a time limit on this job," Sylvie said. "Once his grandmother dies, he's not your boss anymore, so you're free to do whatever you like with him. Even if you're just looking for a bit of fun. Like a friends-with-benefits kind of deal."

"Oh." I shifted my focus to the artwork above the sofa, pretending to be fascinated by its soothing geometry.

"But maybe that's not your thing." Sylvie's smile was reassuring. "A lot of people are strictly relationship-only."

"Well . . ." I wasn't sure I was ready to let this conversation go any further. But if I was going to keep spending time with Sylvie—

and I wanted to—I'd probably have to endure it sooner or later. "It's more that I've never actually done . . . that."

"What, you mean had sex? Or a relationship?"

"Um, neither." Maybe if I mumbled it, it would be less shocking.

"Oh, got it." Sylvie's reaction lacked the judgment I was expecting. "So are you ace?"

"Ace?"

"Yeah, you know—asexual? That's totally cool. I know quite a few aces, actually."

I'd never considered how I'd label myself sexually. "No, I don't think so. I mean, I do feel attracted to people."

"Guys? Women? Everyone? I like to keep my options open, personally." Sylvie grinned. "Binary thinking has never been my thing."

I sifted through all the crushes I'd had over the years—fictional characters, strangers on the subway, college professors, Tim. "I'm attracted to men, I guess." Not exactly a revelation, but speaking the words seemed to stir a part of me that I'd purposely kept dormant.

Sylvie repositioned herself on the sofa so that she was facing me. "So what's kept you from actually dating anybody? You're a total catch—you know that, right? Smart, worldly, kind, perceptive, fun . . ."

The description flattered me—I always felt boringly subdued compared to Sylvie's boundless energy.

"I just never really understood how to go about it," I said, shrugging. "I know you're supposed to just wait and let it happen when you least expect it, but I did that and it never worked. No one ever noticed me in that way."

Sylvie's eyes were kind without pitying. "I'm confident that many people have noticed you, Clover. Maybe you just need to open yourself to actually seeing it. And acting on it."

"But dating is so confusing. I've always preferred things that you can study and learn, where there are set rules." I could feel myself getting flustered. "Love isn't like that—I just can't get my head around how to do it."

"How to do it? Well, that's kind of the whole point. Nobody ever understands love—anyone who says they do is lying or in denial. We're all just working it out as we go."

"What if I make a mistake? Or I'm just really bad at it?" There was no backing out of this, so I may as well be brutally honest. "I've never even kissed anyone."

"You're never going to get good at it if you don't put yourself out there and try." Sylvie divided the last of the wine between our glasses. "Love is kind of like scratching a mosquito bite—painful and euphoric at the same time. You've just got to get out of your head and into your heart."

I didn't bother hiding my discomfort. "But it's also kind of terrifying."

"Of course it is! And that's what makes it so worth it," Sylvie said confidently. "You listen to dying people all the time talking about the things they regretted not doing, right? I bet you'll regret not trying."

I knew she was right, but then I thought about the one time I did try—or almost tried.

I'd listened to my heart instead of my head and I ended up regretting it.

24

It was pouring rain when I arrived at Claudia's house at two on the dot for our third visit. A woman in a floral scrub top and a voluminous topknot the color of espresso answered the door.

"Clover, right? I'm Selma. Sounds like we'll be seeing a lot of each other." Her tone was efficient. "Claudia's in the kitchen. She said to tell you to come on through."

"Thanks—and nice to meet you, Selma." I watched her pull on a navy windbreaker and recognized the emblem of the home health-care service emblazoned on the left shoulder.

"I'm headed out to grab a coffee, but I'll be back in about half an hour. She's supposed to be eating the salad I made her for lunch— don't let her talk you into getting her any junk food."

"Got it."

My footsteps reverberated as I walked through the townhouse, emphasizing the lack of presence, both human and object. The black-and-white photos on the wall reminded me of the lie I'd have to continue—I'd stayed up late last night cramming my brain with the fundamentals of photography.

Aperture. Rule of thirds. White balance.

My plan was to ask Claudia as many questions as possible and then just stoke the conversational fire as needed. Fortunately, I now at least had a prop to help me keep up the ruse. Even though Sylvie had very few possessions, one of them happened to be a moderately fancy digital camera. And she was more than enthusiastic about lending it to me.

"Are you kidding me? Borrow mine!" Sylvie had said when I'd asked if she knew anything about buying cameras. "I'm so hooked on this whole photography charade with the dying woman and her grandson—I'd be honored to play a small role in the saga."

I found Claudia sitting on the breakfast nook banquette in the corner of the kitchen, watching the drizzle crisscross the window pane.

"My darling Clover." Crinkles of delight gathered in her face. "I'm so pleased you're here. Come, sit down."

"Hello, Claudia!" I slid onto the banquette next to her. "I met Selma on my way in."

"Oh, yes, Selma. All business, that woman. Always bossing me around about taking care of myself and eating my vegetables, as if I were a child."

"I'm sure she means well." Working with spirited, stubborn elderly folk usually required a certain level of assertiveness. No wonder Selma was brusque.

"I know, I know—she's just doing her job." Claudia winked. "But life's always more interesting with a little bit of debate. I like to think of her more as a worthy adversary."

I winked back. "Noted."

"So, since the warden's away, how about we have some fun?"

"What did you have in mind?" Better to remain neutral until I knew what I was agreeing to.

There was a nefarious glint in Claudia's smile. "How about you help me bend the rules a little?"

"Oh?"

"I've been craving a little bit of a treat." She nodded to a large ceramic jar on the floating shelves above the sink. "I had Maxwell, the lovely gentleman who comes to do my hair, hide some powdered doughnuts in there for me. Let's indulge in one or two, shall we?"

I considered my options. Really my allegiance was to Claudia, not Selma. And it was my job to help make Claudia's final days as pleasurable as possible, even if she didn't know that.

I pretended to look around sneakily, as if there was a risk of us being caught—even though I knew Selma wouldn't be back for half an hour.

"Count me in."

A fter I'd safely squirreled away the empty doughnut wrappers in my pocket, we sat at the table in front of a makeshift still life comprising a fruit bowl and an ornate china teapot.

"I've never been one for these boring vignettes of inert objects," Claudia said. "But this will help you learn how to shift the depth of field and focus in your photography."

"What's your favorite thing to photograph then?" I peered through the viewfinder, my thumb and pointer finger forming a *C* as I adjusted the lens.

"Human beings, of course," Claudia said, like the answer was obvious. "They're far more interesting than an apple or banana. Or a landscape, for that matter."

"I bet it's an entirely different skill, taking photos of people." I put the camera down on the table. "Those portraits on the wall in the hallway are stunning. What's the secret to taking a good photo of someone?"

Claudia's eyes shone. "Patience."

My mind retreated briefly to my birthday lesson in the park with Grandpa. I shut the sadness away and concentrated on Claudia.

"How so?"

"Before I ever took a photo of anyone, I'd take the time to get to know them—asking them about their childhood dreams, their cherished memories, the people they loved most," Claudia said. "And then, as they were talking, I'd start clicking the shutter."

"So you were kind of tapping into their inner essence."

"Precisely. Engaging people helps them let their guard down and be vulnerable. To feel, to express themselves. And that's what photography is all about—making people feel seen. Of course, we look at people every day, but we rarely stop to really see them for who they are."

"That makes sense."

I wondered what it would mean for someone to see me for who I really was. I worked hard to tuck away my emotions so that they didn't encroach on others—so that my clients could feel seen and understood. Except for Grandpa and Leo, I'd never let anyone in enough to do the same for me.

"The saddest part, my darling," Claudia said, freeing the gold bracelet that had been catching her cardigan sleeve, "is that most of us are guilty of that with our loved ones. We get stuck in a routine and we look at them as we've always looked at them, without seeing them for the person they've become or the person they strive to be. What a terrible thing to do to someone you love."

"I never really thought of it that way." Had I done that to Grandpa? Maybe he was different from the man who constantly occupied my memories. I hadn't really considered who he was outside the role of my caretaker and teacher.

"It's liberating to open yourself up and be truly seen by someone else," Claudia said. "Not everyone gets to experience that in life."

"But it sounds like perhaps you have?"

Claudia watched the raindrops pelt against the window. "A very long time ago." She patted my hand. "And I pray it happens to you too—but the lesson I hope you'll learn, that I didn't, is not to let go of the person who offers that to you just because you don't want to take a risk."

Selma bustled back into the kitchen, ten minutes before expected.

I reflexively put my hand on my pocket, hoping none of the powdered sugar had lingered on the table as evidence.

"Time for your meds, Claudia." She was holding a small plastic cup of pills. "I'll even let you take them with peanut butter this time."

"And what if I wanted them with raspberry jam?" Claudia countered.

Selma sighed, impatient. "Peanut butter at least has some protein. Raspberry jam is all sugar."

The women looked at each other defiantly, neither willing to back down. To avoid having to adjudicate (and to hide my guilt about being an accomplice to Claudia's sugar intake) I busied myself flicking through the images on the camera. I was quite pleased with my progress—maybe there was value to this charade with Claudia after all.

The brief standoff ended when Selma surrendered. "Fine. You can have one teaspoon of jam and one of peanut butter."

"I suppose that's a fair compromise," Claudia conceded haughtily.

After delivering the meds shrouded in breakfast spreads, Selma bustled out of the room again.

Claudia leaned toward me. "I actually like peanut butter better. But it's just so entertaining to push her buttons."

"She's just trying to do her job." I felt compelled to defend Selma again. Home health aides were saddled with extremely unpleasant tasks that I was glad not to have to partake in, especially as a client's body began to shut down.

"Oh, you're so pure of heart." Claudia chuckled. "I'm just trying to have some fun before I go."

Waiting a beat, I kept my tone neutral. "Go where?"

The deep Yves Saint Laurent red gathered in wrinkled rivulets around Claudia's lips. "Because you're so pure of heart, sweet Clover, I'm going to free you from having to participate in this pretense."

Sweat prickled my underarms. "Pretense?"

"I know I'm dying," Claudia said calmly. "And I also know my family thinks that I'm blissfully unaware of that fact."

"What do you mean?" My instinct was to feign ignorance.

"My son instructed the doctor not to tell me the diagnosis—highly unethical, of course, but my boy does have questionable morals at times. I suspected I wasn't being given the whole story and called the hospital myself."

I silently fumed at Sebastian for leaving me to deal with this. I had no choice but to come clean now.

"I'm sorry, Claudia."

"Oh, you're the least to blame." She nodded at the door where Selma had recently exited. "And I do appreciate Sebastian's efforts to provide me with some stimulating company separate from those in charge of my health. I've very much enjoyed your visits."

"So have I." But I still felt complicit in the betrayal.

"The question is," Claudia said, catching my eye, "are you really just a friend of his with a budding interest in photography?"

I squirmed. "Well, I am interested in photography. But no, not exactly."

"I thought as much," Claudia said, pleased with herself. "And?"

"I'm . . . a death doula."

Her wiry brows bounced. "A *death doula*," she said as if trying on the words for the first time. "Now, that was not among the many theories I had about your identity. I must say this turn of events is quite intriguing."

"I'm grateful you see it that way," I said, still ashamed. "I'm sorry for not telling you the truth sooner."

"What's done is done," she said, waving her hand as if shooing a fly. "Now, tell me what it is you're here to do, if not to learn about photography."

"Um, well, like you said, I'm here to keep you company, but also to help you work through any loose ends that you might want to tie up in the time you have left. And also just to talk about it—when you're ready."

Claudia laughed half-heartedly. "My grandson likely informed you that our family has never been amenable to discussing death. It's just 'not the done thing,' as they say." She brushed a wisp of gray hair from her temple. "And though I disagree with their making the decision on my behalf, I understand their intentions. We WASPs tend to express love in somewhat odd ways."

"That's very gracious of you. Is there anything you'd like to chat about or ask me?" I asked gently. "For the record, no topic is off the table."

"Thank you, darling. Today, let's just finish our photography lesson. You're showing some promise—it's a shame you won't be pursuing it."

"You never know; maybe you've inspired me." I paused before picking up the camera. "But first, I have to ask—do you even want me to keep coming?"

"Of course I do," Claudia said. "You're the most interesting thing to happen to me in years. I'm not letting that go so easily."

I wanted to feel relieved, but somehow I felt like I was already more personally entangled with her family than I should be.

25

With the click of Claudia's front door behind me, resentment kindled in my chest. Instinct told me to push it away—to mute my emotions for the benefit of others just like I always did. But as I strode toward the subway, I couldn't stop it from bubbling up to the surface. Leaning into the feeling was liberating and strangely addictive.

Sebastian hadn't just asked me to lie to Claudia. He'd also left me to deal with any fallout of that lie being exposed. All I'd wanted to do was help Claudia and instead I was unwillingly caught up in their family's secrets. I fumbled in my coat pocket for my phone. This exchange couldn't happen via text. I sucked in a lungful of brisk evening air, letting its chill calm me.

Sebastian picked up on the first ring.

"Clover, hey!" His chipper tone was immediately grating. "How'd things go with Grandma?"

I took another deep breath, willing my voice to hold steady. "She knows."

A pause. "Knows? What do you mean?"

"That we've been lying to her."

The staticky phone line abated Sebastian's silence. "Oh, man. How?"

"She called the specialist herself and made him tell her the truth." I still couldn't believe that doctor was willing to lie in the first place.

Sebastian let out a descending whistle. "Geez, okay. How'd she take it?"

"Pretty graciously, considering."

"That's great! I was kind of hoping she'd find out somehow so that none of us had to break it to her. Though I'm not looking forward to breaking the news to my dad."

It stung that he didn't even think about how it might have impacted me.

"You're lucky she wasn't more upset. She could've reacted really badly, you know."

"Yeah, well, Grandma's always been tough. It makes sense that she'd take it in stride." His laugh was uncomfortably forced. "She's still cool with you coming though, right?"

"Well, yes." And I had to admit I was looking forward to spending time with her without the stress of keeping up the pretense. "But you still shouldn't have put me in that position. It's irrelevant that Claudia took the news well because I would've been the one to deal with consequences if she hadn't. Did you even consider that?"

As I said the words, it dawned on me that I wasn't really upset about being caught up in the lie—it was obvious Sebastian thought he was helping Claudia. What hurt more was that he didn't care about how it might affect me when she found out.

"Oh, wow, I guess I didn't." More static. "You're right, Clover— I'm sorry you had to deal with that."

His rapid apology caught me off guard. Maybe he'd simply been preoccupied with the fact that his beloved grandmother was dying. I felt a little selfish for making the situation about me.

"It's fine, really," I said, my resentment shifting to embarrassment. "Like you said, it all worked out in the end."

I was grateful that a garbage truck chose that moment to rumble past, pausing our conversation momentarily.

"So, I'm actually glad you called." Sebastian said, once the noise faded.

"Oh?"

"Yeah . . . because I was wondering if maybe you wanted to get together for a drink tomorrow night? It could be fun to hang out, you know, just the two of us."

I definitely wasn't expecting that segue. Was he suggesting a professional meeting to discuss things going forward with Claudia, now that the truth was out? Or did he mean something else? Was it pathetic that I was approaching middle age and couldn't tell if I was being asked out on a date? The thought of making small talk with Sebastian in a rowdy bar was intimidating, either way.

"I think I might have plans tomorrow night," I said, panicking. I needed to time process his invitation—and to dissect it with Sylvie.

"That's cool," Sebastian said confidently. "We can just do it the night after. Or the night after that."

He was being really persistent, but I could also be reading too much into it. I did have a history of taking narratives about him a little too far, after all. But would I regret saying no? Maybe Sylvie was right: this was my chance to take a risk.

"The night after could work," I said before I could talk myself out of it. "Just text me the details." Better to be casual in case it was just a professional meeting.

"Great, looking forward to it!"

I tried not to put much weight on the excitement in his voice.

"Sebastian, I'm sorry but my train is here so I've got to go."

"No worries—talk to you soon."

"Goodnight."

I tapped the red circle on my phone and walked the remaining half block to the subway, unsure if the giddiness I felt was anticipation or apprehension.

26

Ever since my phone call with Sebastian, a lump of unease had made itself at home in my stomach.

On Sylvie's assessment, his invitation was definitely a date because he'd made a point to say "just the two of us." On mine, it was merely a social drink with my employer, because no one had ever invited me on a date prior to this, and I didn't know why Sebastian would be the exception to the rule.

But on the slim chance that Sylvie was right, I'd taken her up on her offer to lend me a dress that "left just enough to the imagination." Just the idea of being the subject of someone else's imagination was petrifying.

I stood outside the nondescript facade of the Lower East Side bar, wishing I could disappear into the pockmarked bricks. The black dress constricted my middle and its seams scratched my thighs. It felt like I was inhabiting someone else's skin, loose in all the wrong places; my limbs felt even more out of proportion to my body than usual. I envied the innate style and confidence of the other people entering the bar, who could all probably tell I was a fraud.

Sebastian had told me eight o'clock. It was now 8:23 P.M., meaning the fifteen-minute leeway you had to grant everyone in New York City because of the unreliable subway system had well expired.

Surely I wasn't obligated to wait any longer. I considered texting Sylvie for her opinion but I already knew her answer. She wouldn't tolerate the disrespect of her time and would've already left.

But then I spotted Sebastian's now-familiar silhouette hurrying toward me, hunched against the evening cold. He wore an expectedly monochrome palette, but somehow the matching blacks looked neater, more formal. His shoes might've been shinier than usual, but it was hard to tell in the sickly amber of the streetlight.

"Hey, sorry I'm late," he said, face flushed. "I got stuck at work."

"That's fine." A date would have texted to let me know, right? Another point in my column.

We hovered awkwardly in front of each other like teens at a dance.

Sebastian opened the door to the bar. "You're gonna love this place—I come here all the time."

My feet felt nailed to the grimy pavement. *Just get out of your head,* Sylvie's voice nagged at me.

The pavement released its grip.

The dark establishment felt only slightly wider than a school bus. A long bed of oysters on ice lined the narrowest part of the bar, while a man with a waistcoat, white button-down, and waxed mustache shook a copper cocktail shaker with feigned insouciance. Fascinated, I absorbed the scene around me. I'd never had a reason to set foot in this kind of bar, but I'd always wondered what lay beyond their purposefully generic front doors.

Sebastian led me to the back of the enclave, where leather banquettes lined the perimeter. Small tables the size of milking stools sat with a single candle flickering in the center of each. The impractical dimness made it hard to tell, but I suspected that the patina of the tin walls and ceiling was more cultivated than earned.

A trio of brunettes was vacating the table in the corner. The shortest of the cohort stared at us in surprise.

"Sebastian! Hi!!"

I could almost hear the excess of exclamation points.

Sebastian's posture stiffened. "Oh, hey . . . Jessie." From the slight pause, I guessed he'd recalled her name in the nick of time. "How's it going?"

"Great!" Jessie gestured to her friends. "Just out for a girls' night!" Her eyes drifted conspicuously to me.

"Oh," Sebastian said stiffly. "Jessie, this is Clover."

"Hey, Clover," Jessie said, her voice too saccharine to be genuine. She turned back to Sebastian and tugged on his lapel with an exaggerated pout. "It's been so long—call me so we can catch up!"

"Um, sure." He fidgeted with the end of his scarf. "See you later, Jessie."

"See you *soon*." As she breezed past, friends in tow, she trailed her hand down his forearm.

Sebastian quickly directed me to the now-vacant banquette and waited until the women were safely out of earshot.

"We dated for a month last year," he said as if I'd demanded a confession. "Nice, but a little ditzy."

Unsure how to respond to that unsolicited information, I sat down and studied the cocktail menu written in cursive on aged paper stock. "Wow, these cocktails are pretty elaborate."

"Yeah, they really know their mixology here," he said, scooting in next to me.

Was I supposed to move along to give him some room or was the whole point to let him sit close to me? I wished I could surreptitiously text Sylvie for advice, but Sebastian didn't seem to be taking his eyes off me. I split the difference and shifted slightly, but not too far away.

After I downed my first cocktail—bourbon-based with muddled rosemary—the tension in my body receded a little.

"I wanted to say thank you for everything you're doing for Grandma." Sebastian rested his elbow on top of the banquette behind me, right next to my shoulder, but stopped short of touching me. "It's so much better now that everything's out in the open—though my dad still won't really discuss it."

"I'm happy to help—it's my job, after all," I said, distracted by his arm position. "So, how long have you been playing the cello?" Hopefully my tactic of deflecting the conversation away from me was less obvious to him than it was to Sylvie.

"Since I was a kid." He swirled his tropical cocktail—a drink choice I wouldn't have expected of a man in his thirties, but I was no expert. "I was never really athletic—my sisters got our family's share of that gene—and plus I had a lot of allergies, so my mom kept me indoors a lot. On my tenth birthday, Grandma took me to the music store and told me I could pick any instrument to learn and I chose the cello. Since I was the smallest kid in my class at the time, and it looked so big and powerful, I thought maybe if I could make music on it, I'd feel powerful too." Now he was stabbing at his ice cubes with the straw. "Looking back, I really should have chosen something cooler—like a guitar—or at least an instrument that was easier to carry. Getting around the city with a cello is kind of hell."

"I can imagine." I tried to hide my smile, thinking of Sebastian trying to wrangle a large instrument amid a packed train of New Yorkers who were precious about their personal space.

He sipped his drink then licked his lips. "Do you play anything?"

"My grandpa had an old banjo that I kind of taught myself to play." Another YouTube adventure that—judging by the fact that my pets left the room whenever I played—was only slightly successful. "I'd love to learn piano, but there's not really room for one in my apartment."

"Not even an electric keyboard?"

"My apartment is pretty crowded already."

"Oh, you live with someone?" Sebastian's tone was affectedly casual.

"Just my pets. I have two cats and a dog."

"Wow, that's a lot of animals."

"You don't have any pets?" I definitely wasn't going to mention that I was considering adopting a cockatoo I'd seen on Craigslist.

Sebastian shook his head. "I'm allergic to cats and dogs, so I'd be miserable if I did." He rubbed his nose, as if allergic to the thought.

"I'm sorry," I said, genuinely sad for him. "I can't imagine not having pets." They were what helped make my life livable—beating hearts to come home to each day.

He shrugged. "I've never really been much of an animal person anyway, so I'm fine with it."

By the end of the night, three cocktails deep, I still hadn't come to a concrete conclusion about whether we were on a date. His arm was now stretched out behind me, close enough that I could feel the heat radiating from his armpit but still not quite touching me. Each time he leaned forward to sip his drink, I noticed the scent I'd come to associate with him—a fusion of spiced body wash, clothes left in a drawer too long, and a hint of perspiration.

I studied his face as he talked, trying to decide if he was attractive, since Sylvie would likely demand details tomorrow. The way his hair swept across his forehead was quite charming in a boyish way. And his erudite style—gold-rimmed glasses and scarf slung loosely around his neck—reminded me of the owner of one of my favorite vintage book stores in Paris. But it was hard to make a definitive assessment when the light was so dim. I definitely didn't find him unattractive. And I didn't mind his company. Real-life romance was probably more of a slow burn than a cinematic lightning bolt. As a creature of habit, it usually took me a while to warm up to most new things, anyway.

"Sweet," Sebastian said, stuffing the receipt in his pocket after performatively insisting on paying. "They forgot to charge us for one of the drinks."

"Shouldn't we say something to the server?"

"Nah—they should have paid closer attention." He stood up and pulled on his coat. "Ready to go?"

"I'll meet you out front," I said, keeping my jacket over my arm. "I'm just going to the bathroom."

I didn't actually need to use the bathroom, but I spent a few minutes washing and moisturizing my hands with lotion from the chic amber bottles locked to the wall. As I navigated the throng of glamorous urbanites on my way back through the bar, our server—a lanky college kid—was clearing the empty glasses from our table. I slipped him a twenty-dollar bill on my way out.

Sebastian was leaning against the fire hydrant, scrolling through his phone. "All set?"

"Yes, I was just going to walk to the subway." I really should've had a solid exit plan for this part of the night to preempt any awkwardness.

"Oh, I was going to take an Uber. I can drop you." The vapor of his words sailed into the night.

"No, that's fine—it's super out of your way. The subway is only a block from here. Thanks, anyway."

Sebastian twisted his scarf awkwardly. "Are you sure?"

"Positive." My attempt at assertive confidence came out slightly aggressive, but there was no way I wanted him to drop me at my house late at night, even if this was a date. That was too much pressure.

Sebastian nodded obediently. "Okay, cool—I'll walk with you to the subway and call the Uber from there."

Well, I couldn't say no to a chivalrous gesture.

As we walked, Sebastian launched into a story about a college friend who had designed one of the new high rises in the neighborhood, but I couldn't concentrate on his words. My pulse pounded in my ears and I felt a sudden urge to pee, despite having been fine moments earlier.

A handshake seemed too formal after three cocktails. Would he expect a hug? He was walking much closer to me than he ever had before. The uncertainty of it all made me want to break into a sprint. As the green bulbs of the subway entrance came into view, nervousness tumbled in my stomach. The blare of a passing siren—a sound I was generally immune to—felt irritating and chaotic against the shrill laughter of two women standing on the curb.

I wished I was at home on the sofa with my animals, watching someone else's life play out on a screen—or through a window. I wondered what Julia and Reuben's first date had been like. They always seemed so comfortable together, like the world existed only for them. I couldn't imagine them being awkward.

"So, what do you think?" Sebastian was looking at me expectantly.

I was confused. "About what?"

"About the architecture?"

My cheeks flushed. "It's great, I guess."

We paused at the top of the subway stairs, dodging the commuters frantically descending in case the screeching arrival below was their train. Sebastian stood a few feet in front of me and I felt my back against the chilled metal of the entrance railing. For once, I was more uncomfortable with silence than he was.

"Well," I started, "it was nice to see you."

"Yeah," Sebastian said softly. I was pretty sure he was looking at me intensely, but the reflection of the streetlights in his glasses made it impossible to read his expression.

He stepped forward, closing the distance between us. Instinctively, I stepped backward, but there was nowhere for me to go. His hand slid inside my open coat and rested on my waist. It felt cold even through my dress.

Then he leaned in and pressed his lips to mine.

At first, I felt the urge to pull away. But then curiosity set in.

So this was kissing. My first kiss.

I'd imagined a thousand versions of it—and here it finally was. It felt almost surreal. I still wasn't sure if I even wanted to kiss Sebastian specifically. But like Sylvie said, I wouldn't know if I liked it if I didn't at least try it. So I tried to simply observe it, as if documenting it in my notebook like Grandpa taught me to do with every new experience.

It felt wetter than I'd imagined and his saliva tasted faintly of the pineapple juice from his last cocktail. I hadn't noticed any stubble on his chin, but now it rubbed against my face, abrasive like pumice stone. His hands were resting on each of my hips, pulling me toward him. I wondered what to do with mine. Women in movies often ran their hands through the man's hair, but that seemed over the top. Should I grab on to his coat lapels? No, that also felt aggressive. And I didn't want to seem like I was enjoying it until I actually decided if I was.

Just to be safe, I kept my hands by my sides.

His tongue began pushing on my lips, taut, as if trying to pry them open wider. Was I supposed to oblige, since I hadn't resisted the kiss? For the sake of experimentation, I did. And it wasn't totally unpleasant, but it also wasn't igniting the internal fireworks I always imagined I'd feel in this scenario. Maybe kissing was something that grew on you too.

"Get a room!"

The catcall coming from the stairs brought the kiss to an abrupt end. Startled, I pulled away and Sebastian released his grip on my waist. As my face blazed, I shuffled sideways so that I was no longer between him and the railing.

Suddenly everything felt a little too real. My mind flashed to Claudia and the fact that it was definitely a conflict of interest to be kissing her grandson, who also happened to be my employer.

"I've got to go," I said, avoiding eye contact. "Thanks for the drinks."

I bolted down the stairs, head spinning—from the alcohol, the kiss, or the shame of being called out, I wasn't sure.

"Clover, wait!"

Disoriented, I ran toward the turnstile, thanking all the gods and universal forces in existence when my MetroCard swiped smoothly and the bar guided me to freedom.

27

Signs of a nascent spring were emerging from the lonely limbs of trees as I rounded the corner onto Claudia's block, but I barely noticed any of them. Emotions dueled in my body—relief that I no longer had to keep up any pretense about my job and panic about what I'd say to Sebastian the next time I saw him.

Ever since I was a kid, I'd imagined all the different things I might feel after my first kiss: joy, euphoria, excitement. Panic wasn't among them.

Just as I'd rewatched hundreds of movie embraces over the years, I replayed the kiss in my head. It wasn't that it had been terrible, more that I'd thought I'd find it more enjoyable-—that I'd feel some kind of electric current running through my body. But I'd probably built it up so much that nothing would have lived up to my expectations. Or maybe pop culture had just left me ill-prepared, perpetuating the false stereotype that all kisses were wonderful.

I rallied myself before joining Claudia in the garden. In the cold light of day, it felt unprofessional of me to have even gone out with Sebastian in the first place.

"Hello, dear," Claudia greeted me happily. Dappled shade decorated her skin and she briefly closed her eyes, reveling in the sunlight that filtered through. "I've been looking forward to you coming."

The earnest welcome made me feel even more conflicted. "It's lovely to see you too."

"I must say, I'm so fascinated by this profession of yours," Claudia said, rubbing her palms together. "How are we going to approach death today? Goodness, it's just so liberating to be able to talk about it. I regret having left it this long—it would have made things far easier."

Claudia's attitude was admirable, but I didn't believe it. Just like Guillermo's anger had been a mask for his fear and loneliness, her nonchalance was probably a front for her vulnerability.

"Well," I began cautiously, "since I know your family has trouble talking about the fact that you're dying, I was thinking it could be helpful for you to put together a death binder."

Claudia lifted her teacup from its saucer, pinching the handle delicately. "And what, my darling, is a death binder?"

"It's a way of organizing all of the documents and details that your family might need—social security number, birth certificate, bank account details, passwords, and, of course, your will. But it can also be more than that, like a list of all the people you'd like them to notify when you're gone."

"I see."

"And it can also be helpful to compile a list of things that would help them plan your funeral—if you even want one, that is. Like, do you want an open casket? And if so, what would you like to be wearing? And how do you want to be remembered? Do you have a favorite song, poem, or prayer? Or a favorite flower? Things like that."

"This is all very morbid, Clover," Claudia said, mildly amused. "And yet you talk about it so casually."

I blushed, ashamed. I should've eased into the subject more gracefully. The whole thing with Sebastian had really put me off my game.

"I'm sorry, I didn't mean to be flippant. It's just that when your family is grieving, it might be hard for them to recall these details.

So it can provide some emotional relief, for everyone, if we document them now."

"I like your no-nonsense approach," Claudia said. "And a death binder makes a lot of sense. I know they'll all be anticipating the will reading, at least, but they probably haven't thought about much else."

"I think they'll be concerned with more than just your will," I said softly. "From what Sebastian says, you are infinitely loved."

"Oh, I know I am," Claudia chuckled. "My son and grandchildren may be dysfunctional, and a little strange, but I know they all love me in their own way. Even if I hardly see them. But, really, who could blame them for having their eye on this townhouse?" She sipped her Darjeeling.

"It is beautiful." I looked up at the brick-lined rear of the home, curious to know exactly how Claudia would be divvying up her small fortune and New York real estate gold mine. As Claudia's most devoted grandchild, Sebastian could potentially be the beneficiary of a lot of it.

Panic returned as the previous night's kiss looped through my mind.

Claudia laid her palms on the table like a CEO commanding attention. "So, where do we start?"

Grateful to have a concrete task to focus on, I pulled out a notebook and pen. "Well, first of all, have you thought about whether you'd like to be buried or cremated?"

"Cremated." Her casualness made it sound like she was ordering food off a menu. "No need to take up unnecessary space in the world if I'm not here to enjoy it. Though I will say, there's a certain charm to being buried at sea."

"It's possible to do that if it's what you want?"

"Too much effort for everyone. And besides, most of my family gets terribly seasick. It wouldn't be a very poignant farewell if all the mourners were heaving over the side of the boat, would it?"

"Good point." I couldn't help smiling at her pragmatism. "Cremation it is then. And is there a special place you'd like your ashes to be scattered?"

Wistfulness dimmed Claudia's eyes. "I'd like them to be scattered off the cliffs of Bonifacio."

"In Corsica?"

"You know your geography well, I see."

"It's one of my favorite parts of the world—I went there a couple of times while I was doing my master's thesis in Paris. Bonifacio is a cute little town."

"Well, I spent most of my time there on a boat, but it was still very charming," Claudia said, a hint of mystery in her delivery. "What's next on the list?"

"Let's see—we could compile the list of people you'd like us to notify and I can track down their contact details if you don't have them."

"Fortunately, that should be a relatively short task for us both," Claudia said. "When you get to be ninety-one years old, most of your friends and acquaintances are dead."

An echo of Leo's lament. "That must be hard. But I imagine you've had some wonderful friendships over the years."

"Some, yes. Others I wish I'd abandoned long before they dissipated naturally." Her hand shook as she raised the teacup to her lips. "Another lesson for you, Clover—choose your friendships wisely. I'm sure you have flocks of friends at your age?"

I looked down at the iron lace of the garden table, embarrassed. "Not really—I guess you could say I'm a bit of a loner. Most people don't really like being around someone who deals with death all the time."

"A lone wolf, really?" Claudia leaned back, studying me. "I wouldn't have guessed that given the lovely and amenable young lady that you are. My grandson in particular seems to have taken a shine to you."

My stomach lurched. Was this a test? What had Sebastian told Claudia?

Better to play dumb.

"I guess I've just always preferred my own company," I said, still rattled. "I was an only child, so I had to be content with my own thoughts most of the time."

"And your parents didn't encourage you to have playdates?"

"They died in an accident when I was six—that's when I came to live with my grandfather here in the city." I traced my finger over the metal pattern of the table.

"It must have been difficult growing up without a mother," Claudia said in a way that I knew meant she was treading carefully. "Lord knows mine made my life difficult at times, but I can't imagine what it would have been like without her."

I shrugged. "We didn't really spend a lot of time together before she died. It's hard to miss something you never really had."

"Well, I'm glad you had your grandfather."

"Me too. He was a wonderful man," I said. "But he was also kind of a loner—I probably learned it from him."

"Children do tend to emulate the most influential figures in their lives." Claudia reached out to pat my hand. "But he obviously did a great job raising his granddaughter. It's no easy feat to raise a child, especially if you weren't expecting to. I'm sure he would be very proud of you."

"Thank you." I felt the papery texture of Claudia's skin as I clasped her fingers. "He did the best he could."

I knew that was true. But as we sat watching the sparrows play in the garden, it reminded me how hard it would've been for Grandpa to have a six-year-old girl shoehorned into his life out of the blue. And it made me wonder if I was really living a life that would make him proud.

As I walked back to the subway later that afternoon, I thought about Claudia's parents, and mine. While my mother had fulfilled the role of parent biologically, I don't think she ever took to it instinctively. In the six years we had together, I couldn't remember any signs of the tenderness and nurturing that mothers in movies

seemed to exhibit so naturally. No warm hugs, no tying of hair rib-
bons, no baking of cupcakes. Sometimes I liked to imagine that she
might've been that way if she'd been given the chance to blossom
into motherhood. When you fantasize about something enough, it
can almost feel like it's true.

Grandpa had more than filled the role of father in my life—he
had indelibly shaped the way I saw and experienced the world. But I
often wondered what I had missed, growing up without a maternal
figure. I probably still wouldn't be any good at applying makeup, or
care much about clothing, but would I be more attuned to my intu-
ition? Or more comfortable with emotional expression?

Was I somehow less of a woman because I'd never had one to
look up to?

28

"Don't make my drink too strong, Leo." I sat down at his dining table ready for our next bout of mahjong.

He bent industriously over his bar cart stirring a bourbon concoction, a wizard to his cauldron. Ice clinked against the glass like wind chimes. With a satisfied grin, he slid the drink in front of me, the comforting smell of bar soap radiating from his skin as it always did.

"How's that new job of yours going?"

"Claudia? She's a really interesting woman—reminds me of you, actually."

Leo eyed me with a skeptical half smile. "A rich white woman on the Upper West Side reminds you of me?" His tone was playful but his message clear.

"Okay—I mean her cheeky sense of humor, yearning for the good old days, and love of bending the rules reminded me of you."

"Well, of those qualities I'm guilty." Leo sipped his drink, then smacked his lips a few times in deliberation. "A little too much lime, I think."

I sipped mine cautiously. "I think it's delicious." I grinned at him. "Am I disappointing you with my less-than-discerning palate?"

"You'll learn soon enough, my young protégée."

I handed him the dice. "Your turn to roll first."

Cupping them in his lithe hands, he shook the dice dramatically beside each ear as if rattling a coconut. "I hear you've been spending a lot of time with our new neighbor."

He tossed the dice onto the table. A two and a four.

"Sylvie? Yeah, she's really nice." I collected the dice and shook them sideways in my palm. "We've hung out a couple of times—went for coffee, did a yoga class, she made me dinner—things like that."

I dusted my hands with satisfaction as my toss revealed a five and a six. Leo shot me a mock glare.

"Sounds like a budding friendship, if you ask me."

Self-consciousness set my cheeks aglow. "It's probably too soon to call it that." I hoped my shrug appeared sufficiently nonchalant.

"Well, I think Sylvie's a great addition to the building." Leo sipped his bourbon again. "Not least because she shares my love of neighborhood gossip."

"So does that mean you won't be talking my ear off so often about the neighborhood's dirty secrets?"

"I know you just pretend to disapprove of it because your grandpa did. Of course, a gentleman like him would never engage in that kind of behavior. But you know what?" Leo leaned forward and lowered his voice. "I think deep down he enjoyed it as much as you do, but neither of you ever admitted it."

I blushed. There were some benefits to getting the neighborhood news without having to make small talk with strangers.

"I miss him."

"Me too," Leo said. "Good old Patrick. Hard to believe it's been thirteen years without him."

Our game paused as we sat in reflection.

"Leo, did Grandpa ever talk to you about what it was like to have to raise me all by himself?" The ice cubes in my glass formed a lethargic whirlpool. "I mean, I was kind of thrust upon him out of nowhere. I think I'd only even met him twice before that."

Leo's eyes radiated a blend of empathy and sadness. He took a breath as if to say something and then retracted it before the syllables materialized. I didn't think I'd ever seen him at a loss for words before.

After a slow sip, he spoke. "What makes you ask that?"

"Something Claudia said made me wonder. It must've been hard on him, having to deal with a six-year-old girl all of a sudden." I put my glass down and examined the lines in my palms. "Do you think, maybe, I kind of . . . ruined his life?"

Leo exhaled slowly. "I won't lie to you—it was a real challenge for him sometimes. Just like raising a child is a challenge for any parent at one time or another."

"Yeah, but most of the time they choose to have those kids." I was ashamed that I'd never really thought about what it was like for him to suddenly be solely responsible for a little girl he hardly knew.

Leo glanced up at the ceiling as if conferring with a higher power.

"Clover, I think you're the best thing that ever happened to your old grandpa. From what he told me, he worked a whole bunch while your mama was growing up and so he didn't have too much to do with raising her."

I nodded, recalling the conversation from my birthday outing to Central Park. "I remember he told me that he'd traveled a lot when she was young." That was one of the only times I could remember him speaking about their relationship.

"Yup. And your mama turned out a little wayward—only thought of herself is what it sounded like. Your grandpa never approved of the fact that she and your dad were off traveling all the time, leaving you with that neighbor lady. He didn't think they were raising you right. And it was painful for him to see that because it made him wonder if she was just following his example, prioritizing work over family. I think he felt a lot of guilt over it."

I gulped my cocktail without caution.

"And so when it turned out that he was the only family you had left," Leo continued, "I think he saw it as sort of a do-over. Like he had the chance to do right by you and raise you into the best person you could be, to make up for where he went wrong with your mama."

The revelation only deepened the ache in my heart. "I never knew that."

"How could you? You were doing the best you could getting by with the tough hand you were dealt. But I remember sometimes he would come up here for a drink after you'd gone to bed, tearing his hair out over the fact that he had no idea what he was doing. He was so scared that he'd mess you up too."

"But he always seemed so confident about everything he taught me."

"Of course he did—he wanted you to know that you could rely on him no matter what." Leo's irises lit up with amusement. "You know, for most of the female stuff—buying your first bra and whatnot—he got his intel from that woman, Bessie, who owns the bookstore you two always went to."

"Really?" A lifetime of disparate puzzle pieces started to fit together.

"Really. Look, I promised your grandpa that I'd always watch out for you—and I think that includes telling it to you straight." He glanced at the ceiling again. "I'm pretty sure he'd be okay with that."

"Thank you, Leo," I said quietly, my brain whirring as it reconsidered my childhood through a new lens. "I appreciate it. I really do."

He winked. "I got you."

Unsure if I could take any more of Leo's truths, I focused on the tiles between us. "Ready to play?"

"Oh, you bet." Leo rubbed his hands together, then stopped abruptly, holding his neck with a wince.

"Everything okay, Leo?"

He leaned back in his chair, eyes closed, letting the moment pass. When he opened them, I could tell he was rallying his composure. "Fit as a fiddle, like I always tell you. Just some random neck pain I get once in a while. Old age and all that."

I wasn't convinced. "We don't have to play tonight if you don't feel like it. We could watch one of those old British comedies you love instead?"

"I see you trying to wrangle a forfeit out of me." Leo wiggled his finger at me. "Don't think you can get me to surrender my lead that easily."

"Leo—"

He flashed a defiant grin. "Your turn, kid."

Leo's company always made me feel better, but as I closed my apartment door after our game, I was exhausted. Life had seemed so much simpler a month ago. Now I felt slightly untethered.

The binoculars sat on the shelf, benign to anyone else, but contraband to me. Just a few minutes wouldn't hurt. A quick check-in to make sure Julia and Reuben's domestic bliss was still intact. That something in my world was as it had always been.

I executed my routine with precision: lights off, chair positioned, blinds crept open.

A dinner party. Julia and Reuben liked to host them every now and then. Always the same people, always couples. Each pair's nuanced body language its own cryptic puzzle waiting to be decoded.

Yes, this was exactly what I needed.

And there were Julia and Reuben, arms entwined as they chatted with their guests, their quiet adoration for each other burning as strong as ever.

Swaddling myself in a blanket, I settled in for the evening, finding comfort in one of the only relationships I knew I could count on.

29

When Sylvie suggested a last-minute dance class, I shocked myself by saying yes. Between my very public kiss with Sebastian and Leo's revelations about Grandpa, my brain had too many emotions to process. Expending some energy would give me a welcome escape.

"Probably ninety percent of people's first kisses are bad," Sylvie said as we sat cross-legged on the floor of a small dance studio in Chelsea. "Mine was terrible—though, to be fair, we were only twelve. Unfortunately, there are still guys like Sebastian who make it to their thirties without ever learning how to kiss someone properly. You'd think someone would've said something to him by now."

I felt like I'd joined a secret club—one of bad first kisses—that I hadn't realized so many people belonged to. The weight of my disappointment eased slightly.

"So what should I do?"

Sylvie smoothed a wrinkle in her shiny leggings. "You're sure that you didn't feel any kind of chemistry with him? Maybe it was just hard to get past the bad kiss?" A mischievous look came over her face. "Maybe *you're* the one to teach him how it's really done."

I struggled to stop myself from squirming. "I don't know. It all happened so quickly. And it's not like I have anything to compare it to." More than anything, it was anticlimactic. I didn't mind Sebastian's company, and his close relationship with Claudia was endearing, but I wasn't as drawn to him as I thought I would be to the first man I kissed.

"Go out with him again and see how it feels," Sylvie said. "You may as well experiment while the opportunity's there—think of it as a learning process. And at least now you'll know for sure it's a date!"

"I guess I could," I said, not entirely convinced. "But not while I'm still working with Claudia. I need to keep things separate." Besides, that would allow more time for my feelings to develop into something more concrete.

The peeling varnish on the wooden floor felt rough beneath my hands as I looked around at the other women in the dance studio. In the yoga class we'd gone to, everyone wore variations on calming neutrals. Here, the aesthetic was draped black fabrics and deep jewel tones that accentuated the curves of the women's bodies. I hoped my navy leggings and baggy gray T-shirt might help me recede into the background. But then I noticed something even more intimidating than my classmates: two metal poles in the center of the room.

"I see the fear in your eyes." Sylvie nudged me playfully. "Don't worry—this isn't a pole-dancing class. Though we should definitely take one of those. They're super fun."

Her assurance did nothing to quell my nerves. I adjusted my leggings self-consciously and considered tying my T-shirt at the waist, like some of the other women in the studio.

"What's this class called again?"

"Sensual Synch," Sylvie said, wiggling her eyebrows. "Basically you get to feel like a stripper without taking any of your clothes off."

"Wait—I thought you said it was an aerobics dance class." I'd envisioned something closer to Zumba than stripping.

"I said *aerobic*—as in, it will increase your body's need for

oxygen. You just interpreted it with your own psychological bias."
Sylvie grinned. "Plus, I know you wouldn't have come if I'd told you
exactly what the class was. But trust me, it's gonna be so good for
you. Dancing is the best way to get in touch with your body. Well,
except for sex. But you'll love this class—it's so fun and freeing."

On cue, the lights dimmed to an ambience more fitting to a romantic restaurant, revealing candles strategically placed around the
room. I hadn't noticed anyone lighting them.

The grinding, sultry bass of a Beyoncé song filled the room. This
was going to be excruciating. Unlike other things I'd succeeded in
teaching myself, rhythm had proven to be an impenetrable foe. In
theory, I knew you were supposed to clap on the "two," but it was
much harder to put into practice.

A woman sashayed into the center of the room, as if controlled
by her hips. She ran her hands down the sides of her body like she
was savoring the touch.

"Yeeessss," Sylvie whispered appreciatively. "This is going to be
amazing."

"Are you ladies ready to really feeeeeel your bodies?" The woman
purred, eyes closed in pleasure.

Everyone in the room responded with various enthusiastic versions of "Wooooo!"

Except for me. I was pretty sure I was going to vomit. In my
estimation, the door was about ten feet away. I could bolt now and
never look back.

But before I could act on the impulse, Sylvie grabbed my hand
and pulled me up. "I'm so happy we're doing this together, C!"

The tension holding my body captive relaxed and the nausea began to recede. Sylvie was looking at me so earnestly that I couldn't
let her down. Pleading with my nerves to calm, I focused on the
feeling of connection with my friend.

"I am too." I smiled weakly, exhilarated and terrified in equal
measure. It was like I was holding on to a cluster of helium balloons
and had finally let my feet leave the ground.

As far as I could tell, there was no actual routine to the class. It mostly consisted of a lot of writhing in time to the music (or in my case, slightly behind the beat), a few songs spent crawling along the floor like jungle felines (I wished I'd brought kneepads), and running fingers through hair (impractical for me since I had a tight topknot). Sylvie, apparently born with perfect rhythm, embraced it all with gusto, as did her ponytail, which seemed to sway exactly in time. She'd occasionally bump shoulders with me and flash an encouraging smile before striding off confidently as if sensuality coursed through her veins and it was no big deal.

Twenty minutes into the session, I began to feel sporadic flashes of surrender. It helped that we were told to close our eyes (and "just let goooooooo"), and when I snuck a peek, nobody in the room was paying attention to anyone but themselves. Liberated, I allowed my body to move with a fluidity I'd never experienced. Running my hands over my thighs and waist felt newly intimate . . . and pleasurable.

In an unexpected moment of release, I reached up and unleashed my topknot.

As Sylvie and I retrieved our belongings from the locker room, I felt slightly euphoric.

"See? I knew you'd love it," Sylvie said, looking approvingly at my invigorated glow. "Look how relaxed you are."

"Yeah, it was better than I expected, I guess." I didn't want to seem too enthusiastic in case she tried to talk me into the pole-dancing class. But when the chill of evening hit my skin as we walked toward Eighth Avenue, I was keenly aware of my body. The way my clothing felt against it, the way it moved. It was the same rush I'd get from watching a love story unfold on TV, or indulging in Julia and Reuben's tender kisses from afar.

Yet, somehow this was different.

This time, the stimulus had come from within.

30

Sebastian's name flashed across my phone screen for the second time that morning. The first time, I'd sat and stared at it, willing it to stop. I didn't like that he was inserting himself into my day without warning. He didn't even leave a voice message.

I screened his second call, waited fifteen minutes, then texted him instead.

Hi, Sebastian. Did you try calling me? I was in the shower.

The three-dotted bubble appeared under my message. Thank God—a text would at least give me time to think about my response. But then the dots vanished and his name flashed across the screen for the third time. I had no choice but to answer.

"Hey, Clover!" The sound of his voice triggered the nerves of our last encounter. "I figured it was way easier just to call you rather than texting back and forth. How's your morning been?"

"Pretty good, thanks." I waited for him to reveal the reason he was calling.

"So, the other night was really fun . . ." He said it like he was testing a hypothesis.

"Yes, it was." Parts of it, at least.

An ice-cream truck jingled in the background on Sebastian's end.

"Anyway," he cleared his throat. "I'm actually playing in a cello quartet tomorrow night and I was wondering if maybe you wanted to come . . . with Grandma? She always loved coming to my concerts and I thought it might be nice for her to see, um, one last one."

Well, I couldn't deny Claudia that. My nerves eased slightly—suddenly Sebastian and his phone call felt less intrusive.

"That's such a thoughtful idea," I said. "I'd love to bring her."

S ince Sebastian had to be at the concert early, I stayed past my usual visiting time to accompany Claudia in an Uber to the gallery space in Chelsea.

I watched her sit in front of the gilt mirror above her dressing table. She applied her red lipstick with the ease of someone signing their name, then dabbed perfume on her wrists, behind her ears, and on her décolletage. Somehow I felt like a child watching her mother get ready, brimming with adoration for her beauty and elegance. But instead of it being a painful reminder of something I never got to experience with my own mother—or at least don't remember—it felt as if an empty place in me was being filled.

"Help me with this please, darling," Claudia said, holding a string of pearls toward me.

I took the necklace and pinched open the clasp as she held up the wisps trailing down her neck from her French twist. I patted her shoulder once it was fastened. "There you go."

Claudia put her hand on top of mine and held it, catching my eye in the mirror.

"Thank you, lovely girl. How lucky I am to have you."

Words I'd never thought I'd hear. I felt a small lump swell in my throat.

"I'm very happy to be here," I said, unable to quite express how

deep her words had really hit. "Though we should probably get moving so we're there in time."

I helped Claudia up from the antique Windsor chair, catching
the notes of bergamot and tuberose from her freshly applied perfume. I glanced at the name embossed on the gracefully curved
bottle and its emerald green cap: Creed Fleurissimo. It felt too
glamorous for me.

"Well," she said, smoothing the creases in her skirt. "How do I
look?"

"Perfect," I said, taking in her elegant silhouette. Like Leo, Claudia's style was still firmly planted in the 1960s, but hers leaned less
Mad Men and more Joanne Woodward. Tonight she wore a refined,
high-neck silk blouse along with her tea-length skirt and block-heel
pumps. "I'll go ask Selma to help us get you downstairs before she
leaves. I've got your wheelchair waiting in the foyer."

Claudia waved her hand in a shooing motion. "No wheelchair for
me tonight—this could be my last night on the town, so I'm determined to do it in style!"

Without the wheelchair, our grand entrance into the art gallery
was more of a shuffle, with my arm wrapped tightly around
Claudia's waist helping her keep balance. And yet she carried herself
with such grace and confidence, which didn't go unnoticed by the
people gathered at the entrance, who beamed at her with approval.

What was it like to turn heads like that, to assert your presence
with such charisma, so unafraid to be seen and admired?

Inside, folding chairs were lined up in rows facing the back of
the gallery with an aisle carved through the middle. As Sebastian
strode down it toward us, a swarm of moths began flitting about in
my stomach. I'd been so captivated with Claudia that I hadn't had
time to worry about how I'd react to seeing him.

"Hello, Grandma!" He kissed her twice, then turned to me.

Mortified that he would try to kiss me in front of Claudia, I abruptly stuck out my hand for him to shake it.

"Hi, Sebastian," I said.

It took a beat for him to process, but he recovered quickly, switching the phone he was holding to his other hand so he could shake mine.

"I'm so glad you're both here," he said, though his eyes stayed mostly trained on me. "I saved you some seats in the front row."

He moved to the opposite side of Claudia, supporting her other elbow, and together we walked her slowly to her seat. Once we'd made sure she was comfortable, Sebastian hovered awkwardly, hands behind his back as if wanting to say something. I busied myself with the photocopied program that had been placed on our seats.

"'Bach's Cello Suites,'" I read aloud.

Sebastian smiled bashfully. "Yeah, I know, it's kind of the most clichéd cello composition ever—I wanted to do Fauré's 'Pavane.'" He gestured to the other attendees taking their seats around us. "But you've got to give the people what they want—especially when you're trying to get them to donate to charity."

I hadn't realized this was a fundraiser—that was nice of him to be part of it. His awkwardness now felt more endearing.

"Bach was my grandpa's favorite," I said, trying to put him at ease since I was probably one of the reasons he seemed so nervous. "He used to take me to concerts at the New York Philharmonic when I was a kid."

Grandpa and I would sit in the balcony whispering as he taught me the name of all the orchestra sections and their different instruments. My favorite conductor was the one who used to get so caught up in the music that it looked like he was dancing. And every so often, he'd pause to hitch up his pants.

Sebastian's face lit up. "Grandma used to take me there too! I wonder if we were ever at the same concert?"

I imagined us as two lanky kids, passing each other in the lobby of Lincoln Center.

Claudia gazed up at her grandson. "I always tried to get him to appreciate jazz, but he was insistent that classical music was his thing—just like his grandfather."

"Yeah," Sebastian grinned. "Grandad really hated jazz—refused to listen to it." Another fascinating insight into the relationship between Claudia and her husband.

A stocky man tapped Sebastian on the shoulder and gestured to the makeshift stage, where four cellos perched in front of chairs.

"Oh, right," Sebastian said. "We'd better start getting ready." He turned back to Claudia and me. "Enjoy the show!"

We watched him disappear into a side room.

As the lights dimmed and the audience hushed, I closed my eyes and tuned into the ripples of anticipation that always came at the beginning of a live performance. That shared intimacy among strangers where, for just a moment, everyone laid aside the baggage of life to be completely present as one—a communal hopefulness. I breathed in the soothing woody scent of the instruments and the pique of a freshly rosined bow.

The side door opened and Sebastian and his fellow musicians— each dressed in black, all similarly bookish—filed out and took their seats, hanging their heads shyly at the warm applause. The woman seated on Sebastian's left counted herself in and commenced the prelude from Bach's "Cello Suite No. 1," her fingers moving gracefully across the neck of the majestic instrument as if caressing the sound out of it. When the familiar refrain reverberated throughout the gallery space, I felt the audience breathe a collective sigh as they settled into the music's embrace.

The remaining trio of musicians joined in and I took the opportunity to study Sebastian in motion. The way he bent his neck slightly around the cello like he was telling it a secret. How his face crumpled with concentration. The way his foot kept time, alternating between a toe tap and a heel tap as the rest of his body swayed. It was clear that I was watching someone doing something they truly loved.

To observe someone swept away by the thing they're most passionate about, most skilled at—what some call "flow"—is one of life's great privileges. There's an energy that emanates, a magic. As if they're opening their hearts up completely and letting themselves communicate with the world in their purest form—unencumbered by insecurities, stresses, and bitterness. Like time is suspended and they're simply allowing themselves to be.

Watching Sebastian with his cello made me see him differently than before. And for a few moments, instead of constantly debating what I might feel for him, I let myself follow his cue. To let the music sweep me away and simply be.

Once the performance had ended, Claudia and I sat on a bench outside the gallery, waiting for Sebastian.

"What a lovely concert—thank you, sweet Clover, for being my date," Claudia said, linking her arm through mine. "I do hope my grandson is paying you for this, spending time with us after hours."

My shoulders tensed with guilt as I thought about my other evening with Sebastian for which I definitely did not charge overtime.

"Oh, no," I said, scrambling for what to say next. "We're here for a good cause, after all. I couldn't take any payment for that."

"You're very kindhearted, my darling," she said, and I squirmed at the undeserved compliment. "But don't let us keep you—I'm sure you're ready to be done with your workday. I can wait here for Sebastian."

I was tempted to take the opportunity to leave, but I was curious about seeing Sebastian again.

"I'll at least wait until Sebastian comes out here," I said. "I wouldn't leave you all alone."

Claudia looked skeptically around at the polished gallery district streetscape. "I've been in much more precarious situations, believe me."

The gallery door opened and a cello case poked out, followed by Sebastian.

"Ah, there you both are!" He leaned his instrument against the gallery's glass front. "I was looking for you inside."

"I was just telling Clover she could take her leave from us," Claudia said. "We don't want to monopolize her time any longer since she's already working late. And it's cold out here."

I couldn't work out what his expression was trying to communicate to me as he looked between me and Claudia.

"Oh, right, of course." He pulled out his phone. "I'll call us a car."

"I'm just going to take the subway from here," I said quickly, to avoid being sandwiched in the back of a car with Sebastian and Claudia trying to pretend everything was normal. "It's only a couple of stops."

Sebastian held up his phone. "But the car's only a minute away—we could drop you on our way."

"No, no," I insisted. "It's in the opposite direction. The subway is definitely no problem."

Claudia put her hand on Sebastian's arm. "Allow the woman her independence, muffin." She winked at me. "Clover's probably had enough of us."

I watched Sebastian's cheeks flash red. "Right, sorry."

"I appreciate the offer," I said. "Thank you both for inviting me—it really was a beautiful performance." I looked shyly at Sebastian. "You're a very talented musician."

For the first time ever, he seemed to be at a loss for words.

Conscious of Claudia watching our exchange, I panicked. "Anyway, I'd better get home to my dog," I said, buttoning up my coat. "Have a good night, both of you!"

Then, in what now seemed like a habit, I found myself fleeing down the street from Sebastian. Only this time, I wasn't sure what it was I was running away from.

31

When I arrived at Claudia's house the following Wednesday, Selma met me at the door.

"Claudia's in a lot of pain today." Selma spoke from the back of her throat to lower her voice. "Of course, she refused to stay in bed, so we've set her up in the library." She gestured past the foyer. "Up two flights of stairs and on your left."

The library, easily two-thirds the size of my entire apartment, could have been plucked from my daydreams. Grand walnut shelves extended to the ceiling, lined reverently with books. A tasteful assembly of plush seating beckoned hours of reading. Diffused sunlight streamed through arched windows, setting the space mildly aglow. And propped up in the corner was Sebastian's cello.

I was still trying to reconcile my shift in feelings at the concert. Was appreciating his talent the same as being attracted to him? It was hard to know if the resistance I still felt had more to do with working with Claudia than about Sebastian, specifically. I wished I had some experience to compare it to. But since I'd never had a male friend my age, let alone a boyfriend, I couldn't tell the difference between platonic admiration and the lukewarm beginnings of romantic attraction.

Claudia was lying on a mahogany chaise longue, her diminishing frame propped up almost doll-like by an arsenal of ornate pillows.

A jacquard duvet covered her up to her armpits. Though her eyes were closed, her hand tapped in time to the Duke Ellington riff wafting from a small speaker on the nearby side table. The squeak of old floorboards under my feet alerted her to my arrival and she greeted me with a sleepy smile.

"I met Duke Ellington at a party once," Claudia said, her voice soft, dreamlike.

"I bet there's an interesting story there." I sat in a tufted wing-back armchair within her sight line.

"Actually, I mostly remember that evening because of the argument I had with my husband," Claudia said, trying to sit up. I stood to help, supporting her weight as I adjusted the pillows behind her. "He wasn't fond of me chatting with other men, no matter how interesting they might be. It was a sticking point in our relationship—one of many—because I enjoyed conversing with strangers. It's what had made me a good photojournalist."

"It must've been hard, leaving that career behind," I said. "Did you know many other female photographers at the time?"

"There was only a handful in my day, as you can imagine. And really, it was women like Margaret Bourke-White, Dorothea Lange, and Martha Gellhorn who paved the way for the rest of us."

"I just read Martha's book, *Travels with Myself and Another*. What a fascinating woman." It was one of several memoirs by intrepid, independent women that Bessie had recommended to me. "Did you ever meet her?"

"We crossed paths a few times in the fifties—she was prickly. But she was also the only one of Hemingway's wives sensible enough to divorce him."

"I can only imagine how tough it must have been to be a female war journalist back then," I said. "You probably had no choice but to be prickly as a way of self-preservation."

"You're sharp, Clover," Claudia said. "I like that about you."

"Did you ever consider going back to it? After your son was older?"

"Hardly," she responded wearily. "In those days, most women in our social circles didn't even work, let alone go gallivanting across the world without their families, taking photos of strangers. My husband would have never allowed it. It's no wonder Gellhorn and Bourke-White were both divorced twice over. There's an intimacy to being a journalist and photographer that men at the time just didn't understand."

"Still, you must have some pretty compelling stories from your travels before you married." I looked around at the bookshelves flanking the chaise longue. "I'd love to see more of your photos sometime." I hoped it might help her reflect on her life.

Claudia nodded toward the opposite side of the room to a large teak desk. "You'll find a key under the paperweight. Most of my photos are locked away in the basement—I suppose now is as good a time as any to start sorting through them, since the clock's ticking and all that. Lord knows that brood of mine will likely just throw them away as soon as I'm gone."

"I'm not so sure that Sebastian would allow that." I knew he was too sentimental to be that ruthless.

"Ah, yes, he's certainly a dedicated grandson, even if he's a bit of a mess in other areas of his life," Claudia said. "I've been hoping he might find someone to settle down with before I go. It would be nice to know he's happy. But while his lady friends are always very lovely, they never seem to be the right fit for him. I sometimes suspect his relationships have less to do with compatibility and more the fact that he doesn't like to be alone."

I thought of the woman we'd run into at the cocktail bar—I had no idea if she was a good fit for Sebastian. I realized I hadn't even asked myself if he was compatible with me. And what did compatibility really mean? It felt unfair to hold someone's pet allergies against them, but that would definitely make a relationship with him harder.

I walked quickly over to the desk and found the key under a small brass whale. "What should I be looking for in the basement?"

"You may have to dig a little, but you'll see a stack of old bankers boxes—if they haven't all disintegrated by now. It's been years since anyone has gone through them."

"Got it!" I scooted out the door before Claudia could delve further into Sebastian's personal life.

The contents of the basement defied gravity. Furniture, artwork, old leather suitcases, and snow equipment all balanced precariously as if waiting for the faintest of nudges to send the pile tumbling. So this was how people kept their homes so elegantly minimal—by cramming all their real belongings out of sight.

The thick coat of dust on every surface meant that allergy-prone Sebastian likely rarely ventured down here. It even managed to irritate my usually robust senses and I sneezed four times in a row. As I navigated the crypt of forgotten objects, I made a mental note to do an inventory of what was down here at a later date. Claudia might want certain things to go certain places rather than just be sold off at an estate sale or tossed out on the curb. It wasn't officially part of my job, but I'd often watched as lifetimes of memories were unceremoniously discarded by bereaved family members eager to sell a home of the recently departed. The promise of a chunk of money often robbed people of their scruples.

The boxes in question were wedged under an old wooden toboggan. The deep indentation from the toboggan's runner suggested that they hadn't been touched for several decades. I gingerly pried the boxes free and returned triumphantly to the library, stray cobwebs laced into my hair.

"You look like you've been on an adventure," Claudia remarked. "I hope you'll find it worth the trouble."

"I'm sure I will," I said, trying to remove the cobwebs, my eyes gritty from the dust. I rested the first box on the glass coffee table. "Should we dive in?"

Claudia's face flinched with the vulnerability of an artist unveiling a painting for the first time. "I suppose so."

The box probably held close to three hundred photographs, all printed on cardboard stock. Most were matte, all were black-and-white, many were faded to nothing more than ghostly outlines of figures and structures. I selected a stack of photos tied with twine and began flipping through them.

First was an image of a woman in an elaborately patterned dress sitting by the roadside, two voluminous bunches of bananas positioned in front of her.

I read the inscription on the back. "*Tunisia, 1956.* Wow, you were in Tunisia?"

"My first and only trip to North Africa," Claudia beamed. "I'd been stationed in Marseille and I begged my editor to let me go there to cover the tail end of the Tunisian independence movement. When he said no, I traveled there on my own—by flirting my way onto a boat—and sent a telegram from Tunis asking his permission again. Then he had no choice."

"I don't think I'd be that brave." But it did make me miss the feeling of arriving in a foreign country with nothing but the unknown awaiting me. It'd been so long since I'd done that.

"Well, deep down, I knew it was my last hurrah, so to speak." The sparkle in Claudia's eyes weakened. "At the end of that summer, I was due to come home and get married, and I knew my short photography career would be coming to an end. So I figured, what the hell?"

"How old were you?"

"I turned twenty-five that August, which, in those days, was old to be getting married. My husband proposed when I was twenty-three, but I told him I wanted two years to pursue my photography. And if he let me have that, I'd promise to be the faithful society wife he wanted from then onward."

"And you kept your word."

Claudia nodded. "I knew I wanted a child and I wanted them to grow up in a stable environment. So my only choice was to get married. Not like you women these days, freezing your eggs and going it alone in your thirties and forties if you want to. If that had been an option back then, I'd have strongly considered it."

I'd never thought about freezing my eggs. I should probably at least google it since I was nearing forty.

"I needed those two years for my sanity," Claudia continued. "I told myself that I'd pack as many experiences and memories into those years as possible so that they could last me the rest of my life." A wry look. "Of course, I wasn't expecting to live this long."

As we flipped through the piles of photos, Claudia's shrewd photographic vision shone through. A rawness radiated from each of her human subjects, as if they were being seen for the first time. Endearing shyness manifested in slightly bowed heads but hopeful expressions. Others were more life-weary, their eyes betraying deep sadness. Emotion resonated from every image—delight, yearning, pain, bitterness—and I felt each one keenly.

The Tunisian vignettes moved on to more staid portraits of the French Riviera. Children splashing in the shallows of a waveless Mediterranean. An old man napping under an olive tree. A dog stealing a baguette. Basically the analog version of a Francophile's Pinterest board.

"The subject matter was less compelling in the South of France," Claudia said, as if reading my thoughts.

I paused on a photo of a young curly-haired man in a Breton striped shirt standing stoically on the bow of a boat. "I don't know," I said, handing the photo to Claudia. "This swarthy gentleman looks pretty compelling."

The pithy response I anticipated never came. Instead, Claudia had her hand to her chest as she stared at the photo.

"Are you okay, Claudia?" I stood, ready to act. "Should I call Selma? Do you need a doctor?"

Claudia reached for my forearm. "No, darling, I'm perfectly fine." Her breathing steadied. "It's just, well, I haven't seen a picture of him in more than sixty years."

"Who is he?"

Claudia's voice was an uncharacteristic whisper. "His name was Hugo Beaufort."

32

"So, I was telling someone at work yesterday about how cool your job is," Sylvie said while we waited in line at a minimalist SoHo lunch spot known for its deconstructed meals and communal seating. "And I realized I still have all these questions."

"Like what?" I said, flattered that Sylvie was so interested.

"Like, is it true that people talk about how they're going on a trip right before they die?"

"Sometimes."

"So do you try to talk them out of it?"

"No, usually I offer to help them pack."

Sylvie looked skeptical. "Really?"

"Of course—and besides, they kind of are going on a trip. Who knows where, but it's better to let them be excited for the journey and feel like they're prepared for it."

"I guess that makes sense." Sylvie waited for the obnoxious grinding of a passing truck to stop. "And is it true that people can still hear everything that's being said, even when they're unconscious?"

"I can't say for sure, but I've had clients who have been in comas and heard their family members reveal secrets about them."

"Oh, my God, you have to tell me about that."

I realized that I liked having a captive audience—maybe Leo and I weren't so different after all.

"Well, there was one guy who was in a coma and his wife was telling her sister about how she'd never told him that their daughter was another man's child. She thought her husband wasn't going to wake up, but when he did, he remembered every detail of the conversation and got his lawyer to change his will to cut the woman and her daughter out of it. He died the next day, completely bitter."

Sylvie winced. "That sucks for everyone involved. I bet it was awkward for you being in that room."

"Yeah, it was pretty horrible." I'd gotten a little more caught up in that situation than I should have, but the man did have the right to change his will. And I'd mistakenly thought helping make it happen would bring him some peace. I still regretted not encouraging him to discuss it with his family first—instead of softening his bitterness before he died, I worried I'd helped him cement it.

"I read about a woman once who asked for a divorce on her deathbed because she didn't want to meet her death while unhappily married."

I nodded. "That happens more often than you'd think," I said. "Actually, Claudia told me something interesting yesterday. She said she regrets not marrying a guy she met while she was living in France in her twenties."

"That's so romantic," Sylvie said. "But also super sad that she was miserable with the guy she did marry."

"I don't think she was miserable, exactly. Women had less freedom of choice in those days, so she went with the more sensible option."

Sylvie linked her arm through mine as we moved forward in the line. "Tell me everything."

I felt a twinge of guilt at revealing Claudia's closely held secret, but I couldn't resist the urge to impress Sylvie, to live up to her perceptions of me. And it's not like she'd ever meet Claudia.

"Okay," I said, high on the dopamine rush of having Sylvie's attention. "I'll tell you the story exactly as she told it to me."

Even though it had been more than sixty years since she'd met Hugo Beaufort, Claudia had described the day to me with such vivid nuance that it could've been last week. It was clearly a memory that had been replayed thousands of times over the years.

It began with a three-legged dog tied up outside a bookstore in Marseille, France, in 1956.

The absence of any kind of breeze had made the heat of the already-sweltering July day nearly unbearable. Even the vainest of souls had relinquished any concern about their appearance. Everyone wore the same gleaming layer of sweat, so there was no choice but to embrace it.

Claudia regretted her decision to wear trousers that day. Since arriving in Europe to work as a photojournalist, she'd taken to wearing them out of practicality. This was no time to fuss with dresses; a white button-up shirt and linen slacks were far more dependable and easier to pack. Besides, the disapproving comments from male colleagues about the inappropriateness of her attire meant she also wore them out of rebellion. With every brow that creased with censure, she'd slide her hands into her pockets and saunter by with happy defiance.

On this particular day, however, Claudia allowed herself a moment of self-pity as she daydreamed about the ventilation a pretty sundress would've offered in such stifling conditions. (It seemed a further injustice that she was so close to the Mediterranean without even a hint of a sea breeze.)

She also briefly regretted her refusal to let her unseemly landlord give her a ride to the train station. Since she'd managed to rebuff his advances for her entire stay in Marseille, depriving him the satisfaction of carrying her suitcase was a victory she wasn't willing to relinquish. As the leather handle of the battered suitcase slithered in her sweaty grip, she tightened her hand determinedly and readjusted the bulging satchel on her shoulder. Independence was worth a little discomfort, she reminded herself. Besides, she had one last stop to make before she boarded the train to Paris. One final purchase to keep her company on the long journey home to New York City.

Le Bateau Bleu bookstore sat about five minutes' walk from Marseille's Vieux Porte, and ten from the diminutive attic apartment that Claudia had rented for next to nothing. The store had been her retreat, her oasis, her buffer against the waves of homesickness and loneliness. Books had always been her solace during a turbulent upbringing with parents who loathed each other. Amid the constant verbal warfare that carried through the walls of their townhouse, Claudia would tuck herself in her closet with a pillow and a flashlight, and lose herself in a story. Later, as an adult, whenever she needed a moment of calm, she'd escaped to the nearest bookstore (she knew most of them in Manhattan). And though her fiancé didn't really care for reading, he always knew where to find her after they'd argued.

Claudia's heart swelled as she rounded the corner of the narrow rue where Le Bateau Bleu perched exactly halfway up the hill. Its awning was painted an incongruous cherry red, which angered local purists because it didn't match the dreamy pastel Mediterranean palette of the rest of the city. But that rebellious spirit only broadened Claudia's affection for the bookstore.

A sliver of shade—the warped silhouette of a lamppost—slashed the sunbaked pavement outside the store. A shaggy Jack Russell had elongated its body to fit within the slim confines of the shadow—belly pressed into the cool concrete, the pink of its hind paw pads pointing toward the sky. The dog opened a weary eye as Claudia's own shadow crossed its path. Setting down her suitcase, she wiped her damp palms on the linen of her trousers (at least they were good for something) and knelt beside the scruffy pup. Tenderly respecting its space, she offered her hand for an inspective sniff. The dog forwent all formalities, nudging its forehead into her palm appreciatively. As it rose to a seated position, Claudia saw that the dog's right shoulder simply rounded into its chest, like there'd never been a leg there at all.

She took out a flask from the tightly packed possessions in her satchel and poured some tepid water into her cupped hand. The dog lapped gratefully, stopping to lick her wrist as if to say an extra word of thanks. When she took a swig from the metal bottle, only drops remained. She had no regrets about sharing the last of it.

The door of the bookstore jangled merrily as it opened and Claudia stood to avoid blocking it. From the way the dog perked up, she figured that the young man standing in the doorway was its owner. His tangle of curls also matched the scruffiness of the Jack Russell's coat.

"Matelot!" The man addressed his faithful friend enthusiastically, bending down to cradle its face between his tanned, calloused hands. Then, as if remembering his manners, he straightened up abruptly, a broad smile giving way to a slight gap between his top two front teeth.

"Good afternoon, mademoiselle." His English was heavily accented, but spoken with ease.

Embarrassed that her foreignness was so obvious, Claudia wished she'd worked harder on her French.

"Good afternoon," she said, noting the small crescent of a scar disrupting the stubble on his chin. "I was just saying hello to your friend here. Matelot, did you say his name was?"

"Yes, Matelot! It means sailor. Like me!" The scar compacted with his grin. "He's my—how do you say—deckhand?"

The thought of this man sailing the seas with his scruffy three-legged deckhand was enchanting. Claudia nodded at the stack of books under his arm. "I imagine you have plenty of time to read on the boat then?"

"Yes, I plan to sail to Corsica tomorrow." The man clutched the books appreciatively to his ribs. "And these will keep me company."

"I've heard Corsica is a lovely little island," Claudia said. "Regrettably, I've never been."

"Well, it's not too late, you know. I see you're already packed for the trip."

On other men, his forwardness would have been sleazy. But on this lanky, young Frenchman, it was beguiling. "Sadly, I'm on my way to the train station," Claudia said, her disappointment unfeigned.

"Actually," he responded, accentuating each syllable, "you are on your way to the bookstore."

"Guilty."

"Perhaps after the bookstore and before the train station, you will have a drink with us?" Both man and dog looked at her hopefully.

"Well, I don't know you."

"Then let us fix that." The man wiped his free hand on his shirt and offered it to her. "I'm Hugo."

She wiped her own hand before taking his. "And I'm Claudia."

"It is a pleasure to meet you, Claudia." The scar disappeared into a dimple. "And may I say, I like your trousers."

B y the time I'd finished telling Sylvie the story of Claudia and Hugo, we'd reached the front of the café line. We followed the server to one end of a long, oak communal table and took our seats on the aluminum stools.

"'I like your trousers,'" Sylvie repeated in an affected French accent. "What a line! Hugo does sound smooth—no wonder she was tempted away from her controlling fiancé." She unfolded her napkin and draped it across her lap. "Imagine if he's still alive somewhere on a boat in the Mediterranean, pining for her too."

The bittersweet prospect pulled at my heart. What was it like to feel a love so strong that it still lingered with you more than sixty years later?

33

Impending death is a fickle thing. Someone with a terminal diagnosis might be vibrant and robust one day, only to spiral the next, as if mortality had suddenly set its foot on the gas. In the three days since I'd last seen her, Claudia clearly had been at the mercy of that acceleration. Though she was sitting in her usual wicker garden chair, it now looked oversized in comparison. Her body had shed its surplus weight, making her diminutive form harshly angular and her skin pallid, almost translucent. A distinct melancholy dulled the usual cheeky glimmer in her eyes.

No matter how many times I witnessed this rapid decline, it was still jarring to watch someone become a shell of themselves. And it hurt a little more this time, seeing Claudia robbed of her vibrancy. I'd grown attached to her in a way that was unusual for me. I wasn't sure if it was my involvement with Sebastian, her thwarted romance with Hugo, or something else. But even without medical expertise, I'd intuitively learned to estimate how long someone had left. She likely wouldn't see the end of the month.

"I'm a little caught up in the blues today," Claudia said as I joined her at the garden table.

"I'm sorry to hear that." I noticed her shiver against a nonexistent breeze, struggling to pull the blanket higher up her torso. I tucked the thick mohair closer to her chest. "What's on your mind?"

"You mean aside from the fact that my days are numbered?" The rest of her body might be diminishing, but Claudia's dry humor was not. She fiddled with the edge of the blanket, her knuckles like knotted rope beneath her skin. "You know, when I found out, I wasn't exactly surprised—I am ninety-one, after all, and I've known for a long time that my body wasn't working the way it used to." A deep breath rattled in her chest. "It's just that, well, I suppose I feel a little guilty."

"Guilty?"

"I've gotten to live many more years than a lot of my contemporaries, my husband included, and so really I should be grateful for what I've had and should walk toward the end with grace."

"Maybe," I said, resisting the urge to placate. "But gratitude doesn't necessarily free us from sadness—or our fears."

Claudia sighed gloomily. "It's the unknown of it all that's getting to me. The doctor said I had about two months, but it could be more or less than that." I was glad she didn't look at me for confirmation. "Sometimes I feel like I'm just sitting around waiting to die, and that everyone else around me—you included—is waiting for it too. Some mornings I wake up almost disappointed that I'm still here."

"I can see how you'd feel that way," I said, treading a conversational path I knew well. "If you did walk toward death with grace, what would that look like?"

"I don't know, darling," Claudia said with a hint of exasperation. "I suppose dying gracefully would mean squeezing the best out of my last days and not focusing on every little regret—all while wearing a fabulous shawl, of course."

I allowed for a few beats. "What are some of those regrets?"

Claudia eyed me cautiously. "You're not going to force me to focus on the positive things?"

"Believe it or not, you're allowed to think about both the good and the bad right now."

Relief softened her jaw. "It's funny, I find myself going in circles thinking about mundane, inconsequential things," she said, watching the neighbor's cat navigating the fence like a tightrope. "I wish I'd stuck with ballet lessons when I was a child. Or that I learned to speak Arabic better. Or that I hadn't wasted so much time pretending I liked Shakespeare because it made me look intelligent."

"Everyone pretends to like Shakespeare."

The joke earned a small smile.

"Selfish as it sounds," Claudia said, "I mostly regret putting the needs of others ahead of my own. But as a woman, that's what I was taught to do. Your husband, your children, your parents—their happiness all mattered more. You were always someone's wife, or mother, or daughter before you were yourself. It's like I didn't live my life for myself, as myself. Like I wasted what I was given."

"You did what was expected of you for the people you loved. I wouldn't call that a waste." I hadn't had the chance to love many people, but I imagined it would be a privilege to be in service of their happiness.

"Once you've lived a long life, I think you might see things differently."

A murmuration of starlings spread gracefully across the sky and we both leaned back to watch their flight.

"I've never told anyone this," Claudia said, tentative, as if not quite ready to commit to her next sentence. "But when my son was a toddler, every night after I'd fed him, bathed him, and read him several bedtime stories—it was always me, never his father—I'd sit and watch him sleep. And every night, I tried to push away the bitterness that was welling inside me, so that I wouldn't hold him responsible for the life I knew I wouldn't get to live. Watching that little chest rise and fall, the curls so cherublike around his face, I'd whisper to him over and over, 'I will not resent you. I will not resent you.'" Remorse flickered in her face. "But no matter how many times I said it, I never stopped feeling it. I resented him, I resented my husband, and, most of all, I resented this house for all it took from me. It felt like a prison."

I clasped her hand in mine and offered a reassuring smile. People weren't usually looking for a commentary to these sorts of revelations. They just needed someone to sit and listen to them without judgment. It's tempting to try to fix it, to cheer them up. But the truth is, you'll never find the right thing to say—because the right thing doesn't exist. The fact that you're there, and present, says so much more.

Still, I couldn't help also feeling a little deflated by what Claudia had told me. I wasn't naive enough to think all marriages were happy, but lately it seemed like real life was trying very hard to disprove all my romantic ideals.

"My life could have been very different," Claudia continued. "Perhaps instead of sitting here with you, I'd be on a boat somewhere in the Mediterranean with Hugo. If he's even still alive."

I was glad she brought up Hugo again—I was so curious to hear more about him. "What exactly happened after you met at the bookstore?"

It was as if someone injected Claudia with a shot of adrenaline. She straightened in her chair and her face reanimated. "He invited me for lunch at a nearby café, and I drank too much pastis and ended up missing my train to Paris. I think I wanted to miss it, to be honest—to give myself one last adventure before I came home to be married. And I just felt this energy with him I'd never felt before. So when he suggested I come sailing with him to Corsica, I couldn't resist. I was supposed to stay with a family friend in Paris for ten days before catching the ship to New York, and I'd planned to get a haircut and buy some new clothes. Instead, I spent the time on a sailboat with Hugo." The cheeky glimmer returned. "I'll let you fill in the rest with your imagination."

"What was it that drew you to him so immediately?"

"I don't know . . . I haven't thought about him in so long." Claudia watched the starlings again, contemplating. "I liked that everything about him was simple—he enjoyed life, even though his had been tough. The scar on his chin was from when his father hit him with a bottle in a drunken rage. And I liked that he was smart, not from any formal education, but from being out in the world. He learned English from working on fishing boats from when he was thirteen, and taught himself everything else by reading the books the other sailors left behind." A long sigh. "But mostly, it was the way I felt around him—independent, sexy, intellectually stimulated, encouraged. He made me feel free, like myself, in a way my husband never did."

"He sounds very charming." I felt a flare of hope—perhaps I hadn't falsely idealized the potential of romantic chemistry after all.

"That he was," Claudia chuckled, then grew serious. "But then again, perhaps things wouldn't have been as rosy with him either. He told me I shouldn't give up my photography career, but his attitude might have changed if we'd had kids. It's easy to glamorize the path you didn't take. After all, we only spent ten days together." A faint flush of pink spilled onto her cheekbones. "But I did love kissing that scar on his chin."

Claudia closed her eyes and smiled, as if drifting off into a pleasant dream.

As I sat holding her hand while she dozed, I wondered if there might be a way to relieve her of at least one regret before she died.

34

The vigorous knocking on my front door implied urgency. I reluctantly untangled my limbs from the blanket on the sofa and nudged George off my shins.

A brief pause and then more knocking, each time a staccato series of five. I wished I had a peephole so that I could at least prepare myself for the drama that seemed to await me behind the door.

Sylvie stood in front of me, a huge grin on her face and a laptop under her arm. Her messy bun, pajama bottoms, and polka-dot socks felt intimate and comforting. Tacit confirmation we'd reached a level of friendship where we didn't have to worry about appearances.

"I found Hugo!" Sylvie announced. "Can I come in?"

I hesitated. It wasn't that I didn't want Sylvie to come into my apartment. More that, except for Leo and our building's super, no one had really ever stepped inside. I was also painfully aware of the aesthetic differences between Sylvie's minimalist apartment and mine. And then there was that conspicuous odor of cat litter.

But her revelation was too enticing—especially since I'd asked her to look into it.

"Of course."

Sylvie bustled in, then stopped abruptly. "Whoa. Your apartment kind of looks like a museum." She stared curiously at the jars, rocks, and fossils lining the shelves. "I never knew you were into all this stuff. But I guess it makes sense for someone whose job revolves around death."

I bristled at the stereotype. "Actually, most of it belonged to my grandpa. I've just never really gotten around to sorting through it." I hovered stiffly. "Would you like a cup of tea or something to eat?" Was anything in my pantry even appropriate? Sylvie's tastes were likely more sophisticated than Triscuits and cheddar cheese.

"Green tea would be great if you have it! But wait, first let me tell you what I found out about Hugo." She patted the sofa between her and a snoozing George. I sat down beside her.

With the wicked smile of someone about to reveal some sordid gossip, Sylvie opened her laptop partway. "So, this girl I dated for a summer in college—I also dated her brother, but that's another story—lives in France now and she works as an art historian at a museum in Marseille. That's where you said Claudia met Hugo, right?"

"Right." It was hard to keep up with Sylvie's extensive dating history.

She allowed for a dramatic pause. George woke up, startled by his own snore.

"Well, she has access to all kinds of civic and historical records and so I sent her his name and approximate age. I figured he was around Claudia's age, which would have put him in his mid-twenties in 1956."

"That's probably about right." I didn't want to get too excited. "I think Claudia said she was twenty-four when she met him."

"So anyway, she had to do some digging, but eventually she found this . . ." Sylvie opened up her laptop fully and swiveled it on her knees to face me. The screen showed a black-and-white photo of a youngish man with dark curls standing on the bow of a boat wearing a fisherman sweater. A scar interrupted the rugged stubble on the left side of his chin. And at his feet sat a shaggy Jack Russell missing its right front leg.

I peered closer. "That could be Hugo."

"It's totally Hugo!" Sylvie said, rolling her eyes. "There's no way there would be two guys in Marseille with a chin scar and a three-legged dog. And I've got to say, the man looks good in a sweater."

"What did you find out about him? Is he still alive?"

"So, this is where it gets even wilder. It turns out that they don't have many records on this guy, Hugo Beaufort. Because, wait for it—" Another dramatic pause. "He immigrated to the United States in 1957."

"What? He's been living here all this time?"

"Yep. And so I did a little bit of further research of my own."

"And?" I felt uneasy—this was definitely invading Claudia's privacy—but I needed to know more.

"Turns out there's a Hugo Beaufort, born in France in 1931, listed as a resident of Lincolnville, Maine." Sylvie waited for me to catch on. "Meaning we could potentially track him down for Claudia before she dies."

"Oh, wow."

"There's just one catch." Her face turned apologetic. "No matter how hard I searched, I couldn't find a phone number listed for his name. I did find an address, but it was from at least ten years ago, so I have no way of knowing if he's still there."

My conscience battled itself. "Is it even worth mentioning it to Claudia then? Discovering that he was so close by all this time might make her feel even worse."

"True." Sylvie snapped her laptop shut. "But it could also make her feel better. It can't be a coincidence that he moved here a year after they met. Or more to the point, a year after she almost abandoned her fiancé for him."

"I guess you're right." I chewed on my bottom lip. "But her health is getting worse every day—she's probably got less than two weeks left. I don't know if we should even put her through that."

"Or, on the other hand," Sylvie pressed, "are you depriving her of some kind of peace and resolution by not telling her? I would one hundred percent want to know. Wouldn't you, if it were the love of your life?"

"I couldn't say," I said quietly. "I've never been in love." The words sounded kind of pathetic coming out of my mouth.

"Yeah, but you've lived it a million times vicariously through all those rom-coms you devour."

It surprised me how Sylvie seemed to get me in ways that I didn't even get myself. "I need to think about it."

I had to process the logistics, and the ethics, of what Sylvie was saying. But a long-lost lover living in coastal Maine did sound like the ultimate romance plot—even if it was a little clichéd.

"Well, don't overthink it—Claudia deserves closure. I mean, isn't that the whole point of your job?"

I glanced at my notebooks. "It's one aspect of it."

Sylvie stood up and began wandering around the room in awe. "What did you say your grandpa did again?"

"He was a biology professor at Columbia."

"Huh." She picked up a jar and peered at the exoskeleton inside, rotating the vessel above her head like she was slowly screwing in a lightbulb. "It's cool that you keep all his stuff around in his memory, but have you ever thought of, you know, making the place more your own? I'll be honest: it's a little bit creepy for a thirty-six-year-old woman."

Her words stung. "It is my own. I've lived here on and off since I was six. I grew up surrounded by all these things."

"I get that, I do, but it's all still your grandfather's vibe, right?" Sylvie pulled a book off the shelf and read its spine. "Like, have you ever actually read *The Insect Societies* by Edward O. Wilson?"

"No," I said, my cheeks lighting like dormant coals responding to breath. "But I might one day."

Sylvie rolled her eyes again. "Right, I'm sure there's a lot of romance in that one." Returning the book to its place, she ran her finger along the row of spines and stopped on my three notebooks.

"'Regrets' . . . 'Advice' . . . 'Confessions' . . . Hey, what are these?" Sylvie grabbed the first one.

I lunged across the room. "Please don't touch those."

Watching Sylvie audit my space so clinically made me feel raw and exposed. Every single object in this apartment was a thread binding me to Grandpa. And with each thing Sylvie touched, I felt a tug at my heart, like the thread's strength was being tested.

Sylvie shoved the notebook back in the wrong place and stepped away obediently. "Sorry, are they like your personal diaries or something?" She held up her hands in surrender. "I completely respect your privacy if that's the case. I'm all for boundaries."

"They're not my diaries, exactly." I couldn't stop myself from rearranging the books to their proper order. "They're more, well, I kind of keep a record of the last things people say before they die—you know, like their words of wisdom and stuff. And I guess it would feel like an invasion of their privacy if I let somebody else read them."

Sylvie nodded, but looked at me quizzically. "But all of those people are dead, right? So how would they even know?"

"I would know." I glanced over at Grandpa's armchair, my stubbornness solidifying. "Just because no one's there to witness it, doesn't make it okay." Most of the words in those notebooks had been spoken when people were at their most vulnerable. I could never betray their trust.

We eyed each other cautiously for a few seconds before Sylvie broke into a grin.

"Wow, C, I love how your moral compass rarely wavers, even when I try to corrupt it. A very admirable personality trait. I wish I could say I was as decent as you all the time. But, somehow, bending the rules is just more . . . fun."

She winked as she walked toward the windows and splayed the Venetian blinds with two fingers, forming a diamond-shaped portal into the night outside.

"Hey, did you know you can see right into the building across the street?"

I kept my voice even. "Huh, I never really noticed that."

As decent as I liked to think I was, I still felt like I was lying with abandon these days.

"I can totally see *Game of Thrones* on someone's TV. Should I warn them not to waste their lives getting hooked on something with such an infuriatingly unsatisfying conclusion? They probably only watch it for the horny sex scenes anyway."

"Ha, yeah, maybe."

Sylvie grabbed the binoculars from between the jars of animal fetuses. "Should we take a closer look?"

My feet felt stitched to the rug. Was she being serious? Did she somehow know?

Swinging the binoculars by their straps, Sylvie laughed. "God, you should see your face!" She put them down on the windowsill and plonked back on the sofa. "Of course I know you'd never spy on anyone—you're such a good human!"

As I walked over to put the kettle on, shame rippled through my body.

Two hours later, I lay in bed, my mind refusing to disengage from its endless spin cycle. Sylvie was right. I owed it to Claudia to bring her some kind of closure if I could—and I knew I'd regret it if I didn't at least try. But I also didn't want to be the reason she died with even more of a broken heart. The details Sylvie tracked down were vague at best.

I tried everything I could to quiet my thoughts. I flipped my pillow to the cooler side. I cycled through a series of deep-breathing exercises. I counted backward by sevens from one thousand, first in English, then in Japanese. But sleep still eluded me.

Frustrated, I hauled myself out of bed and padded barefoot out into the living room.

There on the windowsill, exactly where Sylvie had left them, sat the binoculars. Maybe a few minutes of Julia and Reuben would be the salve my racing mind needed.

Lights out. Blinds open. Heart swelling.

Even though it was past midnight, they were still up—I knew they would be. They were night owls, after all. The TV was turned off and they were standing in the middle of the room embracing, swaying. I didn't need to hear the music to feel its rhythm. It was there in the movement of their hips, in their steps from side to side as their bodies pressed closely together.

The two of them, lost in a world of their own.

And me, alone in mine.

35

Given my history of running into Sebastian when I didn't want to, I wasn't surprised when he materialized outside Claudia's bedroom door early the next afternoon.

"Hey, Clover." The bags under his eyes aged him a little.

It was the first time I'd seen him since the concert and I was still conflicted. I wished I'd had more time to mull things over, but I'd been distracted lately.

"Oh, hi." I closed the bedroom door and ushered him down the hall. "Claudia's been sleeping most of the day. A doctor came this morning and spent quite a long time with her—Selma can fill you in on the details. I think it's good that your family is coming down this weekend."

"Yeah, I just spoke to my sisters," Sebastian said. "They're driving here tomorrow night after work."

"What about your parents?"

"They're arriving on Sunday. I think my dad's putting it off as long as he can."

"It'll be really hard to see his mother like this."

"I get that." Sebastian frowned. "But it also seems kind of selfish, you know? Avoiding being here for her just because he doesn't want to deal with it."

"Everyone has different ways of processing their grief." Sebastian's father did still sound like a jerk.

We stood silently in the hallway, the space between us pulsing with the weight of what wasn't being said. Things were so much simpler when I had no social life. I knew I had to address it.

"Sebastian, I'm sorry I left so quickly after we went out for drinks," I said, practically forcing out the words. "And after the concert."

He stuffed his hands in his pockets and shrugged. "That's okay, I get it—things were moving kind of fast. We can just take it slower."

As my thoughts spun, I realized that the only thing I was sure of was that I wanted to be completely present for Claudia—especially now she was nearing the end. "Actually, I think it might be better if we just keep things professional for now. My focus needs to be on your grandma."

"But—"

"I'm sorry, but I've got to go—I'm meeting my neighbor." I felt like a coward as I scooted past him toward the stairs.

"Clover, wait." He grabbed my arm, then dropped it quickly.

I reflexively put my hands behind my back as I turned. "Yes?"

"Who is Hugo?"

The bottom of my stomach dropped like I was on a carnival ride. "What?"

"I heard you talking to Grandma about some guy named Hugo. It sounded . . . personal."

As my armpits dampened, I considered my options. I'd already developed a pattern of dishonesty with Sebastian, but this was a chance to remedy that. Plus, I didn't want him thinking the reason I wanted to pause things was because of someone else.

I looked him firmly in the eye, the way Grandpa had taught me to do when owning up to things.

"Last week when we were going through some of your grandma's old photos, I found a picture of this guy from when she was living in France."

"Who was he?"

"I wasn't sure whether to tell you—but he was . . ." I lowered my voice even further. "Her lover."

"What?" Startled, Sebastian gestured for me to follow him down the hall and then continued in a stage whisper. "How? Wasn't she engaged to my grandfather when she lived in France?"

"Yes."

He shook his head vigorously, as if doing so would change the truth. "Wow. I mean, I'm pretty sure my grandfather was unfaithful—he didn't have the greatest morals—but Grandma? I never would've predicted that." He actually seemed slightly impressed.

"Apparently, she was really in love with this guy. She even thought of staying in France permanently instead of coming home to marry your grandfather."

"No wonder they had such an unhappy marriage." Sebastian rubbed the back of his head distractedly. "But I guess it helps me understand her a little better."

"There's actually more to it." I figured I'd already ripped off the bandage so I may as well tell him everything.

"Oh, God, don't tell me there's, like, a secret child or something?"

"No, nothing like that." At least his mind had gone to something more controversial than what I had to say next. "It turns out that this guy, Hugo, ended up immigrating to the United States in the late 1950s. And he might still be living in a small town in Maine."

Sebastian failed to hide his skepticism. "How do you even know all this?"

Guilt crept further under my skin. "I told my neighbor, Sylvie, because . . ." I struggled to explain why. Because it was nice to feel like I had something interesting to share with a friend? "Because it was a really romantic story." It didn't feel like a good enough excuse for invading someone's privacy, but it was all I had. "And she's an art historian, so she has access to all these resources. She looked into it for me."

"So, what are you saying?"

"The thing is, even though she's so grateful for your dad and you—for all her grandkids—Claudia told me that Hugo was, well, the love of her life. And part of her still wishes she'd told him that."

Sebastian's brow furrowed. "I see."

"I know that's probably hard for you to hear, but I was thinking maybe I could try to contact him."

Despite his frown, Sebastian's tilted head hinted at curiosity. "Do you have a phone number for him?"

"No, unfortunately. We tried to find one, but all we came up with was an address in a town called Lincolnville."

He shoved his hands back into his pockets. "What were you planning to do then?"

Was my idea ridiculous? I'd only come up with it a few hours earlier and admittedly hadn't thought it through. "Since your family will be here this weekend, maybe . . ."

"Yes?" He was getting impatient.

"Maybe I could drive up to Maine and see if I could find him." I focused hard on the curlicues of the rug pattern.

Sebastian removed his glasses, cleaning them with his shirttail. It was peculiar to see his face unobscured by lenses—it diluted the professor-like persona that I'd attributed to him.

"How long would it take to drive up there?"

"About seven hours. I'd leave early in the morning and then come back the next day."

"But what will you do if you find him?"

"I'm not sure yet." I was embarrassed I hadn't planned that far. "I was going to figure it out on my way there. But maybe, if I do find him, I could arrange a phone call with Claudia—if they're both open to it."

"I don't know. It could be just opening up a can of worms, especially with my family."

"Right, I get that." It was his grandmother, so it was his decision. I was presumptuous for letting myself get caught up in it all. "Never mind—it was a stupid suggestion anyway."

"It's just a lot to wrap my head around." He slid his glasses back on. "It's a whole side of Grandma I never knew about. Can I think about it?"

"Of course," I said, grateful for a reprieve from the conversation. "I've got to get home anyway. I guess I'll talk to you later."

I hurried down the staircase, my mind weighing the possibilities. I could still go without him knowing. By the time I reached the sidewalk, I was already googling rental car rates, my adrenaline racing at there being even the slightest chance I might find Hugo. Sylvie was going to be so excited.

"Clover, hang on a second."

I looked up to see Sebastian shutting the heavy front door of the townhouse behind him.

I stuffed my phone into my pocket, hoping there was no way he could tell I'd already decided to go against his wishes.

"Yes?"

He descended the stoop and kept his voice low. "I think you should do it—I think you should go to Maine."

The moths started fluttering in my stomach. "Really?"

"Yes," he said, firmly. "If there's a way we can help Grandma find peace, we have to at least try it. She deserves some happiness."

"That's great!" I almost hugged him but stopped myself.

Exhilaration shone in Sebastian's eyes. "And I'm coming with you."

36

I stood in the treat aisle of the pet store, paralyzed with indecision. Would Lionel prefer a seafood medley or a party mix? He was such a fickle cat that he'd probably turn his nose up at both.

I couldn't waste any more time on it. Sebastian was picking me up early the next morning and I needed to get home and pack. So I grabbed the seafood medley, plus some jerky chews for George and a jingling stuffed octopus toy for Lola (unlike the rest of us, she wasn't food-motivated). The offerings would distract them all from my absence over the next forty-eight hours—and hopefully Leo wouldn't mind walking George a couple of times while I was gone. But then again, Leo had been walking so slowly lately that I thought maybe I should ask Sylvie. She and George were obsessed with each other anyway.

I rushed through the self-checkout—no time to politely endure cashier small talk—only to be delayed by a stocky man and his Saint Bernard trying unsuccessfully to use the revolving door together. Even though it was obviously logistically impossible, they kept trying. I bounced on my toes waiting, trying not to glare at them.

When I made it outside after their fourth attempt, I stopped abruptly.

In front of the café next door, a woman stood waiting, hunched into her camel coat while scrolling through her phone.

Julia.

With only a few feet between us, I realized just how many details my decades-old binoculars had missed: the light smattering of freckles across her cheekbones, the fullness of her bottom lip, her slightly crooked nose. It was like I'd only ever seen her in 2D.

Was she waiting for Reuben? Panic rippled through my body as I searched for a place to hide. A mailbox was the only option and I was already standing so close to Julia that any sudden movement would make me seem creepier than I already felt. Clutching the paper bag of treats tighter, I concentrated on keeping my footsteps unremarkable, praying she'd stay engrossed in her phone and I could just walk by unnoticed.

Also unnoticed: the hole in the corner of the paper bag, just big enough for Lola's bell-stuffed octopus to shimmy through and bounce onto the sidewalk in front of Julia.

She looked up from her phone, alerted by the jingling sound. Seeing the fluorescent-pink stuffed octopus at her feet, she bent down to pick it up.

I stood frozen. There might have been a flicker of recognition in her eyes as she handed me the toy, but I couldn't be sure.

"My cat has one of those too," Julia said, confirming what I already knew. "I bet yours will love it."

My muscles softened enough for me to take the toy and form a smile that I hoped was in no way creepy. "Oh, thanks—I hope so . . . she's kind of picky."

Julia's own sunny smile revealed her uneven bottom teeth—another detail I'd never caught. She turned her attention back to her phone.

Instead of sprinting the rest of the way down the block like I desperately wanted to, I kept my pace normal. But I didn't let myself turn around until I'd reached the corner, where I pretended to stop and tie my shoelace so I could take one more look.

Julia was waving to someone across the street.

I held my breath—maybe I'd finally get to see Reuben and Julia together without several layers of glass between us. In the wild, so to speak.

But as I watched the scene unfold, my brain struggled to process the disparate parts coming together, like it was happening in slow motion. The person who crossed the street to greet Julia with an unmistakably passionate kiss was definitely someone I recognized.

But that someone was not Reuben.

It was Sylvie.

Suddenly, my coat felt too hot, too constricting, like the suffocating central heating of department stores in the dead of winter. The grating of a jackhammer against pavement, which I'd barely noticed moments earlier, now felt like an assault on my eardrums.

Without thinking, I ran.

George, Lola, and Lionel watched with alarm as I barreled through my front door and went straight to the windows. I yanked down the blinds—I didn't want to know what was going on in the apartment opposite. As I collapsed onto the sofa, I recognized the searing ache from my solar plexus to my gut—I'd felt it before.

Betrayal.

Julia and Reuben were the one emotional constant I had in my life. I'd seen their love expressed so clearly in their mannerisms, their routines. They were the one piece of evidence I had that real, romantic love existed beyond screens. And it was all a lie.

What hurt even more was that it was all happening with someone I'd trusted. I'd revealed so much of myself to Sylvie—my fears about love, my nonexistent sexual history, the kiss with Sebastian. Parts of myself I'd worked so hard to keep hidden. But she'd told me nothing. I didn't even know she was in a new relationship. What kind of friendship was that?

I pushed my forehead against my palms, wishing I could delete the memory of what I'd seen. But sitting still only made me more anxious. I began pacing laps around my living room, ignoring the concern on my pets' faces.

Unsure how else to calm myself, I did the thing I knew best. I switched off my emotions, pushing them away until I felt numb, and I refocused on the one thing I could control: finding Hugo for Claudia.

I grabbed Grandpa's old leather overnight bag from the top of the closet and started throwing clothes into it. The weathered bag was impractically bulky and couldn't fit in the overhead compartments on airplanes. But his initials were embossed on one of its flanks and though I hadn't traveled in years, whenever I'd carried it, it was as if he was with me, his whispered wisdom stitched into its sturdy seams. I could really use some of that now.

My phone flashed with a text from Sebastian. He'd managed to book a last-minute rental car and would pick me up the next morning at eight o'clock, which would get us to Maine in the early afternoon.

At least I could rely on somebody, even if it was the last person I expected.

I waited an hour before going to ask Leo to walk George while I was gone. No way was I asking Sylvie. I was embarrassed that I'd let myself think we were close friends. I'd been so careful to never let myself make the same mistake I had with Priya.

"You alright, kid?" Leo frowned in concern as I stood in his doorway. "You seem kind of agitated."

"Of course!" I forced a smile. "Just a lot to quickly organize for the trip. Thanks so much for taking care of George while I'm gone. It'll just be one night."

"It better be—don't want you bailing on our next game."

"I would never."

I savored Leo's chuckle as he closed his door. A consistency I could still cling to.

I was halfway through my apartment door when I heard footsteps on the stairs.

Damn. I should've waited another hour.

"Hey, C—I'm glad I caught you!" Sylvie's unfailingly enthusiastic tone, which I usually found soothing, triggered the ache in my chest. I needed to get better at turning that emotion off.

"Hey, Sylvie." I kept my expression neutral.

She had an envelope in her hand. "This was in my mailbox by mistake. It looks like a check, so I figured you'd probably want it sooner than later."

"Thanks." I avoided eye contact as I took it from her.

"So, I'm dying to know what you decided about Hugo!" She leaned casually against the wall by my front door. "Are you going to try to find him?"

"I'm driving up to Maine with Sebastian first thing tomorrow." All I wanted to do was scurry into my apartment and shut the door.

"With Sebastian? No way! I can't wait to hear about that." Sylvie's grin widened. "Hey, I just got a great bottle of tempranillo from the condescending wine guy. Want to come downstairs and tell me all about it over a glass?"

"I can't, I've got to pack for tomorrow." I shuffled farther into my apartment. "Sebastian's picking me up early."

"Okay, no worries," she said, stepping away from the wall. "But could you at least tell me why you're acting weird?"

I fiddled with my watchband, trying to think of an excuse. "What do you mean?"

"Well," she said in a way that was both teasing and serious, "let's start with the fact that you're avoiding eye contact with me."

I forced myself to look at her. As soon as I did, the betrayal I'd felt seeing her and Julia embrace began to flare again. How could Sylvie come between two people who so clearly loved each other?

I sucked in a slow breath, trying to swallow my hurt.

It didn't work.

"How could you ruin Julia's marriage like that?" My voice was unnervingly high-pitched. I hoped Leo had his TV turned up loud.

"She and Reuben are happy together. They've been so happy for years."

Sylvie's eyebrows flattened with confusion. "Who's Julia?"

"The woman you were making out with this afternoon outside the café." I didn't care that my cheeks were bright red. "I saw you."

The look on Sylvie's face was inscrutable at first, then shifted into suspicion. "The woman I was kissing is called Bridget."

Oh. Right. Julia was the name I gave her. When I first started spying on her and her husband in the privacy of their home.

Sylvie cocked her head curiously. "How do you know she's married, anyway?" She crossed her arms against her chest. "And why do you even care?"

The redness seeped down to my neck as shame began to course through my body. I realized how ridiculous I was being. But it felt impossible to turn back—like I'd already unraveled the person Sylvie thought I was.

So in that moment, all I could do was step backward and close the door, sinking down onto the floor into an emotional mess of my own making.

37

woke up before my alarm, mainly because I hadn't slept. Yesterday's debacle with Sylvie and Julia (well, Bridget, if we're being
technical) had looped through my mind the entire night.

Dulled by sleep deprivation, I carried George downstairs and
practically had to force him to lift his leg and pee. Even though
there was no way Sylvie would be up this early, I still held my breath
when we passed her door.

She probably thought I was unhinged after my outburst and the
way I'd ended our conversation. In retrospect, my reaction was melo-
dramatic, even a little childish. But it still bothered me that Sylvie
would come between a happy couple, even if she did like to bend the
rules. At least I had forty-eight hours before I'd have to think about
dealing with her—thank God I had an excuse to leave town.

Leather overnight bag slung over my shoulder, I gave my living
room a final glance. A pang of wanderlust surfaced as I thought about
how long it had been since I'd last gone away on a trip. Five years at
least, and that was only a weekend in Philly to see a museum exhi-
bition on funeral pyres. I missed the freedom of travel—observing
the world and uncovering its magic, decoding its people, all while
still enjoying my solitude. It nourished me in a way that nothing
else did.

I was out on the front stoop exactly one minute before Sebastian's promised arrival time. He pulled up outside the building in a rented black Chevrolet Spark twenty-five minutes later.

He rolled down the window and waved. "Sorry, I had a bit of trouble getting up so early."

"That's okay," I lied. I was annoyed that he didn't care enough to show up on time. Or maybe the thing with Sylvie was making me overly sensitive—at least he'd turned up at all. "Thanks for picking me up."

"Of course." Sebastian reached under the steering wheel and pressed the button for the trunk, nodding at my bag. "There should be room back there next to my suitcase."

He watched in the rearview mirror while I tried to wedge the bag in next to his larger-than-cabin-sized suitcase. (Was he planning to be away longer than one night?) After trying several times to lever my cumbersome bag in beside it, I gave up and slid it into the back seat. When I joined Sebastian in the front, I took solace that his hair was as unkempt as mine.

We sat in relative silence until we'd left Manhattan. Sebastian must've been really tired if he wasn't trying to make conversation—or maybe he felt as awkward as I did about our conversation yesterday at Claudia's.

Once the fugue of tiredness had dissipated from my brain, I pulled out my book. A little rude, maybe, but so was making me wait on the stoop for almost half an hour.

"Wow, you can read in the car?" Sebastian's chattiness had stirred. "I could never do that. I get really bad motion sickness."

"I'm sorry—that must be frustrating." Passing the time getting lost in the pages of a book was one of the things I loved most about traveling.

He adjusted the car's visor to accommodate the sun. "Not really. I'm not much of a reader—I find it kind of lonely, to be honest."

This revelation contradicted several of the scenarios I'd conjured when weighing him up as a potential romantic interest: strolling together through used bookstores, swapping book recommendations, reading side by side in bed.

"You don't even read before you go to sleep?"

"Nah, I usually fall asleep watching TV." Sebastian peered at the mundane strip of suburbia fringing the highway. "Hey, there's a drive-through Starbucks up ahead. Let's get coffee."

We were second in the queue of cars.

"You take your coffee with milk and sugar, right?" Sebastian asked.

My annoyance piqued again. "Black, please—no sugar or cream. Drip is fine." He'd made me coffee several times before at Claudia's, so shouldn't he remember by now?

But also, why did it bother me?

Three hours into the road trip, somewhere in the belly of Massachusetts, I was wishing for the awkward silence of the early morning.

Sebastian launched into a detailed description of a documentary he watched about soybean production, no part of which sounded remotely appealing. I was pretty sure I'd never mentioned an interest in soybeans. But he was probably just dealing with the same nervousness I was about spending an extended time together in an enclosed space. So I indulged him by nodding and making occasional affirming noises, feigning enough engagement to seem polite but not encourage elaboration. At least it was keeping me awake. And it was a distraction from thinking about Sylvie. But as the mile markers ticked by, I wondered how much time would pass before he'd pause to elicit a response from me.

When he finally did—exactly three hours and forty-seven minutes after we'd hit the road—it took me by surprise.

"Want to listen to a podcast?" He picked up his phone from the center console. "I downloaded a few new ones last night."

"Good idea." I tried not to sound too relieved.

He handed me the phone. "There are lots on there. I'm kind of a podcast addict—I'd rather listen to someone else than be alone with my own thoughts. You know how it is."

Not really. I'd spent most of the past decade alone with my thoughts. "Actually, I've never been able to get into podcasts. It always seemed to me like having an unwelcome presence chattering away in my brain." Kind of like going on a road trip with someone who doesn't stop talking.

The list of podcasts was like a window into Sebastian's mind. He subscribed to several on classical music, another on managing life as someone who is allergic to many things, and a few about the economy and cryptocurrency. I stopped scrolling on an NPR episode.

"What about this one on the regrets of the dying? Kind of on theme for the trip."

Sebastian grinned. "Yeah, I thought you might like that one—I downloaded it especially for you."

My bubbling annoyance subsided, as if someone had switched off a hot plate. The gesture was unexpectedly touching.

"Thanks, that's really nice of you." I'd probably heard all of the regrets over the years, but I was curious to see if some hadn't yet made it into my notebooks.

"Before I started going to the death cafés, I listened to a lot of podcasts about death . . . to kind of dip my toe in," Sebastian said, squinting at the road. "At first it was kind of excruciating, and I could only listen to a few minutes at a time. I guess it made all of my fears about death come up to the surface."

I plugged his phone into the USB cable. "What scares you most about it?" This was a conversation I didn't mind having.

"I don't know, exactly." Sebastian adjusted his hands on the steering wheel and tapped his thumbs to a silent rhythm. "It's the finality of it all, I guess." I let him mull further, sure he would continue without a prompt. "Like, when I was a kid, I'd always work myself into a panic thinking about death before I went to sleep at night. At first, it was that Sunday-school guilt, you know—was I doing all the right things to get into heaven? The potential of having a whole life to fuck it up was terrifying to me. There were just so many rules."

"Right." I imagined a child-sized Sebastian tucked into his bed, terrified, and felt a surge of compassion.

"And then, when I was about eighteen and decided I didn't believe in God, that still didn't really take the pressure off like I hoped it would." The white across his knuckles brightened as he gripped the wheel. "Because every time I imagined dying, I would freak myself out by thinking about how that was it for me. You know, like, for the rest of eternity, I would no longer exist. And eventually, everyone who knew me would die, and then I'd be forgotten forever. It just made me feel so isolated."

I was impressed at how well he could articulate his fear. "Did you ever talk to anyone about it?"

"That's the thing." Sebastian glanced at me helplessly. "Whenever I had the panic attacks as a kid, I'd run into my parents' bedroom and tell them about being scared of dying. And my dad would just tell me to be brave like a man and go back to bed."

It fascinated me how parents messed up their children so obliviously.

"And your family never discussed death? What about when your grandfather died?"

Sebastian shook his head. "We're your pretty typical WASP family—stoic to the point of emotional denial and too proud to ever discuss our feelings, let alone see a therapist. I mean, of course they discussed the logistics of it—the funeral, the will, all that stuff. But we didn't talk about it afterward, about what it meant to lose him."

I waited a few beats as a station wagon cut in front of us. "How do you think losing his father impacted your dad?"

Sebastian changed lanes, speeding up to pass the car.

"You wouldn't think it did at all, to look at him. He didn't even cry at the funeral—he just stared straight ahead the whole time during the service and then did his duty as the son, thanking everyone for coming and all that stuff." He kneaded the steering wheel again. "After everyone had left our house when the wake was over, I saw him sitting in his study, just staring. I went in and asked if he was okay and he just turned to me and said, very calmly, 'Of course, why wouldn't I be?' And that's all we ever said about it."

It was a typical male response to grief. No wonder Sebastian struggled with death.

He wriggled his shoulders, shrugging off the emotion. "Anyway, you probably don't want to hear about all of this."

"No, I do." Honestly, I was flattered that he felt comfortable enough to open up to me. It made me feel closer to him. More relaxed.

Our eye contact, though brief, felt weighted.

"Okay, well, I remember when I was a kid and I'd ask questions," Sebastian continued. "Like why we die and all that—and my parents would always just tell me that it wasn't appropriate to talk about. And then I'd ask my teachers, and they'd get all uncomfortable and tell me to ask my parents. The only time we ever really got to talk about death was during Sunday school, and then it was in the context of being sure you were good while you were living so that you didn't end up in hell, which obviously only made things worse."

I shifted in my seat so that my shoulders faced toward him. "Is that why you started going to the death cafés?"

"Yeah. I stumbled across the first one by accident when I was at a restaurant on . . . a date." We both stared at the road. "There was a back room where it was being held, and I overheard the discussion while I was on my way to the restroom. I asked the moderator if I could join the next one. At first, I never said anything at them because I was petrified of talking about dying. As if I said it out loud, it would bring me closer to my death, or something stupid like that. But then hearing everyone tell their stories about why they were there—and being able to discuss it like it was a normal thing—really helped me feel less alone."

Death cafés made me feel less alone too, but for entirely different reasons.

"Well, death *is* a normal thing," I said instead.

Sebastian's posture stiffened, as if the shield he'd temporarily lowered had snapped back into place.

"For you, maybe, but not for the rest of us." His laugh was forced. "It's cool that you're so comfortable with it, but that's pretty unusual, don't you think? Nobody I know ever wants to talk about death."

His words scratched the same wound as when Sylvie questioned the contents of my apartment. Another reminder that I was out of step with the rest of the world. A weirdo.

I let the silence endure, partly in retaliation, while I watched a flock of geese take off from a field beside the highway. Then I picked up his phone. "Should we listen to the podcast?"

"Sure—fire it up."

For once, he seemed happy not to keep talking.

I hit Play and settled back into my seat, grateful for the chance to spend the next forty-five minutes freed from conversation.

38

The NPR podcast featured stories of people who'd had near-death experiences and the regrets they'd felt when faced with the fact they might die. Most of them were recurring themes in my REGRETS notebook—people wishing they'd worked less, loved more, taken more risks, followed their passions. Sadly, regret was pretty predictable. For some of the people, the near-death experience was a wake-up call; for others, it was unfortunately a lesson that was easily forgotten. Habits are hard to change, after all.

The podcast's closing music rang out and I reached over to pause it before the next one began. Sebastian piped up as soon as the speakers quieted.

"Guess you've heard most of those before, huh?"

"A few of them." I didn't want to sound smug.

"What's the weirdest regret you've heard?"

Watching pine trees flicker past the car window, I thought through all the ones I'd documented over the years.

"One woman said her biggest regret was not splurging on the expensive dish soap she always saw advertised on TV." It was a banal revelation, but I still felt a tiny bit guilty for betraying Helena's trust. I promised myself I'd make up for it this week by splurging on the fancy eco-friendly detergent in her honor. I loved the scent—a blend of lavender and lily of the valley.

Sebastian scoffed. "She must've lived a pretty good life if that was her biggest regret."

"I think it was more that she spent her whole life scrimping and saving and never let herself indulge in simple pleasures like that." I felt protective of Helena's legacy. "She ended up dying with all this money in the bank that she never spent."

"At least she could leave it to her family, right?"

I wondered if he was thinking about Claudia. "Actually, she was ninety-five and never married, so she didn't have any family. I think it all ended up going to charity."

"Man," Sebastian said, pushing his glasses up the bridge of his nose. "That would suck, dying without anyone left to miss you."

"It happens to more people than you'd think," I said quietly, feeling an invisible punch to my gut.

"So a lot of the time it's just you alone with the person who's dying?" He shuddered. "No way I could do that over and over."

"If I didn't, they'd often die alone." I reflexively slid my hand back between the seats to touch Grandpa's leather bag behind me.

"It's still a little strange that you spend your days doing that." Sebastian's tone had shifted. His vulnerability from an hour earlier—and the closeness I'd felt—had evaporated. We were sitting the same few inches from each other, but it felt like we were drifting farther apart.

"I think it's a privilege to be with someone as they leave this life." My voice wavered. "And sometimes it's really beautiful."

He resumed his nervous tapping of the steering wheel.

"Beautiful? How?" Agitation underscored his words.

"Well, for some people, especially the ones who love music, I arrange a threshold choir—they sing at people's deathbeds to help comfort them." I figured music was something he could relate to. "It's amazing what a difference that can make, how the music can calm them so instantly, like it's healing their souls or something."

The skepticism in Sebastian's forehead softened. "Music can be healing for sure."

"And even without the music, there's often this kind of serenity that people get, right before they die. Something that you never see in the living—like they're letting go of everything they've held on to so tightly and finally just letting themselves be. I wish everyone could learn to do that sooner."

"But . . ." Sebastian pressed his lips together and then shook his head. "Never mind."

"No, what were you going to say?" Maybe he would open up again with a little encouragement.

Shifting in his seat, he focused on the road. "No offense, Clover, but sometimes you come off as a little preachy. And kind of hypocritical. Like, you've gained all this wisdom from watching people die, but what's the point of having all that wisdom if you're not going to use it?"

For the second time in five minutes, an invisible punch assailed my gut. "What do you mean?"

"Well, except for that old guy, Leo, you said you don't really have much of a social life, right? And I overheard you telling Grandma that you've never really dated anyone. I bet if you knew you were going to die tomorrow, you'd probably have more than a few regrets." He swallowed hard and stared ahead, steeling himself for my reply.

Anger boiled beneath my ribs.

Respond, don't react, Grandpa had always said. But in this instance, my tongue wasn't open to negotiation.

"A successful life doesn't mean you have to date people all the time—or anyone at all." I recognized the unhinged pitch of my voice from my argument with Sylvie. "In fact, I'd say that the opposite is true. It sounds like you date people all the time, just so you don't have to be alone and think about who you really are."

The blaring horn of a truck speeding past us felt like a satisfying conclusion to my statement. We sat fuming in silence.

"At least I've been in love." He turned to look at me, his tone clipped. "You're impossible to get close to. There's a difference between being alone and never letting anyone else in."

His final blow was short, incisive, and hurt the most. Suddenly the car felt like it was closing in around me. I couldn't stand another minute inside.

Through the windshield, a gas station loomed.

"Pull over, please," I said.

"What?"

"PLEASE. PULL. OVER." It was the first time in my life that I'd ever yelled at anyone.

Sebastian turned into the gas station and slowed the car to a stop. I got out and clumsily retrieved my duffel from the back seat.

"Clover, what are you doing?" Sebastian said.

"I'll find my own way back to New York."

I slammed the door and didn't look back.

39

The day I learned that Grandpa was dead was a Wednesday, three days after my twenty-third birthday. I was in Cambodia, crammed with a large man and woman into a bus seat meant for two, my suitcase balanced on my lap and a cage of live chickens lodged in the aisle. We'd been in that same Tetris-like arrangement for the past two hours, rattling along a narrow, winding road somewhere between the southern province of Takéo and the capital, Phnom Penh. Sweat drowning our brows, we collectively dreamed of a vestige of fresh air and I regretted not spending the extra money for a ticket on the air-conditioned bus. The lethal combination of heat, chicken manure, and rank body odor had brought my nausea close to delirium. All I could do was focus on breathing.

The tortuous journey was the last of my two-month stay, during which I'd been studying the Cambodian Buddhist traditions of death. I was booked to fly back to New York via Singapore on Thursday, meaning I'd make it home in time for breakfast with Grandpa at the diner on Sunday.

I hadn't felt the comfort of his presence in almost a year and I ached for it.

Before Cambodia, I had been at the Sorbonne in Paris completing my master's thesis in thanatology. My small suitcase wasn't stuffed with clothing, but rather stacks of notebooks I'd filled with all my observations from my travels. I'd been counting the days until I could share them with Grandpa, imagining him stirring his coffee thoughtfully as he methodically studied each page.

Our most recent conversation had taken place a couple of days ago, early on Monday morning—Sunday evening his time. I'd snuck out of my hostel bunk room and padded down to the old rotary telephone that rested on a stool in the corner of the communal area. It was the only time of day when it was possible to talk on the phone in peace. The way the morning sun streamed in through the curtains reminded me of our apartment in New York.

"Clover, my dear—I was just thinking that it's been more than a month since I heard from you."

The tinny connection robbed Grandpa's baritone of its usual rich timbre, making me miss him even more.

"I'm sorry, Grandpa," I said, soothed by the sound of his voice. "I should've called sooner."

Even over the bad connection, his deep chuckle was as endearing as ever. "I figured you had plenty of other things occupying your brain than your old Grandpa."

"You're always in my brain—even if I don't call often enough to tell you." I'd been so caught up in exploring the world this past year that I'd let our regular phone calls become sporadic.

"Don't worry, dear. When I don't hear from you, I know it means you're enjoying yourself. And that makes me very happy."

I closed my eyes and envisioned him sitting in his green armchair, one leg crossed over the other, the steam of his evening coffee dancing in the glow of the reading lamp.

"So then," he continued. "Tell me what you've learned from your studies in Cambodia."

I switched the phone to my opposite ear, trying to get comfortable. "It's quite different from the Western world."

"Ah, yes, the Buddhists and their reincarnation."

"Right, and so the actual dying process is super important to someone's rebirth in their next life."

"Intriguing—how so?"

"Well, they often have a monk present when someone's dying to help them prepare for the next life." I was proud to be the one to teach him something for once. "And some people believe that after the soul exits the body, it often lingers in the place where they died. Sometimes the soul is confused or frightened, so the monk needs to be there to calm it and guide it onward. It's quite beautiful, really— the idea of helping usher someone into their next life."

"Yes, it is," Grandpa said. "What a privilege it must be to be able to do that for someone."

The bus lurched to a halt outside a gas station surrounded by rice fields. The reprieve from our stifling purgatory on wheels— intended for bathroom breaks and quick snacks only—would last twenty minutes. The thought of dealing with food or a squat toilet made me even more nauseated, so I bought a bottle of sparkling water and stood in front of a small desk fan that was half-heartedly circulating stale air.

Kios Intanet read the neon-pink cardboard sign taped above the old computer monitor next to the fan. The hostel WiFi hadn't been working the past few days, so I hadn't checked my email in a while. I slid the requested two thousand Cambodian riels across the counter to the gas station clerk, earning me ten minutes of infuriatingly slow dial-up internet access.

Six emails sat in my inbox. One was a reminder of my flight on Thursday. The second was an email from a student I'd studied with in France, requesting my input on a research paper. And the remaining four were from Charles Nelson, a longtime colleague of Grandpa's at Columbia University.

The sight of Charles's name made my pulse stutter.

I read his emails in the order he sent them. The first few were variations of "Please call me as soon as you can." The most recent one, sent only an hour ago, was painfully to the point.

> *Clover,*
>   *I know you are traveling abroad, and I regret having to do this via email, but your grandfather passed away yesterday.*
>   *Please contact me when you receive this, as arrangements need to be made.*
>
>   *Regards,*
>   *Charles Nelson, PhD*

My nausea became dread. I fumbled in my travel pouch for my international phone card and stumbled over to the pay phone, dialing the cell number in Charles's signature.

Three rings, then a connection.

"It's Clover," I blurted out before he'd even spoken.

Charles cleared his throat. "Ah, yes, hello, Clover—I see you received my email. I'm very sorry for your loss. And to be the bearer of such bad news."

The oppressive humidity made my panicked breathing worse. "What happened?" I managed to squeeze out the words, but they materialized as only a whisper.

"Stroke, they think." Charles had always been matter-of-fact, but in this moment his brevity felt callous. "He'd been working late in his office on campus and the janitor found him slumped in his desk chair."

I rubbed my sternum, willing myself to find a single, slow breath. "He died . . . alone?"

"'Fraid it looks that way—very sorry."

Outside, the bus blasted its horn as my fellow passengers filed miserably back on board. Somehow, amid my internal chaos, I found a flicker of pragmatism. If I was going to make my flight to New York tomorrow, I had to get on that bus.

"Charles, I'm really sorry, but I'm in the middle of nowhere and my bus is about to leave. I'll call you back as soon as I get to Phnom Penh."

Charles cleared his throat a second time. "Okay then—safe trip, speak soon."

I soon found myself wedged back in with the same two passengers, the cage of chickens squawking next to them. But now I was numb to the unbearable heat, the cacophony of sounds, the stench of sweating bodies. All I could think about was that dark, cramped university office at the end of the corridor. The one I'd visited hundreds of times since I was a kid.

The place where my best friend met his death alone, with no one there to guide him through it.

40

I regretted abandoning the road trip with Sebastian at this particular gas station. Nothing but single-lane highway and winter-lorn fields stretched in both directions. The breeze carried the salty, fetid smell of coastal marshland and a chill that found its way into every crevice of my clothing.

Facing the entrance to the gas station, I focused hard on my phone until I heard the hum of the rental car diminish into the distance. When I finally turned around, the only presence in the parking lot was a lone brown pickup whose dented doors had copped someone's wrath more than once.

Sebastian had really left me.

My armpits prickled with sweat. I hugged the duffle close to my body.

What I would give to talk to Grandpa right now. In panicked moments on my first backpacking trip in Latin America, I'd called him from a pay phone just to hear his calming, rational voice for ten minutes before my credit ran out.

"Your sympathetic nervous system is just manipulating you," he'd tell me matter-of-factly. "A classic biological fight-or-flight response. All you need to do is take back control. Close your eyes to eliminate external stimulation. Then take a long, deep breath and release it slowly."

Though he'd given the instructions years ago, I stood outside the gas station and did what I'd been told.

Eyes closed. Breathe in. Breathe out.

"Now, instead of focusing on all the things that have gone wrong," Grandpa would then say, "think about the next right step forward you could take to move things in a positive direction."

The glass door to the gas station swung open. A hefty, corn-raised type in buffalo plaid strode through it, stuffing a packet of Parliaments into his breast pocket. Sweat stains rose above the brim of his trucker's cap like tide marks on a beach.

"'Scuse me, love," he barked at me and my large bag blocking the doorway. As I stepped aside to let him pass, I caught the combined mustiness of stale tobacco, spilled beer, and questionable hygiene habits.

One small step forward.

I considered the stranger and his battered pickup.

Catching my eye, he winked, grin wide but lacking warmth. "Need a ride?"

On second thought, he didn't look like the type who was headed toward New York City. "That's very kind of you." I tightened my grip on the duffle. "But, no, thank you."

"Suit yourself," the man said, an unlit cigarette now loping from the corner of his unsettling grin.

As the pickup rattled out of the gas station, the adrenaline of a near miss flooded my limbs.

A compact luncheonette sat annexed to the edge of the gas station's boxy cement building. My jitters were probably partly because I hadn't eaten in five hours. A meal was a small step that would do me good. After stopping by the disinfectant-drenched bathroom, I set my bag down in the least sticky booth in the luncheonette.

I nodded through the service window at a waitress/cook in a

hairnet and gravy-stained apron. Steam from the deep fryers rose dramatically behind her, cloaking her imposing silhouette.

"Menu's up top," the woman said, expressionless, pointing an apathetic finger toward the roof.

A blackboard above her head listed a comprehensive selection of misspelled offerings, most of which had a jagged line of chalk struck through them. Only two items were still available: the patty melt and the grilled cheese.

I figured the latter was the least likely to expose me to salmonella. "I'll take the grilled cheese, please."

"You wanna pickle with that?" The woman clearly couldn't care less.

"Sure. I mean, yes, please."

"Coffee?"

"That would be great, thank you."

The woman nodded at the coffee pot sitting on a warmer at the end of the service window. She slid a mug in my direction. "Help yourself."

The burnt aroma indicated the coffee pot had overstayed its welcome. I poured myself a cup for comfort rather than enjoyment. Sitting down in the booth, I sat stirring, thinking. It'd been a sad part of growing up when I realized that the answers to all hard questions didn't really lie at the bottom of a coffee cup. I tapped my spoon on the side of the coffee mug three times.

Here I was, once again, sitting alone in a diner.

Perhaps I'd slightly overreacted to Sebastian's criticism. But he'd basically told me that my whole life was a lie.

Following an incongruously long wait since I was the luncheonette's only customer, a plate with an anemic grilled cheese and miserable pickle plonked down in front of me.

I smiled as politely as I could at the waitress. "Thank you, ma'am."

"Sure." The woman disappeared back into the kitchen.

As I bit gingerly into a corner of the gooey sandwich, my phone, which was facedown on the table, vibrated with a message. I hesitated before turning it over. It could be Sebastian texting to apologize, but I wasn't sure I even wanted it to be him.

I flipped the phone quickly, like a hot piece of toast.

Mike, take advantage of these unbelievable mortgage rates right now.

A spam text. No matter how many times I blocked the number, I still got them weekly. (And whoever sent them clearly thought "Mike" was pretty gullible.) I went back to my sandwich, trying not to notice the plastic-like consistency of the cheese.

I could call a cab and go to the nearest car rental place. Or bus station. Or airport. Of course, that all depended on whether cabs even serviced this gas station in the middle of nowhere.

My phone convulsed with another message, kick-starting my pulse.

Sylvie's name populated the screen.

I grabbed a scratchy paper napkin from the dispenser and wiped the grease from my fingers.

Hey C. Hope you're OK and the road trip's going well. That was weird yesterday—can we talk about it?

Part of me wanted to pick up the phone and tell her about my fight with Sebastian—she'd definitely be on my side. And I could use her calming voice of reason.

But since I obviously didn't know Sylvie as well as I thought—and also because of my behavior yesterday—maybe she'd agree with him about how weird and pathetic I was. As I deleted the message with a resentful swipe, the burning in my chest shifted to the ache I knew best.

Loneliness.

I was right back to where I'd started before I met Sebastian and Sylvie. What was the point of putting myself out there if this was how I ended up? All I wanted to do was curl up on my sofa with my animals and never leave the apartment again.

But then there was Claudia. She was the reason I was doing all of this, not Sebastian. And if I gave up when we were so close to finding Hugo—we'd made it to Maine, after all—I knew I'd regret it.

Breathe in. Breathe out. The next right step.

Motioning to the waitress for the check, I ignored the dread in my stomach. She scribbled on her pad and tore it off, placing it in front of me.

"I know it's hard to admit when you're wrong, sweetie, but sometimes you just gotta do it for the sake of the marriage."

I stared back, confused, then realized she must have seen my dramatic exit from the car. "I'm not married," I said, trying to hide my embarrassment.

"Oh," she replied. "Well, good luck with whoever he is."

I hastily pulled the bills from my wallet. "You didn't charge me for the coffee, so I threw in an extra few dollars—hope that covers it."

I slid out of the booth and headed back to the restroom to scrub the grease from my hands. The duffle on my shoulder was a graceless companion for the gas station's narrow aisles, sending a stand of plantain chips flying like a wrecking ball. The teenaged store clerk rolled his eyes but didn't move from behind the counter to help me resurrect it.

I knew I couldn't stall things any longer. Positioning myself in the corner farthest from the clerk, I took a breath and tapped Sebastian's name on my phone.

He picked up after one ring.

"Hi, Sebastian." I didn't give him a chance to speak. "I'm sorry for . . . overreacting like that." What was left of my pride now lay hemorrhaging on the grimy linoleum floor. "The most important thing right now is finding Hugo."

"I'm really sorry too," Sebastian said cautiously. "It's none of my business how you live your life. I shouldn't have said . . . what I said."

He wasn't exactly saying that he didn't mean it, but I didn't have the luxury of triviality right now.

"I'm not sure where you are, but I'm still at the gas station." I examined the expiration dates on the cans of Pringles, searching for one that wasn't a potential health threat. "Do you think you could come back and pick me up?"

A staticky pause. "Look out the window."

I looked from the Pringles to the gas pumps.

Leaning against the rental car, Sebastian waved at me.

41

The number on the letterbox confirmed we were in the right place. But there was no house, just a dirt driveway lined with soaring birch trees leading down to a lake. Surely this wasn't the place—there was nothing here.

Sebastian double-checked the GPS. "This is definitely it."

I peered ahead through the trees but couldn't see a building anywhere. "Should we drive down closer to the water?"

"There's no house anywhere around here," Sebastian said impatiently. "We'd be able to see it."

I felt my heart deflate. All this time and energy on a foolish quest. Thank God I didn't say anything to Claudia about the trip.

"I was stupid to think we'd find him," I said, ashamed to have to admit yet another shortcoming to Sebastian. "I'm sorry I dragged you up here for nothing."

He nodded toward the water. "Let's go down and check out the lake. Since there's nobody here, we aren't exactly trespassing."

"I guess we could." It was too late to drive back to the city tonight, anyway.

The tang of crisp, woodsy air eased my disappointment as our footsteps crunched against fallen bark. I'd forgotten how comforting nature could be—I hardly even visited Central Park anymore.

"Looks like it's called Megunticook Lake," Sebastian said, peering at his phone. "Home to the landlocked salmon, pumpkinseed sunfish, and the banded killifish."

"Are you into fishing?" I wouldn't have predicted that.

Sebastian wrinkled his face. "God, no. I'm not much of an outdoors guy—I'm probably allergic to about seventy percent of nature. The one time my dad took me camping was torture." He swatted erratically at an invisible insect buzzing near his face.

The driveway rose slightly then fell into a curved slope. We stood at the peak and looked down at a sagging jetty where a retro-looking boat with a faded blue stripe was docked.

"Is that a houseboat?" Sebastian said, adjusting his glasses. "I didn't know anyone even lived in those anymore. My sisters used to make me watch that old movie with Cary Grant and Sophia Loren that was like *The Sound of Music* but on a boat. Man, what was it called again?"

"*Houseboat?*"

"Ha. Yeah. I should've figured. The one with Kurt Russell and Goldie Hawn on a boat was funnier." He started down the slope, the soles of his city-appropriate Oxfords sliding on the damp ground.

Secretly glad for his investigational bravado, I followed him down. A wool sweater slung over the boat's railing signaled that someone had been there recently—or was still there.

Maybe this wasn't such a stupid idea after all.

Just as Sebastian set foot on the jetty, several shrill dog barks fired in succession. A shaggy black terrier jumped from the boat and bulleted at Sebastian, who leaped back clumsily. The dog bounded around Sebastian like its hind paws were on springs while he tried helplessly to escape the exuberant onslaught. I swallowed the tickle of laughter.

"Gus!" A man's voice called from within the boat's cabin. "Calm down, buddy."

A head of dark curls emerged, ducking against the low-set door frame. When the man stood up straight, it was almost like he doubled in height.

"Hi there." His eyes seesawed between Sebastian and me. "Can I help you?"

Gus trotted back to his owner's side, his red collar like a flare against his jet-black fur.

"Ah, yeah," Sebastian said, grateful to be rescued from his excited assailant. "We're looking for Hugo Beaufort."

"Well, then you've found him."

Sebastian frowned. "That's you?"

"Pretty sure it is, yeah." The man squinted, skeptical. "What can I do for you?"

This guy couldn't be older than thirty-five and he definitely didn't sound French. I glanced over at Sebastian who looked as defeated as I felt.

"Sorry, man—I think we've got the wrong person," Sebastian said. "The Hugo we're looking for would be a lot older than you. Like, fifty years older."

"Oh," the man said. "You mean my grandfather?"

"Yes!" Sebastian and I spoke over each other.

The Hugo in front of us bowed his head. "He actually died a couple of months ago."

"I'm really sorry to hear that," I said reflexively.

Gus cocked his head at the sound of my voice, bypassing Sebastian to run up the hill to me. As I bent down to scratch his floppy ears, the dog nuzzled calmly against my leg.

"Thank you," Hugo said. "I mean, he was in his nineties, so it was kind of expected."

"That doesn't make it hurt any less," I said, as much to mitigate my own grief as his.

The three of us stood in silence.

"Wait," Hugo said, puzzled. "Why are you guys looking for my grandfather anyway?"

"It's about my grandmother," Sebastian said softly. "She's dying too." He seemed stunned, as if speaking the words finally made them a reality. I recognized the weight of grief in his slumped shoulders, the way he stared at the ground.

"I'm sorry, man," Hugo said, his tone radiating empathy. He waited for Sebastian to elaborate.

Sebastian looked at me, imploring me to take the lead in the conversation.

I walked closer to the jetty, Gus trotting beside me. "We think Sebastian's grandmother might have known your grandfather for a time when she was living in Marseille in the mid-fifties."

It sounded ridiculous now that I said it out loud, more than sixty years later. I was naive to think this trip would achieve anything.

But instead of looking at me like I was crazy, Hugo tilted his head with curiosity.

"Are you talking about . . . Claudia?"

Sebastian and I stared back at Hugo in disbelief. Gus looked between us, panting in anticipation.

Sebastian stepped onto the jetty. "You know about my grandmother?"

"Yeah—I mean, kind of." Hugo rubbed the stubble on his jaw. "Right before he died, my grandfather said he needed to tell me something that he'd never told anyone. To be honest, I thought he'd killed someone or something like that. But instead, he told me the story of an American woman, a photographer named Claudia, who he fell in love with in France. He said she was the reason he moved here to the United States."

"That's Sebastian's grandmother!" I said, trying to temper my welling hope. "Only, she didn't know that your grandfather moved here."

"This is wild," Hugo said. He'd inherited his grandfather's angular chin—it suited him. "But if she didn't know he moved to America, how'd you guys find out he lived here?"

Sebastian pointed a hitchhiker's thumb at me. "She's kind of an internet super sleuth."

Hugo raised an eyebrow. "She is, huh?"

I deeply regretted not brushing my hair that morning.

"Well, my neighbor was the one who found your address," I said, my mouth suddenly dry. "But I found a picture of your grandfather among some of Claudia's old photos and she told me the story of how they met."

"Wow, I have so many questions. But, first—" Hugo stuck out his hand. "Sebastian, right?"

Sebastian shook it. "Right."

"Nice to meet you, man." Hugo turned to me, eyebrow raised again. "And you are?"

I prayed for my cheeks not to burn. "Uh, I'm Clover."

Hugo's face lifted into an easy grin. "Like the Etta James song, right? 'My heart was wrapped up in clover'? I always loved that one." He reached out his hand. "Great to meet you, Clover."

As the thickness of his calloused palm pressed into the softness of mine, I felt my whole hand tingle. "You too."

"Hey, are you guys hungry?" Hugo raked his fingers through his curls, habit-like. "We're not far from a great pub—maybe we can chat about all this over lobster rolls. I'd love to hear more about Claudia."

Sebastian shifted his feet stiffly. "I'm allergic to shellfish, but a beer would be great."

"No problem at all—they do a mean chicken pot pie there too." Hugo motioned to a decrepit, olive-green Land Rover parked under a tree. "You guys can follow me there in your car." He looked at me. "You in?"

My smile felt goofy, like it belonged to someone else. "I really love pot pie."

I cringed, wishing I could channel some of Sylvie's relaxed confidence instead of being weird and awkward.

More than that, I hated feeling like I needed her.

42

Sitting on a coastal outcrop, the exterior of the Curious Whaler lived up to its seafaring name. Battered by sea spray and salty air, its rusted awnings and peeling paint bore the weathered, world-weary appearance of a crusty old sailor.

Hugo was waiting for us at the entrance, hair blown erratically by a small squall off the bay.

"This was my grandfather's local—he'd eat lunch here nearly every day." Seeing me pull my coat tighter, Hugo pushed open the door and guided me through. "I promise it's warmer inside."

A crackling fire at one end of the pub delivered on his promise. He led us to a mahogany booth parched of varnish. "Can I take your coats?"

Sebastian shrugged out of his parka, handed it to Hugo, and then slid into the booth. "Thanks, man."

As I tried to wriggle out of my duffle coat, one of the wooden toggles caught in my hair; Hugo reached over and eased it free. I felt clumsy and inelegant, like the newborn giraffes I loved watching on the Discovery Channel.

"Thank you," I said, only briefly looking Hugo in the eye. His gaze was steadier than I was comfortable with. I was relieved to see

Sebastian preoccupied with his phone—his presence suddenly felt conspicuous.

"Please," Hugo said, gesturing for me to sit down. I shuffled into the same side as Sebastian, since Hugo's long limbs could probably use the extra room.

A white-haired woman in a faded chambray shirt and decades-old jeans arrived at our table, plastic menus tucked under her arm. Hints of an elaborate tattoo curled up from beneath her collar, distorted by neck wrinkles.

"Haven't seen your face in a while, darlin'," she said to Hugo, her hoarseness likely the mark of a lifelong love affair with nicotine.

He leaned over and kissed her on the cheek. "Hey, Roma—yeah, sorry, it's been a busy few weeks. I've been out of town for most of them."

"Lured by the big city, huh? Well, the important thing is that you're here now." Roma turned to the opposite side of the booth. "And you've brought some visitors, I see."

"Sure have—Roma, meet Clover and Sebastian."

I liked how he introduced us as if we were old friends.

"Welcome to the Curious Whaler," Roma said, forming an opinion of us she was unlikely to share. Instead, she transcribed our orders without fanfare, tucked the pen into her messy bun, then strode back through the swinging doors of the kitchen with the assured swagger of a big-hatted sheriff.

"So, you guys drove all the way from New York today?" As Hugo leaned forward, his fingers laced together on the table, I couldn't help studying his hands. Large, but somehow graceful despite the smattering of scars.

"Yep, we got an early start," Sebastian said proudly, as if a seven-hour drive was an especially impressive feat.

"Yeah, I prefer to try to do it in a straight shot too," Hugo said. "Get up before sunrise and beat as much of the traffic as possible."

Now I was intrigued. "Do you go to New York often?"

Hugo rested his long arm along the back of the banquette. "I have been lately—I'm a landscape architect and I've been consult-ing on a few projects for the city councils down there."

"That's a pretty long commute," Sebastian said.

"You're not wrong. If I were smarter, I'd think about getting a place down there." Hugo gestured to the view of the tempestuous bay out the window. "But I can't seem to tear myself away from my sea-dog roots. Just like my grandfather."

I dared myself to make eye contact with Hugo, unsure why it made me so nervous. It could've had something to do with Sebas-tian's thigh pressed against mine. I pushed my nerves away to focus on the reason we were there.

"So if your grandfather moved to the States for Claudia, why didn't he ever tell her? And how did he end up in Maine?"

"You know, I'm not exactly sure," Hugo said, apologetically. "He didn't give me too many details except to say that his biggest regret in life was letting her go."

The revelation almost made me giddy. We'd done the right thing coming here after all.

Hugo thought for a moment. "It does explain why my grandparents never really seemed that affectionate—more like good friends," he said. "I always just figured that was normal for their generation."

"Yeah," Sebastian said. "I definitely wouldn't call my grandpar-ents' marriage the happiest. My grandfather was kind of an asshole. I think my grandmother has actually been happier in the ten years since he died."

Roma arrived balancing a tray of drinks, winking at Hugo as she slid a beer, a neat bourbon, and a club soda with bitters onto the table.

Hugo raised his club soda. "Cheers."

As we clinked glasses, Sebastian nodded at Hugo's drink. "On a health kick?"

"Not quite," Hugo said, good-naturedly. "I gave up drinking a few years ago. I just don't like who I become when I drink alcohol, you know? Turns out I'm much happier without it, anyway." His relaxed self-awareness was disarming—and made me rethink my bourbon.

"Right. Good for you," Sebastian said quickly.

We all sipped in silence.

"So, it's great that you guys came up here looking for my grandfather," Hugo said, "but what did you hope would come of it? Did your grandmother ask you to find him?"

"No." Sebastian looked at me. "She doesn't know we're here."

"We didn't want to disappoint her if we couldn't find him," I said quickly in defense. "But we thought that if we did, maybe we could give her some kind of resolution before she died by being able to tell him that she always regretted not marrying him. Apparently they spent time together in Corsica."

"Ah," Hugo said. "That'd explain why he asked to have his ashes scattered there. I've been so busy with work that I haven't been able to make the trip yet."

"Claudia requested the same thing." It hurt to imagine an unfulfilled love that had endured more than half a century—loving somebody so deeply that simply being near them was your dying wish.

"You said your grandfather only passed away two months ago?" Sebastian asked Hugo. "We were so close. I wish we'd found out about this sooner."

"It really is a shame," Hugo said. "I'm guessing she doesn't have long left?"

Sebastian looked forlornly into his pint glass. "A few weeks at best, they say."

"I'm sorry, Sebastian," Hugo said. "I know how much it sucks to lose somebody you love."

"Well, I'm kind of lucky," Sebastian said, tracing the top of his glass with his thumb. "Apart from my grandfather, this is the first time I've had to deal with losing a family member." He sighed heavily, shoulders slumping again. "Any chance it gets easier the more you have to do it?"

Hugo looked pained. "I wish I could tell you that's true, but my mother died fifteen years ago and it still hurts." He watched a loose tarp writhe against the storm outside. "The truth is, grief never really goes away. Someone told me once that it's like a bag that you always carry—it starts out as a large suitcase, and as the years go by, it might reduce to the size of a purse, but you carry it forever. I know it probably sounds clichéd, but it helped me realize that I didn't need to ever get over it completely."

It almost felt like Hugo had reached over and hugged me. For a moment, my grief felt a little less solitary.

Sebastian turned to me. "What do you think? You see people die all the time."

"Yeah, but it's my job."

Hugo's eyes widened. "Your job is to watch people die?"

"Not exactly," I said, uncomfortable with the sudden focus on me. "But I do see a lot of people die as part of it."

"She's a *death doula*," Sebastian said, a little too dramatically.

"Oh, wow, that's cool," Hugo said, face lighting up. "I read an article about that the other day. It's a pretty new profession, right?"

Relieved that I didn't have to go into detail, I also felt an inkling of pride. "The term 'death doula' is, but people have been performing the role for thousands of years in one way or another. Priests, nuns, hospice workers, doctors. And even now it's kind of vague—everyone has their own interpretation of what it means."

"Interesting." Hugo sipped his drink without breaking eye contact. "And what does it mean for you?"

I searched for skepticism or judgment in his face but all I found was gentle curiosity.

"I guess it means helping someone die with dignity and peace." My palms felt clammy around my bourbon. "Sometimes it's just about them not being alone or helping them get their affairs in order before they go. Other times it's about helping them reflect back on their lives and work through any unresolved issues."

"Like tracking down a long-lost French sailor to tell him that he was her one true love?" Hugo's kind smile countered his teasing tone.

I managed a shy smile back. "Occasionally, that."

"What a beautiful thing, to help someone die with dignity," Hugo said. "It reminds me of that Leonardo da Vinci quote, what is it again? Something like, 'While I thought that I was learning how to live, I have been learning how to die.' I bet you've learned some pretty great lessons from it all."

Sebastian coughed and stared hard into his beer.

My face glowed pink.

"Yes," I said quietly. "But I haven't always been great at applying them to my own life."

Hugo shrugged. "Is anybody good at doing that, though? Most of us don't ever learn our real lessons in life until it's too late, right? I guess the important thing is that you're trying your best."

Sadness lapped at my throat. I wished I could live up to Hugo's benevolent appraisal, but Sebastian's brutal evaluation earlier that day had been much more accurate.

Observing the world, rather than engaging with it, meant I didn't have to invest emotionally. If I never got close to anyone, they couldn't leave me. Or it wouldn't hurt if they did. Better to be alone by choice—that was one thing I always had control over.

But now I realized I wasn't fooling anyone. The truth was, I wasn't trying my best—I was only living a shell of the life I knew was possible.

And I regretted it.

43

The small squall was a full-fledged gale by the time we stepped outside the Curious Whaler after dinner. Each gust of wind brought fat raindrops that defied gravity by falling sideways.

Sebastian's phone chirped in the pocket of his parka and he dug to retrieve it.

"It's my sister," he said, frowning at the screen. "I'd better take this."

Hugo and I walked a few steps away to give Sebastian privacy, sheltering from the rain under an awning.

"Thanks so much for dinner." Words were tumbling out of my mouth as I basked in the relaxed haze of the bourbon. "That was so kind of you to pay for us."

Though he'd discreetly tucked it under the ketchup bottle, I'd also noticed Hugo's generous tip for Roma.

"Of course," Hugo said. "It's the least I could do since you guys drove all the way up here to find me—well, my grandfather."

"So, this was his favorite place?" Since Hugo was much taller than me, I had to look up when speaking to him. The way he bowed his head slightly, almost deferential, felt comfortably familiar.

"Sure was. He must've eaten thousands of meals here over the years. They even started serving bouillabaisse because of him—it was the thing he missed most about France. And the pastis, of course."

"Sounds like he was beloved."

Hugo grinned. "Completely. Years ago, he basically knew everyone in town, and they all loved being around him, hearing his old sailor stories from the Mediterranean. But by the end, most of his friends had moved into nursing homes or passed away. It was pretty sad, really."

"It's the curse of longevity," I said. For once in my life, I didn't want the conversation to end. "And he lived on that houseboat?"

Hugo's curls bounced in time with his nod. "Before my grandmother died, it was kind of like his retreat when he wanted to escape into his own world. But after she was gone, he sold their old saltbox house and moved to the boat on the lake."

"You'd think he'd want to keep it in the harbor, being a sailor and all." I caught the subtle scent of cedar, and maybe a hint of cypress, rising from beneath Hugo's open jacket. I found myself leaning closer.

"I guess he preferred being surrounded by all those trees," he said. "And I can see why—it's so peaceful. I love sitting in the morning just watching nature do its thing. There's a family of ruby-throated hummingbirds that lives in the trees right next to my boat. Ever seen one of those?"

"Their wings beat up to eighty times a second, right?" *Thanks, Grandpa.*

"Right! Not many people know that."

My confidence buoyed further. "I bet Gus loves being able to run around there too."

"You remembered my dog's name—I'm impressed." Hugo leaned his head to the side appreciatively. "You're a dog lover then?"

"I have a bulldog named George. But he does not enjoy running around outdoors."

Hugo laughed. "Typical city dog."

"Exactly."

Sebastian was frowning in our direction, still arguing with his sister.

"So, where are you guys staying tonight?" Hugo asked, trying not to eavesdrop.

"I booked us a couple of rooms at a motel just outside of Lincolnville." I'd felt safer being in control of the sleeping arrangements.

"Oh," Hugo said, looking over at Sebastian. "I figured you guys were . . . together."

"Definitely not." I giggled. "I'm just doing my job, you know, helping his grandmother."

"Got it." Hugo slid his hands in his pockets. "It's really good of you to go to all this trouble to help her find some resolution before she dies. I just wish we could've somehow brought her and my grandfather together."

I nodded. "Sadly it happens more often than you'd think—people don't realize how they feel about someone or something until their lives are almost over." I pulled my coat tighter against the wind.

"A good lesson for us all, huh?" Hugo positioned himself sideways so that his back was blocking me from the gale. "So, what would you regret, Clover?"

For the first time in months, it felt impossible to lie. The words had already formed on my tongue. "Well . . ."

I felt a firm tap on my shoulder.

"Ready to go?" Sebastian's voice was impatient.

I looked apologetically at Hugo, since Sebastian didn't seem to care that he'd interrupted our conversation. "Yes, I guess so. Is everything okay with your sister?"

"Yeah, she's just being bossy as usual, trying to take control of things with Grandma even though she's hardly visited her this whole time." He scuffed his shoe against the gravel. "Anyway, we should get to the motel, since we have to get up early tomorrow."

Unfortunately Sebastian didn't realize how bossy he could be too.

"Sure—want me to drive?" I'd probably had one bourbon too many to be driving on roads I didn't know in the dark. But from the way Sebastian was swaying, he was even more inebriated, which would only be worsened by his agitated state.

Sebastian frowned unsteadily at me. "Fine." He plonked the keys into my palm and strode toward the car.

I pressed the remote to unlock the vehicle just before he reached it so that he didn't have another reason to be irritated.

"He's probably just stressed about his grandma," Hugo said gently.

His kindness lessened the sting a little. "Yes, probably." Though our argument earlier in the day might have also had something to do with it.

"You know, the roads around here can get pretty hairy with no streetlights and all those potholes—especially after you've had a few drinks." Hugo half smiled as he zipped up his jacket. "How about you guys follow me to the motel? I'm pretty sure I know which one you're talking about, since we don't have many. The one with the blue doors on the way to Camden, right?"

"Yes," I said, recalling the photos on the website. Under other circumstances, it would be a lovely place for a romantic getaway. "That'd be great, if it's not too much trouble."

"No trouble at all," Hugo said, pulling out his own keys. "Some high school friends of mine actually own it—it's a cute little place."

Sebastian and I drove in silence as I concentrated on Hugo's taillights burning against the darkness. The motel was only eight minutes away, but it was down an embankment and the roadside was pitch-black. My dulled senses would've easily missed it if Hugo hadn't slowed to a stop and flashed his hazard lights.

"Great to meet you guys," he called through the open car window. "Safe travels back to Claudia."

The crunch of tires on gravel became the whir of rubber on blacktop as he made a U-turn on the narrow two-lane and waved goodbye.

While Sebastian continued texting impetuously with his sister, I watched Hugo's taillights dissolve into the moonlit fog that floated above the road like cotton candy.

Puzzled by the weight I felt just below my collar bones, I put my hand to my chest.

I'd only known Hugo for a few hours, but somehow I was sad to see him go.

44

For the sixteenth time that day, I watched Kevin Costner stand stoically on the tarmac, arm in a sling, staring at an airplane window framing Whitney Houston's silhouette. As she ordered the taxiing plane to a halt and sprinted down its steps into his embrace—her iconic ballad swelling in the background—I felt a vicarious twinge in my heart.

Painful and euphoric at the same time.

It had been a week since I'd gotten back from the road trip to Maine, and the leather bag still sat on the living room floor, yet to be unpacked.

Sebastian and I had hardly said a word to each other on the seven-hour drive back home, except for one brief conversation somewhere in the southeast corner of New Hampshire. I'd been so deep in my own thoughts, my mind swirling in the romance of Hugo and Claudia, that I jumped when he spoke.

"We're definitely not telling Grandma about any of this," he said abruptly. "There's no point."

Since I'd spent the last three hours excitedly planning exactly how to reveal the news to Claudia, this came as a surprise.

"But it would bring her some peace to hear that Hugo always loved her. She deserves to know."

Sebastian glared at the horizon, clenching the steering wheel. "Deserves to know that the supposed love of her life was living a car ride away for the past sixty years? That she could've lived an entirely different life from the one she apparently now regrets, even though she has a family who loves her? No way."

I swallowed the words of protest forming in my throat. He had a point. It must have hurt to find out that his grandmother had spent most of her married life unhappy. And I'd never forgive myself if I caused Claudia to die with even more regrets than she already had.

But it somehow still felt wrong not to tell her.

"Okay," I said, consciously stripping my voice of emotion. "She's your grandma, so it's your decision."

I slumped back in my seat and stared out the window for the rest of the drive while Sebastian buffered our simmering silence with an endless procession of podcasts.

And for the week since our trip, I'd made sure to schedule my visits to Claudia for when I knew he'd be at work. After his bleak assessment of my life choices, it seemed we had nothing more to say to each other.

S quinting against the darkness even though it was early afternoon, I switched on the reading lamp by Grandpa's chair. I hadn't opened the blinds since my confrontation with Sylvie—I still didn't want to imagine what might be taking place in the windows across the street. I'd timed most of my exits from my apartment to early morning and late evening, so I'd managed to avoid her completely. And I'd told Leo that I'd come down with the flu and didn't want to infect him.

I didn't even feel like going to a death café. I just wanted to be alone.

Snuggling George against my stomach, I resisted the impulse to replay the scene a seventeenth time. Yesterday I'd binged on Tom Cruise's manically earnest declaration of love to Renée Zellweger.

The day before that, it was Hugh Grant interrupting Julia Roberts's press conference to profess his love. But no matter how many times I watched, or mouthed the words along with them, the truth still stung.

Some people just didn't get a happy ending, even if I tried my best to give them one.

And that made my chances of a happy ending, even if I wasn't sure what that would look like, feel even further away.

I forced myself to turn off the TV—this cycle of binge-watching wasn't numbing my loneliness like it usually did. I looked around my apartment for an alternative. All I could see were reminders of Grandpa—his insects frozen in resin, his beloved kangaroo skull, his tarnished brass compass—and it hit me how disappointed he would be in me. Instead of following in his footsteps, engaging my curiosity by traveling the world and decoding its patterns, I'd become a loner with an increasing penchant for dishonesty. Someone who spied on her neighbors and chose to spend her time with dying people so she didn't have to develop lasting relationships with anyone.

Sebastian was right—I was a hypocrite. I spent my days looking death in the face and I still hadn't found a way to manage my own grief. I'd been clinging on to Grandpa's memory, and his possessions, even though he was long gone. And I dedicated more time to honoring the lessons and wisdom of other people's lives than I did to living my own.

But the notebook ritual was the one thing that I knew could help pull me out of this sense of hopelessness.

I grabbed the REGRETS book from the shelf, closed my eyes, and allowed it to fall open to a random page.

Jack Rainer, a fifty-six-year-old lawyer with long eyelashes, a dry sense of humor, and an inoperable brain tumor.

I wish I'd learned my wife's native language.

When he met Ditya, a pastry chef, on a business trip to Kathmandu, her English had consisted of the pop lyrics she'd learned via her passion for karaoke. But when she moved to be with him in New York, she worked hard to learn the language so that she could communicate with him and his friends and eventually open her own patisserie in Midtown.

"You know, I never bothered to learn Nepali because I thought I had no use for it," Jack had told me days before the tumor began to suppress his speech. It had already stolen his eyesight, so he spoke to my general vicinity rather than directly to me. "But I was bored waiting at the dentist last year and the only thing to read was a book of inspirational quotes. And there was one from Nelson Mandela that said, 'If you talk to a man in a language he understands, that goes to his head. If you talk to him in his language, that goes to his heart.'"

I pressed my hand to his arm. "That's beautiful—I've never heard that one."

"It made me realize that all the times I complimented her, it was always in English. I never even thought to ask how to say it in her language. So I never really spoke to her heart."

Balancing the notebook on the chair arm, I reached for my laptop. I'd probably never have a use for Nepali either, but, in Jack's memory, I could learn the basics. I signed up for a two-week online course, starting next month.

One small step forward. I felt a little better already.

I flipped through the notebook, planning how many people's regrets I could honor in the time before my next visit with Claudia.

Alison, a nun who'd always wanted to dye her hair blue.

Una, a bank CEO who'd never gone ice-skating in Central Park.

Harry, a kindhearted carpenter who'd wished he'd ignored his brothers' taunts and learned how to knit.

I might even adopt a hamster for Guillermo.

And when I was finished, maybe it was time I addressed my own regrets.

45

The back of my jeans was still damp from repeatedly falling on the ice. And judging from the ache in my butt and thighs, I'd just used muscles that had been dormant for years. But as I limped away from the Wollman Rink in Central Park later that afternoon, I felt like I'd been useful.

While shuffling around the ice rink, daring myself to let go of the rail, I had imagined Una skating next to me, her high cheekbones flushed with red. I'd breathed in the smell of roasted chestnuts floating from the stand on Fifth Avenue. I'd marveled at the twisted tree limbs contrasting with the clean geometry of shiny skyscrapers. I'd laughed at the toddlers in their puffy coats, envying their low centers of gravity as they glided fearlessly past me on the ice. Thanks to Una, I'd never regret not going ice-skating in Central Park. And hopefully she'd been with me in spirit.

Now I had to find some blue hair dye and knitting needles.

As I dug for my phone in my coat to google nearby craft stores, I felt it vibrating with a call.

I was relieved when I saw it wasn't Sebastian or Sylvie—it was a number I didn't have saved, so probably someone calling about work. But it felt too soon to commit to a new client, even if Claudia didn't have much longer.

I stepped off the sidewalk to let a cluster of neon-clad joggers pass. "Hello, Clover speaking."

All I heard in response was a bark.

"Hello?" I repeated, a little impatiently.

"Oh, hi, Clover." The familiar voice made my heart thump. Another excited bark. "Gus! Chill, buddy." The sound of the phone fumbling. "Sorry, Clover—hang on a sec."

"Um, sure." My mind spun through all the possible reasons Hugo might be calling; perhaps I'd left my scarf at the Curious Whaler.

"Okay, I'm back," Hugo said. "Sorry about that—Gus was trying to chase a squirrel. Oh, and it's Hugo, by the way."

"Hi, Hugo." I waited for my usual phone-call anxiety to kick in, but it didn't.

"I hope it's okay that I'm calling you." I could hear the smile in his voice. "I got your number from my friends who own the motel you stayed at. To be honest, I've been debating whether it was a creepy thing to do, but then I decided that you'd probably want to know."

"Know what?" An inexplicable energy buzzed under my skin.

"Well, a few days after you guys were here, I decided to finally go through a crate of my grandfather's things that he'd left on the boat. I'd been avoiding it for months." I could definitely relate to that. "And there was an old shoebox in there."

"Okay . . ."

"It was filled with letters from Claudia, plus a couple that he wrote to her but never sent. There's a photo of her in there too."

That ice-skating really made my legs feel like jelly. "Did you read any of them?"

"Just one." Hugo's nervous laugh was endearing. "But it was so intimate. Not in a sexual kind of way, thank God, but just the longing of it all. It makes me so sad that they never found their way back to each other."

The low, gentle tone of his voice felt calming. "Me too."

"I was thinking that it might help Claudia to see them, and to know he kept them . . . if it's not too late. It would make me feel like

I did one last thing for him." Another bark from Gus. "How is she doing?"

I thought back to my last conversation with Sebastian. Maybe the letters would be enough to convince him to let me tell Claudia.

"I don't think she has much longer—a week at best. Probably not enough time for you to send them down here." I wondered how much a one-day courier from Maine would cost. Even if it was several hundred dollars, I'd be willing to pay if it meant giving Claudia a small sense of resolution.

"Actually," Hugo said, "Gus and I are in New York right now—I had to come down for a work thing." In the background, a fire engine wailed in confirmation. "We're headed back home tonight, but maybe I could meet you somewhere and give you the letters this afternoon?"

"Um, sure, that would be great." Pulse thumping, I frantically tried to think of an appropriate meeting place. After Sylvie's critical reaction to my apartment, there was no way I'd invite anyone else in there. "There's a nice café in my neighborhood that's dog friendly. I can text you the address."

Was it reckless to agree so quickly to meet up with a virtual stranger? Or since we'd already eaten dinner together, perhaps that bumped us up to acquaintances. I'd only met him once, but it felt like I'd known Hugo for longer.

"Great," he said brightly. "Can't wait to see you, Clover."

My legs didn't hurt so much anymore.

Hugo was wearing the wool sweater I'd seen hanging on the houseboat railing. The cable knit clung to his broad shoulders as he leaned against the brick wall outside the café. When he grinned in my direction, I almost turned to check if it was intended for someone behind me. The warmth of it felt like more than I'd earned.

Gus, who'd been making the most of the olfactory wonderland that is a New York City sidewalk, trotted over and rested his front paws on my thighs. I cupped his face between my hands.

"Hey, Clover!" Hugo looped Gus's leash around his wrist to rein him in. "I'm so happy we could make this work."

"I'm glad you called me." I was also glad that I hadn't had time to dye my hair blue.

"Of course." That grin again. He gestured at the old shoebox under his arm. "Should we go inside and read these over coffee?"

"Definitely." I walked quickly through the door he was holding open and wondered if a heart could beat eighty times per second.

The café was even more packed than the last time I was there, with Sylvie. It felt like years, not months, since that first coffee we'd had together. I missed her company and frank advice.

Anxiety knotted in my stomach as I scanned the room for an empty table. I didn't have a backup plan, but, mostly, I didn't want to disappoint Hugo. The knots loosened as I spied the only unoccupied table: my favorite single-seater in the corner.

"Here, you sit down and I'll find us another chair," Hugo said.

I watched him approach two women across the room, observing how they played with their hair and giggled like he'd made a really funny joke and not just asked to borrow their extra chair. I felt their eyes scrutinizing me, questioning my presence as he sat down across from me. Even the server delivered our coffees like I was an afterthought, her attention trained solely on Hugo as she slid the drinks between us. I was grateful for Gus pressing his head against my leg under the table.

But Hugo seemed to tune everyone out but me.

The times I'd been with Sebastian, he'd always seemed distracted, looking around at other tables, or his phone, like he was checking to see if something more interesting was happening. I liked the way Hugo listened closely to what I said, catching mundane details and asking about them like he actually wanted to know the answer.

I almost forgot that we were there to read the letters.

We worked our way through the yellowed envelopes, piecing together the timeline. After Claudia had come home from France in the summer of 1956, she'd continued to write Hugo's grandfather letters, mostly about how conflicted she was about getting married and giving up her photography career.

"It seems like he must have tried to convince her to come back to France and marry him instead," Hugo said, scanning the letter in his hand. "Are there any more letters from her?"

His knee brushed against my thigh under the small table as he leaned over to look into the shoebox. I concentrated on sifting through the remaining envelopes instead of the feeling of my legs dissolving.

One letter was thinner than the rest.

"Only one." I pulled out the dainty note card and read Claudia's perfectly slanted cursive.

Hugo—
    We are not meant to be in this lifetime . . . perhaps we will meet in another.
    I'll keep you in my heart until then.

—Claudia

We sat wordlessly, processing the finality of Claudia's words. The noise of the crowded café felt distant, inconsequential.

"That's it? No other explanation?" Hugo frowned at the note card. "That's pretty harsh. Knowing how sensitive my grandpa was, that must've really broken his heart."

I imagined the yearning between the two young lovers, letting it spill through my body like it was my own. Even though I knew it ended in pain, I still envied their intimacy.

The remaining letters were addressed to Claudia and still sealed. "None of these have stamps or postage marks," I said, picking up the first one. It almost felt illicit to tear it open.

Hugo's grandfather wrote mostly in English with smatterings of stream-of-consciousness French.

"*You inhabit my waking moments and my dreams*," I read aloud from the letter. "Wow. Except for his slightly indecipherable handwriting, his written English was really good. And for a guy in the 1950s, he was unusually in touch with his emotions."

Sadness tempered Hugo's smile. "Yeah, he was always that way— told me he loved me every time he saw me."

"That's really special." I sipped my coffee, hoping it would soothe the pang of envy.

Hugo nodded. "I was lucky to have him."

I skimmed the letter. "It looks like he responded to her, asking her to change her mind, but he never actually sent it."

"I wonder why?" Hugo bent forward to look at the letter, and I caught the hint of cedar and cypress.

"Maybe just writing these letters gave him closure," I said, noticing a small hole in the shoulder of Hugo's sweater. "Or he was respecting her space and her choice. It's kind of honorable when you think about it."

Hugo looked down at the table, disappointed. "It just kills me knowing that he lived most of his life with a broken heart. Is it weird that I wish he'd fought for her?"

I couldn't help smiling. It was endearing how viscerally he empathized with his grandfather's longing.

"It shows how much you wanted your grandpa to be happy. I think that's really sweet."

Determination wrinkled Hugo's forehead. "He must've tried to tell her that he was in America, otherwise what was the point of him moving all the way here, especially in the 1950s? I know my grandpa—he wouldn't give up that easily." He rifled through the letters. "This looks like the only one we haven't read."

He cleared his throat and began to read.

My dear Claudia,

You'll always think that the last time we saw each other was through the window of your departing train as it pulled out of the station in Marseille on that humid day in July.

Really, it was in New York City on a windy day in November a year later. I went to that bookstore in Midtown, the one you told me was your favorite. The one where you said you went whenever you needed to feel comfort and safety.

It was a way to still feel you even if you weren't there. To perhaps touch the same books that you once touched, to admire the same architecture that you loved so much.

But you were there in the flesh, with him. I stood upstairs on the mezzanine watching with envy. He placed his hand on the small of your back and you smiled up at him with that glint in your eye—the one that I selfishly thought existed only for me.

I came to New York for you. If you couldn't live in France, I would move here for you. But that day in the bookstore I saw that you were better off without me. You were cared for and happy. And so I said nothing. I just watched you walk away with your hand in his.

You were right—this life isn't the right one for us.

I'll see you in the next one.

"Wow," Hugo said, leaning back in the oak chair, which seemed to shrink against his tall frame. "So that's it. He moved here for her and never told her."

"They were so close to being together." The thought of such a near miss made it even sadder.

"He must've wanted me to know about it, or he wouldn't have left that box in the boat." Hugo took the shoebox and began sifting methodically through the letters to make sure we hadn't missed one. When no more materialized, he piled them back in and pushed the lid on, frustrated.

Then he grabbed both my hands and looked me firmly in the eye.

"Clover, you've got to tell Claudia he still loved her."

46

Selma usually answered Claudia's front door, but when I arrived at the townhouse the next day, it swung open to Sarah, Sebastian's eldest sister. I'd never met her, but my first impression was that Sebastian's description of her was accurate—tall, pointy, and perpetually disapproving.

"Clover, right?" The deep lines between her eyebrows indicated that a frown was her neutral facial expression. "Grandma's been asking for you. We should go upstairs."

She turned briskly, beckoning me to follow.

On the third-floor landing, two women who looked like distortions of Sarah stood stage-whispering, their faces red and hair astray. Jennifer was the middle sister, Anne was the stockiest and youngest, and both gave me a conspicuous once-over. All four siblings shared a similar hawkish nose.

"Can we go in?" Sarah motioned impatiently toward Claudia's door.

Anne stood imperiously in front of it, as if stationed there by some higher authority. "Dad's in there with the doctor. You'll have to wait until they're done."

"Is she conscious?" I spoke softly to defuse the obvious power struggle.

The sisters' heads snapped toward me.

"Yes," Jennifer said solemnly. "But she's been sleeping a lot."

"That's pretty normal," I said. "Her body is getting weaker, especially if she hasn't been eating much."

"She refuses to eat anything but doughnuts," Sarah said, face pinched. "I tried to convince her to drink a green smoothie but she wouldn't even consider it."

I hid a smile—I would have loved to see Claudia's reaction to that proposition.

The door opened and a man with the same hawkish nose walked out, another balding man close behind him.

"Dad, Roger, this is Clover," Sarah said tersely. "She's been helping Selma and Joyce take care of Grandma."

"Ah, the death doula," Roger boomed. "I've been encountering more and more of your kind recently. Good folk, you are."

"Thank you." I blushed, avoiding the sisters' collective expression of judgment. "How is she?"

Roger pulled the door shut behind him. "Not great, I'm afraid. I'd say she has only a day or so left." He looked around at Sebastian's family. "I've advised everyone to say their goodbyes while they can."

Anne snorted a sob and pulled a tissue from the pocket of her culottes. Her father watched her stoically but said nothing. Nobody tried to comfort her.

The hallway felt cramped with so many of us standing close together, and I could smell cigarettes on Roger's blazer. The wall blocked my attempt to step backward and reclaim some personal space.

"Is Sebastian on his way?" No matter how I felt about seeing him personally, he needed to be here for Claudia. I'd never want him to miss the chance to say goodbye.

Sarah rolled her eyes. "He said he'd be here soon, but he's taking his sweet time as usual."

The more I interacted with Sebastian's sisters, the better I began to understand him. No wonder he spent so much time at Claudia's house growing up.

"Okay," I said. "I can keep Claudia company if there's anything you need to take care of?" She likely needed a break from all her visitors. "I'll let you know if anything changes with her condition."

"Thanks." Sarah herded everyone else along the hall. "We'll be downstairs in the kitchen with Mom."

Claudia looked even smaller than when I'd last seen her two days ago. When the door clicked shut, her eyes fluttered open and she managed a slight smile.

"Oh, thank the Lord. I thought it was my granddaughters back to inundate me with their overwrought opinions and emotional hysterics." Shallow breaths punctuated her sentences. "I've been dying to see you, Clover—pun absolutely intended, because what's the point of being close to death if you can't make use of wordplay."

I sat in the chair closest to the bed and pressed her hand between mine. "I'm happy to see you too."

"From the looks on everyone's faces, it seems as though my knell is sounding." Claudia shifted her head to catch my eye. "Tell me the truth, my darling. You're the only one who ever does."

I smiled back calmly. "Yes, I think it's almost time. How are you feeling about it?"

It was always hard to acknowledge this moment, to look someone in the eye and affirm that their entire existence was coming to an end. But the conviction that I was giving them the chance to navigate their final moments with clarity and grace always helped me temper my own discomfort.

"Honestly? I know my family means well, but I can't take all of their fussing." The signature glint briefly returned to Claudia's eyes. "I've been pretending to be asleep so they would leave me alone for a while."

"Living on your own terms until the end—good for you." I could see the network of veins glowing beneath her pallid skin. "Is it okay that I'm here? I can let you rest if you want."

Claudia squeezed my hand. "Stay, please." She was slowly becoming more alert. "How about you tell me about that shoebox you're holding? I imagine it's not a parting gift."

I moved the box to my lap. "Actually, it kind of is."

"Oh?" Claudia perked up further. "Do tell."

I'd decided against telling Sebastian about the letters for now. Aside from the unresolved tension following our road trip, it felt unfair to saddle him with more details of his grandmother's lost love while he was grappling with her impending passing. I thought about locking the door behind me, but realized it would be hard to explain if somebody tried to come in. I positioned the chair so my back was to it, giving me time to conceal the letters if necessary.

"Well, after you told me about Hugo, I did a bit of digging with the help of a friend."

Claudia's eyes widened. "And what did you . . . dig up?"

I inhaled, preparing myself to say what I'd practiced in my head so many times. "We found out that he actually moved to the United States, not long after you left France, and was living in Maine up until recently."

I paused to let the news sink in.

Confusion clouded Claudia's face. "I don't understand."

"He came to New York to find you." I may have been gushing a little. "But then he saw you together with your husband and thought you looked really happy, so he decided not to intrude." Not the most romantic telling of the story, but it was a good summary.

Tears teetered on Claudia's lower lashes. "He came for me?"

"Yes!"

"You mean . . . he's still alive?"

This was the part I wasn't looking forward to. I tightened my grip on her hand.

"Unfortunately, we learned that he passed away a couple of months ago," I said softly, wishing there was a better way to deliver the news. "I'm sorry, Claudia."

When she finally spoke, her voice was small. "I'd assumed he was likely long gone, but death is less painful when it's hypothetical."

She gazed at the ceiling as if watching the replay reel of her life, editing it to include the ending she had feared but never confirmed. I sat silently until she turned to face me.

"We did find something else," I said, sliding the lid off the shoebox. "His grandson. And he gave us these letters that Hugo wrote to you. They say that you were the love of his life—that no one ever came close to you."

It was the first time I'd ever seen Claudia flustered. "He really said that?"

I rubbed her shoulder, where barely anything now separated bone from skin. "Would you like me to read them to you?"

Her tears began to spill gently, navigating the wrinkles of her cheeks like riverbeds.

"Please."

47

I spent the next two hours reading the letters aloud, stopping at Claudia's request to repeat certain passages.

"I remember that November day in the bookstore," she whispered as I folded Hugo's final letter. "My husband and I had argued that morning because he wouldn't allow me to leave the house wearing trousers. I was so angry—so I fled to the bookstore, which was the only place that felt like I could be my true self." She closed her eyes, journeying back. "He found me there and apologized like he always did, in his very charismatic way. I realized in that moment that if I ever wanted to have a child, I had few choices but to forgive him."

"Did you ever think about going back to France to be with Hugo?"

Claudia's tired smile balanced melancholy. "After I wrote my final letter to him, I told myself that if he wrote back trying to change my mind, I would go." The smile faded. "But he never did."

"Well, he did—he just didn't send it. But his grandson told me that he loved you until the day he died. You were always his great love."

The curl of Claudia's fingers around my hand relaxed and she closed her eyes again. "And he was mine."

With a steady rise and fall of her chest, she slipped into a contented sleep.

The sudden opening of the bedroom door startled me. I quickly stuffed the shoebox into my tote and tried my best not to look guilty.

"Hey." Sebastian stood gloomily in the doorway, clutching his scarf between his fists. "I hear you met my sisters."

"I did." I offered a small smile. "They must have been a lot to grow up with."

"That's an understatement."

Even through his glasses, I could tell Sebastian was exhausted and it looked like he hadn't shaved in a couple of days. But as he smiled back wearily, I realized the simmering resentment I'd felt since our road trip was gone. Especially because I'd finally admitted to myself that there'd been truth in what he'd said about my life, even if his delivery felt cruel.

Now I just felt sorry for him. Losing someone you loved really sucked, and there was nothing anyone could say that would make it hurt any less. I was almost tempted to hug him.

Instead, I stood up from the chair and motioned for him to sit. "Claudia just drifted off to sleep, but I'm sure she'd love for you to sit and talk to her."

Sebastian's body tensed, but he followed my direction. As I closed the door on my way out, I heard him begin telling her about a podcast he'd just listened to.

The early evening light caught the caramel wood of the cello in Claudia's library, where I sat paging through a biography of Henri Cartier-Bresson.

"It's weird, right, how my grandmother's literally on her deathbed and no one in my family wants to talk about it?"

Sebastian was leaning against the bookshelf by the door. When I'd gone downstairs to get a drink of water, his family had been discussing everything except the very thing they didn't want to acknowledge.

"Not really," I said, setting the book down. "Lots of people find it hard to talk about death, even when it's happening. But you did your best to help your grandmother through this. I know she appreciates it."

"I guess so." Sebastian sat down next to me and picked up the whale paperweight, which had somehow made it to the coffee table. "But it was really you who spent all the time with her."

"True, but you were the one who found me—because you wanted to help her."

He passed the whale distractedly from one hand to the other. "I just feel like I could be doing more, you know? Instead of just sitting here, waiting for her to die."

I looked down at the tote bag by my leg, debating whether to tell him about the letters. It would still probably just complicate things. Maybe I could tell him one day when the wound wasn't as raw.

"Do you feel like you've said everything that you need to?"

"I mean, I told her how important she's been to me and that I'm grateful to have had her as my grandma." He looked at his hands, embarrassed. "We don't really ever say 'I love you' in this family. It'd kind of feel forced if I did."

And I'd feel like a hypocrite if I tried to convince him otherwise.

"She knows how much you love her, even if you don't say it."

"Maybe." His deep breath and exhale seemed exaggerated—until I realized he was preparing to say something else. "Clover," he said, putting the paperweight back on the table. "I'm sorry for the way things turned out on our trip to Maine and for what I said. I was kind of a jerk to you. But I want you to know that I think you're great, and that it's pretty amazing what you do for people like Grandma."

I definitely didn't see that coming.

"Oh, thank you," I said, slowly processing the compliment. "And I'm sorry for reacting the way I did. I think it hurt so much because a lot of what you said was true." It felt surprisingly cathartic to admit that. "I do use my work as an excuse not to get close to people. And there's a lot of things I probably would regret if I knew I was going to die tomorrow."

Tick-tick. Tick-tick. Tick-tick.

The rhythm of the old pendulum clock on the wall suddenly seemed much louder than usual.

Sebastian's leg started jackhammering. "So, there's also something else I should probably tell you."

Since the past few weeks had been full of sensational revelations, I wasn't really surprised there was another one. I steeled myself for whatever was to come.

He moved to face me. "I know you said you wanted to cool things down between us until after Grandma . . . you know."

"Yes."

"Well, it turns out that I'm kind of back together with Jessie." He eyed me warily as I tried to place the name. "We ran into her when we were at the bar that time, remember?"

The trio of brunettes. "Right, I do remember." I braced myself for everything movies and TV shows taught me I should feel in response to this news—rejection, jealousy, betrayal, heartache.

But all I felt was really, really relieved.

I even double-checked to make sure I wasn't lying to myself by just numbing the other feelings. Nope, definitely relieved. But maybe I should pretend to be a little disappointed.

"I really appreciate you letting me know." I hoped it didn't sound indifferent.

"Of course." Sebastian's leg stopped jackhammering. "I'm sorry things didn't work out for us—I guess it just wasn't the right timing, huh?"

The knock on the door, on the other hand, felt like excellent timing. Until I saw the look on Selma's face.

"I think you'd better come," she said to us soberly.

As soon as we walked into Claudia's room, I noticed it—that distinct yet indescribable smell.

Though her breaths were labored, Claudia was still conscious.

"I'll go get everyone from downstairs," Selma said, her usually officious demeanor softer.

Sebastian stood frozen in the doorway. "Uh, I'll be right back." He turned abruptly and left.

I sat beside Claudia, resting my hand on her forehead.

"Thank you for bringing me some peace," Claudia whispered. "There's so much I regret about this life, and you're helping me leave it with my soul a little less burdened for the next one." She stopped to catch her breath. "And I'm ready for the next one."

"I bet he's waiting for you there." It didn't even feel like a merciful embellishment.

Claudia settled back on her pillow. "Learn from my mistakes, my darling." Each word was quieter, more staccato than the last. "Don't let the best parts of life pass you by because you're too scared of the unknown." One last wink. "Be cautiously reckless."

Sebastian reappeared, lugging his cello into the room, its spike catching against the ridges in the carpet. He pulled another chair next to the bed and balanced the instrument between his knees.

"I thought you might want to hear some music, Grandma," he said tenderly.

Claudia nodded sleepily.

Sebastian positioned his hand high on the neck, his fingers hovering over the strings. His head nodded as he counted himself in. Then he pulled the bow across the lowest string in one long note that merged into a slow rendition of Billie Holiday's "I'll Be Seeing You."

I stood up and receded into the corner next to Selma, as the rest of the family shuffled into the room.

Gathering around Claudia's bed, they allowed Sebastian's music to say what they could not.

48

The walk from Claudia's house on the Upper West Side to my apartment took almost two hours, but I barely even noticed the time passing. I didn't mind being slowed down by the gaggle of schoolkids walking in a serpent of pairs along the edge of Central Park. They couldn't have been more than seven years old. If they were lucky to live as long as Claudia, that meant they'd still have eighty-four years of life ahead of them. I wondered how long it would be until that look of wonderment in their eyes dulled and their curiosity stopped burning. When living became a habit rather than a privilege and the years ticked by unnoticed.

The world felt a little emptier, like it always did when one of my clients had just passed, but this time the hole was more pronounced. It's funny how you don't notice how significant someone's presence is until it's no longer there. I already missed Claudia's wit and warmth. Yes, she'd died with regrets, but she had still lived out loud, unafraid to take up space in the world, never losing her sense of adventure and playfulness. As I walked home, I began to realize that this was first time I'd encountered a woman whose approach to life I could aspire to.

"How about a photo, baby?"

A man in a cheap Batman costume stood in front of me, hands on his hips and chest thrust outward.

I'd been so caught up in my thoughts that my feet had somehow taken me right into the neon-drenched triangular block that any self-respecting New Yorker avoids. But despite the flashing billboards, the competing street musicians, the mishmash of languages and accents spoken at obnoxious volumes, today I found Times Square oddly comforting. The energy, the noise, and the frenetic movement were all symbols of the living. Of paths crossing, of memories being etched into psyches, of the beginnings of youthful dreams. And most of all, of a blissful ignorance that your time could be up at any moment.

I stood still, right in the thick of it, allowing myself to be the swaying seaweed for once instead of the darting fish. Closing my eyes, I breathed in the comfortably familiar blend of smoky pretzels, rotting trash, and car exhaust, and let the auditory chaos beat against my eardrums.

I was still here, still living.

But was I just existing out of habit?

George was sitting in darkness on his dog bed when I arrived home—I'd forgotten to leave a light on in my apartment before I left that morning. He squinted when I switched on the lamp, but otherwise didn't move. As my own eyes adjusted, I noticed something resting under his chin: the REGRETS notebook, lying open. It must have somehow fallen from the shelf—strange, since it was jammed in pretty tightly. I hurried over to rescue it, praying that it wasn't saturated in drool, rendering the entries illegible. George grunted as I eased it out from under him.

I exhaled in relief—everything was intact. Settling onto the sofa, I looked at the notebook in my hands, and its ADVICE and CON-FESSIONS counterparts still on the shelf.

Those books weren't just a collection of people's final words. They were also a record of some of my most meaningful encounters.

From the outside, I might have helped those people, but, really, they'd helped me more. They had helped fill the void of intimacy that I felt so keenly in my own life. And by carrying out rituals inspired by their regrets, advice, and confessions, I wasn't just honoring my clients' memories. The truth was, I'd been using the notebooks to avoid the fact that, subconsciously, I knew exactly which one I'd end up in.

I'd accepted regret as the foregone conclusion of my life.

The question was, how could I change that? I'd spent the last thirty-six years coming to grips with the idea that it was difficult to be anything other than what the world already thinks you are. But what about what you already think you are—was it possible for me to change what I believed about myself?

I took a deep breath, then grabbed the pencil I usually used for crosswords.

Turning to a blank page in the REGRETS notebook, I wrote my name at the top.

Clover Brooks

I regret not taking more chances.

I regret closing off my heart.

I regret existing out of habit.

An invisible weight lifted from my shoulders. As I sat rereading my entry, I felt something other than the despair I'd been expecting to consume me.

Hope.

Documenting my regrets didn't make them inevitable. It gave me a gift that I hadn't been able to give anyone else in this notebook—a chance to do things differently before it was too late. My regrets were written in pencil, after all.

I stood and walked to the window, slowly raising the blinds so that the streetlight spilled across the floorboards. My pulse thundered in my ears as I prepared myself for what I might see. But while the window opposite glowed, the living room was empty.

The sound of clinking glass rose from the street below. I looked down to investigate and saw a familiar figure standing next to our stoop, her ponytail swinging as she dropped several bottles into the recycling bin.

Next right step forward.

Before I could overthink it, I grabbed the bag of recycling from the kitchen and forced myself out my front door.

Sylvie was about to walk up the stoop when I stepped outside. We stood—me at the top, her at the bottom—watching each other, as if waiting to see who would draw first. I knew it had to be me.

"Hi, Sylvie."

I'd never seen her look surprised until now. "Oh, hey, Clover." The exclamation point that usually accompanied her greetings was noticeably absent. "It's been a while."

"Yeah, it has." I desperately wanted to break eye contact but forced myself to hold it. "I'm sorry I haven't been around much." Not quite the apology I'd intended, but I could work my way up to it. I lifted the bag in my hand. "Ugh, these cat-food cans really stink."

I thought I detected a smile in Sylvie's eyes. "I figured you were busy with work." She leaned against the banister. "How's Claudia doing?"

"She actually passed away this afternoon." It felt too soon to say those words, even though they were true. Death felt oddly temporary at first. It would be a few days before I would feel ready to document her words in the ADVICE notebook.

"Oh, C, I'm sorry." I'd forgotten how soothing it was to hear her call me that.

I shrugged. "It's all part of the job."

"Yeah, but that doesn't make it easier—I know you cared about her." Sylvie walked up a step then stopped. "Did you end up finding Hugo?"

It took me a beat to realize she was talking about Claudia's Hugo—she didn't even know the other one existed. I hated how much I'd kept from her.

I moved down a step.

"Kind of. It's a long story." It was so tempting to weasel out of the apology I owed her, but if Sebastian could do it, so could I. "But first I want to say how sorry I am for the way I acted the last time I saw you."

Sylvie crossed her arms and grinned. "Yeah, that was kind of weird."

"It's none of my business who you kiss and who they're married to."

"You're right," she said, frank but not unkind. "You know, I mentioned your name to Bridget, and she said she didn't know you."

"Oh, she's right—I don't really know her." The sweat of my palms clung to the plastic bag. "I think I've seen her at the bodega on the corner a few times. I must've confused her with someone else."

"I guess you did." A slyness shone in Sylvie's eyes. "But when I mentioned that you lived upstairs from me, Bridget realized that you must be directly opposite her and Peter, her husband. And she asked me if you watched a lot of nineties romantic comedies."

A strange giggle escaped my throat.

Sylvie seemed to be enjoying watching me squirm. "Apparently they can see into your apartment from theirs. She said that they've never really seen you because you keep your apartment so dark, but they've got a pretty good view of your TV screen."

"Really?" I wasn't sure if I felt relieved or violated. "I guess I've seen them a few times too. They must be the ones who watch *Game of Thrones*."

Confident that Sylvie wouldn't buy my lie, I readied myself for the interrogation. But it didn't come.

"For the record," she said instead, "Bridget and Peter have an open relationship—I met them on Tinder. And I've actually been hanging out—and making out—with both of them these past few weeks. I really like how I feel around them. We're going away together to the Catskills next weekend."

"Oh." God, I was naive. "I'm sorry I implied . . . otherwise. And I'm glad they make you happy." I actually meant it.

"I appreciate your apology." Sylvie moved up so we were standing on the same step. "Now can we go back to being friends?"

"That would be nice." The world suddenly felt brighter.

"Great—come over for dinner tomorrow night and you can tell me all about Hugo!" It was so nice to hear that exclamation point again.

Sylvie continued up the steps to the front door, then stopped.

"Oh, and Clover, you know what's funny? Bridget said they'd always joked that they should get binoculars so that they could see into your apartment better."

As she disappeared into the building, I was pretty sure she winked.

49

Despite Claudia's assertion that all her friends were dead, the funeral service was packed.

I only attended my client's funeral if the family requested it, or if no one else was likely to show up. Claudia had made the request in person—and it was hard to turn down an invitation from someone to their own funeral.

"Someone needs to keep an eye on things," she'd told me.

Still, I preferred to keep a low profile. Navigating the grand front steps outside the Gothic Revival church on Amsterdam Avenue, I spotted Sebastian caught in polite conversation with two elderly women in elaborate hats. From his constant nodding, it was clear that he couldn't squeeze a word in. Though I felt sad for him, especially today, it was amusing to see he'd met his oratorical matches. I caught his eye and gave a small wave as I claimed a place in the last row of pews.

Claudia's family had observed at least some of the funeral service wishes we'd noted in the death binder. The vases of hydrangeas along the altar. The lively jazz in place of the usual "perversely depressing" organ refrain. No enormous photograph of her on an easel next to the coffin.

"Those photos are always incredibly disconcerting and rarely well shot," Claudia had proclaimed when given the option. "I don't want everybody to feel like I'm looming over them."

But she did allow for a selection of her favorite photos to be printed in the program. I grinned as I flipped through it. There were a couple of Manhattan street vignettes, but the remaining black-and-white images were all distinctly taken in the South of France. The final image—the only one of Claudia herself—showed her in her mid-twenties sitting on a rock looking out at the Mediter-ranean, a silk scarf tied around her dark hair. Even in monochrome, her skin had a sun-kissed glow. And tucked in beneath the arch of her knees was a three-legged Jack Russell.

Claudia had made it clear whom she planned to meet in the afterlife.

Mourners slotted in alongside one another like Scrabble tiles on wooden racks. A good portion of the crowd was gray-haired, but there were plenty around my age, likely friends of Sebastian and his sisters. I tried to imagine what it would be like to have so many people willing to come out and support you in your grief.

The service itself definitely did not reflect Claudia's wishes. In-stead of being short and upbeat with very little religious affirmation, it was long, somber, and pious. And also kind of boring. That was the thing about funerals—no matter how much you try to control the run of show, once you're dead, it's out of your hands.

The rustle of fidgeting paper programs rippled around the church as Sebastian's father delivered a dry, self-referential eulogy that didn't capture any of Claudia's best qualities. I hoped everyone was silently meditating on those instead, but it was hard to glean people's emotional states from the backs of their heads.

The eulogy dragged on—Sebastian's verbosity was obviously an inherited trait. Scanning the front pews, I spotted him wedged be-tween Jennifer and Anne, whose shoulders shook with the rhythm of their sobs.

To stop myself from yawning, I started counting the arches in the cathedral's soaring vaulted ceiling. Since Grandpa had raised me agnostic, I hadn't spent much time in churches. The architectural drama of this one seemed to match Claudia's extroverted persona. But as I turned to the back of the church, I quickly lost count.

A familiar silhouette stood against the sunlight in the doorway. Tall, but not quite lanky. A head bowed deferentially, curls coaxed into formality with the heavy-handed use of hair product.

Hugo. Here in spirit and in blood—via a grandson, at least.

As if he felt my eyes upon him, he raised his head and looked directly at me. Keeping his hand close to his waist, his wave was discreet but his smile genuine.

After I returned the smile and we both looked back to face the altar, I realized my entire body was tingling.

F ollowing the recessional, I slipped out the side door of the church and tried not to be obvious in my search for curls in the sea of heads. It wasn't hard to spot Hugo at the bottom of the steps—it's difficult to blend in when you're a foot taller than most. I'd always suspected that the reason Grandpa wore neutrals and muted greens was to camouflage his notable height in the urban environment.

This time Hugo's wave was enthusiastic. He walked up toward me, stopping one step below so that the gradation partially dissolved our height difference.

"Hi, Clover," he grinned. I liked how the volume of his voice was consistently gentle, as if he was speaking in a library or as the lights dimmed before a theater performance.

"Hi, Hugo." It was strange to feel such familiarity with someone I hardly knew.

"I hope it's okay that I'm here," he said, looking around at the other mourners. "After you texted to let me know Claudia had passed, I thought about how much it would've meant to my grandfather for me to pay respects on his behalf. When you sent the link to her obituary and I saw that the funeral was being held here, I figured I could probably blend in." He patted the top of his head. "Well, as much as my height lets me."

"Claudia would've loved that you're here." Now that we were almost at eye level, I noticed the flecks of amber in his gray irises. "Reading those letters and knowing that your grandpa came to find her really did help her find some peace."

"I'm just happy she got to see them before, well, you know . . ." Hugo adjusted the collar of his coat—he looked quite distinguished when he dressed up.

"We got there just in time." I glanced over his shoulder, hoping the brief break in eye contact would settle my jitters. "I have the letters at home if you want them back? I was going to mail them to you."

"Yeah, I'd love to have them, if you wouldn't mind? Reading them made me feel so much closer to him—you know, being able to get to know him as a young man instead of just as a grandfather."

"Of course." I spotted Sebastian climbing the steps in our direction, Jessie trailing behind him in a short pink dress that, despite my limited fashion knowledge, didn't seem funeral-appropriate. "I was thinking I might scan them first if that's okay? I haven't told Sebastian about them yet, but he might like to see them one day."

"Great idea." As Sebastian arrived next to him, Hugo reached out to shake his hand. "Hey, Sebastian, I'm so sorry for your loss. Even when you know it's going to happen, it doesn't make it any easier."

"Thanks, man, appreciate it." Sebastian glanced sideways at me then back at Hugo like he was piecing together a puzzle.

"Hope you don't mind that I came," Hugo said. "I saw the funeral notice and wanted to pay my respects."

The explanation seemed to relax Sebastian a little. "Not at all— it's a shame you didn't get to meet Grandma."

Hugo patted his breast pocket. "I'm looking forward to reading the program—her photography was beautiful." He turned to Jessie, who was hovering stiffly behind Sebastian. "Hi there, I'm Hugo."

Sebastian looked like he'd only just remembered she was standing there. "Right, sorry—this is Jessie." He looked quickly at me. "And you guys have already met."

Jessie entwined her arm possessively around Sebastian's elbow. "Oh, yeah, at the bar—what was your name again?" Her voice was as saccharine as I remembered.

"Clover."

"So cute," she said in a way that made me wonder if it was a compliment.

"Sebastian!" Sarah was walking briskly in our direction, balancing her feet in stilettos and a squirming toddler on her hip. "We're heading back to the townhouse to finish prepping before everyone arrives for the wake. Oh, hi, Clover—so good of you to come." Sarah looked at Hugo uncertainly.

"Hi, Sarah," I said quickly. "This is Hugo."

Sarah's eyes flicked between Hugo and me. "Nice to meet you. Will the two of you be joining us for the wake?"

Hugo's face lit up. "Definitely."

For once, Sarah's face implied that she approved of something. "Wonderful!" Her expression turned authoritative as she faced her brother. "Sebastian, are you coming with us?"

He straightened like a puppy being called to heel.

"We'll be right there," he said, looking at us as if trying to understand what his sister had found so pleasing. "I guess I'll see you guys later."

I'd planned to spend only a courteous hour at the wake, so I was grateful when Hugo told me he had to leave and asked if I wanted a ride.

"You said you live in the West Village, right? I'm staying with a friend in Brooklyn, so I can drop you on the way if you want?"

"That would be great." I wouldn't even get him to drop me a few blocks away from my apartment.

I searched for Sebastian in the crowded living room and realized it was the first time I'd ever seen it with any sign of life. He was being commandeered again by the big-hatted twosome from the church. When I caught his attention and made the motion that I was leaving, he looked back helplessly and then gave me a resigned wave. Though I was secretly relieved our farewell could be kept to a simple exchange of hand signals, I still felt a twinge of sadness. We'd been through so much in the past two months—it would be strange not to have him around. Maybe we could be friends one day.

As I sidestepped through a gauntlet of well-heeled New Yorkers in the hallway, a hand clasped my forearm. With a different squirming toddler on her hip, Sarah leaned away from her husband toward my left ear.

"That guy of yours is handsome." She nodded at Hugo waiting patiently by the front door. "Good for you."

"Oh, thanks." I blushed, but didn't bother correcting her. My embarrassment morphed quickly into quiet pride.

While Sarah and Claudia didn't see eye to eye on green smoothies, their taste in men still appeared to follow the same bloodline.

When the Lyft pulled up in front of my building, it felt like only a few minutes had passed since we'd left the Upper West Side. Hugo leaned between the front seats to address the driver, a cheerful soul named Dimuth. "Hey, man, could you just wait a couple of minutes, please?" He handed Dimuth twenty dollars. "So you get paid for the extra waiting time."

We stood at the bottom of my stoop, the afternoon radiance muting into twilight.

"It was really great seeing you," Hugo said. "I wish I didn't have to drop you off and run, but I promised my buddy I'd meet him for drinks and I can't really say no, since I'm sleeping on his sofa and he's watching Gus right now."

"No problem." I did my best to sound nonchalant. "I really appreciate the ride home—thank you."

Dimuth was watching us expectantly.

THE COLLECTED REGRETS OF CLOVER 281

Hugo put his hands in his pockets and glanced briefly at the tree-tops. "So, I'm going to be in town for the next week." He looked back down at me. "Maybe we could meet up for coffee again . . . and I could get those letters?"

Of course, it was the letters he wanted. I was embarrassed that I let myself think otherwise, if only for a second. "Yes, sure—I'll scan them tomorrow so they're ready for you to take whenever."

"Perfect! I'll text you." Hugo lightly touched my shoulder. "I'm glad we get to see each other again so soon."

Disappointment and hope dueled in my chest. "Me too."

Long after the Lyft drove away, I could still feel his presence.

50

True to his word, Hugo texted, suggesting we meet in Washington Square Park on Sunday. But I wouldn't have minded if he'd called. I was also scheduled to play mahjong with Leo that evening—I'd been so busy with Claudia that it had been several weeks since we'd had a game. An afternoon with Hugo followed by an evening with Leo felt like the makings of an almost perfect day.

As I threw my wallet and keys into a tote along with the letters, I recognized the feeling in my stomach. It was the same one I felt whenever I was about to board a plane for a destination I'd never been to—a giddy blend of nerves and excitement. I didn't realize how much I missed that.

That Sunday was the first day of the year warm enough to be outside without a coat. Bathing in soft sunshine, the park was shrugging off the sedation of winter. The lawns were a patchwork of picnic blankets, couples perched on the edge of the fountain, and musicians dotted the walkways.

I spotted Hugo leaning under the archway holding two take-out coffee cups while trying not to get caught in tourists' photos. As I walked toward him, I felt a strong breeze propelling me forward. And yet the treetops were still.

"Hey!" Hugo's wave was more of a wiggling of fingers, since his hands were full. The sleeves of his sweater were pushed up to his elbows, revealing a small tattoo of a botanical line drawing on his right forearm.

"Hi!" A little more enthusiastic than I'd intended.

"It's such a sunny day that I thought maybe you'd like to walk around the park instead of sitting in a cramped café somewhere?"

"Great idea." I always felt less nervous when my body was moving.

He handed me a cup. "Black, no sugar, like your grandpa, right?"

The thoughtfulness caught me off guard—I'd only mentioned it briefly at the wake. "I'm surprised you remembered."

Hugo shrugged. "I kind of have a knack for observing small details." He bent his head forward and lowered his voice. "But please don't tell anyone. Some people find it creepy how much I remember about them."

"We all have our secrets," I said with mock solemnity. "Lucky for you, I'm really good at keeping them."

"Well, in that case, I'm looking forward to hearing yours." Hugo pointed his coffee past the fountain in the park's center. "Should we go watch the drama unfold at the dog run? A guilty pleasure of mine."

Usually, visiting the dog run would just remind me how much I missed Grandpa, but today the prospect ached a little less. "I'd love that."

"We should've brought Gus and George so they could get to know each other." Somehow his eyes looked happy even when his mouth was neutral.

"Maybe another time?" I wasn't sure why the suggestion felt so intimate. Flustered, I handed Hugo the tote with the letters. "I'd better give you these, since that's why we're here."

He examined the logo. "Repping the New York Public Library, huh?"

I blushed. Thank goodness I hadn't grabbed the Trader Joe's bag. "I'm a bit of a bookworm."

"Glad to hear it," Hugo said as we walked toward the dog run.

"We're rare creatures now that everyone's attached to their phones. What's the last great book you read?"

I liked being included in his "we."

"I just finished one by Martha Gellhorn that I loved." Did he order me a double shot of espresso? My brain felt hyper alert.

"The journalist, right? She wrote about the Spanish Civil War?"

"Yes, that's her." He really did have a mind for details. "Claudia reminded me of her, actually. It's a shame she gave up her photography career."

"For so many reasons," Hugo said, squinting up at the sun. "Do you think they're together now? Claudia and my grandpa?"

"I hope so," I replied, though I was confident they were.

He sipped his coffee. "You know, I really like what she said in her final letter. 'We're not meant to be in this lifetime . . . perhaps we'll meet in another.' It's actually super pragmatic. Like, maybe we have different business with the same souls in each lifetime. And it doesn't always work out how we want it to in every one of them."

"I wonder what their business was in this one?"

"Great question." Hugo grinned. "I guess only they can answer that. Maybe they'll tell us in the next one when they get a do-over."

"Maybe they will." I loved that idea.

"So, what would be your do-over? In this life, I mean." Hugo asked it casually, as if such deep questions were normal between relative strangers.

It surprised me how easily the answer came—and how natural it felt to share it with him.

I drew in a slow breath.

"I wish I'd been with my grandfather when he died." We walked several beats in silence but Hugo didn't try to fill them. "I was traveling in Cambodia at the time. He had a stroke in his office at Columbia late at night and he died . . . alone."

A few more beats.

"Clover, I'm so sorry. It must have been so devastating not to have been there with him."

My whole body tensed. "I know it sounds stupid, but I wish I could ask him to forgive me for being on the other side of the world when he needed me." As I said the words out loud, it was as if someone had unhooked a weight from my shoulders. One I'd been carrying unknowingly for years.

Hugo considered his words. "Is that part of why you've dedicated your life to being with other people when they die?"

I was embarrassed that he'd seen through me so quickly. That, in a way, my work as a death doula was selfish. It wasn't just the regrets of the dying people I was trying to resolve—it was my own.

Of course I knew that Grandpa could still have died alone in his office even if I'd been in New York. But at least I would have spent time with him in the days leading up to it. Instead, I hadn't seen his face in an entire year, and I'd taken it for granted that he'd still be there when I got back. Worst of all, I hadn't cherished the small details that felt inconsequential then but that I missed so dearly now—the way he stirred his coffee, the sound of him rubbing his stubble, the deep rumble of his laugh. When someone has always been there for you, it's easy to assume they always will be. And then, one day, they're not.

"I guess it is," I said. Finally acknowledging it out loud shifted something inside me. Hugo had posed the question so gently, without judgment, that the embarrassment began to dissipate.

"You know, from what you've told me about him, it doesn't sound like there'd be any issue of him forgiving you." Hugo stopped walking and looked at me. "Maybe it's more a question of you forgiving yourself?"

One sentence and the emotions I'd neatly tucked away for years rushed through my body like a river freed from its dam. I was afraid I would unravel in the middle of the park.

"I'm sorry," I said, sucking in a sharp breath. "I'm not sure I can talk about this."

Hugo put his hand lightly on my shoulder, shifting his posture until I finally made eye contact with him.

"You don't have to," he said quietly. "Your grief is yours to process in your own time, in whatever way works for you. No one can tell you how to do that. But if you do ever feel like talking about it, I'd be happy to listen."

"Thank you." Though Hugo was smiling, there was a hint of pain in his expression.

He looked down at his coffee cup. "My mom died when I was in college—ovarian cancer," he said. "And I remember getting so angry about people trying to comfort me. They'd say things like 'she's in a better place now,' or 'at least you had the time you did together,' or 'she wouldn't want you to be sad.' And I just wanted to scream at them. It was like they wanted me to get over my grief so they didn't have to deal with it." He ran his hand through his hair. "I think that's why I ended up drinking so much alcohol back then—to numb myself because no one understood what I was experiencing."

"I can understand that." I paused. "Except my way of numbing myself is binge-watching romantic comedies." It was the type of thing I never would have shared before, but Hugo's vulnerability had inspired me.

"Well, there's nothing wrong with a Sandra Bullock marathon." Hugo nodded in the direction of the dog run. "I bet we're missing some serious canine drama right now. Should we keep walking?"

"Definitely." I already felt calmer—how did he do that?

When we reached the dog run, two golden retrievers were overwhelming a gray short-haired poodle with their boisterous play. The poodle stood perfectly still as the other two romped around her, like she was praying to blend into the landscape.

"I think someone needs to have a word with those two goldies about learning to play it cool," Hugo said.

I twisted the cardboard collar on my coffee cup. "Or maybe it's a good opportunity for the poodle to get outside her comfort zone."

"I like the way you think," Hugo said, leaning his forearms casually on the fence, at ease with himself and the world.

I suddenly became conscious of my coffee breath. "When are you headed back up to Maine?"

"Turns out I'm going to be here for a few more days," he said. "I got a pretty sweet job offer—building rooftop gardens for some public schools here. I have a couple of meetings this week to talk through the details and see if I want to take it."

"That sounds really interesting," I said. "What's holding you back?"

Hugo watched a tubby corgi waddling proudly with a stick twice the length of her body. "I guess it would mean committing to living here for at least six months to oversee the project. I've got to figure out if I want to venture out into the world again, so to speak. I've kind of been loving being a recluse living on a houseboat and not seeing anybody. It's getting a little weird, actually."

Each small detail he shared about himself felt like catching a firefly in a jar. "I don't think that's weird at all."

He nodded at the poodle. "Yeah, but I think it's time I pushed myself outside my comfort zone again. That's where all the best things always are, right?"

"So I've heard," I said. "Though I haven't really done that in a while—I'm not much of a risk taker."

"Then maybe it's time for both of us to start?" He raised his eyebrows as if issuing a challenge. "What about you? What's in the cards now that this job is done?"

The corgi waddled over to us to show off her stick. I bent down to pet her through the fence.

"Except for a mahjong game with my eighty-seven-year-old neighbor, Leo, and hanging out with my pets, I'll probably be reading as many books as possible and hardly leaving the house for a few days."

"Sounds perfect to me." Hugo bent down to pet the corgi too. "I totally get how you'd need time to decompress after a job like yours—especially when it required a last-minute road trip to Maine."

I looked over at the poodle. The timid pup had given in to the golden retrievers' friendly persistence and was now playing with them—albeit very awkwardly.

I thought back to a few days earlier when I'd written Claudia's final words in my ADVICE notebook.

Don't let the best parts of life pass you by because you're too scared of the unknown.

Maybe the biggest risk in life was taking no risks at all. I summoned Claudia's fearless confidence and dared myself to leap.

"So, my grandpa's favorite bookstore is right near here and it was kind of our tradition to go on Sundays." I looked up at Hugo. "Would you like to come with me?"

He tossed his coffee cup into the nearby trash can with one clean shot, then grinned.

"I'd love to."

T he bookstore was surprisingly quiet for a Sunday—empty except for two middle-aged women chatting in Mandarin by the historical fiction. Based on their excited whispers and hand gestures, it sounded interesting.

I looked around for Bessie but couldn't see her. I was a little relieved, since I'd been slightly dreading her reaction to the fact that I hadn't come alone. She was always just so . . . exuberant. And I didn't want to scare Hugo away.

"Clover, honey!" My pulse sped up as Bessie materialized from behind some shelves. "I figured I'd run out back to the powder room while there was a lull in customers." When she registered Hugo standing next to me, she stopped so quickly that I could almost hear the cartoon-like skidding of her heels. "Well, hello there."

Hugo gave his usual relaxed grin, apparently not sharing my embarrassment.

"You must be Bessie," he said, reaching out his hand to shake hers.

"Great to meet you—I'm Hugo. I'm looking forward to exploring your book selection." He smiled down at me. "It comes very highly recommended."

Bessie beamed. "Well, Clover has been shopping here since she was six!"

"So she said," Hugo replied. "That's good enough for me."

I thought Bessie might strain a muscle, she was smiling so hard.

"Hugo is an urban landscape architect," I said, hoping to move things along quickly. "I remembered you had a few good books on landscape architecture." I may have looked into it after the Maine trip.

"Oh, yes, I definitely do," Bessie said. "There's a wonderful monograph of Roberto Burle Marx that I love."

Hugo's face lit up. "Burle Marx is one of my favorites—I love the joy and optimism of his work." I made a mental note of the name to google later.

"I thought he might be." Bessie looked pleased with herself—she did have a sixth sense for people's reading taste. "Let me show you where it is."

For a second I was worried she was going to embarrass me further and take Hugo by the hand. Fortunately, he just followed her lead toward the back of the bookstore.

"Don't let me buy too many books, Clover," he called to me over his shoulder. "Or there won't be room for Gus in the car!"

The bell above the door jingled several times as more people filed into the space. In an instant, the tiny bookstore felt crowded.

In between reading various blurbs, I snuck glances over at Hugo who was happily paging through some of the books Bessie had recommended. It was almost as if I had to keep checking that he was really there and that this wasn't all just a fantasy I'd concocted in my mind. The whole day had felt kind of surreal.

After about thirty minutes of browsing, I was lost in the first chapter of Françoise Sagan's *Bonjour Tristesse* when I breathed in the familiar scent of cedar and cypress.

I looked up to see Hugo standing next to me, a book in his hand. He held it out to me.

"I think you'd like this one." Although I knew he was keeping his voice quiet out of respect to the other browsers, it felt intimate, special. "It's about Gertrude Bell, the archaeologist and travel writer from the early 1900s."

"Oh, I haven't read that," I said. But it sounded perfect.

"My mom loved reading books about adventurous women in history too." The pain had returned to his eyes. "Even though she's been gone for a long time, sometimes I forget for a moment and go to buy her a book she'd love."

"I get that." I'd done the same, many times. "You know, in Samoa some people believe that the spirits of loved ones stay with you even after they die, so you can still chat with them whenever you like."

Hugo's smile returned. "I love that—and I do still tell her things sometimes," he said. "I think she would have loved to meet you."

I dared myself not to look away. "I wish I could have met her." There was no use trying to hide the spilling of pink across my cheeks.

A throat cleared. Behind us, a balding man with a toddler in a stroller was trying to maneuver past in the narrow aisle.

As Hugo shuffled closer to me to let them through, I felt our pinkies lightly touch.

51

Standing outside Leo's front door, I knocked for the fifth time. That was odd. I couldn't recall a time when I'd had to knock more than twice before the door swung open to his gold-toothed grin.

"Leo?" I knocked once more. "It's me. Is everything okay in there?"

Maybe he just wasn't home or we'd gotten our wires crossed about the time. But he'd never stood me up before. On our agreed terms, a last-minute cancellation meant an instant forfeit, adding an extra point to the opponent's score. Since we were currently tied at sixty-seven games apiece, and both of us were intensely competitive, I doubted he'd give up a point unless something was seriously wrong.

I pulled my keys from my sweatpants pocket, trying to remember which one was Leo's. My hands shook as the search became more panicked.

"Leo? Are you there?" I fumbled with them again, finally sliding the right one into the lock and turning it the extra rotation that was a quirk of doors in our building.

I stepped into the empty living room. The box of mahjong tiles was already on the table, but there was no sign of Leo. The only hint that something was amiss was the insistent whistle of the kettle on the stove. I threw my keys on the table and ran toward the sound.

Leo was bent over the kitchen counter clutching his chest. Sweat clung to his forehead.

"Leo, what's wrong?"

"It feels like . . ." He put a hand on the cabinets to steady himself. ". . . an elephant is sitting on my chest."

I quickly turned off the stove, then guided him to the living room, holding his forearms as he lowered himself down onto the sofa. "You could be having a heart attack." I reached for my phone, hands trembling again. "I'm calling an ambulance, just hold on. You'll be alright."

Leo's breath found fleeting depth. "Don't call them, please." He waved his hand weakly. "Just sit with me."

"But you need a doctor."

"I don't."

Dread weighed in my gut as my breaths matched his shallow ones. "At least let me get you some aspirin and water. If it's your heart, that will help."

Leo reached out a frail hand and put it on mine. "Just stay with me, please." My dread turned to despair—the serenity enveloping his demeanor was one I knew well. I'd seen it many times in the faces of the dying.

When our eyes met, he confirmed my question without me having to ask it.

"Leo," I whispered. "Please, no."

"It's time, Clover," he implored. "I'm ready to go."

Desperation surged through my body. All my years of experience and all I could feel was panic.

"But you can't—I need you."

Leo smiled sleepily, his hand to his sternum. "You should know better than anyone that when your time's up, your time's up."

"I know," I said softly. "But you're all I have."

"And what a ride we've had, huh?" His eyes blinked rapidly, but his smile remained. "I've lived the hell out of my life and now it's time for me to take the next exit." He gazed up at Winnie's portrait.

I clasped his long fingers as he drew in a ragged breath, like an aluminum can was knocking about in his lungs.

"You really have lived the hell out of your life," I said, returning his smile as best I could. There was no use trying to persuade him. When someone decided to walk confidently toward death, you couldn't hold them back.

"Clover—I want to tell you something."

I squeezed his hand. "Of course, Leo."

For once, the constant city noise outside quieted. Reverent silence enveloped the apartment as I waited for Leo to form his words.

"I've watched you spend your life trying to help people have a beautiful death—the thing you couldn't give your grandpa." Even now, his brown eyes managed to sparkle. "But the secret to a beautiful death is to live a beautiful life. Putting your heart out there. Letting it get broken. Taking chances. Making mistakes." Leo's breaths were becoming too labored for him to speak. "Promise me, kid," he whispered, "that you'll let yourself live."

I rested my head on his shoulder. "I promise."

His grip loosened as he managed one last grin. "I love you, Clover."

"I love you, Leo."

What began as a trickle down my cheek soon became a deluge. And for the first time since I was a child, I let the tears fall freely.

52

The spice of early spring seasoned the afternoon breeze as Sylvie and I walked home after the celebration. Leo's funeral had overflowed with people from the neighborhood who'd grown to love him dearly over the years. It had been doctors' appointments—not out-of-town visitors—that had been keeping him busy. Heart disease, the specialists had told him.

But Leo hadn't told anyone. Instead, he'd quietly gotten his affairs in order, set aside a sizable sum for his funeral—or "celebration of life," as he'd specified, with ample food and drink—and donated the rest of his money and all his possessions to a community center in Harlem.

Well, all his possessions except for two—he bequeathed me his bar cart and his mahjong set.

"That was the perfect farewell for Leo," Sylvie said, linking her arm through mine. "I'm honored to have spent even just a couple of months in his orbit. Wherever he is now, I'm sure he's smiling like crazy with that gold tooth of his."

The image was comforting. I wasn't sure I'd have been able to make it through the past few days without Sylvie. Our apartment building felt like it was missing its heart.

"I hope so."

We walked the next block without talking until Sylvie stopped outside a bodega. "Should we buy some ice cream then get in our pajamas and binge on nineties rom-coms? I vote for something with Cameron Diaz."

Words welled up in my throat several times, only to meet a wall when they reached my lips.

"Actually," I said tentatively, "there's something I wanted to ask you. A favor."

"Is it to watch a John Cusack movie? Because you know I can't stand him." Sylvie grinned. "But I would be willing to endure two hours of sad-sack Cusack for you."

"No, not John." The joke relaxed me a little. "I was thinking about what you said about all the stuff in my apartment—my grandpa's things."

Sylvie stroked her chin theatrically. "Go on."

"And I guess you're right. Maybe I've been holding on to the past so that I don't have to think about what I really want in the future."

Sylvie graciously feigned nonchalance. "I see."

"I think maybe it's time . . . I got rid of some of it."

"And?" She was consciously teasing the words out of me.

"And I was wondering if you could maybe help me? Some of it might be valuable to museums or universities, which you would know better than me. But also . . ." Long, deep breath. "I think it's going to be hard to let go."

"Oh, C, of course it will be," Sylvie said. "Your grandpa was the love of your life—how could it not be hard?" She draped her arm across my shoulders. "I'd be honored to be there to help you through it. What are friends—and neighbors—for, if not to help you declutter your emotional baggage?"

It was a relief to know I wouldn't have to deal with it all alone. And for a moment, I let myself imagine what it would mean to have a space that was truly my own.

53

Sylvie was a ruthless adjudicator. After I spent each day sorting things into Donate/Throw Away, Definitely Keep, and Undecided, she'd arrive in the evening to sit with her imaginary gavel on the sofa that was now her judge's bench.

The process quickly developed a pattern—Sylvie immediately relegated anything I'd categorized as Undecided to Donate/Throw Away and frowned skeptically as I tried to plead my case for most things in Definitely Keep.

"I'm almost positive that what you're holding contains a biohazard that should only be handled while wearing a hazmat suit," Sylvie said, unswayed by my argument that the specimen jar with some kind of sea creature was one of Grandpa's favorites. "Add it to the donation pile and the NYU biology department can deal with it."

Through her contacts, Sylvie had found a home for the more rare scientific paraphernalia at a museum of biological oddities in a gentrified corner of Brooklyn. Bessie had arranged for a secondhand bookseller to take the hundreds of reference books and make them accessible to niche bibliophiles who'd hopefully appreciate them as much as Grandpa had.

Some things were easy to let go of. Items that had always been there but that I'd never really seen—anonymous parts that composed a significant whole. Others felt like a merciless cutting of another vital thread that tied me to Grandpa. What now remained of his possessions were the most sacred, the things even Sylvie knew better than to try to evict. Grandpa's notebooks, decades of painstaking observation now pared down to neat leather-bound rows stored in the sky-blue suitcase that began our journey together— I'd read them all one day, but not just yet. His tweed winter coat that I'd gripped onto as a child while he strode confidently through the sidewalk throngs, always guiding me to safety. The old leather overnight bag, his love and wisdom forever etched into every one of its wrinkles and scuff marks.

As the clutter diminished, the space grew bigger. Sunlight bounced off swaths of white wall long hidden by dusty objects and compendiums. Arboreal shadows danced on the hardwood floor, finally liberated from beneath the towers of bankers boxes.

On the top of the last crateful of books I was taking to Bessie sat *The Insect Societies* by Edward O. Wilson—I'd finally admitted to Sylvie that I'd probably never read it. But I could at least skim it. I picked it up and flipped through it, imagining Grandpa's index finger poised at the top corner of each browned page, ready to turn it long before he'd finished reading it. I always liked to think it was a sign of his insatiable curiosity, forever wanting to know more.

Wedged between page 432 and 433 of the book was an old cardboard coaster from an Argentinian bar in the East Village. Since I'd never read the book, the coaster had to be at least thirteen years old. Someone had written on the back of it, but it wasn't Grandpa's neat capital letters. It was a distinctly loopy cursive that I recognized from the lone Christmas card I received every year without fail—from Bessie.

My sweet Patrick. I couldn't ask for a better tango partner.

I stared at the heart dotting the *i* in Grandpa's first name (a flourish that never appeared in my Christmas cards), and reread the coaster several times, unsure if it was better if the message was literal or a euphemism.

Grandpa and Bessie? Surely not. He was as much as a loner as I was—that's where I learned it from.

But then again, Leo did mention that Grandpa asked Bessie's advice when shopping for my first bra. Oh, God. Does that mean he'd seen Bessie *in* her bra? I tried to remember any other sign that might've hinted that their relationship transcended that of book-seller and devoted customer.

But also: Grandpa and tango? I'd never seen him dance a step in his life.

Suddenly his memory sat differently in my mind—and I began to see him not as a grandfather, but as a man.

54

As I lugged the crate four blocks to the bookstore, I convinced myself I'd play it casual with Bessie. There was probably a really boring explanation for it all.

"These are the last of the books, I promise," I said, heaving the crate onto the counter as the coaster burned a hole in my pocket. "I really appreciate you helping me find homes for them all. It would've been so sad just to throw them in the recycling."

"Of course, honey—I'm glad you asked." Bessie's beam felt as welcoming as ever, but I couldn't help wondering if she had a different one especially for Grandpa. "How are you feeling with this whole cleaning out of the apartment?"

"Okay, I guess." I'd been so busy that I hadn't allowed myself to process any of my emotions. "A friend helped me with it all."

I stopped to appreciate my last sentence—months ago, it would've seemed completely ridiculous to say that.

Coy, Bessie lifted her shoulder to her cheek. "Ooooh, that handsome young man you brought in here the other day?"

"Ah, no, not Hugo," I said shyly, but secretly thrilled she'd mentioned him. In the weeks since, he'd texted me several times to tell me how much he was enjoying one of my book selections (along with several photos of Gus), and that he'd taken the job offer. We were planning to meet up when he was back in New York and take George and Gus to the dog park.

"I see," Bessie said, her dimples deepening. "Well, he seemed like a perfect gentleman to me. I think your old grandpa would've approved."

Tracing my fingertips around the edge of the coaster in my pocket, I debated whether I was invading Grandpa's privacy. I'd just have to be subtle about it.

"Actually, Bessie, I found something while I was going through his things." I slid the coaster onto the counter like it was contraband—I didn't want to embarrass her in front of the other customers.

Bessie clasped her hands to her chest. "My goodness," she said, laughing. "That brings back wonderful memories."

Memories that were appropriate to share with a granddaughter? I kept my reaction neutral.

"Oh?"

"Well, you've probably already figured it out." As she bent forward conspiratorially, I couldn't help noticing the hefty cleavage peeking through her blouse.

"Figured out what?"

"That your grandpa and I were . . . special friends." Bessie's eyes darted around the room. "I think you younger folk call it 'friends with benefits.'"

Her air quotes were very unnecessary.

I fought the urge to put my hands over my ears and hoped I wouldn't live to regret my next question. "Did Grandpa like to dance the tango?"

She looked dreamily at the coaster. "He sure did. We went dancing every Thursday evening for almost ten years."

"I never knew that," I said quietly. He'd always told me he had a late faculty meeting on Thursdays. I wasn't sure whether I should feel betrayed that he'd been living a double life or elated that he hadn't been as lonely as I'd imagined.

"He always looked so happy when he was dancing," she said, eyes shining in recollection. "Like he was allowed to shed his armor." Bessie patted my arm. "You know, I remember the last time we went . . . before he passed. He'd just spoken to you on the phone a few days earlier—you were in Thailand, I think?"

I tensed. "Cambodia."

"Cambodia, yes! Anyway, I remember he was just so happy to know you were off traveling, learning about the world. He couldn't have been prouder of you and what you were doing. I know he regretted not being a better father to your mom, and I think it somehow gave him a sense of peace that he'd done right in the way he raised you. It was such a joy to see."

The room began to spin as emotions flooded my body, the reality of the past few decades suddenly rearranging itself in my mind.

I pretended to look at my watch. "I'm sorry, Bessie—I'm running late for something."

"Of course, don't let me keep you, honey." She squeezed my arm tightly, pulling me in closer. "But I'm always here if you need me."

I walked all the way to the Hudson River and back again, trying to sift through what I was feeling. And to imagine what Grandpa might've looked like dancing—and flirting.

I considered again how I'd never asked him anything about his own life. I knew nothing of his fears, his challenges, his goals.

It's so easy to see your parental figure through that lens alone, to think that their existence has always revolved around yours. But before they were parents, they were simply human beings trying to navigate life as best they could, dealing with their own disappointments, chasing after their own dreams. And yet we often expect them to be infallible.

It was selfish of me to assume I was the only important person in his life for all those years—Bessie had lost Grandpa too. But I was infinitely grateful for what she had revealed. Even though he died alone, he didn't die lonely.

And while I'd never know what his exact last words were, I knew he was proud of me.

I t was a little jarring to arrive home to my newly decorated apartment. By most people's measure, it wouldn't have appeared empty at all. Plenty of my own books still lined the shelves, along with select mementos from my travels. The amount of furniture was reflective of an adult my age, with a few new pieces—thanks to Sylvie's nudging—that made the apartment seem almost modern. But compared to what it looked like just a week ago, it felt bare.

And there was one item still slated for departure.

When Sylvie first suggested we donate Grandpa's armchair to Goodwill, I defiantly refused. It was the one thing in the apartment that made me feel closest to him. But as the weeks passed, my defiance faltered. So many times I'd watched family members refuse to leave their deceased loved one's side long after their life—their essence—had left, and all that remained was a body. Inevitably, they'd face the agonizing moment when they had to accept that the only way to keep that essence alive was to carry it in their own hearts.

So I sat in his beloved green corduroy armchair, tracing its threadbare fabric and allowing myself to feel his embrace one last time. And as I stood in the hall, watching the movers maneuver it out of the building, I felt like I was being given a chance to redeem myself.

To be present as the final sigh of breath departed Grandpa's body.

When I got back up to my apartment, I noticed a large UPS package resting next to the door. Strange. I hadn't ordered anything lately—the whole point of the last couple of weeks was getting rid of old stuff, not acquiring new stuff.

I placed it on the coffee table and stared at it, trying to guess what it could be. Then I looked at the sender's name on the label.

Selma Ramirez

Why would Selma be sending me something? I sliced my house

key through the packing tape and found another box inside. As I
pulled it out, a folded note card fell to the floor with my name neatly
inscribed on the outside in Claudia's elegant hand.

> *My darling Clover,*
> *I love the way you see the world—I hope this helps you*
> *share that vision with others.*
> *(Never too late to pick up a new hobby, eh?)*
>
> *Sincerely,*
> *Claudia Wells*

From beneath the layers of paper, I unearthed a brand-new digital camera, several lenses, and a small bottle of perfume with an
emerald-green cap.

I sat back on the sofa, processing everything. Maybe Grandpa,
Claudia, and Leo had teamed up on the other side.

Now I just had to work out how to live a life that would make
them all proud.

55

ola and Lionel watched curiously as I wheeled my brand-new lightweight suitcase out into the living room. George was already comfortably settled into his three-month sabbatical in Sylvie's apartment, but the two tabbies would stay here with the subletter, Sylvie's colleague from Chile, whose soft spot for animals rivaled mine.

The apartment no longer felt bare, but I also didn't feel as tethered to it as I once had.

Grief, I'd come to realize, was like dust. When you're in the thick of a dust storm, you're completely disoriented by the onslaught, struggling to see or breathe. But as the force recedes, and you slowly find your bearings and see a path forward, the dust begins to settle into the crevices. And it will never disappear completely—as the years pass, you'll find it in unexpected places at unexpected moments.

Grief is just love looking for a place to settle.

Even without all of his possessions, I still felt Grandpa's presence— I'd been carrying it with me all along. But there were still three books on the shelves that I'd never get rid of.

Leo had spoken his final words more than a month ago, but I still hadn't been able to bring myself to write them down. I closed my eyes as I stood in front of the shelves, summoning my strength, then pulled the notebook marked ADVICE from between its two counterparts.

Flipping to a clean page, I uncapped the fountain pen Grandpa had gifted me for my ninth birthday, now on what must have been its hundredth ink cartridge.

Then I noted Leo's name, address, the date he died, and his words of wisdom.

The secret to a beautiful death is living a beautiful life.

I reflected on the words for a few moments, etching them onto my heart for safekeeping. Then I blew briskly on the ink and snapped the book shut. As I returned it to its rightful place, my eyes fell on the binoculars on the shelf next to the notebooks. I'd forgotten they were there. I couldn't care less what was going on in the apartment across the street—my own life was proving to be far more compelling.

Sylvie answered as soon as I knocked.

"I was waiting near the door listening for your footsteps because I was worried you'd try to sneak out without saying goodbye." She crossed her arms. "I know you're good at being stealthy when you want to be."

I cringed, hoping she'd let me forget it one day. "I'd never do that—I promise."

"What time is Hugo picking you up?" she asked with the sing-song of a teenaged girl.

"In about five minutes, so I'd better get downstairs." I could see George snoring contentedly in a patch of sunlight on her sofa. As much as I wanted to give him one last hug, I didn't want to confuse him when he'd already made himself at home with Sylvie. "Thanks again for taking care of George."

"Are you kidding? It's a dream—and I'm pretty sure three months is enough time to convince him to enjoy doga." Sylvie flashed the sly smile I already knew I'd miss. "And for the record, despite my minimalist decor, George and I expect to receive a postcard from every place you visit."

I felt a mix of sadness and exhilaration. "I can do that."

"Great. Now, I know you're super awkward about hugs, so I'm giving you fair warning that I'm about to give you one."

Thank God she brought it up first—initiating a hug felt so unnatural. I put down my luggage in anticipation. "That's okay with me."

She squeezed me tightly, resting her chin on my shoulder. "I'm going to miss you so much!"

It felt like such a privilege to have someone to miss me. "I'll miss you too."

Sylvie inhaled deeply as she loosened her grip. "Mmmm, you smell lovely—I didn't think you were a perfume person!"

I blushed. "I wasn't, but I thought it might be time to try something new."

She winked at me. "I love it."

Hugo arrived outside my building exactly on time, his battered Land Rover incongruous against the manicured West Village streetscape.

"You packed light," he grinned, lifting my suitcase into the back seat then opening the passenger-side door. Gus squeezed in at my feet.

"Thanks so much for driving me to the airport." I scratched Gus's chin and committed his adoring canine gaze to memory.

"Of course!" Hugo maneuvered the Land Rover around a double-parked delivery truck. "I'm happy I get to spend an extra fifty minutes with you before you go—depending on traffic, that is."

A wave of sadness washed over me as we turned out of my street. I sat with it and let it recede.

I looked over at Hugo. His curls were more contained than usual—he'd probably gotten a haircut before starting his new job. "So, how are you settling into city life?"

"Well, Brooklyn isn't quite as peaceful as a houseboat on a lake, but it's been treating me well so far," he said. "And it's nice not having a seven-hour commute."

"I bet."

The independent cinema on Sixth Avenue sailed past my window and my nostalgia surfaced again. I was going to miss this city and being just one bead on its infinite abacus of inhabitants.

"So, first stop, Nepal, right?"

"Yes!" Excitement soared through my limbs. "My first time there."

"And after that?"

"Who knows?" For once, the thought of no fixed plan was exhilarating. "Wherever I feel like going next, I guess."

Hugo tapped his thigh nervously. "But you're definitely going to meet up with me in Corsica in three months, right?"

"I always keep my word." And I was saving the best of my trip for last. In the pocket of my backpack was a small jar of Claudia's ashes that Sebastian had given me. She'd accompany me on my global adventure before joining her beloved in the Mediterranean Sea.

"Great," Hugo said, still tapping his thigh. "That's great." For some reason he was lacking his usual ease.

As we pulled up to the curb at JFK, anticipation bubbled in my veins. The passport in my hand felt like a skeleton key ready to escort me into myriad new experiences. And the camera on my shoulder was ready to document them. How could I have waited so long to feel this again?

Hugo set down my suitcase and pulled up the handle.

"Oh," he said, flustered. "I can't believe I almost forgot." He reached into the back seat and retrieved a paper bag. "I got you something for your trip."

The liberal use of sticky tape and asymmetrical folds of the wrapping paper tugged a familiar heartstring, as did the contents of the package: a leather-bound notebook featuring the word ADVENTURES written on the spine.

I welcomed the spring of tears in my eyes. I'd only ever mentioned the notebooks once to Hugo. This must be what Claudia was talking about—what it felt like to be really seen by someone.

"Thank you," I said, stroking its smooth cover. "It's perfect."

"My pleasure." He slid his hands in his pockets and looked down at his feet. "I'm really going to miss hanging out with you, Clover."

Missed by two people. That felt almost unbelievable.

Flipping the notebook open, I saw a handwritten inscription flowing across the bottom of the first page.

Here's to living a life with fewer regrets—Hugo

Amid the impatient honking, yelled farewells, and general chaos of the JFK departures drop-off, I heard a chorus of familiar voices urging me forward: Leo, Sylvie, Bessie, Grandpa, Claudia.

Be cautiously reckless.

The hummingbird's wings fluttered beneath my ribs.

With a deep breath, I stood on tiptoes and put my hand to Hugo's cheek, looking him confidently in the eye.

And my second first kiss was exactly what I imagined it would be.

EPILOGUE

The scent of sunbaked eucalyptus mingled with the salty breeze as I stood on the cliffs of Bonifacio, Corsica. The delicate stillness was far from the urban din I'd grown up with. Leaves brushed softly against one another as if in a loving caress. A bird called out to the vanishing sun, bidding it farewell for another day. The ripples of the Mediterranean washed gently onto the rocks, carrying with them the sparkle of dying sunlight.

In the air below the cliffs, two distinct clouds of ashes danced together before descending gracefully into the sea.

Claudia and her great love were reunited at last.

Beside me, Hugo squeezed my hand, the golden glow from the horizon reflected in the traces of tears on his face.

I squeezed back and watched as the last of the ashes disappeared into the water.

In the distance, a small sailboat eased its way out to sea. I imagined Claudia sitting on its bow, happy to finally be where she belonged. But while the vision was heartwarming, it also felt bittersweet.

If Claudia and Hugo had reunited, the Hugo next to me wouldn't exist. I wouldn't have spent the past three months traveling the world, documenting my adventures in my notebook that I couldn't wait to share with him. And I wouldn't be standing here on this

French island, about to return home to New York to begin my photography studies.

Their fate had somehow determined mine.

People who were complete strangers to me less than a year ago
had forever shifted the trajectory of my life. The fact that all of
us were entangled—that everyone on the planet somehow shaped
the course of one another's lives, often without realizing it—felt like
almost too much for me to comprehend.

But perhaps that's the point. Do we actually need to understand
the world and all its patterns?

You can find meaning in anything if you look hard enough; if you
want to believe that everything happens for a reason. But if we completely understood one another, if every event made sense, none of us
would ever learn or grow. Our days might be pleasant, but prosaic.

So maybe we just need to appreciate that many aspects of life—
and the people we love—will always be a mystery. Because without
mystery, there is no magic.

And instead of constantly asking ourselves the question of why
we're here, maybe we should be savoring a simpler truth:

We are here.

ACKNOWLEDGMENTS

To the death doulas, hospice workers, nurses, doctors, home health aides, spiritual practitioners, and all those who refuse to look away from other people's pain—thank you. You are some of the noblest among us, and yet so often don't receive the support, recognition, and compensation you deserve. Thank you for all you do to make people's final moments a little more bearable, and sometimes even beautiful.

What I love most about this book is that its pages hold the fingerprints of so many people who have so generously shared their wisdom, stories, expertise, and lessons with me over the years.

To Katie Mouallek, thank you for spending all of those early-pandemic Sundays with me, socially distanced in parks across New York City, envisioning Clover's world and her journey. Thank you for sharing so much of yourself, and for reading so many versions of the story that you know it almost as intimately as I do. This book wouldn't exist without you.

To Michelle Brower, thank you for plucking my manuscript out of the slush pile and for imagining what it had the potential to be— and taking a chance on that. You truly are a dream agent, advocate, provider of necessary truths, and the person I would always want in my corner. A huge thank you also to the wonderful Jemima Forrester for championing Clover throughout the Commonwealth.

To Sarah Cantin, Harriet Bourton, and Beverley Cousins, thank you for lending me your astute editorial brains and for your vision that challenged me to reach higher so that I ended up with a final manuscript that I truly love. You all made the editing process a pleasure and a masterclass.

Thank you Danya Kukafka for your expert notes, to Allison Malecha for finding Clover a global voice, and to Natalie Edwards and Khalid McCalla and the entire Trellis Literary Management team.

Thank you to the tireless and talented publishing folk who have helped bring the book into existence, especially Jennifer Enderlin, Lisa Senz, Anne Marie Tallberg, Jessica Zimmerman, Sallie Lotz, Drue VanDuker, Rivka Holler, Brant Janeway, Tom Thompson, Kim Ludlam, and everyone in the Creative Studio, Ken Silver, Gabriel Guma, Jonathan Bush, Alex Hoopes, and Kirsten Aldrich, at St. Martin's Press; Lydia Fried, Georgia Taylor, Sam Fanaken and the UK sales team, and Linda Viberg and the international sales team at Penguin Viking UK; Dot Tonkin, Janine Brown, Jo Baker, and Deb McGowan at Penguin Australia; and everyone at Bertrand Editora, Cappelen Damm, China Translation & Publishing House, Dioptra, Droemer Knaur, Éditions Eyrolles, Euromedia, Globo Livros, Influential Press, Lindhardt & Ringhof, Muza, Planeta México, Sperling & Kupfer, Vulkan, and Znanje.

To my mum, Jillian, thank you for so enthusiastically supporting every creative whim and career dream I've ever had and for always encouraging me to pursue what lights me up, rather than what seems sensible. Thank you for reading many versions of this book and for your pragmatic, detailed feedback. I'm so grateful to have grown up with such a wonderful example of what it means to be a curious, independent, resourceful, and successful woman—I love you.

To Jeremy, thank you for entertaining me for hours when we were kids by crafting elaborate imaginary worlds for our toys—my first foray into storytelling—and for all of your excellent feedback on this book. I'm so fortunate to have such a wonderful big brother. Thank you also to Kirsten, Hugo, Amélie, and Reuben for your love and support throughout this journey.

To all the aunts, uncles, grandparents and extended family who stepped in to help raise us, thank you for instilling us with an insatiable sense of adventure, curiosity, imagination, and love for storytelling, and for making us feel cherished.

To Jamie Farnsworth Finn, Trisha Ray, and Jesse Steinbach, thank you for reading early versions of the book and for your immensely helpful notes and relentless cheerleading along the way. To

Claudia Cosgrove and Cara O'Callaghan, thank you for graciously entertaining my cross-continental texts containing odd medical questions and hypotheticals. To Danielle Katvan, thank you for sharing your experiences of growing up in New York City. To Stephanie Ogé, Anna Caradeuc, Shannon Sharpe, and Carilyn Garrett, thank you for your infinite enthusiasm and encouragement.

To Emma Brodie, KJ Dell'Antonia, Annabel Monaghan, Ruth Hogan, Meredith Westgate, and everyone who took the time to read or blurb early copies of the book, I deeply appreciate your support and generous words. Thank you also to Georgia Clark, Rosalind McClintock, and Allison Warren for so generously sharing your publishing industry knowledge.

To Christine Arroyo, Meredith Craig De Pietro, Tara Crowl, Dani Fankhauser, Lydia Gidwitz, Suzanne Martinez, Eva Munz, Irina Patkanian, Nayomi Reghay, Liana Rodriguez, Natalia Sandoval, and Kabira Stokes—thank you for responding so positively on the first day I joined the writing group and announced I was trying to write "a book about death that's fun and uplifting." Your support and perceptive feedback in those very early stages helped me believe it might actually work. I can't wait to see your novels alongside mine on the shelves one day.

To Joe Veltre, Olivia Johnson, and the team at The Gersh Agency, thank you for your dedication to helping Clover reach the screen. Thank you also to all the foreign literary co-agents: Ania Walczak and Beata Glińska at Anna Jarota Agency, Mira Droumeva at Andrew Nurnberg Associates, Vanessa Maus at Berla & Griffini, Sophie Langlais at Books and More Agency, Duran Kim at Duran Kim Agency, Evangelia Avloniti at Ersilia Literary Agency, Clare Chi at The Grayhawk Agency, Kristin Olson at Kristin Olson Literary Agency, Antonia Girmacea at Livia Stoia Literary Agency, Rik Kleuver at Sebes & Bisseling, and Miguel Sader at Villas-Boas & Moss Literary Agency.

To Imani Williams, thank you for your attentive sensitivity reading and immensely helpful feedback.

To Chafin Elliot and Dorothy Hinz, thank you for your company, your wisdom, and your stories. To the staff and residents of the Fray Rodrigo de La Cruz nursing home in Antigua, Guatemala, thank you for teaching me so much about helping people to age with dignity.

To Jeanne Denney, thank you for so generously sharing your insights in what it means to walk beside someone as they journey toward death and how to help them do that with peace and grace.

To all those who have shared their own experiences with death and the dying, via books, podcasts, and webinars, especially Megan Devine, Atul Gawande, Michael Hebb, Scott Macklin, Bronnie Ware, and Karen M. Wyatt—thank you for making conversations around death easier. Thank you also to the folks at Doula Givers, Doula Program, Carter Burden Center for Aging, and Citymeals on Wheels in New York for your excellent, much-needed work. And to the New York Public Library, the Open Center, the New York Society for Ethical Culture, and all those who open their spaces to death cafés and discussions.

To Jane Birkin, who shared her wisdom to be "cautiously reckless" with me years ago when I interviewed her for a magazine. It has guided me ever since and became Claudia's wisdom in this book.

To Tamara Salem, thank you for your golden friendship and for all the adventures we got to enjoy together—though you'll never travel by my side again, you'll always be in my heart.

To Carl Lindgren, it's ironic that so much of what you taught me exists in this book and yet you'll never get to read it, therein proving the very point of it: we often lose the people we care about much sooner than we expect to, so we should cherish them while we can. I wouldn't be where I am had you not given me a chance all those years ago and continued to believe in me. Thank you for teaching me to write with my heart instead of my head; thank you for everything.

And finally, lovely reader, thank you for dedicating a portion of your precious hours on this earth to reading my book. I hope you've found your own version of living a beautiful life.

THE COLLECTED REGRETS OF CLOVER
by Mikki Brammer

About the Author
• A Conversation with Mikki Brammer

Behind the Novel

Keep On Reading
• Recommended Reading
• Reading Group Questions

Also available as an audiobook
from Macmillan Audio

For more reading group suggestions
visit www.readinggroupgold.com.

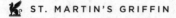 ST. MARTIN'S GRIFFIN

A Conversation with Mikki Brammer

Could you tell us a little bit about your background, and when you decided that you wanted to lead a literary life?

I'm from Tasmania, Australia, and now live in New York City, with a few years in France and Spain before that. Like most writers, I've always loved books, but I actually didn't have literary aspirations until a few years ago, at least in terms of penning a novel! I've spent most of my career as a journalist writing about art, design, and architecture and had always admired people who wrote novels but never really imagined writing one myself. The thought of sitting down and writing about the same thing, living with the same characters in your head for years, seems a behemoth task when you're used to writing magazine articles. It wasn't until I had the idea for *The Collected Regrets of Clover* that I felt like I had something to say—and that's when the thought of writing a novel felt a little more possible.

Is there a book that most influenced your life? Or inspired you to become a writer?

I've always loved books that encourage readers to look for the magic in the world. Not necessarily in a supernatural sense but the idea that the universe works in mysterious ways. As a kid, I always loved books by Enid Blyton and Roald Dahl, but the book I loved most was *Possum Magic* by Mem Fox, which is perhaps the most classic Australian children's story. I was very close with my grandparents and great-aunts, all of whom helped my single mother raise me and my brother, and *Possum Magic* captures the beautiful

relationship between grandparent and grandchild so well (and I think is perhaps the root inspiration of Clover's relationship with her grandpa!). As an adult, I've always loved books by Martha Gellhorn. Though she didn't write fiction, her writing is so evocative and vivid yet admirably economical, and it's something that has inspired both my journalism (especially as a travel writer) and now fiction writing.

I've also always enjoyed books that give me the chance to see the world through characters whose lives and perspectives are so different from my own. To me, that's the point of good literature and art—to challenge you to look at the world differently and to reconsider your own perspective and biases.

About the
Author

How did you become a writer? Would you care to share any writing tips?

Becoming a writer wasn't something I'd considered until after I finished university (I studied international business and Spanish), even though I'd always enjoyed writing. But then my mum hired me to edit her PhD, which I enjoyed doing, and I then got a job working as a copy editor for Boeing, where I had the very unglamorous task of editing airplane manuals. Boring as it was, the great thing about it was that I used the time to learn the rules of spelling and grammar inside and out, which has served me very well ever since. I was fortunate to then get a job as the editor of an Australian pop culture magazine in my mid-twenties, where I got to interview and write about many inspiring, well-known people—actors, musicians, chefs, artists, designers, authors (I remember we featured Kate Morton when she was an "emerging" local novelist!). After that I worked as a freelance travel journalist and photographer in Europe before moving to New York City, where my focus became art, design, and architecture, all of which I love. And I've been doing that ever since and will hopefully continue it alongside writing fiction!

My writing tip would be to write what your heart has to say, not what you think people want to read. Readers are very intelligent and perceptive and I think can tell when something isn't written from the heart or when they are being manipulated in a story. With *Clover*, I approached it like a conversation with the reader—and the meaningful, insightful responses I've since received from people who have read it have been so rewarding in that sense!

What was the inspiration for this novel?

It began as an exercise in exploring my own anxieties about death, which I'd had since I was a kid. I decided that instead of avoiding everything about the topic, I should try to be curious about it (I have that approach with everything I'm scared of!). So I started to dip my toe in and began listening to podcasts and reading articles and books about the topic, and that's when I came across the concept of a death doula. I'd never heard of it before, and I was so intrigued by the fact that someone would dedicate their entire professional existence to watching people die on a regular basis. It struck me as such a noble thing to do. I wondered what kind of people would choose

to be a death doula, and that's when the character of Clover began forming in my mind. I realized that perhaps I could write a story that encompassed all the things I'd learned in my attempts to be more curious about death and mortality, with a death doula as the protagonist. But it was very important to me that it wasn't a depressing or maudlin story—it would have to make the topic of death palatable for a reader like me, who would generally avoid it. So, in short, I challenged myself to write a fun, uplifting, and hopeful book about death!

Can you tell us about what research, if any, you did before writing this novel?

As part of my attempt to become more curious about all things death-related, I went down a bit of a rabbit hole in New York City. I attended death cafés, message circles (kind of like séances), lectures on the Stoics (who loved to discuss mortality), and talks by hospice doctors. I also listened to a lot of podcasts and webinars and spoke to death doulas, nurses, and doctors about their experiences being with the dying. What I discovered was that there are many interpretations of what it means to be a death doula. So I took everything I learned and then wrote the character of Clover to reflect how I would approach being a death doula if I was one (which I never could be!).

Are any of the characters based on people from your own life?

I've always been close to the elders in my life— grandparents, great-aunts and -uncles—and have done a lot of volunteering with the elderly, so the older characters like Grandpa, Leo, Claudia, and Bessie are kind of a tribute to many of those people (with a dash of my mum in there too).

What is the most interesting or surprising thing you learned as you set out to tell your story?

The most valuable thing I learned was how to be with someone who is grieving or dying. As humans, our inclination is to help or fix a problem, so we often try to give people in these situations pep talks to make them feel better. But I was surprised to learn that this is often more harmful than helpful. Though it may be more uncomfortable for us, it's actually often more helpful to let people be sad and talk about their fears and regrets and negative feelings, as Clover does with Claudia in the book. Listening is often the most healing thing you can offer them. I also learned that it depends on the day—people might want something different depending on how they're feeling, and it's nice to give them the choice by asking them what they need. Something like: "Would you like a cheerleader, someone to just listen, or do you want to just talk about how much this sucks?" I've also heard it put as "Would you like to be hugged, helped, or heard?" They may even want you to do all three. The most important thing is realizing that there's no "right" thing to say and that your presence is often more meaningful than anything else.

Are you currently working on another book? And if so, can you tell us what it's about?

I am! It's about mothers, sisters, the ocean, wanderlust, the search for knowledge, and squeezing everything you can out of this beautiful life.

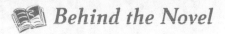 *Behind the Novel*

FROM THE JOURNAL OF
CLAUDIA BARTLETT

June 1956: Marseille

It's been a week since I arrived in France and I still can't quite believe I'm here.

How glorious it is to be living beside the Mediterranean. I swore I'd always be a New York City girl—I knew it was home as soon as I arrived. But there's something about the South of France, the way the golden light bathes the beautiful old buildings, dances on the surface of the sea, and imbues the people here with such a vibrant passion for living.

Life is so much slower here. I thought I thrived on the bustling energy of New York, but perhaps there is something to be said for taking your time and savoring things, whether it's a deep conversation, a beautiful view, a glass of wine, or a twinkling smile from a stranger. I feel as if I'm being shown another approach to living that's so foreign to how I've been raised.

And yet, in spite of all of this beauty, there's a small sense of dread growing in my chest. These past two years have been the happiest of my life. But not for the reasons most people might think—that I'm a young woman in the blissful throes of love. These two years have been the first time I've had the chance to know myself. The first time I've felt freedom. That was the deal I made—two years to pursue my photography career as I pleased before I came home and got married and became the dutiful wife everyone has always told me I'm destined to be.

*Behind the
Novel*

I'm not sure a bride-to-be is supposed to be counting down to her wedding day with a sense of doom. But, to me, these last few months before I go home to get married feel a little like a farewell to that freedom. I went from belonging to my parents, to now belonging to my soon-to-be husband, and soon enough I'll belong to my children.

This will be the last time my name belongs to me. Soon Claudia Wells will replace Claudia Bartlett, and everything I've earned under that name will be discarded as if Claudia Bartlett never existed.

So I'm going to make the most of this time. To seize every adventure, savor every experience, and say yes to everything. I have this unshakeable feeling that there is something for me here in Marseille. What, I don't know—perhaps it's a career opportunity, a new friend, a mentor or something more. Regardless, I'm going to live these three months with one driving philosophy:

To be cautiously reckless.

 **Recommended Reading**

Convenience Store Woman by Sayaka Murata
Loneliness is a prominent theme in *Clover*, and
there are many books that explore the topic so
perceptively, but this one in particular felt like such
a fascinating and original perspective to me. It's
particularly interesting to read it in the context of
Japanese culture and the expectations it puts on
women in terms of marriage and children. I found
the story both hilarious and heartbreaking.

Shark Heart by Emily Habeck
I adored this debut novel for so many reasons.
Habeck is so inventive in crafting a tale that
embodies an experience many of us have
encountered or will likely encounter—nursing
a loved one through an incurable illness—but
presenting it in such a fresh, creative way that
is both comforting and unexpected. It's also a
touching rendering of grief and the many ways it
shapes us.

A Single Man by Christopher Isherwood
A beautiful, poignant examination of grief, love,
and what it feels like to be on the outside looking
in, observing the world rather than participating in
it. Though it was published in the 1960s, so much
of this book still resonates as a deeply human story,
and I often revisit it. The film version by Tom Ford
is also excellent!

The Safety of Objects by A. M. Homes
I was never a short story reader until my friend
insisted I start reading this book while she was
making us dinner—and by the time dinner was
ready, I understood why she loved it so much.

Homes somehow manages to take many taboo topics and turn them into enthralling, clever, and fun short stories (I will admit that my sense of humor is a little twisted). I often thought about this while writing *Clover* because death is such a taboo topic in Western society and I wanted to find a way to make it palatable.

The Secret Lives of Church Ladies by Deesha Philyaw
This cemented my love of short stories and is a master class in what you can pack into such a limited word count. Philyaw creates such fascinating, vivid characters that draw you in immediately. My favorite story in this collection is "How to Make Love to a Physicist."

Vladimir by Julia May Jonas
It's not often that we get to read through the eyes of a fifty-eight-year-old female protagonist, and this story hooked me from the beginning. Jonas does such a fantastic job of questioning the moral standards society has for men and women while also endearing us to a character whose behavior is at times morally questionable.

Intimacies by Katie Kitamura
When people describe books as being a "vibe," this is one of the ones I think of. Though its plot is relatively uneventful, I like to think that's exactly what Kitamura intended because it really examines what it means to exist between worlds, in that interstitial space where you feel like you don't quite belong anywhere, whether it be in relationships, language, identity, or even home. I also loved her elegant yet economical prose.

You Exist Too Much by Zaina Arafat
I admire Arafat's way of diving deep into the topics
of addiction, obsession, sexuality, and religion,
never shying away from the thornier aspects but
doing so with such humor and wit. I laughed
out loud several times in this book but also felt
deeply for the protagonist, who makes bad choice
after bad choice in a quest to find a place—and
someone—who feels like home.

Limberlost by Robbie Arnott
My family has lived in Tasmania, Australia, for
eight generations, in the island's north-east region,
which is where this book is set. The descriptions
of the land and wilderness are stunning and are
a great comfort to me when I'm feeling a little
homesick! It's also a lovely, simple story of family,
childhood dreams, and how the choices we make
when we're young can shape our entire lives.

Bonjour Tristesse by Françoise Sagan
Not only does this classic perfectly capture the
sensory experience of a lazy Mediterranean
summer, but it's another book driven by the
reckless choices of youth and their consequences.
I could read this for the setting alone, but the
story itself also happens to be captivating and
thought-provoking.

# *Reading Group Questions*

1. How does the first chapter set the tone for the rest of the novel? What role do you think Clover's early exposure to death plays in her ability to feel comfortable talking about it?

2. Clover believes that one of the reasons she has had trouble forging connections with others is because of her job as a death doula. Why do you think it's socially unacceptable to discuss death as an inevitable experience we will all face? How is Western society different from others in this sense?

3. Does the colloquial discussion of death and people dying in this novel make you uncomfortable? How about when you read the casual descriptions of the various ways people die on page 48? Do you feel (even just a little) more comfortable with death after reading this novel?

4. Sylvie is the first real friend her own age that Clover has as an adult. What does their friendship teach Clover about vulnerability? Discuss Clover's evolution when it comes to opening herself up to human connection.

5. What effect do you think traveling and learning about various cultures' perception of death has on Clover?

6. After a series of events, Clover begins to see her grandfather as a multifaceted man rather than just her caregiver. Is there someone in your life you've had this experience with? Is it common for people to view the elderly in a two-dimensional way in Western society? If so, why do you think that is?

7. "But the thing is, we all know we're going to die—that's guaranteed. So shouldn't we be making the most of our lives anyway?" (p. 63). How did your perspective on time and the way you lead your life shift, if at all, after reading this novel?

8. Books and movies are a viable way for Clover to escape and gain new perspectives. Did you learn anything new/valuable from experiencing the world through Clover's lens? How often do you inhabit your imagination, as Clover does?

9. "Someone told me once that [grief is] like a bag that you always carry—it starts out as a large suitcase, and as the years go by, it might reduce to the size of a purse, but you carry it forever. . . . It helped me realize that I didn't need to ever get over it completely" (p. 241). How does it feel to consider grief as something you learn to deal with rather than setting an end goal of ridding yourself of it? Has your perception of grief shifted at all after reading this novel?

10. When Sebastian's paternal grandfather died, his father "didn't even cry at the funeral" (p. 214). Clover considered this "a typical male response to grief" (p. 215). How does this example of handling grief "like a man" affect Sebastian's relationship with death and the way he navigates his life?

11. Sebastian mentions feeling "that Sunday-school guilt," worrying if he was "doing all the right things to get into heaven" (pp. 213–14). How has your upbringing, spirituality, or religion influenced the way you think about death?

12. Clover compulsively rewatches romantic scenes in movies as a type of coping mechanism. What did you make of this behavior? Do you ever find yourself returning to TV shows, movies, or books?

13. "Don't let the best parts of life pass you by because you're too scared of the unknown" (p. 268). Consider where you are in your own life. If tomorrow was your last day, which of Clover's three books do you think your final words would belong in?

14. "But the secret to a beautiful death is to live a beautiful life. Putting your heart out there. Letting it get broken. Taking chances. Making mistakes" (p. 293). How important do you think it is to be "cautiously reckless" with your life? How do you plan to do so moving forward, if at all?

15. By the end of the novel, Clover realizes she's spent most of her life operating as the person the world told her she was rather than who she believed herself to be. How does Clover's character shift after she begins to reevaluate herself?

16. Do you think Clover still needs those vitamins she went out twice to get? Or did she receive them in a different way?

ABOUT THE AUTHOR

Mark Wickens

Mikki Brammer is an Australian journalist based in
New York City, by way of France and Spain. She writes
about design, architecture, and art for publications such
as *Architectural Digest, Dwell,* and *Elle Decor. The
Collected Regrets of Clover* is her debut novel.